Wheels and Circles

Paperback   ISBN 0 9553418 5 X
Paperback   ISBN 978 0 9553418 5 4

First published in Great Britain by
Petan Publishing
20 Dorchester Crescent
Baildon Shipley
West Yorkshire
BD17 7LE

petanpublishing@blueyonder.co.uk
www.petanpublishing.co.uk

Sole Distributor
Liberato
16 Middle King
Braintree
Essex
CM7 3XY
liberato@talktalk.co.uk
www.liberato.co.uk

Wheels and Circles

Second Book of the Trilogy *Closed Circuits, Cluttered Minds*

by

Roz Colyer

Petan Publishing

The Trilogy
Closed Circuits, Cluttered Minds

Book One
Riding the Wheel

Book Two
Wheels and Circles

Book Three
Full Circle
(Out in 2007 from Petan Publishing)

PART ONE

1987 and 1976

1.   March 1987

When questioned later about that night, Leo will remember certain things – a shushing sound like doors quietly opening and a certain whispering in the air. What time was it? Gone midnight, she will say; yes, definitely long past midnight. She had been writing in her Diary until about quarter to eleven, then she had gone to sleep. No, she hadn't been dreaming; something must have woken her up. But her room is at the front of the house. The library is at the back. The house is large and thickly carpeted. Noises don't usually travel.

The next morning she got up at her usual time when not working – about half past seven. She had a shower, as usual, then did five minutes' yoga breathing, ten minutes on her exercise bike, ten minutes with her weights. So it was just gone eight when she went downstairs. Mrs Wainwright was in the kitchen; she always arrived at eight o'clock sharp to cook the breakfast.

Leo hadn't spoken to the housekeeper, she rarely did, apart from ordering a poached egg on toast and half a grapefruit. Her father was back to prunes and low-calorie orange juice, but it was a self-imposed diet, one ordered by his doctor because of his knees.

He usually came down earlier, about seven. He liked to read the papers in the lounge or the library before breakfast, and then he would appear in the dining room at about eight-fifteen, already dressed in his business suit as if he were going to the gallery. To her knowledge, he hadn't been there for months.

But that morning he hadn't appeared. Leo had sat at the table, eating her grapefruit, then her poached egg. No, she hadn't been worried; not then. Not even when she had a cup of coffee because Mrs Wainwright said it was going to waste in the percolator.

When had she started to get worried? Not until about quarter to nine, Leo thought. Until then she'd assumed he'd had a late night, and overslept. The papers were still on the hall table. She had taken a copy of *The Times* to read over her breakfast – no, she wasn't interested in current affairs as a rule, but her sister was in Moscow and there might be an article written about Gorbachev that Gemma might have had a hand in. Well, half-sister really, Leo amended. They weren't at all alike.

It would have been about ten to nine, then, or just after, when Leo had gone upstairs and knocked on her father's bedroom door. When there was no answer, she peeped around. He wasn't in bed; in fact his bed hadn't been slept in at all.

And she still wasn't worried, not really. He sometimes sat up all night, either in the lounge or the library, when he couldn't sleep. He hadn't slept well for a while now, because of his knees. Leo had heard him sometimes going into the kitchen for a glass of milk. His doctor had told him that if he didn't give up the whisky he'd be dead in five years, but she didn't say this to the police.

So she had gone downstairs, and into the lounge, and he wasn't there. So then she had gone into the library.

They hadn't questioned her too much about what happened next. She couldn't have told them anyway; when it came to this part in the story her throat closed up and she found it impossible to go on. She had written it down in her Diary, instead.

Mon 2 March 8.53am (approx) (ritten Wed 4 11.43pm)

I thort he was asleep. He sometimes worked on his book all hours of the night, one of his Old Masters, and would fall asleep at his desk. I thort he had a pen in his hand. He had something in his hand, but until I droo the curtains I couldn't see wot.

So I went behind the desk and droo the curtains and then I turned round and said, Daddy, wake up or your brekfast will be in the bin, becoz he's as scared of the old bat as I am. Both Wainrites scare us to bits and I don't know why he took them on. Probably becoz their name also begins with a W and Daddy has never liked change, he likes everything to stay exactly the same

O God

Then I throo my arms round his neck and kissed his cheek. And it was cold. Like marble. And then I saw the hole in his temple and the black oozing mess spred out underneeth his head and his outstretched hand holding the gun. And the world stopped spinning and everything holted, suspended,

like an image cort in a camera shutter and then I screemed and screemed and
Mrs Wainrite came in and the camera clicked and the world somehow went
on spinning
But I don't know how
I don't know how I'm going to
O my Daddy my darling Daddy how am I going to

******

It seems that the world and his wife have come to the funeral. The crowds outside the crematorium include a BBC camera crew and a bunch of journalists, even though Daddy hadn't done any new TV shows for a long time. It makes you realise how popular he was, Huwie says, guiding her along the path, his arm round her waist.

All through the service he stands by her side, holding her up against his comforting solid bulk. He takes after Daddy, while she is small like Mummy, who stands behind with Uncle Alun. They aren't coming to the house afterwards, but are catching the next train back to Swansea. The Groosomes haven't come, thank goodness.

Somehow she makes it through the interminable service, keeping her eyes fixed on the coffin. The coffin, containing her father, is covered in flowers. She tries to imagine him lying there like he lay in bed, flat on his back, hands crossed over his stomach, snoring... Oh Daddy, she thinks, how will I bear it?

With Huwie's help she makes it through the worst part, when the curtains close and the coffin is winched down to the flames. As they wait to file out, she can hear the machinery creaking. She feels as if her heart is being torn from her body. She must be trembling, because the hand at her waist tightens. Tears are scorching the backs of her eyes but they won't fall. If they did, they would burn her cheeks like molten lava.

She is steered through the crowds outside; they are a blur in front of her eyes. Then she is being handed into the car and she presses herself into the corner until Huwie climbs in next to her and when he's seated she presses herself against him although this time his arm doesn't go round her. He's turning away, talking to someone on his other side. She feels the car start, crawl forwards. She turns her head away from Huwie, away from the other occupants of the car; she stares through the back window, through the blur of people thronging the front of the crematorium, back to the place she has left her heart.

"…couldn't believe it, still can't get my head round…"

"…same here, completely gutted, must have been health prob…"

"…worried about that damn operation…"

"…didn't know about that, thought it might be – you know – the big A…"

"…gave it away like that, bloody good business, what the hell…"

"…TV'd dried up, but funnily enough he was never comfortable with that, he told me once…"

"Ssssssh!"

All heads turn towards her. She can see them clearly, old friends, old colleagues, some faces she doesn't recognise. As she passes through the room, Daddy's lounge - where he had held his parties - she bestows smiles on everyone, acknowledges every condolence, returns every kiss. In the knot around Huwie she sees Pudge and Ralph and the profile of someone she doesn't immediately recognise; behind them, Hilary Frost and the Jacobsens. Where's Gemma?

"Okay, sis?" Huwie gives her a glass of white wine, holds it until he realises her hands are quite steady. His other arm is around Pudge.

She smiles. "Fine."

"Lovely service," says Isabel Jacobsen.

"Such a lot of flowers," says Hilary Frost.

"Just what he'd have wanted," says Ralph.

The someone she doesn't recognise turns round and, with a shock, she realises it's Miss Rottweiler. She's dressed sombrely but that's nothing unusual, and her face is half-hidden by a close-fitting hat with a veil, but there's something different about her that Leo can't place. Her usually acute powers of observation have deserted her. And then the slim black-clad figure of Gemma swims into her vision in the background, deep in conversation with Crispian Pyke from the BBC. Of course.

Pudge takes her hand in both of hers, a gesture that shows off her engagement ring to perfection. "You were so brave, Leonora."

"Thanks."

George says, "Never thought it of Larry. The last thing..."

"Quite," says Huwie, heading him off.

After a short silence, Ralph says, "The mind's a funny thing..." and stops.

Leo says steadily, "My father didn't commit suicide," and watches their faces express polite sympathy and embarrassment.

"Well," Ralph says at last, "I would never have believed it either, but the police..."

"Leave it, sis," says Huwie.

So she will leave it. Nobody is on her side. Daddy's side. She turns away, leaves them to whisper amongst themselves about how her mind has been affected, poor thing. Only, as she turns, she catches Miss Rottweiler's eye behind the veil and sees an expression there of – what? Complicity? Warning? That woman is dangerous; Leo has always thought so.

She will get through this by appointing herself Daddy's guardian. She has already refused to speak to the press. Laurence Bassett's private life has always been public knowledge anyway, but she won't give the media hyenas any more than necessary. She had done her duty; told the police all she knew, even about the noises. There had been noises, she is quite sure about that. But it was the fact of the gun, with no other fingerprints on it, that is apparently incontrovertible proof. The gun he'd kept in his drawer, the gun she'd seen him gazing at when she went into the library only a few weeks ago, the one he'd knocked to the floor when she startled him (Daddy had always been clumsy), the one she had been so eager to pick up and hand back to him before she knew what it was. The gun he'd locked away in the top drawer of his desk.

11

It was a small, rather beautiful object, metallic grey with a pearlised handle that rested snugly in her palm with a reassuring weight and presence. Daddy had told her with a kind of wry shame that he kept it in case burglars got in; silly, really, as he didn't know how to use the thing anyway.

Oh, why had she told Huwie? Why hadn't she kept this knowledge to herself? She would have lied quite brazenly then; no, she had never seen the gun, her father would never have had a gun, he hated violence in all its forms. But Huwie had felt obliged to tell the police that the gun was Daddy's, and that was enough for them to be satisfied. Even without a suicide note.

And the Man is there again tonight, as she knew he would be. Standing beneath the street light at the end of the driveway, looking in. The drive is at least twenty yards long and the overgrown hedges limit her view but it is Him, back again. He stays only long enough to see the light is on in Gemma's bedroom window and then walks off, quickly but not at all guiltily. She draws the curtains, blots out the dark, the drive, the lonely street light. Then she looks down at her Diary, open at those last words she wrote only a few moments ago.

He killed my father and I'm going to proove it.

2. July 1976

Peering out of the taxi's window at the weary queues at bus stops, women in limp sundresses that showed off pasty arms and men sweating in suits, Laurence Bassett felt a smug contentment with his life.

"Poor buggers," he smiled.

The summer was turning out to be one of the hottest on record. Beginning in May, there were no signs that the heatwave would end soon. Reservoirs were drying up, foundations of buildings being eroded; standpipes would have to come into use in some parts of the country. The great British public, more used to complaining about their miserable climate, was becoming uneasy. The Seventies, so far, had been a pretty depressing decade: three-day weeks, miners' strikes, sugar shortages. Flying anywhere was dangerous because of terrorist hijacks, drinking in pubs because of IRA bombs. Now the sun was shining in summer. Where, Laurence ruminated aloud, would it all lead?

Ralph was leafing through a stack of continuity sheets. "I think we've covered all angles. If the backroom boys do their stuff we might be on a winner here." He lifted a worried bespectacled face. "We anywhere near Highgate?"

"Not far." Laurence bestowed his smile on Ralph. Weinstock had worked at the BBC for years but still got himself tied into knots before the launch of every new programme. Laurence, the front man, a mere newcomer, had never felt more relaxed. "Don't worry, Ralph. It's my personal view, don't forget."

"It's my head on the block, though."

"Oh, hardly."

"You don't know the backstabbing that goes on. And this is a departure from the norm, you know that. Arts programmes are the kiss of death anyway, we're lucky to have got the slot. Art and religion, the two great no-no's in tellyland." Ralph leaned forward and tapped the driver on the shoulder. "Drop me at the corner." The clasps of his briefcase gave him trouble after he'd stuffed the papers back, but at last he conquered them. "Thanks for the lift, Larry, see you next week."

He opened the door and made to leap out but found that he'd trapped the end of his tie in his briefcase. Laurence helped him extricate himself. That was one of the things he liked about Ralph; he was almost as inept at the intricacies of everyday living as he himself. A good producer, though, knew his job inside out.

"I'm giving a party Saturday night," Laurence said as Ralph launched himself on to the pavement. "Not really a celebration, but we can treat it as such. Hope to see you and Viv there."

"I hope you're not being premature."

"Have faith, dear boy."

"Hardly your career on the line. You'll still have your business even if we go down like the Titanic."

"Saturday, Ralph. Champagne and caviar." Laurence pulled the door to and left Ralph receding on the steaming pavement. A hot blast of melting tar had belched in with his exit. "Hampstead," he said to the driver, and relaxed back into the seat.

It still gave him a thrill, being driven through London streets to his large Hampstead house. He often wondered what would have happened if he'd remained in Swansea. Would he still be a lecturer at the university, or would he have risen a little to become an art historian, possibly publishing a few books? Would he still be married? But celebrity had its perks. Notoriety had helped, too. Surely a small price to pay for the life he now led.

This programme Ralph was so het up about was a new departure for him, but he had no doubts about its success. Up till now he'd been the doyen of afternoon television, the housewives' favourite, chairing quiz shows or being one of a panel of 'experts' guessing the value of the contents of people's attics. Well, the money was useful and he'd certainly noticed an upturn in his antique shop's sales, enough for him to sell it at a nice profit and buy the gallery in Cork Street.

His 5-year contract with the BBC had come at a good time, too. On the basis of that he'd sold his bachelor flat and bought his house overlooking the Heath. Too big just for him, obviously, but he told himself he had bought it as a place to bring his children, still marooned in Swansea, for the school holidays (although he hadn't done this yet, notwithstanding his daughter's weekly letters threatening self-harm and half-sibling murder if he didn't let her come and live with him), and to give lavish parties at least once a month. If anyone had said he was doing that to buy love and friendship, he would have said yes, of course it was, that was the whole idea.

So life was good. He was happy. Well, he had regrets, but who reached the age of forty-seven without a few regrets? He regretted what he had done in the past that had taken his life in a different direction, but not what this new life had brought him. He regretted what he had done to his wife and children, but it was only what thousands – millions – of other men had done before him. And he at least had made sure that Cait and the kids were well provided for, and now she had remarried and produced twins he could make himself believe that it had all happened for the best. Even Leonora would come to forgive him in the long run.

Damn and blast! He'd forgotten the date – yesterday was his daughter's fourteenth birthday, and it had completely slipped his mind. He tapped the driver on the shoulder. "Stop at the next florist's, will you?"

Through Interflora he ordered the biggest bouquet they did, wrote a card saying *Happy Birthday to my darling Leo, love and kisses, Daddy,* and then, feeling virtuous and self-satisfied, was driven on to Hampstead.

******

The preparations for his parties were carried out by Deborah Routledge at the gallery and by Mrs Wetherby at home. He, Laurence, was superfluous, as far as the work went – all that was required of him were the contents of his wallet or his signature on cheques. He was used to it by now – used to sitting behind his desk on the first floor of his office at Gali-Leo's while Miss Routledge ran his business downstairs, used to getting under Mrs W's feet in the kitchen at home and being gently chided to go into his library and relax. What was it about him and women?

15

Why did they persist in treating him like an endearing but useless dog? Well, he knew why, of course, and he couldn't complain.

So now he sat at his desk in his first floor office doodling on his pad and reading the paper while the telephone rang almost incessantly below. Only a few calls were put through to him. Ralph: "You sure about Stockhausen for the credits? Wouldn't Sibelius be safer?" Pieter Merck from Amsterdam: "I will send you the outline, Mr Barsett, and you will contact me with the green light, okay?" Mrs W: "I thought I'd better let you know, Mr B, the deli can't do Parma ham, there's a shop in Mayfair, or could you possibly try Harrod's – and, if you remember, could you see what you think about cheese, some of that French camembert would be nice…" Well, at least he was thought capable of running errands.

Rising from his desk and shrugging into his jacket (why didn't he go in shirtsleeves? – much cooler in this heat), his errand was aborted by Miss Routledge bringing in their lunch on a tray. He shrugged his jacket off again.

"Were you going out?"

"No. No. It can wait."

She set the tray down on the desk. Chicken and ham sandwiches for him, purchased in the café over the road, two Ryvita with cottage cheese and a pot of natural yoghurt for her.

"Rosemary can hold the fort for half an hour," she smiled. "About time she took on some responsibility."

He sat down again and pushed the newspaper over to her. "Have you seen this?"

She drew up a chair and, sitting, unfolded the small half-glasses she wore on a chain round her neck and perched them on the tip of her nose. She looked like a prim convent-educated schoolgirl as she peered at the article he'd pointed out; then, sitting back and folding the glasses into their chain again, reverted to prim Miss Routledge, forty-something spinster.

"Extremely interesting."

"Do you think we've had any of these fakes?"

"Would you be hoodwinked by this conman, Mr Bassett?"

"Lunch time, Deborah."

She smiled. She wasn't prim when she smiled. "Would you," she amended, "be hoodwinked, Laurence?" She pulled back the lid of her yoghurt and slowly inserted her spoon.

"Oh, I'm hoodwinked all the time. Nothing easier."

"Not about painting."

"No. Perhaps not." He slid the paper back and ran his eyes down the columns of newsprint, trying not to watch her stirring the yoghurt in slow, deliberate circles. "I'd like to have a look at some, though. I've always wondered how easy it would be. They say all the art galleries in the world have forgeries on their walls, masquerading as the real thing."

"But if they're as good as the real thing…"

"And isn't art supposed to be about pleasure? Or is it just about money?"

She knitted her brows together thoughtfully. He liked the way she gave his apparently throwaway remarks all her attention. "I would say, both equally," she said at last. "A lot of the pleasure is because of its price." Then lifted a loaded spoonful to her mouth and closed her lips round it.

"I thought great art was price*less*."

She swallowed slowly, letting her tongue rest for a second on her lower lip, then pressed a paper napkin to her mouth. "Not in this gallery."

He laughed. "No, indeed. And you're right. The higher the price, the more punters we get. Strange world we live in now, Deborah."

"Don't knock it, Laurence. We both make a good living."

And just then there was a knock at the door and Rosemary the junior peeped round. "Sorry, Miss Routledge, but there's a man…"

Deborah rose from her chair like a missile. "You haven't left the gallery unattended? How many times have I told you to ring through – oh, never mind, I'm coming…" and she swept from the room, those stilettos flashing like knives. The spoon remained upright in her abandoned pot of yoghurt for maybe a second or two before giving in to gravity.

Laurence remained at his desk for maybe a minute or two,

before once again rising up, pulling on his tie, shrugging into his jacket, and preparing to go off on his errand.

The man was a stranger to her. When she arrived downstairs he was standing in front of a Bridget Riley, hands shoved in the pockets of his flared trousers. He wore a black roll-necked jumper and a light unstructured jacket with the sleeves pushed up, which nevertheless didn't disguise a rather pronounced hump to his left shoulder. He turned round when she approached but didn't remove his hands.

"Can I help you?"

"You the owner?" His voice had a trace of an American accent, although he wasn't American, she thought. The Americans who came into the gallery were usually large, tall and open-faced, and this man was shorter than average, longish hair, quite thin, with almost hawk-like features. He was wearing sunglasses, which he hooked up with a forefinger and left on the crown of his head as he turned towards her.

"No. Mr Bassett is out, I'm afraid. Can I help?"

He brought his right hand from his pocket and proffered a business card between index and middle fingers. "I'm here on behalf of my client. He's looking for art."

"That's what we deal in, Mr – Simmons?" Not having her glasses, the words were blurred.

"Symons. Dave Symons. I'm over from Denver."

"So what exactly is your client looking for, Mr Symons?"

"Contemporary stuff. Not things like this," he jerked his thumb back at the Riley, "more your Francis Bacon. He's partial to Freud, too."

"Oh. Well, I'm sorry, we don't rep…"

"No, you misunderstand me." Was he chewing gum? He moved his tongue round his mouth as if dislodging something. "He wants to patronise new painters, the younger lot, but nothing too Jackson Pollock, if you get my meaning. He can get plenty of that over there. He's looking for…"

"Perhaps something more like this?" Definitely not American, she thought, as she led him towards the back of the gallery. A definite East End accent coming through. And he didn't know much about painting. He gave a cursory glance to everything she showed him, even the best Timberlakes, and didn't want to see the back catalogue.

"Yeah, that's the stuff. Keep the card, I'll be back."

After he'd gone she put her glasses on and looked at the card more closely. *David Symons, Personal Representative, Venn Pegasus Agency.* Addresses in New York and Denver. Nothing given away there. But not surprising. Big business was moving into the art world and prices were set to rocket. And a lot of moguls didn't want their names attached, obviously. Tax evasion, perhaps, or money laundering...? Was it any of her business? Of course not. Her loyalty was firstly to her employer, then to the gallery's clients; through them, they were patrons to the next generation of artists. Laurence might dislike the way art was used as collateral and not merely enjoyed for its own sake, but it was ever thus. She liked to think she shielded him from the grubby commercial aspects of the business, but she knew he'd done a few dodgy deals in his time; her first week in the job, she'd realised that. But his deals were small scale; a valuation a little on the low side, a sale with a few more noughts attached, a couple not going through the books. Show me a businessman who doesn't play the system, she thought, and I'll show you a bankruptcy statistic.

"Disaster averted, Miss Routledge?" Laurence was coming down the stairs, pulling up his tie.

"Everything running smoothly, Mr Bassett."

"I'm off on the trail of a couple of elusive ingredients. Parma ham and camembert." As he passed, he winked at her. "I could be some time."

Rosemary was loitering behind the desk. Deborah had set her the task of sorting out the drawers, but she was taking her time over it. Had she seen the wink? Oh, did it matter? And, for a second, she had rather enjoyed being seen not as Miss Routledge, prim spinster, but a desirable woman worthy of a wink.

But of course Rosemary knew Laurence was homosexual,

that was why he was such a hit with the housewives. What Rosemary was thinking, of course, was poor old trout, the only man who gives her any attention is gay.

******

One thing old Larry could do, he'd heard on the grapevine, was throw a good party. Usually last-minute affairs, sprung on guests at the eleventh hour, they nevertheless dropped other commitments to attend. He tried to invite a good mix of interesting, creative people, and this one was no exception.

Laurence surveyed his lounge from behind the drinks bar. By the door was Cyril Lyttleton, theatre impresario, chatting to Angie Witt, fresh from the Slade; next to them, political cartoonist Xavier Dodd was haranguing recently elevated Labour MP Ken Young; in front of him historian Nathaniel Brookes was exchanging tortured vowels with art *aficionado* Frederick Swainton while blond, blue-eyed Hugo draped himself on a bar stool looking gorgeous. Laurence, conscious of those sapphire eyes fixed on him, hurried over to extricate poor Janis Brodwicz, émigré Polish novelist, holed up in a corner by Hilary Frost, BBC news researcher, who had evidently taken exception to his latest book.

"My dear Janis," she was saying, "why waste your talent trying to emulate the sort of sexist trash everyone in the western world is writing? You have the perfect opportunity to do something positive for a change! Your main protagonist should be a strong-minded woman leading a revolt against the forces of male bureaucracy but instead you have her fighting with another wretched female over a bar of soap..."

Janis murmured apologetically, "Maybe a bar of soap is more important than politics."

Hilary snorted. "Only a man would say that! Only a man would have the *gall*...!"

"Top up, anyone?" Laurence held aloft the Dom Perignon.

"Did you hear that, Laurence? Janis here thinks soap more important than politics. That's either the most fatuous statement

I've ever heard in my life or a feeble attempt to placate women's anger by elevating their status to some kind of universal matriarchy. I can tell you, Janis, that sort of male condescension won't wash with the sisterhood any more."

"With or without soap." Laurence's attempt to lighten the mood evidently fell on deaf ears. Hilary had no sense of humour anyway, and poor Janis was too bewildered by this unexpected hostility to his previously well-reviewed book to do anything but look cowed. Laurence threw an arm round his shoulders and steered him towards the more congenial company of Ralph and his long-suffering wife Vivian, leaving them together to compare neuroses.

He looked over the milling occupants of his lounge, overflowing on to the terrace. Outside, Mr W had rigged up lines of coloured lights which had attracted swarms of mosquitoes. The tables and chairs on the terrace were mostly empty. Despite the heat, most people were firmly ensconced in his lounge, dropping crumbs and spilling wine on the carpet, using his ornaments as ashtrays. As usual, he had changed the art work on the walls; he used his parties as informal viewings and a couple of Timberlakes were displayed, as well as a Witt lithograph and a small Van Kratzenberg.

He felt one of his panics coming on. About this time in the evening, when his party got into its stride, he began to feel superfluous. He could make his exit, leave them to it, and not be missed. The only person who anchored him, made him feel safe, was Deborah. Where was she?

"So how many fakes have passed through your hands, Larry?" George Jacobsen, curator of Renaissance art at the National, was at his elbow.

"None, George. Apparently I can't be hoodwinked."

"This fellow's pretty good, by all accounts."

"I don't deal in anything before the nineteen hundreds. You'd better look to your hangings, though."

George laughed. "Oh, no doubt we've got a few rogue Raphaels and Rembrandts. They're not the problem. It's the turn of the century lot that can undermine the market. They could be your problem, Larry."

"I never buy anything without a certifiable provenance. Don't worry, George, I'm very thorough."

"A lot of charlatans muscling in on the market now. It's not the gentleman's club it was."

"For God's sake don't let Hilary hear you say that, she'll have your gonads for ping pong balls."

"Ah, the lovely Hilary…" and George drifted off towards the bar, where Hilary had found a kindred spirit in Antonia Latimer, publisher of the feminist magazine *Red Monthly*.

About this time in the evening Laurence always felt the need for solitude; today was no exception. He filled his house with people, fed them canapés and champagne, allowed them to mix and mingle and then, around midnight, felt this gnawing tedium, this undefined panic. Who am I, he thought, what am I doing here? One day I shall be unmasked as the charlatan I am. I am the fraud. I know nothing much about anything; I tiptoe over the surface of things, leaving the hard work to others. When things become too complicated, I run away. I throw money at problems and think that will solve everything. And it does, it has. But one day…

He needed a drink, desperately. Whisky, not champagne. Something hot and fierce to melt the icy fist in his gut. He slipped away from the party and hurried along the carpeted corridor to the deserted back of the house, to his library. He needed darkness and silence, and the bottle in the bottom drawer. So he didn't switch on the light, and went to pull the long curtains across the window. And bumped against somebody crouched over his desk.

…that predatory old fart Swainton, inhaling a line of coke into one of his elegantly flared nostrils. And he wasn't even apologetic, he reared up with an expression of extreme annoyance on that equine set of features. "Have a care, old chap, stuff's fucking expensive."

"What are you doing in my library, Freddy?"

"Would think that's obvious, old boy. Clearing out the sinuses."

"I'd rather you didn't do it in my house, that's all."

"Why?" Swainton's large ascetic head swayed belligerently on its long neck. "Invited any detective johnnies to your luvvy do? Drugs squaddies? Disguised as fucking artisans?" He held out his wrists and overlaid a mockney accent on his impeccable tones. "It's a fair cop, guv'nor, I'll come noice and quiet."

"Freddy…"

"You old ponce, Larry. You fucking cock teaser. I see you've invited just one of your delightful young catamites tonight. Never share them out, do you. Never pass them round…"

"Go home, Freddy. I'll get a cab…"

Swainton pushed off his arm and reeled towards the door. "Piss off, you Judas! Piss off, the lot of you! Liars and swindlers all!" He lurched back towards Laurence, almost fell. Laurence took him by the shoulders to hold him up. Swainton's breath fanned against his face, his rheumy, bloodshot eyes bulged into his. "But I've found him, Larry, not you. I've got him."

"Who?"

"Boy. Marvellous boy. Paints. Bloody good." His legs were giving way; he slid down Laurence's chest, that blade-like nose scything against his breastbone.

"Glad to hear it, Freddy."

"Next Dermot fucking Timberlake. Better. Better than Dermot fucking…" Now he was on his knees, nose pressed against Laurence's thigh. His eyes were closed, that enormous head lolled to one side. Hoisting him up by the armpits, Laurence dragged him over to the sofa. Swainton was a heavy, ungainly weight; he could only drape the top half on the sofa, the legs splayed out like long spindly stilts.

Wondering how the hell he could manoeuvre Swainton on to the sofa, let alone out of his house, Laurence heard the door open. He looked up to see – oh, thank God – Deborah.

"I thought you might be hiding in here." She had obviously failed to see who he was grappling with – she had put the outside light on, but the library was still in darkness. She had obviously failed to see him grappling at all, but when she did her shock was palpable.

23

"No, Deborah, wait – it's Freddy, he's collapsed…"

She exhaled in relief. Poor Miss Routledge, what was she thinking? That he'd brought one of his – Freddy's quaint term - 'catamites' in here? Surely she knew he hadn't ever 'had' a catamite. Hugo was here purely for decorative purposes, and knew it.

"Help me get him on the sofa. He can sleep it off in here."

They took one of Swainton's legs each and hoisted them up. It was only when he was horizontal, with a cushion under his head and his long, fluted hands laid on his chest, that Laurence took a good look at her.

She was dressed in an eggshell-blue figure-hugging frock unfashionably short, showing sculpted knees and good legs balanced on precarious heels. She'd always had good legs, of course, he'd admired them from the first time he'd hired her, six years ago. But they were usually below rather intimidating skirts and mannish jackets, and even her feminine blouses had a touch of the nanny about them. Even to his parties she had worn long unflattering dresses, with her hair pulled back in its usual severe chignon. But now her hair was loose, just caught back on one side with a pale blue comb. No sign of the spectacles.

"Why, Miss Jones," he said. "You're beautiful."

And she was, to his surprise. She must have done something to her face – something different with the make-up, possibly. She had never been pretty, but tonight she was beautiful.

"Thank you."

And there was a slight embarrassment between them, different in quality to their self-conscious games at the office. He'd thought she led him on, with those teasing little rituals of hers, secure in the knowledge that she was safe; everyone knew Laurence Bassett liked boys – but boys of a certain type, and not the ones he paraded for public consumption. But she had seen him at his lowest ebb; she must have realised it was all a sham. There *had* been a boy – long ago, in another country – which was what had brought about the downfall of his marriage, his infamous divorce, and had set him on the road to notoriety and wealth. But that was a long time ago. The boy was now a man, and lost to him forever.

He said, to overcome the embarrassment, "Freddy's found himself a painter. The next Timberlake."

"He was always jealous of you, Laurence."

"Do you think it's true?"

"Do you?"

Laurence sighed. "Very possibly. We've done well out of Dermot, but he's not exactly the young Turk any more. There's signs of him becoming just another tired old has-been. His last exhibition didn't excite much comment, did it?"

She didn't reply. Of course she hadn't come here to talk shop, but what else could they talk about? He realised he knew nothing about her, apart from the fact that she lived in a flat in Baron's Court, inherited from the mother she had spent the best years of her life looking after. Realised, too, that he didn't want to know, preferring to keep her domestic life mysterious. He enjoyed that aura of mystery about her and it saved him the bother of having to pretend interest in arrangements that didn't interest him in the slightest. He kept his own life in compartments and preferred that other people kept theirs under wraps, too.

And just as the silence was becoming oppressive, another figure appeared in the doorway. He recognised the short, pugnacious silhouette, the cropped hair, the baggy working man's trousers, with relief.

"What are you doing in here, Laurence? Everyone's looking for you." The overhead light was snapped on, and Hilary surveyed the room – Freddy snoring on the sofa, he and Deborah kneeling beside him on the floor. "Oh, Miss Moneypenny! Good God, what have you done to yourself?"

God bless Hilary. She had no qualms about speaking her mind. He could sit back and let them slug it out, with no input from him.

"At least I've made the effort." Deborah's voice was neutral.

"Yes," Hilary sneered, "and it must have been an effort. That shade of blue doesn't suit you, by the way. It's a much younger colour."

"And what would you know about fashion?"

"Fashion!" Hilary snorted. "That length went out in the Sixties. You must keep up with the trends, Debs."

"If you have the legs," Deborah murmured, "you shouldn't hide them under hideous navvy's coveralls. But of course you haven't the legs, Hils."

First round to Deborah, Laurence thought.

"If I had, I wouldn't flaunt them like you. The rest needs to match up."

"Oh, I think it does."

"You need new specs, then."

"They're easy to change. Unfortunately, Hilary, you need a whole new body."

"Oh, but I'm not desperate to court men's approval. So what's your excuse, Deborah?"

"Girls, girls!" Laurence thought it about time he waded into the fray; Deborah's face had flushed an unbecoming puce. One round all, perhaps. "Time to call pax, I think." He lumbered to his feet.

"Just as I'm getting into my stride." Hilary placed her two hands on his arm, stood on tiptoe and kissed his cheek. "Darling Larry. You were always the exception."

"To what?"

"My general aversion towards the male of the species."

"Ah."

"But don't get me wrong. I'm not a complete lezzy. I have been known to enjoy the odd screw."

He couldn't resist a joke. "How odd does it have to be?"

He'd obviously said the wrong thing; Hilary's little ferret-face darkened, she pulled her hand away. Damn. He stooped towards Deborah, grasped her elbow and helped her to her feet. Then, taking both of them by the hand, tucked their arms through his on either side and steered them out of the library, closing the door behind him.

They were halfway down the hall when the doorbell rang. Late guests, obviously, but who hadn't already arrived? He left Deborah and Hilary standing two feet apart and hurried towards the door, seeing two shadows against the stained glass, one slightly taller than the other, but neither of even average height – two midgets? Had dwarves been invited to his party? – and opened the door, peered into the darkness beyond. He'd drunk more than he thought. He couldn't even recognise them.

"We're not going back," said a voice from waist height. "We've run away. And you forgot, didn't you? You forgot my birthday."

His daughter Leonora was standing there, hand in hand with her brother Huw. They were carrying suitcases. She'd done what she'd been threatening to do for years – she'd run away from home and come to live with him.

******

7 Aug 9.31pm

Sorry I've not ritten in you for a wile but not been in the mood. Hope you haven't felt abandonned like me for the last week. Thort Daddy would be pleesed to see us & he made out he was but he wasn't. Begged him not to but he foned Mummy & told her & they had a rite go. She said we must go back at once but I said I wouldn't, I'd throw myself off London Bridge first & Daddy said I was histryonic but thort he ment moronic so throo a rite fit & he sent me to my room but found out since it means something else but forgotten wot. Anyway, it's not nice so won't forgive him. But it's nicer here than rotten Swansea even with Daddy in a mood tho he pretends he's not but he is coz Mrs W sez he's not eating like he used to. I like Mrs W & she likes me coz she cooks things I like even tho Huwie doesn't & solks a lot. He can go back, I don't mind. He said he wanted to come but he did nothing but complane all the way down, saying every 5 mins he wanted the toylet & he was hungry & everything but so was I but didn't care. Won't boor you with the detales but the jerney was HORRENDUS. And it cost me all my pokit money. Will get it back from Huwie when he's older coz I'm not paying for the ungratful little brat. Anyway, Mummy says we can stay for the hols but we've got to go back after but I won't, Huwie can but I won't. She can go down on bended nee but I'm staying here. I'll say Uncle Alun was aboosing me, don't really no wot it means but it's something norty men get put into prison for. And Mummy won't want that coz she needs help with the Groosome Toosome. So that's how it stands now & I'll let you no wot happens next. WOTCH THIS SPASE!!!

3.   March/April 1987

Leo hadn't asked Huwie anything about the funeral arrangements; she didn't want to know. Of course she knew all Daddy's friends and colleagues would come, but what about the side of his life he had kept secret all those years? What about Gemma's mother, who is now down in Sussex with the Wetherbys, who had broken the news to her, Leo supposed. In the end, neither the Wetherbys nor Gemma's mother had made it. The Ws had sent a beautiful bouquet, *From Barbara and Bernard, with love and gratitude,* and expressing their sadness that they couldn't attend. Accompanying this was a small brown teddy bear with a pink ribbon round its neck tied in a large floppy bow. A handwritten note was pinned to it: *Sweet dreams and flights of angels - your Beggar Maid, always.* For some reason this little bear had brought Leo closer to tears than all the floral tributes put together.

She had left Huwie to make the initial phonecall to Gemma, who had flown off to Russia a few days before Daddy – It - happened. She'd gone up to her room, keeping the door open so she could hear his voice. He had been on the phone for over twenty minutes. Twenty minutes to Moscow! – and yet of course he couldn't just recount the bald facts and hang up. She listened to his low, soothing voice, but couldn't hear the actual words. She had paced her room, impatient for him to finish the call, to come up and use those same words, those same sympathetic tones, to her. But when he *had* tried to comfort her she had turned away, accusing him of being cold and unfeeling.

He hadn't come up the stairs. She heard him put the receiver down and had peered from the landing as he stood there in the hall, head bowed, staring at the phone. Now she was annoyed that she hadn't stayed downstairs, hadn't heard his exact words.

Give Gemma her due; she had caught the next available plane back, arriving after midnight in a taxi from Heathrow. She and Leo had embraced, both too exhausted to say anything. Gemma was wearing a long wool coat with fur collar and cuffs and matching hat, which she swept off as soon as she arrived – a bit over the top in London but probably just the thing for Moscow – and the taxi driver had brought in two Vuitton suitcases and a smaller vanity case and left them by the door. Even in the midst of her all-consuming grief, Leo had noted Gemma's clothes and luggage. And Gemma herself, although pale, looked poised and wanly beautiful. She had lifted her head as Huwie came into the room after paying the fare; had gently pushed Leo away and silently gone to him, encircled his waist with her arms, rested her face against his shoulder. And he had gathered her into himself, his chin resting on the top of her dark head. They looked, Leo thought, with a sudden diamond-hard clarity of vision, like a Rodin statue – Grief Personified. Or Love Denied.

******

"Of course I didn't know he had a gun," Gemma says, stopping beside the desk and staring down. Leo hovers in the doorway; she hasn't been near the library since that terrible morning. "How would I have known?"

"Huwie might have told you."

"Well he didn't."

"He kept it in case of burglars. But he didn't know how to use it."

Gemma smiles. "That's so typical of him. What happened to it?"

"The police took it."

"Did he have a licence?"

Leo hesitates. She doesn't like lying, but perhaps she can equivocate. "I don't know."

"And anyway surely everything is insured?"

"Oh, you know most things are sentimental to Daddy. The value isn't important." A sudden constriction in her throat makes speaking impossible.

Gemma is now looking at the newly papered wall. "What happened to the picture…?"

"The Murchison?" Leo forces the words out. "Huwie took it

29

to be cleaned. There was b-b-blood…" And suddenly the tears that have been threatening for so long are pouring down Leo's face and she can't stop them. She stands, wracked with sobs.

Gemma's arms are around her. "Oh, Leo, I'm so, so sorry." Now she is shaking too, and Leo knows she is also weeping. It feels so good being able to release all these unshed tears and to share them with someone who understands. Leo can almost forgive Gemma for being her half-sister, for having had to share Daddy for the last eighteen months. She was Daddy's princess, for twenty-three years his one and only precious princess. But Gemma is so beautiful and clever that he couldn't help being proud of her. He couldn't help showing her off. Leo knows she isn't pretty, she is too small and dark and intense-looking, but she could always make Daddy laugh, even when he was in one of his depressions – more frequent as the years had passed – no, not exactly depressions, she had hastened to assure the police, he was never *depressed*, just sad occasionally. Sometimes just so sad…

"I still can't – can't believe it," Leo sobs. "I just – it's so…"

"I know, I know," Gemma soothes. "I do know."

And of course she does. Because just after what Leo always refers to as the Bombshell had dropped, Gemma herself had gone through a protracted period of grief. But she had lost a boyfriend, someone she'd only known for a couple of years. Not in the same league, surely, as a beloved father whom Leo had known all her life. No, not *all* her life, she has to admit, and if she were being scrupulously honest she would confess she hadn't loved him at all for the first fourteen years, and then for the next two or three she had merely tolerated him. That horrendous journey from Swansea with Huwie in tow had been in vain – they had been packed back to Mummy and Uncle Alun at the end of the holidays like unclaimed baggage and she had spent the next few years being shunted between London and Swansea and not wanted at either place. Oh, Daddy had pretended he enjoyed having her in the holidays but she could see through him – he never gave parties while she was there, never took her to see any of his friends, never introduced her round like he had Gemma, when *she* first arrived. The only thing he had done was name the gallery after her, but that was only because Gemma hadn't been around when he bought it, otherwise he might have called it Precious Gems, or something.

Oh, she is being spiteful again, and she shouldn't be – Gemma can't help being Daddy's long-lost daughter, and by all accounts she had a miserable upbringing, too. Stuck in Silly Suffolk with a doollally mother can't have been much fun. But why does she have to be so clever – and beautiful?

"So here you are!" sings a voice from the doorway, and Pudge appears with Huwie hovering behind. "Leonora, darling, do you think it wise to be in here? So soon? Look at the state of you – and you, too, Gemma!"

They pull apart, but not before Leo has seen the same expression on Gemma's face as she knows is on her own – amused annoyance. For a split second they have both exchanged mutual glances that conceal the same feelings, and Leo recognises with a joyful leap of her heart a hope that all is not lost between them. Perhaps they can go back to that easy friendship they'd had those first few weeks, when Leo had taken Gemma in hand and given her a whole new persona. And done too good a job, obviously.

Pudge hurries them out like a mother hen. "I've brought some home-made brownies and I'll make us all a nice hot chocolate drink. Forget the calories! Let's stuff ourselves rotten!" The Roedean accent is redolent of jolly larks in the dorm and for once Leo is grateful. She glances back at Huwie, bringing up the rear, and suddenly has an unfamiliar flash of understanding. Poor Huw, he hasn't had such a great time of it either and yet, being a man, can't show his feelings; being younger than her, too, he must have suffered the same rejection without being able to articulate it. The Groosome Toosome had arrived at an even worse time for him, when he still needed mothering. Instead of which, he had been shunted to and fro in the wake of his bossy sister. No wonder he had so easily allowed himself to be swallowed up whole.

She feels as if she's been given new eyes; sealed in a crystal-hard bubble, she can sit on a kitchen chair and watch them all with this new clarity of vision. She is sitting at a play, and they are acting out an already written script - but one that they haven't even seen, the undercurrents of which at least one isn't even aware of. She can remember it in its entirety, and will write it down in her Diary tonight.

CAST LIST:
PUDGE (Prudence Ursula Denby-Jessop, PR to Lord Havergo or some such, something high up in the law corts. Recently engaged and wants everyone to know it.) Tall, angular, lots of dark awburn hair held back by girly alice band, something of the thurobred about her but charmingly goshe – irritating but good-harted
GEMMA (Gemma Belling, thinking of changing her name to Bassett. Been thinking of doing this for months but don't know why she hasn't. Hope she doesn't. Daughter of the artist Drusilla (who Daddy calls Deirdre) Belling. Half-sister to yours trooly who wishes she wasn't. Left Cambridge to work for the BBC oversees news dept in some kind of research capasity.) Taller than me (tho who isn't!!), black hair, china doll face, fabulus figure (do I sound jelus? – I don't think I am, really. I think I'm acshully quite fond of her)
HUWIE (Huw Bassett, my younger brother. Works for some big civil engineering company dezining bridges and tunnels and things. Has flat in Barbican but doesn't yet live with Pudge, who has flat in Chelsea) Big like Daddy, broad sholders, good fizeek, looks more capable than he is. Just like Daddy
LEONORA (your narrator, who you should know quite well by now. I keep no secrets from you!! Freelance independant fashion co-ordinator, currantly between assinements, wondering if any more in the offing, possibly will have to apply for job on some gastly glossy celeb-model-obsessed mag) Small, dark, elfin features, pointed ears, forked tung…

SEEN: Kitchen. All sitting round table while Pudge hands round the cakes, won't take no for an anser. Even Huwie takes 1, tho he's not a sweet tooth. Gemma takes 1 but doesn't eat it. I take 3 and evenshally eat them all, first crumbling them to bits between my fingers

PUDGE: *Well, isn't this nice! We don't offen get a chance to have a good gossip. How long are you here for, Gemma?*

GEMMA: *I don't know. I'll have to apply for another visa. I left them a bit in the lerch...*

PUDGE: *I know what it's like to be indispensable. Lord Hav...*

ME: *O don't start on him again.*

PUDGE: *I don't know what you meen.*

ME: *We all know how indispensable you are to his lordship, you don't have to go on about it.*

PUDGE: *I don't! I don't, do I, Huw?*

HUWIE: *Keep me out of it, girls. (Smiling at Gemma) If you need help with arrangements...*

GEMMA: *Oh, please. I'm all at 6s and 7s...*

HUWIE: *I guess we all are.*

GEMMA: *The thing about Russia is it's still so hard to get permits and things, there's so much hanging around...*

PUDGE: *But it must be so interesting! Being on the threshold of world affairs! Glaznost and peristroyka and everything...*

GEMMA: *But the reality is still gloomy. The ordinary Russians...*

ME: *O who cares! I don't care about ordinary sodding Russians! Doesn't anybody care about what happened to Daddy?*

PUDGE: *O Leonora, darling, of corse we do! It's just that life must go on...*

ME: *Why?*

PUDGE: *(In saintly tones) Because your father would have wanted it.*

ME: *How do you know?*

HUWIE: *(Smiling at Gemma) So you'll be staying on here for a few more days...?*

GEMMA: *(Smiling at Huwie) If you don't mind...*

HUWIE: *(Smiling at Gemma) Of course not. I'll stay on till you go. (They smile at each other so long that even Pudge smells a rat)*

PUDGE: *(Gayly) Have another brownie, Huw!*

HUWIE: *No thanx.*

PUDGE: *(Less gayly) What about you, Leonora? O what a garstly mess you've made, o tut tut!*

ME: *I'll eat the crums. I always do.*

HUWIE: *Stop being a brat, Leo.*

PUDGE: *Darling Hooboo. (Kisses him, a real smacker on the lips) Wuvooooo.*
HUWIE: *(Extricating himself) Yes, all rite.*
GEMMA: *(Standing up) I'm a bit tired, I think I'll have a lie down.*
HUWIE: *(Standing up) You must be. That long flite, then the funeral – you look all in. (They stand smiling at each other for ages before Gemma goes out. He looks after her, stroking the place on his arm where her hand had rested) I think I'll go for a walk. I need some fresh air.*
PUDGE: *I'll come with you! Will you be all rite, Leo darling?*
ME: *(Between clenched teeth) Yes. Obviously.*

END OF SEEN

******

The Man is there again tonight. He doesn't stay long, and this time there is a purpose to his visit. He's looking towards the house, obviously towards Gemma's lighted window. Then he goes up to the big oak just inside the driveway and bends down, then straightens. At the gate he stops for a few seconds, then walks quickly away. As Leo peers through the window she can see something white fluttering on the gate – a piece of string or something, probably a signal they've arranged. He obviously doesn't want to phone or knock at the door like ordinary people.

She's aware that her heart is hammering. She feels violated, as if he's invaded her sanctuary, just like she felt when he'd actually invaded the house eighteen months ago.

She knows who he is, of course. She knows his name and what he's done but she doesn't know where he lives and why he hates Daddy and exactly how he fits into Gemma's life. The one fact she knows about their relationship only makes it more puzzling.

The first Invasion occurred only a week or so after the Bombshell. She had taken Gemma out on a shopping trip to buy a whole new wardrobe, and to have her long hair cut short, and they had come back to find this alien presence in Daddy's lounge, drinking Daddy's whisky and making Daddy unhappy.

But Gemma had been pleased to see him, had actually thrown herself at him and dragged him off into the garden. Daddy had watched them go with an expression on his face that had almost broken her heart, but he wasn't looking at Gemma, he was looking at Him. And with sickening clarity she remembered those terrible days in Swansea when Mummy wasn't speaking to Daddy and the house was silent and she knew something terrible had happened, and something even more terrible was going to happen. She hadn't even been three when the something even more terrible happened - when Daddy left home for good and never came back - but that nameless terror, that bottomless insecurity, had lurched up inside her then and is lurking still.

The second Invasion had gone on longer. The Man had actually lived in the house, slept in it, for a week or so. That was when Gemma was prostrate with grief, after the boyfriend had been killed in a car accident. Gemma had blamed herself because she'd stayed on in London while the boyfriend went off to the Lake District. They'd been spending the vacation with the Mad Mother in Suffolk and the boyfriend had sent some of her paintings to Daddy, and that was how Daddy had come face to face with the daughter he'd forgotten he had after twenty years.

The Bombshell had been dropped over the phone, and had appeared in person hours later – pale, slim, dark hair falling down her back in a long plait, wearing something elegant and expensive like a dowager duchess might have chosen. But there had been a naivety about her, a strange lack of confidence, which had given Leo a straw to cling on to. She, Leo, might have feelings of insecurity and terror inside, but on the outside she is streetwise and sassy and doesn't suffer fools gladly.

And she had felt so sorry for Gemma. They had all tried to comfort her but nothing had helped, until He had arrived. Why had Daddy allowed him to come in, to take over, to make them all feel so inadequate? It wasn't as if he was grateful; he hardly spoke to Daddy, let alone her and Huwie, he treated them as if they didn't exist. The house was like the labyrinth in that Greek myth, an alien structure containing a terrible monster – but in fact he was quite short for a man, much shorter than Daddy, and although he was well-built in a kind of athletic, boxer-type way he didn't have Daddy's bulk. And with his dark brown curly hair and deep brown eyes he could have been angelic, except that he wasn't, he looked stern and remote and unfriendly. But he had helped Gemma recover, he had sat by her bed day and night and let her weep and wail against his shoulder until she had surfaced from the depths of her grief, and then he had taken her off to Australia.

And that had been the start of Daddy's sadness. He'd had periods of depression before that - she could remember a very bad time a few months after she'd first come to live with him, when there had been a lot a kerfuffle in the papers about the artist who had painted the picture in his library - but she could pinpoint the actual deepening of his unhappiness to that period when Gemma was in Australia, those three months when the house in Hampstead had taken on that terrible silence of the house in Swansea and her nameless lurking terror had resurfaced.

She is nearly twenty-six, unmarried, still living at home. Daddy had offered to buy her a flat, like he had Huwie, but she refused. She wanted to stay with Daddy. She wanted to look after him, keep him safe. She had known he was in danger.

Who is he? What hold does – did – he have over Daddy? Was he one of Daddy's 'boys', those blond, blue-eyed Adonises Daddy invites – invited – to his parties? But that was all a sham, put on to keep up his reputation. He had told her so, hadn't he? He wasn't gay – how could he be, when he had three children? She's often wondered about his relationship with Miss Rottweiler, the old spinster at the gallery – there was something going on there, she is sure. She will get to the bottom of it, she owes it to Daddy.

And now, just as she's about to switch off the lamp by her window and draw the curtains, the door of Gemma's bedroom, next to hers, is flung open and footsteps are flying along the landing and down the stairs. A beam of light is thrown along the drive from the front door, directly beneath her window, and Gemma is running along it towards the oak tree by the gate. She bends, and is screened from view by the bushes, but when she straightens she has something in her hand – a piece of paper, which she is so eager to read she can't wait until she's in her bedroom but stands in the light by the front door. Then, smiling, she clasps the paper to her heart and steps inside the hall. The light goes out; the drive is in darkness.

4.   September 1976

Laurence leant back in his chair and stretched out his legs and arms, then folded himself up, elbows on desk, and plaited his fingers through his hair. He hadn't done this for a while – he paid his barber too much to keep his full head of chestnut hair in impeccable order – but he was expecting a phonecall from Caitlin at any moment, to report that the kids had arrived safely back in Swansea. Oh thank God, thank God! – the school holidays were over and his life could get back to normal.

He had realised quite soon that he wasn't cut out for fatherhood. Even with Mrs W's indulgent vigilance, he found his routine turned upside down, his tranquil home thrown into chaos: slamming doors, phonecalls at all hours, slanging matches between the pair of them, histrionics from Leonora when she couldn't get her own way. It was easier all round if he capitulated to her incessant demands, but he knew he was making a rod for his own back.

With the money she'd inveigled out of him, Leonora had bought leather trousers festooned with chains and straps, had her hair dyed orange, cut short and waxed into spikes, her upper arms tattooed with snarling wolves and naked mermaids (only semi-permanent, she had assured him, they'd wash off after a few weeks). Most afternoons, he found out later, she hung around Trafalgar Square being photographed by tourists for 20p a time in the company of other similarly clad Goths ('*punks*', she'd told him, witheringly). She had thrown tantrums when he'd forbidden her to stay out after 9pm. He had a feeling even that was too late for a fourteen-year-old; he'd spent every evening dreading a visit from the police or the social services, the full weight of the law descending upon his clearly inadequate parental head.

But in a way, Leonora had been easier to cope with than Huwie. She at least gave full vent to her feelings, be they exuberant enthusiasm – throwing her arms round his neck, kissing him extravagantly, calling him her darling Daddy (when she had got her own way); or shrieking invective at the top of her lungs, accusing him of being the worst father in the world, she wished he was *dead* (when, on the few occasions he'd put his foot down, she hadn't). At least he knew where he stood with her.

With Huwie he was completely out of his depth. The boy was polite but withdrawn. Sometimes, when he didn't know Laurence was watching him, the expression of abject misery on his face caused Laurence's heart to miss a beat. At just twelve, he was clearly in what Mrs W called a 'growth spurt' – his hands and feet were enormous, and his limbs weren't fully under his control. He was taller than Leo by a good six inches. And Laurence had remembered his own tortured adolescence, when he'd been the biggest in his class by a full head, and he ached to take his son in his arms and reassure him that one day all would be well. But he couldn't, and didn't. Did fathers hug sons these days? – his own father hadn't. And besides, what had Caitlin told them about their father's sexual orientation? – and how much did they understand what it meant? Oh, during these endless four weeks Laurence had been forced to confront the meaning of parenthood, and had been totally traumatised by the experience.

And he couldn't even expect help from Deborah. She had been a willing pair of ears but completely incapable of offering advice. Her own adolescence had been a world away from Leonora's; he'd learnt only now that she *had* been convent educated at a High Anglican order somewhere in Surrey, and had gone straight from there to the all-female environs of Girton College, Cambridge. Men and children were unknown beasts to her. His other ally, Hilary, was no use either. The only person who had steered him through the whole ghastly ordeal had been dear Mrs Wetherby, who called his offspring 'little lambs'; Leonora was a 'highly-strung little pet who'll settle down in her own good time', and Huw was a 'poor little soul who just needs a big cuddle'. Needless to say, both little lambs behaved beautifully when in her care, which unfortunately didn't stretch to evenings and weekends.

Thank goodness Ralph's new project – *Whither Art? A*

Personal View – had been shelved for the foreseeable future. Ralph had been plunged in gloom, but Laurence had breathed a sigh of relief. He could do without further complications in his life at the moment.

The telephone rang. Deborah put it through without comment. For the next few minutes he listened to a catalogue of paternal incompetence: What was he thinking of, sending his daughter back in that state on public transport? Why had he given her so much money to spend on such disgusting garbage? How on earth could she go back to school with *orange hair*? And why had Huwie become such a clingy, affection-seeking child? He would never be entrusted with his children ever again if that was what he let them get away with... and just as his heart had given a joyful leap, he could hear Leonora in the background shouting, "Daddy, I love you, I'm coming at Christmas I promise, she won't keep me away...!"

Dropping the receiver back into its cradle he slumped over the desk, hands covering his head as if to ward off blows. He remained like that even after the door opened and Deborah came in, taking the chair opposite. Eventually he lifted his head, rubbed his face, pulled his nose, and gave her a defeated smile.

"Worse than expected?" she murmured.

"I've just gone ten rounds with Cassius Clay."

"Mohammad Ali."

"Both of them." He remained smiling at her, relishing the way she returned his gaze and his smile; they were, he thought, on the same wavelength. She didn't want him to change. She valued him for what he was. Only one other person, a woman – a girl – had made him feel precious, and that was a long time ago in another country. Was she also lost to him? – up to now he had thought not, had clung to a hope that she could be restored to him. But that hope was now withering.

"I've got some news that might cheer you up."

"Oh, tell me, please."

She pursed her lips. She had her schoolmarmish look today; the feminine Deborah of his party had been completely erased beneath a severely cut suit and pearl choker.

"Have you been a good boy, Laurence?"

"Not particularly, Miss Routledge."

"Then perhaps you don't deserve to hear it." She stood up and smoothed her skirt over her hips, then walked to the door on those silk-encased legs balanced on those knifeblade heels.

On an impulse, he slid to the floor, crawled towards her on all fours, nudged her hand with his nose. Without turning, she bent down, grasped his tie in her other hand, gave it a sharp upward tug. He put out his tongue and panted.

She mussed his hair with forgiving fingers. Then slid down the door to sit, knees elegantly sideways, on the floor beside him. He rolled over, then sat next to her, knees drawn up to his chin. For a while he couldn't bring himself to look at her; he had made a fool of himself, probably. But her face in profile was softened, a little pink.

"If little Rosemary could see us now..."

She said quietly, "The *News of the World* would have a field day."

"So what is the news, Deborah?"

She was going to make him wait a little longer, evidently. He sat, hands dangling between his knees, trying to look remorseful.

"I've found," she stated at last, "Freddy's boy."

"Ah. The painter."

"There's a student exhibition in Whitechapel. He's included."

"Any good?"

"By all accounts, yes."

"Name?"

She smiled at him. "You haven't been that good, Laurence."

"You're a hard woman, Miss Routledge."

"Go along. Have a look. Freddy can't keep you away, much as he'd like to."

"Will he be there?"

"Freddy? Or the boy?"

"It'll be both, or neither. You know how possessive the old goat is."

She got to her knees, then stood, smoothing down her skirt. "It starts Monday. You've got four days." The door opened at

41

his back and she vanished, leaving him stranded on the floor.

******

Whitechapel was in a part of London untrodden by Laurence. Anywhere south of the river, north of Watford or east of St Paul's was uncharted territory. He decided to take a taxi; he found driving anywhere in London a pain, even in his nearly-new Rover. The taxi deposited him outside an old warehouse in a decrepit side street opposite what seemed to be a hostel for itinerant sailors. Only a few sad flags over the door, and a handwritten sign stuck with sellotape to the frame with the words *Art Exhibition, Second Floor* under a black arrow pointing up a flight of grimy stairs, indicated that this was indeed the place.

What exactly was he doing here? He didn't need to trawl the outer reaches of the city desperate to find the next Big Thing in art. Was it just because, as he told Deborah, Dermot was now pushing forty and losing his edge? Artists, like everyone else in this modern world, had to be young, good looking, outrageous. Prodigious talent was less important than shock value. But he, Laurence, wasn't at the cutting edge of art; he bought and sold what appealed to him, not merely the latest trends, and managed to make a comfortable enough living.

Reaching the long gallery at the top of two flights of stairs, trying not to pant too heavily, he gave his card to the bearded fellow at the door and was nodded through to join the smallish crowd inside. At the door he was accosted by a young girl carrying a tray of wineglasses. He took one with 'Riviera Hotel Torquay' stamped on its side, and sipped at the wine which was warm, sweet and virtually undrinkable. He was reminded of his own student days in Cambridge where he had helped out at amateur exhibitions, and the wine had been crap then, too.

He made his way round the room, giving each painting at least thirty seconds'-worth of attention; some didn't even merit that long. Only one held his gaze for a minute or so - a portrait of an old man, quite competently done. But it wasn't Deirdre's.

And now he knew why he was here. Freddy's boy was just an excuse; he was here to find Deirdre, and would be searching for her at every obscure viewing he could attend from now on. Why now, after nearly twelve years? But up till now he had been confident of confronting her art sooner or later, at any of the student exhibitions or first viewings he had attended, without having to put himself out; talent like hers would surface without any effort from him. She would surely have gone on painting, it was as natural as breathing to her. One day, he had thought, he would open the arts section of the paper, or be confronted by a portrait, and she would be back in his life. Her, and the child.

Why should this unknown daughter have risen in his mind so insistently? Possibly because, having just unburdened himself of his legitimate offspring, he had realised it would be her eleventh birthday soon, if not already. He had trained himself not to think of her or her mother, not to dwell on his life before his rise to fame, not to confront the ghosts. Because he knew where these thoughts would lead. They would take him inexorably back to the figure outside his gate on those Fridays in Swansea when he was supposed to be teaching Deirdre about art - that small, fierce, hostile presence with the face of an angel and the patience of a saint.

He stopped in front of a large, garishly-painted canvas and took three or four deep breaths. Anyone watching him would take him to be suffering the ailments of late middle age – breathlessness, angina, creeping emphysema. He had smoked cigarettes in his youth, then had taken up cigars, but nowadays his only vice was perhaps an over-reliance on alcohol. But it wasn't anything medical that caused him to stop and breathe deeply, to get a grip on incipient vertigo; just the jolt these memories always gave him, and the knowledge that time had moved on and life had progressed and yet he was still locked in the past, still awaiting forgiveness.

The moment passed, as always; his head cleared, helped by a gulp or two of the execrable wine. The painting in front of his eyes swam into view. It was modern art gone mad; two great swirls of red surrounded by thinner stripes of gold and orange, a thread-like stripe of an almost luminous white snaking across the canvas horizontally. And smaller circles of red in the background, a livid red changing imperceptibly to the clotted black-red of dried blood, again trailing thinner stripes, almost tumbling off the sides, melting into the cheap hardboard frame. But always that thin white thread, almost invisible, keeping the whole thing together. It was some moments before he could tear his eyes away to read the small postcard tacked up at the side: *Closed Circuits of the Cluttered Mind #2: Will Murchison.*

There was no one around this corner of the room. When he sneaked a look, most people were now grouped in the middle, a few clustered round a couple of paintings near the entrance. He wondered how they had managed to move on; his own feet refused to budge. He would have remained here all day and night, had not a figure sidled up to him, holding out a tray on which were small bowls of crisps and peanuts. He took a handful, his eyes still gripped by *Closed Circuits of the Cluttered Mind #2.*

"Why is it," he said at last, the figure still at his elbow, "that young British artists insist on giving perfectly good paintings outlandish Americanised titles?"

It was a rhetorical question that required no answer. And it didn't get one, not right away. But something made Laurence tear his gaze from the canvas and look down; the boy at his elbow was obviously trying to frame some kind of reply. And at the instant he looked down, the boy looked up.

It wasn't the mop of light brown hair, the hazel eyes, the straight nose and finely-drawn mouth. The features weren't quite the same. The body wasn't the same either, it was looser, thinner, less dense. There was nothing of that watchful hostility of gaze, just an intense eagerness to please. This boy didn't tell him to "fuck off", he was trying to frame a polite response. And this 'boy' was at least four years older, maybe more – nineteen or twenty – and obviously taller. But the resemblance was enough, and for the second time in just over as many minutes Laurence felt the floor slide away from his feet and his lungs empty of air. Again, he had to make a superhuman effort to breathe.

"The c-college c-called it that."

"Ahhh." It wasn't a response, just an exhalation.

"I c-call it W-wheels Number Two."

And Laurence had to summon up every ounce of his strength to ask, "Is there a Wheels Number One?" and to keep his voice on a level, the word 'wheels' from almost mimicking the boy's stammer.

A tentative smile lifted the anxious face at his side. "No, but I can d-do one if you want."

The room was almost back to normal; Laurence almost back in control. "Are there any more of yours here?"

"Just one, along there." He indicated a smaller canvas hung on the opposite wall. This one had two or three people round it and Laurence felt a sharp stab of proprietorial jealousy. "I think it's b-been sold."

The painting titled *Cross Currents in a Stoned Sea* was mainly in tones of blue, waves of indigo and lapis with depths of black and that same livid red, the luminous white this time in tiny dots scattered randomly across the canvas. Except that Laurence realised they weren't random, but had been placed with extreme care and probably over a fairly long period of time. But this painting had a small red dot on the bottom right-hand side of the frame.

"Do you know who bought it?"

The boy glanced round the room. "That b-bloke there, I think." He pointed towards a shortish, squattish fellow in a black turtle-neck sweater and grey flares, wearing sunglasses, who was in conversation with a couple of people, one of whom Laurence recognised as Maudie Madison from the *Guardian*.

He turned back and smiled. "It's your lucky day, Will. I'm buying Wheels Two, as long as you paint me a Wheels One to go with it."

"Not on your fucking life, you old pisspot." And Swainton was hurrying in from the door marked *Toilets*, doing up his fly. "I've only got to turn my back and give the old bowels a good workout and here you are, muscling in on my territory." He draped an arm round young Will's shoulders. "Fuck off, Larry, I found him first."

"I'm only buying a painting."

"Not for sale, old boy. Not to you."

"For God's sake, Freddy…"

"Not to God or his archangels or the whole heavenly fucking host. Piss off back to Mayfair." An expression of deep satisfaction settled over Freddy's long horsy features. "Never clapped eyes on you before in the underworld of lost tribes. You must have been mightily intrigued." He gathered the boy into himself. "And mightily pissed off, I fervently hope."

Was it only his imagination, or was there a look of despair, of entreaty, in those green-brown eyes under the tumbling curls as Freddy ushered the boy away in the direction of the turtle-neck sweater? - for whom Laurence felt a sudden almost pathological hatred. As he made his way out into the foreign landscape of east London, he made a mental note to remember to invite Maudie to his next party.

******

Deborah Routledge had lived in Baron's Court all her life, in this same flat and with almost the same furniture. Wherever she looked her mother stared back at her: in the old-fashioned dresser in the kitchen, the ugly three-piece suite in the lounge, the mahogany wardrobes and chests in the two main bedrooms. None of these huge ungainly items were antiques, or worth anything much – the modern taste was for light, plain furniture set against highly patterned wallpaper and carpets. The wallpaper in the flat had once been highly patterned, but now had faded and crumbled to a uniform ochre, and the carpets – what could be seen of them – were mostly threadbare. Once every two years or so she promised herself to get rid of the lot and buy new, but somehow had never got round to it. And now it was probably too late. She was at the same age her mother had been when she took to her bed, and she, Deborah, had had to leave university to look after her. After those long years of what she had assumed was malingering (and had hated her mother for), and then the

46

protracted dying of the motor neurone disease that might have been there all along, the flat had been left as a museum to the past and she saw no reason to disturb it now.

Of course, if she'd had many visitors, she might have freshened the place up a bit, but visitors were scarce at Hurlingham Mansions. All the old great aunts were long dead, her mother's only sister living down in Devon. She had no siblings and no friends of any note. She knew plenty of people in the art world but none she liked well enough to invite back. And she preferred it that way. Over the years she had cultivated an air of mystery, an aloofness, that was now second nature. She knew she was no beauty, but she had a good figure for her age, light brown hair that showed no grey, and dressed conservatively but with a certain élan. She enjoyed turning men's heads but had no desire to enter the competitive world of dating.

When her mother had been taken into the hospice, she had had to look to her future. Without a degree, she couldn't apply for the posts she'd assumed she was suited for – museum curator, custodian of antiquities. She scoured the Sits Vac for something interesting, but it wasn't in the classified pages that she found the answer. It was on the front page of the paper, then on the inside pages, which carried the story of a scandalous divorce and photographs taken outside the court. The principal character was always shielding his face from the camera, or half-turned away. This intrigued her; he seemed the twin of herself, someone who also craved privacy. He was a big man, too, and handsome, with a good head of hair and an expression, where she could see it, of bemused amiability. He was *unthreatening*. The allegations of homosexuality, of his obsession with boys, all unproven, only added to his fascination. The divorce had made the newspapers after his inheritance of a large sum of money, and was settled in the end fairly amicably. But the press had found a *cause célèbre*, and from then on regularly reported Laurence Bassett's movements in the gossip columns. There were also thundering editorials in the broadsheets along the lines of: *Do we now reward sexual deviants? Has our national character sunk so low?* - but these were soon overwhelmed by an avalanche of sacred cows tumbling down. Laurence Bassett's alleged misdemeanours were small fry, but still the press pursued him because now he was a national treasure, 'the unthinking woman's Quentin Crisp', as one wag had dubbed him.

And Deborah Routledge, too, pursued him. Unobtrusively, invisibly. She located the Islington shop and watched him from a safe distance, noting his movements. Behind a large hat and dark glasses she jotted down his lunch-time preferences for chicken sandwiches on rye bread and low-calorie juices and then, guiltily, a bottle of good claret, paté and cheese. He was a man after her own heart, enjoying secret pleasures. She watched him change from shunning the camera to playing up his flamboyant image – he took to wearing yellow waistcoats and floppy cravats and smoking cigars – but only for television, for the amusement of his customers. Away from public gaze, she was sure, he reverted to type.

He sold the Islington shop, moved from Kentish Town to Camden, became a regular face on afternoon television. And bought the lease of a gallery in Cork Street.

She made her move; bumped into him as he came out of his solicitors after signing the contract. He apologised profusely, assuming, of course, that *he* had bumped into *her*. The heel of one of her shoes hung loose. A long, narrow sandal with ankle strap, it dangled fetchingly from her long, narrow foot. She felt like Cinderella as he knelt down beside her, examining the damage. The three-inch stiletto came off in his hand.

He insisted on accompanying her to the mender's, paying for the repair and inviting her to lunch. It was fate, he maintained, that had brought them together. No sooner had he bought the gallery than he found the perfect assistant – an art history graduate, unemployed for a number of years from necessity but desperate now to find a proper job. He would, he told her with a rueful laugh, be largely dependent upon her expertise; she probably had more qualifications than him. She smiled and gently remonstrated, saying they complemented each other and he, under the influence of rather too much Chateauneuf du Pape, declared it was a marriage made in heaven.

Which it was, Deborah thought, flicking a duster round a group of sepia photographs on the grand piano she couldn't play. Better than a marriage. She knew his mind more intimately than any wife while he knew next to nothing about her. She catered for his needs in ways he didn't even know he required. She was a willing servant, biding her time. There had been occasions, over the six years she had worked for him, when she nearly showed her hand. That time, just six months after she started the job, when he'd rushed off to Wales and returned sunk in despair – it would have been easy to persuade him to come back with her to Hurlingham Mansions. She was almost tempted. But glad now that she hadn't.

She hesitated, duster arrested in mid-flick. She laid it down, carefully, and went through to the hall, into the kitchen, opened a drawer in the hideous Welsh dresser. Holding the key, she retraced her steps to the hall, past mother's bedroom, to the locked door at the end. She inserted the key, pushed open the door, took a deep breath, and entered.

******

"Laurence Bassett, please."

"May I ask who's calling?"

"Maudie Madison." A pause. Then, irritably, "The *Guardian* arts editor."

"Ah, yes. Well, I'm sorry but Mr Bassett isn't available."

A frustrated sigh. "Get him to call me…"

"If you can give me some indication what…?"

"It's personal."

"I see. Well, in that case, I'll get Mr Bassett to call you back as soon as he returns, Ms Madison."

Another pause. "When will that be, do you think? Oh, just tell him I won't be able to make the party but thank him for the invitation."

"Oh, that's a shame. Mr Bassett's parties are legendary."

"So I believe."

"You haven't previously attended one, Ms Madison?"

49

"No, I – I'm always too busy." A blatant lie, of course. She'd never been invited. "Perhaps the next one…" Ah. It was pride that would be her downfall.

"Oh, I'm sorry. The guest list always exceeds limits, unfortunately. Non attenders go back to the bottom and have to await their turn." Deborah paused. "Unless, of course, he can be persuaded…"

"What do you mean?" – spoken much too quickly.

"I believe Mr Bassett may have wanted to talk to you about something. In an informal setting, possibly."

A longer pause. Then, "To whom am I speaking?"

"His personal assistant, Miss Routledge."

"Do you know what he would have wanted to talk about, Miss Routledge?"

"I believe Mr Bassett might have wanted to know a little more about a young painter - Will Murchison? - and the identity of the purchaser of a painting…?"

"Oh, I see. The exhibition in Whitechapel – I thought I caught sight of him there."

"If you have any information, I'll make sure Mr Bassett is appraised of it as soon as he returns. And I'm sure your name will be reinstated at the top of the guest list."

Another sigh, this time of relief. "The young man lives in Hackney, Cawston Street I believe, and the purchaser was a Mr Symons, David Symons, over from Denver. I have his card…"

"So do I." Deborah allowed herself a small smile. "The Venn Pegasus Agency. I don't suppose you know who the client would be…?"

"I'm afraid not. But he did indicate that his client might be buying more, if he likes what Mr Symons shows him. I got the feeling he's an American businessman, probably also Denver-based. Mr Symons seemed on quite intimate terms with him."

"But I thought Mr Symons himself was English."

"Yes, from East Ham, he told me."

"It seems rather strange that he's on such good terms with an American businessman. Possibly his client is also English…?"

"Possibly." Obviously Maudie Madison knew no more.

"Well, I'll certainly let Mr Bassett know how helpful you've been." Deborah hung up briskly, certain that on the other end of the line the arts editor of the *Guardian* would be fuming. Those types were usually the ones to terminate a call, not be left wrong-footed by a mere minion. It was these small victories that made her job all the more pleasurable, Deborah thought, as she mounted the stairs to the office.

He was standing by the long window looking out over the street. His whole stance was one of defeat – a stoop to the shoulders, a downward incline of the head, hands stuffed into trouser pockets as if he didn't know what else to do with them. Although he must have heard her enter – a small twitch of the cheek in profile told her that – he remained unmoving for several seconds. Then, hauling his hands from his pockets, he turned and walked back to the desk.

"Maudie Madison," she said. "Can't make the party."

"Ah." He sat on the edge of the desk, hands dangling between his legs.

"But a good try, Laurence."

He smiled ruefully. "But I failed."

"Oh no. You identified the right painter."

"He's good, isn't he."

"Very." She leaned back against the desk, next to him.

"Do I have to beg, Miss Routledge?" He half-turned towards her. The desolation in his eyes smote at her heart.

"Cawston Street, Hackney. I don't know the number." That look in his eyes – it took her back to that time over five years ago, when he had heard news that had sent him dashing off to Wales. To Caernarvon, in North Wales. What was in Caernarvon, she had wondered, that was so irresistible? – and had found it to be the location of the circuit court, and a case was being heard that had hit the front pages of the papers, before they lost interest. She had read up all about it – an IRA arms cache had been discovered on a farm near Conwy and the owner, a young man of twenty, had taken the blame. There was some doubt about this; the farm had been the site of a commune, although everyone else had apparently left. There was a photo of the man but obviously taken when he was younger: an unsmiling, tousle-haired boy with a wary intensity in the eyes. He had been brought up in an orphanage in Swansea. Laurence had lived in Swansea; his ex-wife and children still lived there. The ex-wife had cited his alleged interest in boys as grounds for divorce. Deborah's highly-tuned antennae detected a connection.

But what was the connection now? Did this Will Murchison remind him of that lost boy? She tried to recall the name, but it escaped her. No matter, it would be easy to look up. And she must find out more about Will Murchison. Although, of course, she wouldn't need to. Laurence would do it for her.

******

Cawston Street was one of those short depressing thoroughfares of faceless terraced houses in the vicinity of Mare Street, not the elegant Georgian terraces near the Wick or solid Victorian houses facing a rather nice park. Laurence thanked his lucky stars that at least it wasn't one of the Sixties high-rise blocks of soulless concrete or Fifties sprawling estates of red-brick flats he had driven his Rover through, windows rolled up and door locks engaged.

The populace of this part of London seemed a colourful mix – colourful in the sense of nationality, not dress, which was uniformly drab. Even the saris Indian women wore peeping out from beneath buttoned cardigans were faded and limp. African and Caribbean faces looked rusty and forlorn under north European skies, which now threatened rain after the glorious summer.

He had consulted the telephone directory but of course Murchison was not listed as one of its residents. He decided to take pot luck and drive down on a Sunday, when there was a chance more people would be at home. So now he was parked halfway down Cawston Street, wondering what to do next.

A loud rap on the window made him jump. A large West Indian face was pressed against the glass. He wound the window down half an inch.

"Wouldn't park here, man. Not wheels like this, know what I mean? You lookin' for somethin'?"

"No, I'm…"

"Don't say I don't warn you, man. Come back after dark, know what I mean? Keep cool." And he thumped a fist on the car roof and reeled away, bouncing on the soles of his trainers as if on strings.

Laurence wound the window back up, pressed himself into the seat and tugged his collar over his ears. Five minutes. If he didn't see anyone he could ask in the next five minutes…

"Want your car washed, mister?" And now an urchin was peering in, a cheeky-faced lad with no hair and a stud in his ear.

He again wound the window down half an inch. "No thanks. But could you tell me…"

"Only fifty pee. Me and me mate…"

"No thanks. But I'll give you fifty pee if you can tell me…"

"Don't say nuffin' for less than a pound."

"You live round here?"

"Just round the corner. Know everyfing, me."

"Do you know a painter who lives in this street? An artist, who paints pictures? Young, about twenty?"

"Might do."

"A pound if you tell me where he lives."

"This your car?"

"All right. Two pounds."

"Shame if it got done up. Me and me mate could look after it, see nobody does it up."

"How much?"

"A fiver." The urchin waited while Laurence dug into his wallet and threaded a five pound note through the gap. "Deposit, innit."

"Another fiver after I come back, if the car's in one piece." He waited for the kid to pocket the money and run off, but he didn't. "So where does he live?"

"Who?"

"The painter."

"Number 34."

"34 Cawston Street."

"Yeah."

Laurence wound the window up, climbed out of the car and locked it. No sooner had he walked a few paces away than a United Nations of urchins was swarming all over it. He'd probably been well and truly conned, but it was too late now.

Number 34 looked no better but no worse than its neighbours. Laurence searched in vain for a bell or knocker, then rapped his knuckles on the rippled glass insert. He stood for a while, then made a tunnel of his hands and peered through into a deserted hall. On the floor underneath the letterbox was a drift of envelopes, newspapers and junk mail.

"No one in?" The urchin was beside his elbow.

"No one's been in for weeks."

"Yeah, I just remembered, they moved out." Then, probably seeing his financial prospects in danger, said hastily, "You could try Number 41."

"Why?"

"I think he lives at Number 41."

Laurence, the urchin at his side, walked across the road and found Number 41, and got the same result.

"Number 16! I remember now, it's Number..."

"Why don't we try every house in the street?"

The urchin's face stretched in a wide smile. "That's a good idea, mister! I'll do this side, you do the other..."

Laurence laughed ruefully. "A good try, young man. You'll go far." He started walking back towards the Rover, the urchin dancing in front of him.

The other kids fell back as they approached. Laurence inserted his key. The urchin held on to his arm.

"Give us a ride, mister."

Laurence looked down into the lad's face. A lively, intelligent face with startling blue eyes and a mobile, generous mouth. His heart missed a beat. His own son's face rose up in his mind, with that closed inward expression of misery, and suddenly he was desperate to have his children with him again, to make up to

54

them for his years of absence.

"Didn't anyone tell you not to get into cars with strange men?" He opened his wallet and took out another five pound note. To his surprise, the boy didn't take it.

"Didn't do nuffin', did I."

"The car's still in one piece." Then he took out his pen and wrote the Hampstead telephone number on the back of an envelope and tore it off. "If you do find out the address of this painter, give me a call." He placed both notes into the boy's grubby hand.

It was only as he was driving away that he realised what that little scene might have looked like to anyone watching.

5. April 1987

In the end, Gemma won't go back to Moscow for another few weeks at least as there is some trouble over visas and permits, so Huwie is staying on and Pudge, although going back to Chelsea most nights, is a regular visitor. The Wainwrights are staying on, too. Leo had assumed that Huwie would terminate their contract of employment or, when their wages weren't forthcoming, they would leave of their own accord, but neither he nor they have said anything. Huw has always buried his head in the sand when it comes to changing arrangements and Leo herself has never looked far into the future, especially when that future looks bleak.

She has never even thought about Daddy's Will, and what arrangements he had made about the house and its contents. She doesn't even know who his solicitors are. But Huwie must know, because he has informed her this morning that his solicitor is coming to the house in a couple of days to see the pair of them. And Gemma, of course.

It seems to Leo that there has been a clear division in her life. BB and AB: Before and After Bombshell. BB, she had been happy and settled, making her own way in the fashion world, living with Daddy, Huwie and dear Mr and Mrs W. She'd had a succession of boyfriends but none of them serious. AB, her life had been turned upside down: Gemma had moved in, Huwie had got himself ensnared, the Wetherbys were replaced by the Wainwrights. Everything changed. Gemma had been the catalyst; no sooner had she appeared than the Mad Mother had made an entrance and the Man had invaded their lives.

Had he also lived here after he and Gemma had returned from Australia, after Daddy had put up his bail? – she didn't know, because at that time she'd been in the Bahamas on a fashion assignment, and then had gone on to the States. By the time she'd come home, five weeks later, he wasn't there; he was staying with a friend, Gemma said. And then he'd pleaded guilty and was given eighteen months, of which he served about ten – less than a year, for doing what he'd done! It didn't bear thinking about. And he already had a record as long as her arm.

He killed my father and I'm going to proove it. Easy to write, of course. But how to go about proving it? But she's quite sure he did it. From the day she had seen him in Daddy's lounge she knew he hated Daddy. And anyone who'd done what he had was capable of anything.

So what exactly does Gemma see in him? Because she loves him, there's no doubt about that, even though he's fifteen years older than her. The Mad Mother is involved somewhere, too. It was only after he'd been jailed that she went completely bonkers and Daddy had arranged for her to be looked after by the Wetherbys.

Leo has never asked Gemma about him, not even after Gemma's return from Australia when she'd had to turn to Leo for help. She felt she would be showing disloyalty to Daddy by meddling in his business, and Daddy was sad enough already. That was about the time he'd started withdrawing from the gallery and cut down his television appearances. He'd taken up his project on the Old Masters, to give himself some intellectual credentials, he'd told Leo. But she already knew quite enough about the Man, anyway.

When she was about eight there had been all that fuss about the commune case in North Wales, which had been big time news in 1970. Mummy and Uncle Alun had read about it in the papers and talked about the guns that were found and the probable IRA connection. The IRA was hitting the headlines then too, and every night the telly showed pictures of bombed buildings in Belfast and elsewhere. The Man had pleaded guilty to hiding the guns, but obviously he had also been covering up what they found on the farm fifteen years later, when he and Gemma were in Australia. He had been arrested as soon as they'd arrived back but she didn't know any more details because she'd been in the States. Huwie had helped Gemma over her shock at the Man's arrest, and then she, Leo, had arrived back just in time to help Gemma over the next big shock.

Had Daddy seen the Man hanging round the street light, after his release at the beginning of February? Daddy's bedroom, as

57

well as the library, is at the back of the house, and the Man only turned up after dark. The first time Leo had seen him she'd written in her Diary: *There's someone lerking at the end of the drive, under the lite. I'm sure it's Him, tho I can't see properly becoz of the hedge. If he hasn't gone in 10 mins I'll call the police.*

But she hadn't, because when she glanced up again he'd gone, and the street light looked somehow bereft. A couple of days later, there he was again: ***Mon 9 Feb 9.22pm*** *He's back. I'll wotch to see wot he does.* ***9.24pm*** *He's still there.* ***9.28pm*** *Still there.* ***9.31pm*** *Ditto.* ***9.34pm*** *Ditto* ***9.37pm*** *He's gone. He's hoping to see Gemma of corse, but she won't be back for another 12 days.*

Gemma had a job in the BBC overseas news department covering events in Eastern Europe and was away quite a lot on different assignments. This time she'd been in Poland. The Man had turned up another four nights before the light had been on in her bedroom. He obviously knew her bedroom, he'd spent enough time in it during the Invasion.

Mon 16 Feb 9.27pm *Gemma's come back early. She told us she was staying on for another week but she arrived back this a.m. Perhaps she knows he's been let out. Shall I tell her he comes here about this time every nite? No, I'll wait to see wot happens.*

9.31pm *There he is. He's looking up at Gemma's window but she's not looking out or else her curtains are drawn. But he's seen the lite on. Now he's walking up the drive – no, he's turned back. Why doesn't he just come up and ring the bell like a normal person? I wish I knew what she thinks of him now. Her feelings mite have changed. Perhaps he's afraid of that too…*

But then Leo had heard Gemma's door burst open, her footsteps fly down the stairs. She watched her run down the drive and throw herself at him. They had clung together for a long while. Then they walked away from the lamp post, arms entwined, heads bent together, and Leo had waited up way past midnight for Gemma's return, watching her walk alone up the drive, flushed, excited, radiantly happy.

After that the street light remained lonely and bereft until the night of the funeral.

******

"Will you be around tomorrow morning, Gem?" Huwie asks at breakfast.

"Yes, why?"

"Old Cardew's coming – Dad's solicitor. He wants to talk to all of us about the Will."

"Oh."

"Ten o'clock. Okay?"

Concentrating on her grapefruit, Leo nevertheless catches Gemma's sideways glance towards her.

"Yes." Gemma finishes her muesli, then says to Huwie, "Could you give me a lift into town? I've still got a few things to do."

Leo says, "When are you going back to work, Huw?"

Both pairs of eyes turn to her. Huwie says, "Probably next week. They gave me a couple of weeks' compassionate leave but said not to worry if it takes longer." And then he adds, quite unnecessarily, she thinks, "What about you?"

"I'm waiting for the itinerary of my next assignment." It isn't true; she hasn't chased any of her contacts up for weeks. She honestly can't see how she can go back to work as if nothing had happened. Daddy has only been dead just over a month, and people already assume the period of mourning is over. *Pull yourself together,* she can read in their eyes, *get on with life,* but they don't understand. She has no life without Daddy.

She takes her bowl to the sink and runs the tap. Upstairs, the vacuum cleaner hums; Mrs Wainwright is doing the bedrooms today. Gemma and Huwie remain seated at the table, and Leo is well aware that behind her back they are exchanging looks. She goes back to the table and gathers up Gemma's bowl and Huwie's plate. They both rise as of one accord.

"Come on then, Gem," Huwie says, and takes her arm.

"Have a nice day.," Leo calls after them. There's no response; the front door slams.

She stands at the sink, watching it fill with suds as her eyes fill with tears. Doesn't Huwie know Gemma's heart belongs to another? And besides, they're half-siblings; the relationship is doomed. And poor Pudge, unaware she's second best. Oh, life is so complicated! Oh Daddy, I miss you!

On a sudden impulse, she turns off the tap, wipes her hands on a teacloth, and speeds upstairs. Mrs Wainwright is busy in the en-suite of the small guest bedroom, which Huwie is now using. Leo slides into Gemma's room next door (which used to be Huwie's) and quietly shuts the door. Mrs Wainwright has obviously been in here already; it has the air of a hotel room. In Mrs Wetherby's day the bedrooms still felt as if they belonged to their occupants, but Mrs Wainwright has a more professional approach. In fact, both Wainwrights carry out their duties as if they are employed by a corporation, not a family. No wonder Daddy had never taken to them.

What would Gemma have done with that letter? She has watched Gemma like a hawk since its delivery to the oak tree on Monday but she hasn't done anything out of the ordinary. And she goes back to Moscow soon; if they have made an assignation, it will be in the next few days. He won't come to the house any more; he had come on the night of the funeral just to make sure Gemma had returned. It's strange how she can put herself into his mind, see his actions through her eyes. She had felt this during the Invasion, even though he had never said two words to her in all that time. Why is that, she wonders; is it because they are two of a kind, living on the periphery of other people's lives, ever watchful, ever prepared for disaster?

The wastepaper basket has been emptied, but Leo is sure Gemma wouldn't have thrown it away or even destroyed it. Where would *she* put a love letter, if the positions were reversed? In her Diary, probably – but Gemma wouldn't keep a diary, or only one listing engagements and meetings. What, then? A book? There are a few books piled up on the bedside cabinet, hardback tomes with titles like *Politics of the Eastern Bloc* and *Communism in Crisis*. Surely no place for a *billet doux*. Gemma's underwear drawer? – now that is a possibility. But no – her pastel wisps of silk and lace reveal no letter.

And of course she could be carrying it around on her person, which is what Leo herself would do, and has done in the past, until she'd tired of their authors. Most of them had realised they could never compete with Daddy in her affections, anyway. She won't think about the one whose love letters she *would* keep in her knickers for always and ever. Operation Hooking Masterson hadn't even got off the ground.

She is just about to give up when her eyes fall on the table beneath the window, stacked with neat piles of notebooks, a small dictaphone machine, a pen holder and day-to-day calendar. And there it is, poking out underneath the anglepoise lamp – a lined page torn from a spiral-bound jotter, hastily folded, and with an oil-smeared thumbprint at the top.

Gem: If you want to meet me before you fly off, I'll be at the usual place on Friday about 12.30. I'll wait about 20 minutes. I'll understand if you don't come. It must be a rotten time for you. NW.

That is it. No 'dear' or 'darling', no 'love', no tender words of sympathy. Well, that is to be expected. But somehow Leo feels cheated. And angry. 'A rotten time'! – an understatement if ever there was one. How dare he! She realises she is trembling, and that Mrs Wainwright is coming out of the guest room, closing the door behind her. She thrusts the scrap of paper back under the lamp, shrinks against the wall while the long angular shape passes the door and, as the housekeeper goes down the stairs, slips back into her own room and gives herself up to silent, wracking sobs.

******

4 April 10.02-11.06am.
Old Cardew (who isn't that old, but about 10 years younger than Daddy) explained the will to us in words of one sillable but still most of it went over my head. I think I got the general jist. Daddy has left the house to the 3 of us but as it's my home (and Gemma's too when she's not away), he's left me the half-share and divided Huwie's up with Gemma, as he's got the flat. He'd already made financial arrangements with the Ws and Gemma's mother so apart from the house and the car which he left to Ralf Winestock, who can't even drive, there isn't much left. Deborah Routledge has already got Gali-Leo's, so there was nothing else for her.
The will was the easy bit. What stix in my mind is what happened after.

OLD CARDEW: *Of corse when you want to sell the house, we'll have to draw up an appropriate document...*

ME: *Why should we want to sell the house? (Everyone turns to look daggers at me)*

OLD CARDEW: *Well, I assumed it would be much too big — and the memories... (He stops, obviously alerted by my expreshun to the fact that his assumshun is, to put it mildly, premature) ...but of course it's early days yet. When you come to decide, then we'll...*

ME: *But if I don't want to sell, it can't be sold, can it? If I have the largest share? (There is an uncomfortable silence)*

OLD CARDEW: *(Choosing his words carefully) This house is worth a lot of money, Miss Bassett, espeshully in a rising market. You could buy something much more sootable...*

HUWIE: *(Getting up hurriedly) Well, we'll think about it. As you say, it's early days...*

OLD CARDEW: *(Snapping the clasps of his breefcase shut in releef, then opening them again) O, I almost forgot. There's a letter here I must give to Miss Belling. (He takes out a long brown envelope and holds it out towards Gemma) Your father asked me to give it to you after his (paws) um, demise.*

(Old Cardew shuts his breefcase again and struggles into his coat while 3 pairs of eyes stare at the envelope)

OLD CARDEW: *Well, goodby. When you need me again, just call.*

HUWIE: *(Leeping towards the door) Oh, yes, thanx. I'll see you out.*

(2 pairs of eyes stare at the envelope)

GEMMA: *(Staring at it) I wonder what...?*

ME: *(Staring at it) Why don't you open it?*

GEMMA: *Well, I (paws) I think it might be private.*

ME: *O.*

GEMMA: *I'm sorry, I think I'll go to my room... (She scuttles out, still staring at it.)*

It seems as if I'm still staring at it, too — at the large, loopy writing, Daddy's writing, across the front: TO MY DEAR DAUGHTER GEMMA - TO BE OPENED AFTER MY DEATH.

Nothing for me. Nothing for his dear daughter Leonora, his one and only preshus princess.

Only the largest share in the house, of corse.

9.17pm *Daddy's letter really has been a Bombshell. Gemma hasn't come down for dinner (Mrs Wainrite's left a miserable salad – I don't think she'll be here much longer), and has only called throo the door, when I nocked, that she's not hungry. I can't hear any sounds from her room, altho this house is so well-bilt sounds don't travel... But she must be sitting on her bed, staring at the wall, the letter in her hand. I wish I had xray eyes. I wish I knew what Daddy has ritten.*
She'll go to meet the Man tomorrow, I know.
I shall go too.

******

Gemma makes no move to leave until just before midday, so the assignation must be fairly close. Leo has kept watch all morning, since Gemma appeared at breakfast, pale-faced and hollow-eyed. There was no Huwie to relieve the gloom, of course. He had slammed off back to his flat first thing this morning, after he and Leo had quarrelled. It was such a silly quarrel and she is already regretting it, but wasn't it his fault in the first place? Accusing her of being jealous! Jealous of Pudge, jealous of Gemma! And why? Because they'd elbowed her aside, replaced her in his affections! What rubbish!

And nothing had been said over breakfast. Gemma had picked at a slice of toast and drunk half a cup of coffee and gone back up to her room. For the rest of the morning Leo has skulked downstairs. She has laid her clothes out on her bed – a pair of scuddy jeans, one of Huwie's old sweaters he'd worn as a teenager, an anorak with a hood. As soon as Gemma makes her move, she can dash upstairs and change in the time it takes Gemma to reach the end of the drive. There is no bus stop near enough for there to be any danger of her getting on a bus before Leo can also gain the pavement and ascertain which way she goes. She must be careful not to be spotted until they reach the safety of the high street, or wherever Gemma is bound. Once in a crowd, Leo is sure nobody will take her for anything other than a young boy.

At five to twelve Gemma comes downstairs in black trousers,

63

white tee-shirt and white cropped cord jacket and looks in at Leo, reading in the lounge. "I'm going out for a while," she says, and Leo looks up and nods.

"Okay."

She remains curled up on the sofa until she hears the door shut; then springs up, sprints upstairs, flings off her bathrobe and dons her disguise, pulling the hood over her head. Then flies downstairs, through the front door, tiptoes along the grass at the side of the drive, peers round the gate.

Gemma is walking towards the Village. She has a leather bag with a long strap slung across her torso and is wearing mid-calf soft leather boots. Although she looks like a model on holiday, it is hardly the outfit to wear for a romantic liaison. But then the Man will not be in suit and tie; most of the times Leo has seen him, he has been in jeans and jumpers.

It is quite easy to keep Gemma in her sights. She doesn't look round but keeps her eyes fixed firmly in front of her, elbows at right angles and hands in the pockets of her jacket. Even when she crosses the road she only glances left and right, hardly breaking stride, as if her surroundings don't interest her. But she's obviously making for the tube station and Leo has to quicken her steps to catch up. By the time she arrives in the foyer, Gemma has joined the queue at the ticket office and two other people have tagged on behind. But luck is on Leo's side. Although she can't hear Gemma's destination, the bloke behind the glass is young and seems to be trying to chat her up. At any rate, the people in front become restless and, when Leo eventually arrives at the window, she lowers her voice an octave and says, "Same as my sister, please," indicating Gemma's receding figure with a nod of her head.

It's a return ticket to Euston, a few stops down the line. Leo breathes a sigh of relief; she can take it easy now and catch up with Gemma when she gets off. She dawdles down the escalator and hovers in the tunnel, letting people push past her on to the platform. When the train rattles in she jumps inside it at the last moment and sweeps her eyes round the carriage; no Gemma. So far, so good.

64

When they arrive at Euston she is the last to leave the carriage. In front of her the crowds surge towards the exit and there is Gemma, dark head bobbing along about ten yards in front. Now she must keep her in her sights, or all is lost. Thank goodness she chose to wear a white jacket; it stands out a mile.

Out on the mainline concourse it's a battle to keep up, but Gemma doesn't seem to be going anywhere. She has slowed down, almost stopped, and is looking towards the station café. Then she pulls the strap of her bag further up her shoulder and walks quickly towards the door. Leo looks at her watch; it's nearly twenty to one.

So the assignation takes place in a station café! How romantic! Shades of *Brief Encounter!* And how handy, if Leo can get inside without being spotted. She can buy a coffee and sit unobtrusively somewhere nearby, as long as she keeps her back towards Gemma. The Man will never recognise her, he'd always looked through her.

Pulling the hood further down her face, she walks up to the door and pushes it open. The place is fairly crowded, and she doesn't want to look round too far. But Gemma's white jacket is over to her left, by the wall. Leo joins the queue for the coffees and sandwiches, taking a tray and selecting a currant bun and a square of butter; she might be here some time. She asks for a cappuccino and, stretching out to lift it, her hand brushes the hand of the man in front who has also ordered two coffees and as soon as it does so she goes cold. It's Him! She recognises his workman's fingers with the square blunt nails and the round flat face of his wristwatch – the hand that had wielded a knife and an axe to cut up a body...

...but he doesn't notice her and goes on to pay at the till while she stands frozen, the mug of cappuccino shaking in her grip until the press of people behind nudges her on. But he's already gone, carrying the cups over to a table by the wall where Gemma waits, facing towards the window. Leo picks up her tray with her mug and plate and, keeping her head lowered, moves towards them. But the tables nearby are all occupied; she must take one three tables away, where there is already another man

65

seated reading a newspaper. Good; she won't look too conspicuous. She sits, sideways on to Gemma, three-quarters facing the Man.

He doesn't look the sort to chop up bodies or possess offensive weapons destined for the IRA, she has to admit. In fact, when he smiles (which he's doing now), he could almost be fanciable. She's never particularly gone for curly-haired men, but there's some quality about those unruly corkscrews that makes her wonder what it would be like to run her fingers through them, like he's doing now, leaning on one elbow, listening to whatever Gemma is saying. And those dark brown eyes, all concentration, all concern, hardly blinking; not many men have the virtue of patience, which he has in spades. How many hours did he sit beside Gemma, during the Invasion?

And now he has taken the hand from his hair and has covered one of hers, lying on the table. The hand that brushed against Leo's at the counter, clean but with ingrained dirt outlining the nails, grimed into the knuckles... There is something about him now that is slightly *disreputable*, that is the only word that comes to mind. The leather jacket he is wearing is cracked and scuffed, has seen better days. The collar of the open-necked shirt underneath looks unironed. He obviously hasn't shaved today.

It is Gemma who's doing all the talking. And crying. He's offering her a couple of paper serviettes to blow her nose and wipe her eyes. The hand that chopped up a body – the same hand that held the gun to her father's forehead and pulled the trigger – is now holding out tissues to stem the tide of grief caused by the second of those actions. Leo finds herself trembling, has to put down her mug to prevent spillage. How dare he! How *dare* he!

Her companion lays down his newspaper, gets up and walks off. She pulls it towards her. It could provide good cover, if she can get closer. She must hear what they're saying, get a gist of the conversation. But they're whispering anyway; their heads are almost meeting across the table.

And now the couple only one table away are preparing to

move. With a swift glance at Gemma and the Man (who have eyes only for each other), Leo picks up the paper and her half-finished coffee and slides across to occupy a chair opposite Him.

After a good blow into a serviette, Gemma seems to have regained some composure. The Man leans back, smiling – but it's a hesitant, wavering smile that sometimes gets pressed into concern, sometimes pushed out into an expression of compassion. It's a *tender* smile. Tenderness is something she hasn't seen on the Man's face, ever. It's probably the expression he'd kept solely for Gemma's bedroom.

Her hands shaking, she lifts the newspaper and pretends to be reading, straining her ears to catch a few words. "Shock," she hears, and "never forget", "happiest time", "always so good", and then, "father."

Who has said this? The thing about whispers is that male and female voices sound the same, especially when you're not looking at the speaker. But now Gemma is bending sideways, and delving into the bag she's sloughed off and hung on the chair. Leo's eyes slide from the newsprint. Yes, she's bringing out the long brown envelope and is holding it out to him.

Newspaper aloft, Leo slides round in her seat and peeps over. He's opening it, taking out a folded sheet of paper. He looks at Gemma, eyebrows raised, then unfolds it and reads.

How dare he! How dare *she!* And now he's reading words her father wrote, her father's murderer is reading words that she, his dear daughter Leonora, has never seen. Rage dances in front of her eyes, staining the newsprint red.

But his reaction is strange. He folds up the paper and remains staring at it, his breath exhaling in an elongated "Aahh," while Gemma seems visibly to shrink into her chair, pressing both forearms against her stomach as if in physical pain. She is gazing at the Man as if for reassurance, for an answer to an unasked question. Which she doesn't get. He's sliding the paper back into the envelope, pushing it towards her with his fingertips. Then he brings his hand to his face and rubs the dark stubble on his cheek.

"I'm sorry, Gem," is what he says.

And she says, "Did you know?"

He hesitates. Both Gemma and Leo wait upon his words. Eventually he says, "Your mother told me…" They both wait for more, but it doesn't come.

"All this time," she says. "You've known all this time. Like him. You all knew…" And now she is stuffing the letter back in the bag, grabbing it from the chair at the same time as she's getting to her feet, her face twisted and flushed with anger. The Man doesn't move, doesn't try to detain her. As she dashes blindly out of the café he remains sitting, staring at the tabletop. The expression on his face is now one of defeat.

How long do they sit there? It seems hours but, when at last he gets to his feet and Leo snatches a look at her watch, it's only quarter past one. He walks quickly out of the café, across the concourse, down into the tube. He's already got a ticket, but so has she, and she follows him as he takes the escalator, almost runs down it, passing the stationary people on the right as if they don't exist. Leo can't keep up but she sees him take the Northern Line northbound exit and, panting, follows him on to the platform. The train rattling in has Edgware on the front but he doesn't take it. He prowls up and down the platform as if he can't keep still, like a tiger in a cage; there is something pent up in him, a rattlesnake getting ready to strike. People are giving him a wide berth. The next train has High Barnet on the front, and he can't wait for the doors to open; he stands, flexing his fists, until at last he can board, shouldering the alighting passengers out of his way. There are empty seats but he doesn't sit; he stands at the door as if he can't wait to get off again.

Leo takes a seat down the carriage and peers at him from under her hood. His face in profile is closed and hard. Difficult now to remember the tender smile; his every pore exudes thinly suppressed violence. The train rattles on, past Mornington Crescent, Camden, Kentish Town, Tufnell Park… The next station, Archway, is the one; he prises open the doors as they begin to part, sprints along the platform and up the escalator, out into the street beyond. Leo, trying to keep him in sight, breathes a sigh of relief at the lack of ticket collector and wonders why all her exercising, jogging and cycling hasn't made her as fit as he obviously is, all of twelve years older.

But as she gains the street she sees he's slowed down and is walking quite normally. It's the tube that has obviously made him nervous; some people of course are claustrophobic... but it's not that, it's the confinement, the lack of fresh air – he's spent quite a few years of his life in prison. He's still walking quickly but his head is bowed, his hands are in his pockets, he kicks out at stones and cigarette butts in his path. Again she has that odd feeling of kinship. She tries to summon up hatred but only manages curiosity.

He walks along streets she doesn't know and she follows at a distance, at first darting from shop door to alleyway until she realises he's completely unaware of anything going on behind. He must be sunk in his thoughts. The streets are getting more squalid, litter-strewn, and then they're approaching an industrial estate, a hideous squat of prefabricated buildings. She can't follow him in there, he would see her in a trice. She lets him escape from her, keeping watch at the gates to see which way he takes. It's only a small estate; on one side there's a carpet warehouse, a wine depot, a kitchen showroom. On the other, where he's going, is an office supplies wholesaler, a light engineering works and, at the end, a car repair lock-up. It's towards this that he's walking, and she watches him take a key from his pocket, open a small side door and disappear. After a few minutes there is a grating, slipping noise, and the whole frontage slides up to reveal the interior of the garage and the back end of a car. The Man has now changed into a dark blue oil-stained boilersuit and, as she watches, slides himself underneath the car and out of sight.

For some reason Leo is loath to leave, but there is nothing more she can do. But at least she knows now where he works. And, as she walks back along the alien streets towards the tube station, realises that what Gemma had told her when she arrived back from Australia is true. She and the Man are no longer lovers.

******

Huw has never been so glad to be back in his flat. This is his private domain, his bachelor pad, and although he's tidy by nature he doesn't have to pick up every single thing he puts down or keep his shoes in a cupboard by the door. Mrs Wetherby had never minded tripping over his size 12s, but Mrs Wainwright had made it perfectly clear that shoes were to be taken off by the front door and stowed neatly away; she wasn't going to vacuum up every day, she had better things to do than be everyone's skivvy. His father, used to being Mrs W's darling, had learned to tiptoe round in his socks in his own house until Leo had bought him a pair of felt slippers. Remembering his big bear-like father in his pin-striped suit and stockinged feet brings a lump to his throat and for a moment Huw has to steady himself on the hall table before picking up his post that has accumulated on the doormat.

Nothing of any importance, only bills – but there is one he doesn't recognise, or only vaguely. The handwriting on the envelope seems familiar, but for the moment he can't place it. But he isn't in the mood to open his post. He flings it on the table, goes through to the kitchen and takes a can of lager from the fridge.

The answering machine is winking at him from the sitting room and he goes through to press the button. A couple of condolence calls from friends recently back from abroad who have only just caught up with the news… a message from work, telling him not to go back until he's ready, but there's a rush job and can he possibly call in on Monday just to set it in motion… the local library, telling him the book he ordered is now in… and Pudge.

'Huw, darling, I called the Hampstead house but no one's *in!* Where is everybody? Don't worry, my pet, there's nothing wrong, I just wondered… oh, do give me a ring, darling, I do so worry about you all…!'

He realises he is grinding his teeth and has to take a swig of lager before he erases the messages. He flings himself down into the nearest armchair. Oh God, how has he got himself so involved with Prudence Ursula? He can't even remember proposing, but he must have done, and bought the ring to prove it. His credit card had revealed a diamond-shaped hole in his finances, so he must have signed the chitty of his own free will. No one had held a gun to his head.... oh God.

Dad had held a gun to his head and pulled the trigger. Why? – but for years Huw has known there was a well of sadness inside his father, the source of which he never divulged, and was probably endemic. There were other things, too – his retirement from the business, his television career at an end, his sixtieth birthday looming – all these, combined with his health worries, all serving to deepen his depression. Was that explanation enough?

Yes, it has to be. He wishes Leo would also believe it. But she has acted since as if she were the only one to have feelings, and accused him this morning of betrayal, and he had countered with her jealousy of Pudge and Gemma; an accusation he now feels ashamed of. In fact, as soon as he'd slammed out the door he felt ashamed, and had driven to the Heath for a long walk round the ponds before driving back to the City.

He hates being at the Hampstead house; the memories are too painful. How can Leo live there? More to the point – how can she continue to live there in the future, alone? She will have to agree to sell, she's just being stubborn. She'll see sense soon enough. When Gemma goes back to Russia...

Oh God. His life is a mess. Recently of course he hasn't had time to think about it, but now he has to confront the reality: his life is a mess. And it's all his own fault, at least as far as his engagement to Pudge is concerned. But he can't be blamed for what he feels for Gemma, can he? He has no control over that.

Thank God he'd answered that fateful phonecall, not Leo. Possibly it was a man thing; his first thought, when told he had another sister, was - well, the randy old sod! Good for you, Dad. And when his father had brought her home, she'd just seemed a pretty girl with a rather nice figure.

But Leo had given her a make-over so thoroughly that the

caterpillar had turned into a butterfly in front of his eyes. He could still remember his pride on the night of the party when he had escorted her downstairs on his arm dressed in something shimmering, slinky and red, and all heads had turned. He'd been murderously jealous of the attention she'd received and couldn't say a word. And when that creep Tony Masterson had taken her off into the garden…

And what about the bloke who'd seen her through her first bad patch, after the death of the posh boyfriend, and had taken her off to Australia? Huw had been grateful to him, doesn't see him as a threat. Dad had told him Gem had always looked on him as a big brother. And although Huw is her real big brother, he doesn't mind the bloke taking on that role. That frees him up to be – what? What does she see *him* as?

Afterwards, when they'd returned from Australia and the bloke had been arrested for unlawful burial and dismemberment of a body, Gemma had gone through another bad patch. And it was he, Huw, who had got her through that one. He had taken time out of college to be there for her, and they had grown close. As brother and sister? No, surely more than that. On his part, at least.

The discovery of the body on the farm in North Wales where Gemma had spent two of the first five years of her life had seemed to release some terrible memories, something evil that remained shrouded in the fog of the past that he, Big Brother, had rescued her from - she thought. She didn't remember what or how, just the impression that it was he who had saved her. She had been whisked off to Suffolk with her mother and spent the next two years pining, waiting for him. She had only just learned that he'd been imprisoned on charges of possession of offensive weapons, but she couldn't believe he'd had anything to do with that. Now she realises he'd obviously pleaded guilty to stop the police discovering the dismemberment and burial. The name of the victim meant nothing to her.

Huw realised fairly soon that he was falling in love with her – hopelessly, impossibly – and that no other girl would do. He'd thought he had hidden his feelings successfully, but he was not a good actor. He was too much like his father, an open book in the emotions department. Had Dad guessed? Possibly. But although they were close, they didn't have the kind of relationship for heart-to-heart talks.

To try to smother these feelings for Gemma he had played fast and loose with a succession of girls who had begun to throw themselves at him at college. Up to the age of twenty-one he'd been diffident around the opposite sex, but then, without much effort on his part, began to gain the reputation as a bit of a Lothario. On no evidence whatsoever; again, he is like his father. Until Prudence Ursula had loomed on the scene. She has clung like a limpet, impossible to prise off, and he has taken the coward's way out.

With a start, he realises he has been sitting in the armchair for almost two hours. And will go on sitting, staring into space. When the doorbell rings, he is relieved to have an excuse to get up, but also annoyed at being disturbed. He peers through the spyhole in the door, but whoever is outside is too close; all he can see is a textured white surface.

She falls upon him as soon as he opens the door. At first he is too bewildered to speak, and then too elated. He can only hold her close, smell the honeysuckle of her hair, feel the bliss of her body against his. She gives in to wild sobs as he guides her into the sitting room and, making sure she is still tucked against him, sits her down beside him on the two-seater sofa. He says nothing. He can say nothing. He kisses the top of her head, strokes the hair from her face, wanting this moment to go on forever. He doesn't even care, for the moment, what has happened to cause her such anguish.

7. October 1976

Mrs Wetherby was answering the telephone as Laurence was coming downstairs, reciting the number dutifully. She quickly replaced the receiver. "It's another of those calls," she said.

"Calls?"

"Those heavy breathers."

"How many have there been?"

"That's the third one. But this time he said a rude word as well. Shall I call the police?"

"Oh no. They're probably wrong numbers." He went through to the dining room where she had laid out his breakfast just as he liked it, bless her. "This looks delicious as always. But what do you think, Mrs W – should I go on a diet? Grapefruit and lemon juice? It's getting an effort to do up my trousers."

"Never! A man needs a good lining to his stomach to start the day."

His mind at rest, Laurence tucked into his eggs and bacon. "I'll need a good lining today – Ralph at the Beeb, Pieter Merck coming to the gallery to talk about this book project. I might bring him back tonight, Mrs W – could you make up the bed in the guest room just in case?"

"I will, Mr B. And I'll leave a little something in the oven just in case, too."

"You spoil me, Mrs W."

She twinkled at him. "You're worth it, Mr B."

His breakfast set him up for the day. He drove to Shepherd's Bush for his meeting with Ralph, who was optimistic about obtaining another slot for *Whither Art?* He looked in on Hilary on his way out to see if she had any news. He had set her the task of tracking down William Murchison, and she had come up with his birth certificate – he had been born in Newcastle-upon-Tyne to Diane Jane Erica Hallam and Graham Murchison, electrician, in February 1957. Enquiries at local art schools had drawn a blank. But a survey of scholarships for the year 1975 listed a William Murchison from Newcastle as having been granted a bursary to study at the London School of Art, although it seemed he hadn't taken it up. He had obviously come down south, though, to live in Cawston Street, Hackney.

"He might have relatives in London," Hilary said. "There's a Diane Jane Erica Hallam who was born in Forest Gate in 1940."

"I wonder how young Diane from Forest Gate met her electrician from Newcastle? There's a story there, Hilary."

"Everyone has a story, Laurence."

Yes, and Hilary was the one to ferret them out, he thought as he got back in the car and drove on to Cork Street, where Pieter Merck was awaiting him, settled in the gallery with a cup of coffee, talking to Deborah. Pieter was an expert on the Dutch Masters and wanted Laurence's help in editing a book he was writing – "You can do the light touch, Mr Barsett, I am just an old academic foddy-doddy, as you say." Yes, he was an old foddy-doddy, but Laurence was quite fond of him, and they spent an enjoyable afternoon laying out colour plates and discussing the text. And Pieter, although already booked into a hotel, was quite amenable to staying the night in Hampstead before catching his plane back to Amsterdam the next morning.

And the next morning, Saturday, Laurence came downstairs just as Pieter was replacing the handset of the telephone. "I called you," he said, "but you were performing the ablutions."

"Who was it?"

"He said he will call later."

"He didn't give a name?"

"No. He asked who I was and I told him I was a guest of Mr Laurence Barsett and he said he would call later." Pieter frowned. "I do not think he is a very nice man."

"Oh. Right."

Later, after dropping Pieter off at Heathrow, Laurence arrived back to find the telephone ringing and, unthinking, picked it up.

It was Hilary. "Do you want me to trawl through the relatives of Diane Jane Erica? I've already searched for Hallams in Hackney and come up with sod all. I'll have to go through the mother's line. It'll cost you!" Yes, he told her, spare no expense. As he put the receiver down, it rang again.

There was a background of raised voices, obviously from a television, and a nearer voice snarling, "Turn that fucking thing down!" And then, before Laurence could react, "Who's there? Someone's there!" And, as Laurence held the receiver against his ear, "If that's you, you fucking pervert, leave my son alone! Bastards like you should be put down. If I find out where you live I'll bloody come round and tear 'em off, you got that, you wanker?" Heavy breathing, then, "For Christ's sake turn that fucking row down you bleedin' little bugger, before I give you a boot up the arse!" The connection was cut, and Laurence was left with the telephone buzzing in his ear.

******

Deborah Routledge was also making enquiries. She had rung the Venn Pegasus Agency in Denver to ascertain the whereabouts of Mr David Symons and was told he was in Europe at the moment, expected back in a couple of weeks. Where exactly did he stay while in London, Deborah asked; she needed to speak to him urgently about some paintings he had expressed interest in. After a hesitation on the other end of the line, she was told he usually put up in the Holiday Inn at Swiss Cottage. Oh and by the way, Deborah asked as an afterthought, was there any chance she could speak to Mr Symons' client directly if she couldn't get hold of Mr Symons himself? – it really was most urgent.

"I'm sorry," the girl drawled on the other end of the line, "but I'm not at liberty to divulge that information."

"I quite understand, but could you possibly make Mr Symons' client aware of my enquiry? I can leave you my number…"

"I'm sorry," the girl drawled again, "but I don't know the identity of Mr Symons' client. And in the absence of Mr Symons himself…"

"Yes, I do understand. Thank you so much."

So the mysterious client was a mystery man even to the Venn Pegasus Agency, Deborah thought. Curiouser and curiouser.

She was about to call the Holiday Inn at Swiss Cottage when

she thought better of it. In all likelihood David Symons would not know the address either, and she didn't want to alert Freddy to the fact that they were stalking his boy. Besides, Mr Symons might make another visit to the gallery before he left for the States, and she could assure him then that, if his client liked the Murchison painting he had bought, Gali-Leo's could guarantee the supply of quite a few more.

She had also spent her afternoons off at the British Library, going through back editions of newspapers, reading up about the arms cache discovered on the farm in Wales in September 1970. They told her nothing she didn't already know, except the name of the guilty party. Nicholas Woollidge. Yes, that was him, staring out of the newspaper at her as she remembered, that look of closed hostility so disconcerting in one so young (it was a photograph taken when he was fourteen, the caption read). And he didn't look Laurence's type at all, judging by the blond, blue-eyed young men Laurence invited to his parties. But that was all an elaborate act, Deborah was sure; the young men were obviously resting actors or male models, and to be seen at one of Laurence Bassett's bashes could set them up on their chosen careers, if they mingled wisely among the invited. Laurence, she was fairly convinced, had been celibate since she had worked for him.

Excitement had started to tingle along her spine. If Will Murchison did resemble Nicholas Woollidge, and if Laurence had done something in the past he bitterly regretted, then there would never be a better time to show her hand. He would need her help. He would need the comfort of the third bedroom at Hurlingham Mansions.

The comfort of the soft, high, wide four-poster bed with its feather mattress, Egyptian cotton sheets, cashmere blankets and plum silk quilt under a damson canopy the size of a tent, the deep wine-red carpet and long heavy drapes, the fat velvet sofa piled with cushions. Maroon flocked wallpaper with no pictures, no distractions for the eye; matching crimson shades on four lamps strategically placed, controlled by a dimmer switch. To walk into the room was like walking into a mouth, an enticing red orifice that swallowed you up. No, that wasn't quite right. She had subconsciously made it a place for Laurence to go back to the womb.

It was lunchtime. Little Rosemary had gone off for her break, and Laurence was in Shepherd's Bush for another meeting with Ralph Weinstock. Deborah was at the back of the gallery checking the catalogues when the door bell bleeped, telling her someone had entered; she straightened, turned, and saw a figure silhouetted against the glass with a large flat parcel propped against one leg.

"Can I help you?" The sun was slanting off the windows, and she had to shield her eyes against the glare.

"Is Mr B-Bassett in?"

"No, I'm afraid not." Moving closer, she saw the mop of light brown curls and below them, a curious intensity blazing out of greenish-brown eyes. For a moment it was Nicholas Woollidge staring back at her. "But I'm sure I can help…"

"I've b-brought something for him." He held out the parcel awkwardly, but also with a shy pride.

"It's Will, isn't it? Will Murchison?"

"Yes. T-tell him it's W-wheels Number One."

"Well, thank you, Will. Mr Bassett will be very pleased." She took the parcel from him. "How did you know where to find us?"

"He left his c-card at the exhib-bition."

"Ah."

"I was going to t-telephone, but I'm not very g-good at it, I c-can't get the words out, so I thought I'd b-bring it instead. I t-took a t-taxi."

Deborah glanced out at the pavement. The taxi was at the kerb, the driver waiting impatiently beside it.

"I think he wants money," the boy said.

She took her purse from her bag, went out and paid him off. Coming back into the gallery, she turned the sign to Closed and pulled the blind.

The boy was walking slowly round the room, studying the

78

pictures. She noted the fragile back of his head, the way his skinny neck rose out of his collar like the stem of a plant.

"How much did Mr Bassett say he'd pay you?" she asked.

He turned. "Oh, it's not for sale. It's a p-present."

"How nice." This poor young innocent, she thought, he needs looking after. His trousers were frayed and baggy, his trainers falling apart. He wore a knitted striped pullover under a thin plastic parka. "Did you know Mr Bassett has been looking for you? He's very impressed with your work. In fact, if you have any more…"

The lad looked nervous. "I d-don't know, I'm not sure…"

"Do you have an agent?"

"I'm not sure…"

"Does Frederick Swainton represent you?"

The lad gulped. "He gives me m-money…"

"Yes, I'm sure he does. Did he arrange for you to be exhibited in Whitechapel?"

"N-no, that was the c-college. They had some p-p-pictures and said they c-could show them…"

"So Mr Swainton isn't your agent? You haven't signed a contract with him?"

"No, he j-just – l-looks after me." The poor lad was agitated, the words seemed to be stuck to the roof of his mouth. "I've g-got to g-go…"

"Oh, do stay for a cup of coffee, please. Please." Deborah realised she was pleading, something she hadn't done since mother was alive. She felt a rush of – what? Was this what was described as maternal love? She wanted to put her arms round this lad and keep him from harm. He had been the innocent bait to Freddy's circling shark, which had swallowed him whole.

Whether he wanted to or not, he allowed himself to be guided towards the back of the gallery where he sat in one of the comfortable chairs while she poured the coffee from the percolator little Rosemary kept topped up. As she did so, she was aware of his eyes taking in the paintings on the wall and stacked up on the floor. A couple of Timberlakes arrested his attention; she had to give a discreet cough before he tore his gaze away and took the cup she was holding out to him.

"You admire Dermot Timberlake?"

She was rewarded with a quick flash of a smile. "Oh yes! He's my hero."

"Would you like to meet him?"

The smile froze as a red tidal wave washed over his face. "Oh yes!" It was hardly more than a breath.

"I'm sure he'd like to meet you." Oh no he wouldn't, she thought silently. "I could arrange it, if you want."

He just stared at her, those green-brown eyes wide as saucers. There were obviously no words to express what he felt; he lowered his head and took a slow gulp of the coffee.

Sitting down opposite, she asked, "How long have you been painting?"

"All my l-l-life."

"You come from Newcastle?"

He nodded.

"So how long have you lived in London?"

"Not l-l-long."

"Why didn't you take up your scholarship?" This was going to take some time, but it would be worth it. And it didn't take as long as she thought. The more he talked, the less he stammered, and she allowed herself to think it was because she was kind, and patient, and gentle.

He had lived with his mum in Newcastle, but she had originally come from Hackney, in London. She'd got pregnant and followed his father to Newcastle but they weren't wanted and she couldn't go back to London because her family had disowned her. So she'd got a job up there and brought him up alone but money was tight and they couldn't afford art school fees. But he'd entered an art competition, and won, and was awarded a bursary by the college, but his mum had married by then and her new husband wouldn't give him the money he needed for expenses although he'd put him on a train and given him an address of an aunt who still lived in Hackney, and she'd put him up for a while but it didn't work out because the man she lived with didn't like him, and then he met Mr Swainton at

80

an exhibition and Mr Swainton had told him he could live with him if he painted for him and well, that was how it stood at the moment but...

The flow of words ceased.

"Do you still want to live with Mr Swainton?"

He shook his head.

"What would you say if I told you I could find you somewhere else to live, perhaps somewhere you could paint?"

He stared at her.

"No strings attached. Except, of course, whatever you paint, Gali-Leo's would have first option to sell."

He stared.

"Do you want to think about it?"

He stared a few seconds more, then shook his head.

"You don't want to think about it?"

"No." Quickly.

"You'd rather go back and live with Mr Swainton?"

"No." Quickly and violently.

"You want to take up my offer?"

He nodded.

She sat back, relief flooding through her. She'd done it! As meticulously as she planned, sometimes it was just good fortune, serendipity, that caused things to fall beautifully into place at the right time. She instructed Will to go back and collect his belongings without arousing Mr Swainton's suspicions – "Oh," Will said, "he's out, he won't be b-back till tonight," - and meet her outside the gallery at six o'clock. She would put him up at her flat until they could sort out a suitable studio. He could have mother's room. The third bedroom, the one at the end of the corridor, would have to wait – but not, she thought, for very much longer.

Whither Art? – which, Laurence told her, had been on the point of withering completely - was now firmly back on the cards. He rang her from the BBC with the news, and to ask if she'd like to meet him at the Savoy Grill at eight o'clock for a celebration dinner. Make it eight-thirty, she said, she had a few things to do first.

Will was waiting for her as she locked up, a battered suitcase and a couple of blank canvases under his arm. She had already secured Wheels One in the boot of her car, parked round the back of the gallery. As they walked to the car he told her Freddy had provided him with canvas and oils and ordered him to paint every day, but he hadn't been able to produce anything for him yet. Mr Swainton hadn't been best pleased, "but I can't p-paint to order, it d-doesn't work like that, I get t-too tense," and, when Deborah remarked that he'd painted Mr Bassett's picture to order, "oh but that's d-different, he was nice about it, I wanted to d-do it for him."

At first he was daunted by the sheer size of Hurlingham Mansions, but once up the stairs (he wouldn't take the lift) and into the flat he relaxed, and even seemed at home among the bric-a-brac. Deborah showed him to his room and then went into the lounge to take the ornate mirror down from over the fireplace and hang Wheels One there instead. Its minimalist impact was incongruous amid the clutter, but that made it stand out all the more; no one entering the room could fail to see it.

A great red circle, like an eye, gleamed from the centre of the canvas. At first sight, that seemed all there was to the painting; a great baleful eyeball staring out, with a small pure white dot at the centre. Closer, however, she could see other colours round the rim of the circle; oranges, browns, dirty yellows, mixed in with great care and deliberation, yet executed with a kind of hurried dash so it looked as if they were in danger of peeling off like the skin of an orange. And there was also a very thin white line separating the red from the colours but also holding them on, snaking round the rim and trailing behind. It was the kind of painting you could look at for hours and not get tired of, she thought. The kind that gave back more than it took, that you could read in it whatever you liked and yet never get to the bottom of.

"How did you learn to paint like that?" she asked, as she heard him come in behind her.

"I d-don't know. I've always done it."

82

"How do you choose the subject?"

Silence. She tore her eyes away, looked back at him. He stood hunched, hands in pockets, head lowered.

"All creative process is a mystery, isn't it? I wish I could do it. I wish I could paint like you, Will."

He lifted his head, gave her a fleeting smile.

"Can you look after yourself tonight? There's plenty of food in the fridge. I've got to go out, but I won't be late."

He nodded. She went up to him and, after a second's hesitation, drew his head to her breast. The bones beneath the springy hair were surprisingly fine. The nape of his neck brought tears to her eyes. As she felt his thin arms encircle her waist she was shaken by the fierceness of her reaction, a mother tiger defending her cub. Maternal love, she thought, must be the most violent force on earth.

******

In the end, Laurence drove from the BBC instead of taking a taxi. He wanted to have to concentrate on something mechanical to take his mind off art, programme scheduling, business, or – that telephone call. But driving, he found, was instinctive; his limbs performed their duties without his mind being actively engaged. He threaded his way through London streets with his brain still trying to picture the scene. Had that lively, intelligent lad got a boot up the arse? Or a clip round the ear? Or worse? Did it happen on a regular basis? Oh, it happened all over the country, in wealthy shires as well as inner city districts; he'd read in the papers only recently of a little girl starving to death in a locked room while her parents watched television. Such stories gave him a physical punch in the gut. And yet, wasn't that what he'd done to his own kids? Neglected them, left them to cope without him? He'd never hit them, though. Surely he could feel virtuous for not doing that.

He arrived too early, and was seated at his usual table when Deborah arrived. She was wearing the Miss Jones creation, the pale blue dress she had worn to his last party, with her hair down and secured with combs. As she made her way towards him, he was proud to see that heads turned; mostly the older, male heads, those who appreciated a fine-looking woman and not a dolly bird. She had slightly too pronounced features for conventional beauty, a too beak-like nose and square jaw, but there was, tonight, something of the Lauren Bacall about her, a softening of the edges probably to do with the lighting. He stood up and pulled out her chair before the waiter arrived.

"You do me proud, Miss Routledge."

"Thank you, Mr Bassett."

The food was, as always, superb. He ordered a good vintage wine. The Grill was one of his favourite places and he was well known; the service was impeccable, the ambience just as he liked it.

They talked about business during the meal, and Laurence brought her up to speed on his new programme. He tried to sound enthusiastic. He *was* enthusiastic, but that phonecall was still on his mind. It lingered in the background, souring even the taste of the *boeuf en croute.*

"I'm making progress," he announced over coffee, "on the Murchison front."

"Good."

"Probably by next week I can close in. Do you think Freddy will ever forgive me?"

"Oh yes." Deborah laughed. "Eventually. If I know Freddy, he'll be expecting it. Another poisoned arrow to shoot you with. He couldn't enjoy life without being jealous of you, Laurence."

He said suddenly, "Am I a wicked man, Deborah?"

"Wicked!" She sounded incredulous. "You?"

"I've done wicked things." He stirred his coffee.

"Surely not."

"I left my wife and children for a life of idleness."

"You're not idle, Laurence."

"I have a large house, a big car, a business that makes money out of other people's talent. If I didn't lift a finger for the rest of my days, I'd have enough to get by – more than enough. And now it seems I will lecture the nation on its cultural heritage, as if

84

I know what I'm talking about. I don't know why I've had all this good luck. I've done nothing to deserve it." Oh God, he sounded maudlin; he must have drunk too much of the damn vintage. "I'm sorry, Deborah. I asked you out for a celebration and you're stuck with a dribbling idiot."

She smiled. There was genuine fondness in that smile. "I think you deserve everything you've got. I can't believe you could do anything remotely wicked."

"If only you knew."

"Then tell me."

Oh, to unburden himself of over ten years of guilt! The prospect was tantalising. And why not? He hadn't committed murder. But he might have done. What was abortion but the murder of an innocent foetus?

He said, before he could think better of it, "I fathered a child on a fifteen-year-old girl."

She wasn't smiling any longer, but she didn't flinch. "Go on."

"She was a girl who came to me for lessons in art. I was supposed to teach her, but in the end she was teaching me. She had an exceptional talent. I think I put an end to that." He called the waiter, asked for a whisky chaser. Deborah refused another drink. She was a social drinker who knew when to stop, unlike him.

He took a gulp of the whisky to give him courage to go on. "I look for her everywhere, but I've never seen her work. She would have won scholarships, Deborah. She should be painting portraits of the Queen."

"Did she have the child?"

"Yes. It was a girl."

"You've seen her?"

"No. I found out – later. I set Hilary on the trail."

"Ah."

"But that's not the worst part. It's bad enough, isn't it? – taking advantage of an under-age girl who was infatuated with me. But I also lied and sent a boy to borstal. I set him on the path to prison."

She was silent. He finished the rest of the whisky.

"Deirdre ran away to London before she knew about the baby. When she did, she wrote asking for money for an abortion."

"She wrote to you?"

"No. The letter came to me, but it was addressed to a mutual acquaintance."

"The boy."

"Yes."

"And did you give her the money?"

"I gave it to him to give to her. But he already had a record – fighting, vandalism, petty theft. The police picked him up and found the money. He told them I'd given it to him, which was the truth."

"But you lied."

"Yes. What else could I do? I couldn't tell them what it was for – abortion was illegal in 1965. And my wife already suspected – well, you know. She thought I'd given him the money for services rendered. So I had to tell the police he'd stolen it. I swore a written statement and he was sent to borstal."

"It sounds," she said gently, "as if he'd have ended up there anyway."

"Possibly. But that doesn't alter anything, does it? I tried to get the money to Deirdre, but I failed on all counts. She had the baby and gave up painting. He went to borstal and ended up in prison."

"But what happened later wasn't your fault, surely."

"Oh Deborah, if only I knew." He motioned the waiter for another whisky chaser. Unburdening guilt was thirsty work. "No, the IRA thing had nothing to do with me, but I still blame myself for setting him on that path. He was only young. He could have turned out well, he was an intelligent lad. He had an appalling childhood – his mother was an alcoholic, his father abused him sexually as well as physically. I didn't lay a finger on him, let me add. I've never laid a finger, let alone anything else, on any boy, whatever you might have heard. My fault again – I played that image up for all it's worth, and was rewarded for it."

"I didn't believe all that for one minute."

"But we can rise above our upbringing, can't we?" Those clear blue eyes, that engaging grin – he must believe this.

"Our fate is in our own hands, Laurence."

"Yes, but only if we receive proper guidance. And luck must come into it too, as I know only too well." He tossed off the whisky in one gulp as soon as it arrived. Confession was good for the soul, he supposed, but no good for the nerves. He was going to regret this tomorrow.

But Deborah didn't seem to be judging him. She wasn't looking at him as if he were a monster. But then she hadn't known Deirdre. Or Nicholas.

"I think," she said, "I should get you home." She stood, and gave him her hand to help him to his feet. He stumbled; the room swam.

"Damn. I brought the car."

"I've got mine. Leave yours here, you can collect it tomorrow."

"I'll have to remortgage the house to pay for the parking."

"Serves you right."

"I keep hoping," he said as, having been helped into their coats, she steered him out into the street, "that one day I'll get my comeuppance. That one day I *will* be served right. But I just go on making more money."

He dribbled on like this for the whole journey. Folded into the front seat of her little Vauxhall Viva, he watched the streets peel past the window as he dredged up more charges against himself. Confession was addictive. What a disappointment he must have been to his parents. His mother had died the year after his divorce – of shame, he was sure. And this unknown daughter – what kind of life was she living? If only he could make it up to her and her mother. Send them money. Money solved everything. He could absolve that guilt with a stroke of the pen. With a stroke...

The car had stopped. He gazed out at unfamiliar buildings. This wasn't Hampstead.

She was helping him out, through a doorway, into a lobby where she summoned the lift. He leaned heavily against her as she opened its old-fashioned wrought-iron doors and guided him through, then bundled him out when it stopped. She leaned him against the wall while she unlocked her front door.

Wonderful woman. None of your fragile flowers – she was tough, she was a woman you could lean on. He could put himself entirely in her hands, those strong capable hands. Oh, how good it felt to give himself into her hands. He had wanted to do this for years – be treated like a child, a slobbering, blubbering infant. She would sit him down, make him cocoa, tuck him up in bed... oh God, he was going to regret this tomorrow, but for now he was in seventh heaven.

The painting hit him between the eyes. That great red accusing eyeball, staring back at him. His knees buckled, but she held him up. She took him closer. It wasn't an eyeball, but a wheel. A wheel that had collected debris that would one day engulf him. Debris sticking to the rim, held on by a thin white line, the line between goodness and evil, a line trailing back to the innocent past, a past that could never be revisited. The wheel rode on, gathering more rubbish. On and on and on, gathering more and more and more...

"I hope you l-like it, Mr B-Bassett."

He turned. He would have fallen, had not her strong hands been holding him up.

He was looking at Nicholas Woollidge.

No. No, no. He was looking at Will Murchison.

PART TWO

1987 and 1979

1.   April 1987

Leo has arrived back home, changed, and is reading a magazine sprawled along the longest sofa in the lounge when Gemma returns. She hears the front door open and thinks that Gemma will go straight upstairs to her room, so she will never know what Gemma's been doing since she ran from the café.

But she doesn't. In fact, Huwie's voice calls, "Leo?" and Leo scrambles up from the sofa and says, "In here", hugging an overstuffed cushion to her stomach as a shield. And the two of them come in, Gemma with her hand through Huwie's arm in a kind of trustful dependence.

And Huwie looks – well, dazed with happiness. She's never seen her brother so transparent before. He's always looked like Daddy, apart from his hair which is dark like hers, not chestnut like his, and his nose that turns up a bit at the end like Mummy's, not a 'great Julius Caesar of a conk', as Daddy used to describe his. But she had never seen Daddy so happy. (Well yes, she has; when he had brought Gemma home to meet them, eighteen months ago.)

She looks from him to Gemma. Gemma's face is pale and her eyes are reddened and washed-out, but she, too, is smiling, although it's a watery smile. They come into the lounge like a couple of newly-weds.

"Hi, Leo." He has obviously forgotten their quarrel; forgotten he called her a jealous, spiteful little brat. So it seems she must forget it too.

"Hello."

"What have you been doing all day?"

"Nothing."

He perches on the arm of the sofa, keeping Gemma's hand firmly encased in his. She pulls up an armchair next to him and sits. So this is going to be two against one, obviously. "Gemma has something to tell you. It's going to come as a bit of a shock."

Everything to do with Gemma is a bit of a shock, she nearly says. There's been nothing but shocks since she landed on us.

She smiles at her half-sister. "Oh?"

And Gemma says, "You remember that letter Mr Cardew gave me? That Laurence had given him?"

Oh yes, she remembers that. "Oh – yes."

"I couldn't tell you yesterday. I didn't want to believe it. I sat on my bed all afternoon and into the night. I still don't want to believe it, but I suppose…" She looks towards Huwie, who pats her hand encouragingly. "The thing is, Leo – the thing is…"

"She's not our sister." And Huwie says this in a voice of such happiness and relief that, for a moment, Leo is disconcerted.

"What do you mean? Of course she is!"

"No. Dad thought she was, when he met her, but apparently he was wrong. The dates don't match. He didn't realise until her birthday when Gemma told him she was three weeks' premature. It couldn't have been him, do you see? She should have been a couple of weeks overdue."

Leo is silent. The words have yet to sink in.

Gemma delves in her bag and brings out the long brown envelope, now looking a little the worse for wear. She holds it out towards Leo. "Read it."

And Leo is taking the envelope – the same envelope Daddy had written on and sealed the paper up in, the same envelope the Man had held in his dirty murderer's hands – and is sliding the paper out, unfolding it and bringing it to her eyes.

My darling Gemma. You will think I'm a coward, or worse, and I am. I couldn't bring myself to tell you. Please don't think badly of me. You were so happy, as we all were. It didn't seem to matter – but it does. You have a right to know.

I'm not your father. I was wrong. I've known this since your 20th birthday, only a few days after I made that momentous announcement. I should have made sure of my facts first, but – well, I was always an impulsive old fool. I'd spent years thinking about you and your mother, and I just assumed I was her only conquest. Of course that was foolish. Your mother ran away to London, so who knows what happened there. All I know is that, before she left, we shared a very special moment that I have remembered with joy and fondness. Your mother is a special person, Gemma. She's always had a place in my heart and so have you.

I have always thought of you as my daughter. You've been as precious to me as Huw and Leonora, and I hope I've treated you exactly the same...

There is more, but she can't read on. The letter is blurred and Daddy's loopy handwriting is dancing in front of her eyes. Huwie takes it out of her hands and folds it back into the envelope.

"Oh," she says. It is more of a gulp.

"It explains a lot of things," Gemma says. "Why he didn't want me to change my name, for instance. He told me it would upset my mother."

"And why," Huwie says, "you don't look much like any of us. Just because you're dark, and fairly tall, we just assumed... but let's face it, you haven't got the Bassett tendency towards clumsiness, or gullibility, or..."

"Brattishness," Leo finishes. This second bombshell is slowly sinking in. It's a delayed detonation, not like the first. And there's a ray of light hovering over the crater. Too late, of course, but apparently Daddy had known the truth almost as soon as the Bombshell had been dropped. So she, Leo, had still been his only precious princess. Even if outwardly nothing had changed, inwardly he would have felt differently about Gemma. How could he not?

"I feel such a fraud," Gemma says sadly. "I've lived here all this time, let you treat me so well, spent Laurence's money... of course I won't take the share in the house. He shouldn't have left it to me. I'll sign my share over to you, Leo."

"Rubbish," says Huwie, before Leo can open her mouth. "Dad wanted you to have it. He said he always thought of you as his daughter. And that was his last will and testament."

Leo says slowly, "But if you're not Daddy's daughter, whose are you? And fancy your mother not telling you – she must have known."

"She did," Gemma says. There is a hard edge to her voice. "So now I'm back to square one. I'll never know now where I come from."

93

"Why don't you ask her?" Gemma's relationship with the Mad Mother is still a mystery to Leo. She doesn't go to visit her very often, and when she does she comes back in a strange mood. Leo, when she telephones Mrs W, always asks after Gemma's mother and is told, "Oh, she's lovely, pet, she brings a breath of fresh air every day, always picking flowers and making lovely soups out of nettles and things and keeping Bernard cheerful. We wouldn't be without her for the world!"

Gemma gives her a sour look. "I'll never ask her. She didn't tell me for twenty years, why should she now? She was probably relieved Laurence thought it was him, it let her off the hook. She's either ashamed of who he was, or doesn't know because she had so many. Either way, I'd rather not know."

Leo's heart suddenly gives a lurch. Something falls into place. It's such a simple explanation that she nearly gives a shout of glee, but manages to suppress it in time. And Huwie and Gemma haven't even noticed. They are gazing into each other's eyes like love's young dream.

*****

Contrary to appearances, Leo is not a confident driver, especially in London. She prefers to take the bus or the tube – never taxis, like Daddy. He had bought her a little second-hand Triumph TR7 for her twenty-first birthday but she rarely uses it, except to the odd assignment out in the sticks. But today she has decided to drive, and is cautiously making her way along Archway Road trying to remember the route.

For the first time in weeks she's had to think what to wear – apart from her boy's disguise, of course. At home she's been lounging around in tops and denims, the same ones two or three days in a row. Her hair, usually carefully gelled and spiked, has grown longer (softening her face, according to Huwie). She doesn't wear such outrageous gear as she used to – the Vivienne Westwood creations have gone to the local Oxfam shop along with the feather boas and platform shoes. She's dressed today in black trousers, a white tee-shirt and her favourite short biscuit-coloured jacket. On her feet is a pair of boots similar to Gemma's.

It takes a few wrong turns, and angry hoots behind her, before eventually she finds what she's looking for. She drives carefully through the gates, turns right and stops outside the garage. The shutters are up, but she can't see any sign of life beyond. There are a couple of cars inside, one up on a ramp, the other with its bonnet raised.

She slides out of the Triumph and walks towards the garage, stands in the entrance. No sign of the Man. She takes a couple of steps forward. The smell of oil, grease, rubber, hot metal, assails her nostrils; smells she's unfamiliar with, but somehow they're evocative and rather exciting. The deeper she penetrates into the gloom, the more she feels she's entering the first circle of hell – everything is strange, dirty, menacing; there is screwed-up black sticky paper tossed on the floor, fearsome-looking tools lying in pools of oil. She jumps as the sound of rushing water suddenly erupts from somewhere at the back of the garage; a door slams and the Man appears, wiping his hands on a paper towel.

"Sorry," he says without looking up, "can't take any more on until the day after tomorrow." He flings the towel into an overflowing bin, then comes towards her and stops. "Oh," he says. He doesn't sound surprised.

Speech has forsaken her. She just stares at him, unblinking. He's wearing the dark blue boilersuit and his hands (although obviously he's just washed them) are stained black.

"What do you want?" His tone is neither friendly nor hostile.

She swallows, but words still don't come. What *does* she want?

He says in the same even tone, "I'm sorry about your father."

Now the words do come. "No you're not."

He shrugs. "I meant I'm sorry for you." He looks at her steadily for a few seconds, then turns away. "I'm a bit busy at the moment. It's a bad time."

She stands her ground, just watches as he picks up a large chrome implement and bends over the car's engine. Then he straightens. "Oh, bugger it," he mutters, flinging it down, "I'll put the kettle on. Do you want tea or coffee?"

"Tea."

She follows him towards the back of the garage. There's a little room boarded off to one side that contains a rudimentary kitchen – electric kettle, two-ring hob – and, just outside on a ledge running along the back wall, a sleeping bag and a couple of folded blankets. On the far side there's a desk overflowing with papers, an adding machine, ledgers, and a shelf containing manuals, car parts catalogues, a row of keys.

From outside the room she watches him scrub his hands with Swarfega, then fill the kettle from a jug, set out two chipped mugs and drop a teabag in each. He takes an opened bottle of milk from a small fridge underneath the hob and sniffs at it. "I think it's okay. Do you take milk? Sugar?"

"A little milk. No sugar."

He gives a quick smile. "Same here."

And the tea is just as she likes it, hot and strong. She cradles the mug between her hands as he brings out a couple of folding chairs from a passage that presumably leads to the loo (the pipes are still gurgling), and sets them side by side near the desk. He sits.

After a moment's hesitation she sits down next to him, aware that somehow he's taken the advantage. As she takes small sips of the tea she tries to get her bearings. She is sitting next to her father's murderer, drinking tea like she's at some church fete. Well, not quite – the surroundings don't fit, and the cumbersome mug definitely isn't bone china – but she has the same feelings of inadequacy that she would no doubt have at a vicarage.

She glances at him. His face gives nothing away; he doesn't look guilty, uneasy, discomfited. But neither does he look smug or self-satisfied. And although he's dressed for the part, he doesn't quite fit here, either. He's certainly not her idea of a garage mechanic. His voice, for one thing – there's a trace of a Welsh accent, like hers, a nice rhythmic quality to the words, not the usual glottal-stop estuary English. His face, too, has a poetic edge to it, a dash of the Byronic. It's his hair, of course. Hair like that isn't meant to be thrust into the innards of cars.

He says, reading her mind, "I'm looking after this place for someone."

"Oh. Is he on holiday?"

"He's inside."

"Oh."

"He should be out soon. Then I'll have to find somewhere else."

She looks at the sleeping bag. "You live here too?"

"I'm between digs." He smiles again and rubs his unshaven chin. "The sanitary arrangements leave a lot to be desired. I go to the public baths once a week. You came a day early, I'm due for a scrub up tomorrow."

There's no answer to that. She sits, sipping tea. It has a bitter, metallic quality that isn't unpleasant.

"God, that's diabolical." He suddenly gets up, takes her mug with his and flings the contents of both into a nearby bucket. "Come on," he says, "let's go to the pub."

For some reason she can't refuse. He takes a set of keys from the board, thumps the bonnet down on the car he's working on, and opens the passenger door. It's a rather old but sporty MG, its interior smelling pleasantly of sweet malt and tobacco. She slides into the passenger seat as he settles into the driver's side and switches on the ignition. He listens to the engine attentively.

"It needs a bit of a run," he says, backing the car out into the road. Then he leaps out, strides back into the garage, appears a minute later minus overalls, in jeans and the scuffed black leather jacket. He pulls down the shutters.

As he drives out into the main streets she can't keep her eyes off his hands. They rest on the steering wheel, square, blunt, capable hands that seem to have an affinity with whatever is going on under the bonnet. He changes gear deftly, manoeuvres with the skill of a racing driver. This isn't his car, she's well aware, he's obviously not insured to drive it, they are a couple of carjackers, but she feels quite safe, even pleasantly comfortable. The London traffic holds no terrors for him; he seems to know instinctively when to overtake, when to slow down, exactly what the vehicle is capable of. She settles back into the seat in contented silence.

97

A couple of times, on a smooth stretch of road (where are they going? – she's never been in this part of London, if it *is* still London) he presses his foot on the accelerator and gives the car its head. They roar up hills, take bends at terrifying angles; then he decelerates, listens again and mutters, "Timing's still out. Damn."

"Do you take all the cars on test runs?"

"Only the fast ones." He favours her with another quick smile.

"Do the owners know?"

He shrugs. "They've no need to. The gauge is easy to fix. I make up the petrol." His foot goes down again and they take off on another mile or so of exhilarating speed. Despite herself, she can't help laughing and, glancing sideways, sees a smile of adolescent pleasure on his usually stern features. The boy Daddy knew is sitting beside her in the body of a thirty-seven-year-old man. The laughter dies in her throat.

After about forty minutes they arrive at a large rambling country pub somewhere far beyond Barnet. This must be Hertfordshire. She's well away from her bearings now, but it's too late to turn back. He might be planning to murder her, chop her up into bits and bury her over a wide stretch of land, but she follows him into the pub and lets him buy her half a pint of lager. She knows she has more money to spare than he has, but knows equally well that an offer to pay will elicit no thanks from him.

"So," he says, sitting down on a stool opposite the banquette she's settled in, "perhaps you can tell me now what you want."

She takes a long draught of the lager, looks him steadily in the eyes and says, "Are you Gemma's father?"

A shade passes over his face, though his gaze doesn't flinch.

"She showed me Daddy's letter."

"Oh." He too takes a long pull of his pint. "I see."

"It all makes sense now."

"Does it?"

"Of course. It explains why you hate him."

He smiles. "I don't hate him. I did once, probably. A long

time ago."

"If Daddy told Gemma he was her father, and then found out he wasn't and didn't tell her, then you'd hate him for that, wouldn't you?"

"Possibly. If I were her father."

"Are you?"

He gazes at her for a long moment, then says, "No."

She's not disconcerted. She's more certain than ever. "I think you are. That's why you came to the house, why Daddy let you stay. Why you took Gemma to Australia. And," she takes a deep breath, "why you made her get rid of the baby."

For the first time his gaze falters. There's a loosening of the muscles of his face, a shifting in the depths of those dark brown eyes. "What baby?"

She snorts. "Oh, come on! You knew she was pregnant when she came back. It must have been yours. It *was* yours, she said so. It happened only once, she said, but she hadn't taken the pill for weeks, she'd left them in Suffolk. Sod's law, of course, but there it is." She glares at him, willing herself not to be taken in by his obvious shock. "So if you're her father, she couldn't have the baby, could she? It's incest. You made her have the abortion."

He stares down into his glass. She's not sure he's even listening.

"She said she had to get rid of it," she goes on, "so I arranged it for her."

He lifts his glass and takes a long slow gulp. He sets it back down, wipes his mouth with the back of his hand and mutters, "Christ." When he lifts his face again the look in his eyes gives her a first inkling of doubt. There's shock there, and horror, and desolation.

"Don't pretend you didn't know."

"I didn't."

"She must have told you before I came back from the States."

"She didn't."

"And then you went to prison for a year," she goes on implacably, "so it's a good job she had the abortion. No kid deserves a jailbird for a father, or even a grandfather."

"I knew nothing about it. Believe me."

She's fighting all her natural instincts, but in the end has to admit she does believe him. "But you did have sex in Australia. She told me you did."

He doesn't deny it, just sits looking down at his hands, fisted on his knees.

"And you are her father."

He doesn't bother to reply. He's already denied it. Does she believe him about this? He's not the sort, she realises, to tell lies.

Her marvellously simple explanation is in tatters. If he's not Gemma's father, then there must be another reason for his hatred of Daddy, which means Daddy must have done something to him in the past. *I hated him once,* he'd said, *a long time ago.* So it was true. Daddy *did* have boys – or at least, this one boy. Daddy had lied to her. Mummy was right. Those terrible accusations – they were all true.

They finish their drinks in silence. He gets to his feet and she follows him out of the pub. They climb back in the car. He drives back to north London skilfully but not fast, observing speed limits like a model citizen. His profile is cold and hard, as she remembers it.

He drops her off outside the garage and watches as she unlocks the Triumph.

"I'm sorry," she says, not knowing what she's apologising for.

He doesn't answer. He stands watching as she fires the ignition. She realises she has to do a three-point turn, a manoeuvre she's not fully competent in, and only succeeds in doing it in five points under his impassive gaze. Then she puts the car into first (with a small scrape of the gear) and pulls away not quite as smoothly as she would like. It's not until she's past the gates and signalling left that, in the rear view mirror, she sees him turn away and fling up the shutters of the garage in a gesture of barely contained violence.

2.   July 1979

"So, Ralph," Laurence said, making his turn into Hampstead Lane, "what do you think?"

"It's a car, Larry."

"Wrong. It's a Jag."

"It has four wheels and an engine. It's a car."

"You Philistine." Laurence smiled fondly. "If you can't say something nice, I'll throw you out at the next set of lights."

"The seats are comfy."

"What about the air conditioning? The improved leg room? The cleaner, crisper, sexier lines? Not to mention the whisper-quiet ride."

"You'd make a good salesman, Larry."

"No, I make a gullible purchaser. But you must admit, Ralph, she's a beauty." Laurence really didn't need Ralph's approval, in fact he knew he wouldn't get it; Ralph was a fully-paid-up member of the Green brigade. But his Green credentials didn't preclude him from accepting a lift, he noted. "I'm glad you could come tonight. My last night of freedom before I go into purdah."

"Glad you asked me."

Laurence glanced across at Ralph. Poor fellow, he looked half-starved; since poor Viv died six months ago he couldn't have been looking after himself properly. Laurence himself was aware that he'd been stacking on the weight recently; people at the Beeb had started calling the pair of them Laurel and Hardy. Well, for the next five weeks no doubt he'd be run ragged, so it was as well he'd got a bit of ballast to shed.

Although if truth be told, he was looking forward to having his kids again, and he never thought he'd admit that. Of course he could afford to feel like this, knowing he'd be able to bundle them back to Swansea at the end of the holidays. They were getting older and, although Leo was still a handful, at least Huwie was starting to grow into his skin. He was getting closer to his son, and as for his daughter – well, for five weeks he could put up with her moods; she could be amusing, and she might well have grown out of her tantrums by now. Leo was still young for her age, still fairly malleable. He could cope for five weeks. How parents coped with teenagers on a full-time basis, though, was a mystery, and one he had no intention of solving.

His life, over the last three years, had continued to be good. He was still popular on his television shows, even though *Whither Art?* had finally hit the buffers. Ralph, however, was still determined to raise his profile on the box from quiz shows and the odd 'celebrity' spot, but Laurence was quite content now to let that coast along. His business had grown and prospered, thanks of course to Deborah, and even more to Will Murchison. He felt he deserved his Jag, a present to himself for his forthcoming fiftieth birthday, the only piece of grit in the oyster.

Letting himself and Ralph into the house, he felt no premonition of impending doom. The suitcase and three bulging carrier bags by the door failed to impinge on his consciousness. It was only when a whirlwind hurled itself down the stairs and launched itself at him that his world fell apart.

"Daddy!"

"Leo?" He held her away, gazing with incomprehension at her ballerina skirt, rugby jumper and clogs. Her hair, black at the roots, was held up by beads and ribbons into clumps of Dayglo pink and purple. "I thought you were coming tomorrow...?"

"I came down a day early because – listen to this – *I don't have to go back!* I've left school! I've got a place at college – the London Design College no less! – I start there in two months, it's all arranged so you can't get rid of me! I'm here to stay!"

Laurence was temporarily bereft of words. Caitlin had given no indication of this. But then why would she? Chances were she was pleased to see the back of this volatile daughter.

"Huwie?" was all he managed.

"He's gone on a school trip, didn't Mummy tell you? So you've got me all to yourself for two whole weeks! Oh Daddy, isn't it fabulous? Oh, I'm so happy happy happy!" She waltzed round and round the hall.

Ralph said, "You lucky man, Larry. Both my kids have flown the nest." He was looking at Leonora with amusement tinged with sorrow.

"Leo, I'm giving a dinner party tonight…"

"I know, Mrs Wetherby told me. I've been helping her."

"I've got the Jacobsens coming, and the Lyttletons, and Dermot…"

"I know! I'll be good!"

"You'll have to be *quiet.*"

"I know! I can be quiet!"

"And you'll have to – tone yourself down a bit."

This was exactly the wrong thing to say. Leo stopped waltzing and stood like a disgruntled gremlin, scowling. "You're ashamed of me! Aren't you? I'm not good enough for your high-and-mighty dinner party guests! Well, don't worry about it. I won't show you up. I'll stay in my room. I'll stay in my room till I start college, you won't need to see me at all. You won't need to see me ever again, not till the day I *die*…" She flounced off up the stairs, her fluorescent bunches and stiff layered pink tutu quivering with offence.

Ralph laughed. "How old is she?"

"Seven-bloody-teen! I thought she'd have outgrown tantrums by now!" Shit, he thought, I've forgotten her birthday yet again. I'll give her some money to buy something with.

"Oh God, Larry, you've got a few more years of it yet. And how old's the boy?"

"Fifteen."

Ralph looked pitying. "Slap bang in the middle of the terrible teens. You have my sympathy."

"Thanks. Something tells me I'm going to need it."

Although, halfway through the evening, he was beginning to think he'd got away with it. Leo was as good as her word; there was no sign of her. Mrs W told him she'd left a tray outside her room which had disappeared ten minutes later. The little lamb, she said, wouldn't go hungry.

The conversation round the table was stimulating, as always. Wine flowed freely. Even Dermot had left behind his brown corduroy jacket and trimmed his beard and looked quite presentable, although he insisted on puffing on that disgusting pipe between courses. He had become quite an establishment figure, Laurence thought, voicing doubts about the wisdom of electing a woman prime minister and concerns about the fundamentalist revival in the Middle East. So if even Timberlake, *enfant terrible* of the art world in the Sixties, could transform himself into a reactionary old fart, there was hope for Leo – twenty years down the line, unfortunately.

Ralph was in animated conversation with Isabel Jacobsen about environmental issues – oil pollution on the high seas and nuclear disaster only narrowly averted being high on his agenda – and the voracious Dermot was turning his attention to diminutive Cynthia Lyttleton while Cyril was safely visiting the downstairs cloakroom. Laurence leaned back in his chair and lit up a cigar. He hadn't done this for years, but now he felt he deserved one. He'd also treated himself to two nice fat Havanas in honour of his half-century.

"So," George said, leaning over the table, "you're keeping your boy close to your chest, Larry."

"Boy, George?"

"Little Will Murchison. Exciting plenty of comment, I hear."

"He's coming along."

"I saw his name mentioned in the *Observer*. Exciting new artist whose paintings can't even be seen, let alone bought. By the home market, at least."

Laurence glanced towards Dermot. He didn't seem to have heard. He lowered his voice. "I'm going easy with Will. He's not the sort you can hurry. He only paints well when he's happy. Unfortunately that's not very often."

"Oh?"

"He's prone to depression. Gets himself in a real black hole sometimes. Not easy to dig him out of it." He hoped George would take this analysis at face value. The medical diagnosis had been discouraging, the prognosis devastating.

George lit up a cigarette. "I would have thought you could jolly him along, Larry."

"What do you mean?"

"Well – you know. Lad's infatuated with you, by all

accounts."

Laurence laughed – rather too loudly, damn it, both Dermot and Ralph had turned towards him. "Oh no, George. You've got that wrong. He's just grateful to me."

"Hah!" George blew smoke to the ceiling and smiled knowingly.

"So what do you think, George," Dermot asked, leaning across the table towards him, "about our young protégé?"

"Oh, not my field. Ask me about long-dead daubers and I'm your man."

"If you ask me, he's over-valued."

"If people want to pay…" More smoke spiralled upwards.

"It's these nouveau-riche Yanks," Dermot said bitterly. "More money than sense, most of them. They've got to be told what's good and then they buy it up by the lorry-load. Unbalances the whole market."

"Oh now, I don't go along with that. The New York art scene is thriving at the moment. It's us Brits in the doldrums, isn't that so, Larry?"

Laurence, pulling on his cigar, refused to be drawn.

"And this forger Johnny hasn't helped," George went on. "He's being brought to book soon, I've heard. Too late, of course. Damage has been done."

Laurence said, grateful to get off the subject of Will Murchison, "I can't help but admire the man, though. Nobody saw through him, even though he left clues all over the place. Makes you wonder if he would have got away with it…"

"They're like burglars," George said, "going back to the scene of the crime. Can't make it on their own merits so they borrow someone else's. Then of course they want their fifteen minutes of fame, so they own up. Become more famous than the poor sods with the talent. That's the way the world's going, Larry – the less talent you have, the more you'll be famous."

The cigar had lost its savour; perhaps he'd lost the taste for them. Laurence put it out in the ashtray.

"You're right, George," Dermot nodded sagely, pipe dangling from his lower lip. "Young upstarts don't know the meaning of the word talent." Then, taking the pipe from his mouth and pointing the stem towards Laurence, "I'll prove it to you if you like. Let you be the judge."

Just then Cyril said from the doorway, "Look what I found in the hall." All eyes turned to see a forlorn barefoot waif, dressed in something that looked like a white pillowcase, being dragged in by the hand.

"Nooo!" the waif wailed heartrendingly, "he'll beat me!"

"Oh, the poor child!" said Cynthia, getting up.

"Daddy, I didn't mean to disturb your dinner party! I just wanted a morsel of bread and cheese…"

"For God's sake, Leo…"

"No! No!" The waif cringed back against the wall. "Don't hit me, Daddy! Don't let him hit me," she pleaded to Cynthia, who put her arm round her shoulders with soothing noises, then frowned accusingly at Laurence.

"Who's this, Larry? Cinderella?" George asked, amused.

"Stop it, George! The poor girl is terrified!" Isabel was aghast.

"Oh, for pity's sake. It's all an act…" Laurence rose to his feet as Leo, with a strangled yelp, disappeared behind Cynthia. He'd kept both his children away from his friends and colleagues; for three years, during the school summer holidays, he'd become a recluse. Anger at Leo, however, was turning to amusement; the little minx had spirit, he had to admit.

In a loud booming voice he demanded, "Come out from there, you little trollop! I'll whip your backside!"

A howl rose from behind Cynthia, who stood her ground before Laurence like a pocket-sized Valkyrie. "Mr Bassett, I would never have believed…"

"Stand aside, Mrs Lyttleton. My daughter must be taught a lesson."

"I will not, Mr Bassett!"

"He beats me," wailed the waif, "and sends me to my room without any supper! Ooh, he's a cruel, cruel man…!"

"Laurence Bassett!" Cynthia was ablaze with righteous indignation. "I will report you to the authorities! I had no idea – Cyril, did you know about this? This is child abuse! This is…"

"This is a complete charade," said Laurence. "Leo, the game's over. It's not funny any more."

Leo crept out from behind Cynthia, her face stricken. She'd blacked her eyes with boot polish and wound her hair in paper curlers. The pillowcase *was* a pillowcase, he realised. The sight of her skinny limbs and bare feet made him give a sudden snort of laughter.

"Daddy!" Leo threw herself at him, arms wound round his neck. She began kissing him all over his face. "Can I stay? Can I stay?"

"Go and put on something decent, then you can come down and have coffee. Mrs Wetherby says you've eaten."

"My darling Daddy!" Leo beamed at Cynthia, who stood dumbfounded. "He can be so cruel, but he's kind too." And she dashed off up the stairs, coming down a few minutes later in demure skirt and blouse.

Later, when his guests had departed (congratulating him on having such a lively, intelligent daughter), Laurence sat Leo down for a heart-to-heart talk.

"Leo, we must lay down a few house rules. If you're going to stay here, there's got to be some understanding…"

"Yes, Daddy."

"It was amusing tonight, but they are my friends. Others might not be so – forgiving…"

Leo looked suitably chastened. "Yes, Daddy."

"You're old enough now to realise… well, my reputation… I've got to be careful, Leo. In my position…"

"I do understand, Daddy."

"It's not true, what you might have heard. None of it. But mud sticks…" He had never spoken of his past before, and felt slightly embarrassed now. But it was true; she *was* old enough to realise his position. "Just remember, Leo, I'm in the public eye. And there's nothing the tabloid press likes more than to bring people like me down…"

"Oh Daddy! I'll never bring you down." Leo looked mortified.

Laurence had a sudden, overwhelming rush of love for this

strange little creature he had brought into the world. He looked with fondness at her elfin features, too sharp and intense to be pretty, but with a striking vitality of their own; life with this daughter might be exhausting but would never be boring, he thought. And surely this was a small penance to pay for the life he now enjoyed.

******

The summer holidays, when Laurence spent most of his time in Hampstead, were an opportunity for Deborah Routledge to catch up on unfinished business. The gallery more or less ran itself, and she had trained up little Rosemary to take over a lot of the day-to-day tasks; for the next five weeks Deborah could spend much of the day upstairs in Laurence's office. Today she was tidying up his filing cabinets and sorting out his drawers. By doing this she felt as if she were delving into his deepest secrets, but of course there was nothing secretive about any of it; just pads of doodles, jotted down phone numbers, letters that didn't get as far as being filed, odd crumbs and sweet wrappers that hadn't gone into the bin. Surfacing from his bottom drawers, she was aware she was rosy and dishevelled and was sure she caught a smirk on Rosemary's face when she brought up her lunch tray. Well, let the girl think what she liked. Deborah really didn't care any more.

During the next weeks she must make sure everything was in place for the continued smooth running of the business. She must, of course, contact David Symons at the Venn Pegasus Agency and tell him another two Murchisons were ready to be transported, a third expected at any time. Over the last three years he (or his client) had made major purchases of new art and their haul of Murchisons now totalled half a dozen. If only Will could be persuaded to work more quickly! Poor boy, he did his best, and his best was superlative, and if only he could double his output... But genius could not be hurried, she supposed. And after completing a work, he needed at least a couple of months to recover.

Months he spent at Hurlingham Mansions, in mother's room. He had his studio in Wapping that Laurence had taken the lease on, the top of an old warehouse with huge glass windows on all sides, overlooking the docks, a large space containing a fully-fitted kitchen, a partitioned-off bedroom and bathroom. There he painted in a manic frenzy, eating and sleeping on the premises (she kept the cupboards stocked with tins of spaghetti, meatballs and peas and the fridge with fruit juice, cheese and bars of chocolate but she didn't know how often he bothered to eat when he was working) - emerging hollow-eyed and gaunt after five or six weeks, weak and trembling and on the verge of psychosis. She nursed him back to health with nourishing broth, stews and hot milk. And, of course, his medication. She was sure he didn't take it when he was painting, and perhaps just as well – those great explosions of colour and vibrancy were pulled out of some dark corner of his psyche which the pills kept at bay – but she was a solicitous nurse at home, watching him swallow his tablets night and morning with the regularity of a stopwatch. After a couple of weeks he was calm, and soon back to his meek, lovable self.

Most evenings they would just curl up together on the big settee watching television. She had never owned a television before but now she couldn't imagine life without it. Cradling Will's almost weightless head in her lap, her fingers dabbling idly in his lovely curls, laughing with him at the situation comedies that were his favourite programmes, she felt herself to be the luckiest person on earth.

Her love for Will was different to what she felt for Laurence. One was wholly maternal, the other – what? Something different. Let little Rosemary think she was a pathetic old maid – she knew better. Laurence had spent quite a few nights at Hurlingham Mansions since the evening of his confession in the Savoy Grill, the night she had unlocked the door of the third bedroom and illuminated the lamps. He had been slightly drunk, of course, and what with the shock of the painting and seeing Will, his wits had entirely deserted him.

It had been easy to persuade him to lie down on the damson

quilt, unlace his shoes, pull off his socks... and, glancing up to make sure he was asleep, or too far gone to resist, unzipping his trousers, sliding them down his legs, folding them up neatly on the sofa. Then unbuttoning his shirt, loosening his tie, divesting his heavy upper limbs of encumbrances, working smoothly and silently with all the efficiency she had learned with mother. But with more tenderness, more love, more – oh yes, she could admit it – excitement... seeing him lying there, helpless as a baby, in his singlet and striped boxer shorts...

...and how natural it was to slip her fingers through the opening in those shorts, her breath held in her throat, her tongue between her teeth as they encountered an extraordinary pile of strange flesh – a kind of loose bag, velvety to the touch, with something round and pebbly contained in it that she could roll with a finger, and on top of that a thick curled cylinder, not as soft but more with the texture of moist dough that was hardening even as she weighed it in her hand...

He had given a loud groan and she had withdrawn, both out of his shorts and the room, her heart racing, her body trembling and her mouth bone dry yet full of saliva, and it had taken her quite a few minutes before she was able to go back to the kitchen and join Will, drinking his hot milk at the table.

"D-do you think he l-liked it?" he had asked, meaning the painting, and she had replied, "Oh yes, Will, I know he did," meaning something else entirely.

That first visit, and all the rest over the course of the next three years, was never referred to in their everyday lives. What happened in the Red Room took place in another life, on another timescale. She knew when he was coming; he would leave a little note in her account book (which she kept in the safe, forbidden to Rosemary): *It's been a bad day; I need some wine and plums* – and she would make up the bed and light the lamps and then, after sharing a bottle or two of the best Pinot Noir, she would lead him back into the womb, and undress him, and fondle him (she had become an expert in this), and murmur sweet words of comfort; afterwards tucking him up nice and safe under the sheet and blankets. He never reciprocated, nor did she want him to. Her satisfaction came from satisfying him; anything else might be a disappointment, for both him and her, which she did not want to risk.

After a few visits, possibly after a year or so, he had remarked that, with a figure like hers, it might be nice if she dressed in something more suitable – a nurse's uniform, perhaps, with starched bosom and black stockings, or one of those Norland Nanny outfits, just for a laugh... And she had done, which had certainly spiced up their sessions, except that now she was running out of ideas for costumes, and she didn't want him to get bored...

Now, spooning her yoghurt idly into her mouth, she glanced at his pad of doodles. He did this when caught in a telephone call he couldn't bring to a graceful conclusion – she had seen him grimace, pull his nose, pick up his pen and draw great loops and swirls on this pad. Turning the page over, she saw faces with dashes for eyes and question marks for noses *(meaning: what the hell is he on about?)*; the back ends of cats with tails high and crosses for anuses *(this fellow's an arsehole!)*; great looming tower blocks with matchstick men about to leap off *(boring git!!)*. Flipping over another page, she saw circles of all sizes, chasing each other to the margins, all joined by an exuberant, swooping line *(a good day, obviously)* – the next one full of teardrops – no, possibly nooses – some with faces drawn in them (a bad/sad – Red Room? - day).

And the ones at the back – well, the spoonful of yoghurt remained in her mouth, she had lost the ability to swallow. Surely these were shoes – long narrow shoes with impossibly high heels, and boots – a row of tall black riding boots marching off to the left. And jodhpurs and riding crops and black hoods and masks...

When little Rosemary came up to collect her lunch tray, she was sitting in Laurence's high leather chair with a pink, moist, spaced-out expression and she didn't care. The only thought in her mind was that it might be time to change the theme of the third bedroom at Hurlingham Mansions.

111

******

Will always knew when it was time to go back to Wapping. There was that slight itch first of all, not something to scratch but more like an itch in the mind, a restlessness, an urge to get away from what was becoming the stifling atmosphere of the flat. He began to withdraw into himself. When Miss Routledge - who wanted him to call her Deborah, but it was hard to bring himself to do this, just as it was hard, for another reason, to call Mr Bassett Laurence - brought him his milk and medication last thing at night, he found it harder and harder to obey, and when he started refusing to swallow the pills they both knew it was time he went back to Wapping.

So she wouldn't be surprised tonight to find he had gone, because he hadn't taken his pills for three days and that was the Sign that told him he should start painting. He gathered up his possessions in two plastic bags. Just his clothes, toothbrush and toiletries – he didn't bother to shave when he was working and anyway he didn't have many whiskers, he would never be able to grow a bushy black beard like Dermot Timberlake.

All his paints and canvases were stored at Wapping, and Miss Routledge made sure there was food in the cupboards but when he was working he wasn't hungry although sometimes he was told to eat, especially when he couldn't hold the brush any more because his arms were tired. But he never bothered to heat anything up, he just spooned it out of the tin. He never looked at the labels and probably ate meatballs with custard, or baked beans with pineapple chunks. It didn't matter because everything tasted the same.

He knew how to get to Wapping, because Miss Routledge had left the phone number of the local taxi firm, and all he had to do was dial the number and the taxi would take him. When he'd arrived in London (after his mum's new husband had bought the ticket and put him on the train), a man in the station had asked if he wanted a taxi, so he said yes, and gave the address of his aunty's in Hackney because he knew it was in London. But when he arrived his aunty was surprised and his uncle was angry because he'd had to pay the taxi man a bloody hell of a lot of money, he said. And his uncle had tried to phone his mum but there were new people in the house who didn't know where she'd gone, so he couldn't go back even if he knew how. And then he had met Mr Swainton at an art exhibition somewhere, although he didn't like to remember what happened after that. He supposed Mr Swainton only did it to be friendly, but what he did wasn't friendly at all although Mr Swainton seemed to find it nice.

But he didn't paint for Mr Swainton.

The bell rang, so he knew the taxi was waiting downstairs. Miss Routledge had told him not to worry about money, they would pay all his bills, so he gathered his bags and made sure the door was shut behind him, and went down the two flights of stairs and into the taxi, which took him to Wapping.

He knew what to do when he got there. He would ring the bell on the door, and the man who looked after the building would give him the key to the top floor.

He rang the bell and the man came to the door and said, "Oh, it's you. I suppose you want the key?"

And he said, "Yes p-please."

And the man said, "A bloke is looking for you. Told me to tell you when you arrived. You want me to call him?"

"A b-bloke?"

"Big fellow. Corduroy jacket. Black beard."

"Oh! Oh, y-yes, you can t-tell him I'm here." His heart was bursting as he went up the stairs. Dermot Timberlake was calling on him! *The* Dermot Timberlake, who Miss Routledge had introduced him to when he first arrived but who hadn't seemed too pleased to meet him. They had met again a few times since, and always Mr Timberlake had been too busy to exchange more than a few words. Which of course suited Will. In a way it was better *not* to meet people he admired because he always disappointed them, he could tell by the embarrassment on their faces and they way they shuffled their feet when he tried to answer their questions. Mr Bassett – Laurence – was different. He didn't mind how long it took Will to answer his questions,

113

and Will always found he could answer them almost without stammering, because Mr Bassett – Laurence - didn't mind how long... oh, anyway.

And Mr Timberlake must have been really dying to meet him because no sooner had he emptied his bags and put things away and set out his painting stuff in its proper places and filled the kettle and boiled the water and measured a teaspoon of coffee in a mug and added the water (there was no milk because it would go off while he was away, but he didn't mind it black), and then had taken the mug over to the window to make sure the sky was still there (he had put off doing this when he first came in because sometimes he spent so long gazing into the grey white blue ultramarine of it that he didn't exist any more and that was scary, so he had done all these other things with his face turned down to the floor) than the entryphone buzzed and the man who looked after the building said, "He's here, do you want him up?" and he said, "Yes please," and pressed the button on the door so Mr Timberlake could come in.

While he was waiting for Mr Timberlake to climb the stairs he went back to the window and looked down this time, over the river, at the cranes and things that weren't used any more because no ships came into the docks. He might make his next painting a river scene with lots of ships, but of course they never turned out like he meant them to. It didn't seem to matter, people liked them anyway. Mr Bassett had told him that a few of his pictures had gone to America. He couldn't even begin to imagine that.

But he was beginning to tremble now. He knew the time had come to take up his painting because someone else was standing close to him, at his elbow, telling him not to do everything so slowly, that was stupid, why was he so stupid? He knew he would have those terrible grey days which he had tried to capture in paint, before the someone else took over entirely and then he could paint properly although he could never remember afterwards how he had done it.

"So you're back, Will! Taking up the painting again?" And there was Mr Timberlake coming in the door. Will was always surprised, and a little intimidated, by the size of him, and his booming voice, and the smell of stale tobacco he brought with him. Mr Bassett was as big, if not bigger, but he never felt intimidated by Mr Bassett. Laurence.

"Oh hello, Mr T-t-t..."

"Dermot, please."

"D-d-d-d...."

"Oh, I haven't got all day. Nice place you have here. Lucky lad, aren't you? A room with a view. I could have done with something like this when I was your age. Had to make do with a cellar, hah!" He laughed loudly as if he had said something funny, but Will never got jokes. He liked to hear other people laughing though. "Well then, I won't keep you. Busy as usual. Just wanted to know if you..." and as he was speaking he was walking round the room, poking among Will's old canvases, "...had anything to spare. An old canvas you don't want? Something not quite up to the mark?"

Will nodded.

"Can't pay your prices, unfortunately, so it's got to be something you would have thrown away..."

"Oh, I d-don't throw anything away. I p-paint over the t-t-top..."

"Well, something you haven't got round to painting over the top of." Mr Timberlake was now looking at him, smiling expansively. "I'd just like to tell my friends I've got a Murchison, that's all. The way you're going, us mere mortals won't be able to afford you."

Will nodded eagerly. He wanted to say he could have anything he liked, he'd be honoured for *the* Dermot Timberlake to own one of his pictures, but there was no way he could get this out, so he hurried to a stack of his old canvases and indicated with a nod and a sweep of the hand that Mr Timberlake could choose any one he liked.

And he was pleased that Mr Timberlake chose the best, the one he was going to show Mr Bassett when he next visited to ask his opinion. It had been painted when Will had first arrived in Wapping, when he still missed Miss Routledge and the flat, before he had turned into the somebody else who didn't care about the silence and loneliness of this place in the sky.

"One thing, Will," Mr Timberlake said, hefting the picture under his arm, "let this be a secret between us, okay? No need for that dick Bassett to know anything about this."

"Oh, it's L-l-l-l-l-l..." but of course the name wouldn't unstick itself from the roof of his mouth.

Mr Timberlake laughed, mussed his hair affectionately, and left. And Will, in a daze of rare happiness, didn't even need the somebody else to tell him to get on with his painting.

3.   August 1979

Leo had been in his house only a month, but already Laurence felt under siege. His lifestyle had undergone a drastic change the very next day; at breakfast his fry-up had been replaced by half a grapefruit, a bowl of prunes and orange juice. She was putting him on a diet, she announced, and would be counting every calorie that passed his lips. Mrs W had been instructed to cut out all saturated fat, dairy produce and red meat. Portions had also shrunk. No good appealing to her motherly side; Mrs W had fallen under Leo's spell and agreed with her that Laurence must, for the sake of his health, shed at least a couple of stone.

His home was also under threat of a facelift. Not content with redecorating her own room in stripes of acid green and sherbet pink, she had announced her intention of giving the whole house a makeover and, when he remonstrated, contented herself with replanning his library. His library was his den, his individual gentleman's club. He forbade her to touch it under pain of death.

"You're such an old stick-in-the-mud, Daddy! The only twentieth-century thing in there is that picture! Everything else belongs to Dickens!"

He had hung Wheels One in his library and yes, it was incongruous. It belonged in the lounge, which room at least earned a grudging 'well, I suppose it's *tasteful* crap' from Leo. But Wheels One was his painting and he wanted to enjoy it away from prying eyes. In this he knew he was exactly the same as those collectors of art he despised, who kept priceless paintings away from public gaze, but what the hell. In his defence he quoted Benedick from *Much Ado:* man was indeed a giddy thing.

Forbidden the library and the lounge, Leo had to be content with redesigning the conservatory and Huwie's bedroom. Gone was his comfy bamboo armchair with matching upholstered pouffe; the conservatory was now full of potted ferns and climbing ivy, with Art Deco fringed lamps and a sofa shaped like a pair of lips, and delicate wrought-iron chairs that Laurence would never entrust his backside to.

Huwie, after his school trip, had elected to stay with a friend and spend only the last week of the holidays in London; Laurence was surprised at the disappointment he'd felt at this decision. What Huwie would think of his bedroom obliterated in black and grey, and posters of pop groups whose names were lost on Laurence, was anybody's guess. "He *likes* Black Sabbath and Iron Maiden," said Leo, "or he *should* do."

"I've given birth to a pint-sized Boadicea," he told Deborah, escaping to his office one lunchtime for a couple of chicken sandwiches on lethal white bread, followed by a cholesterol-packed Stilton and salted crackers, washed down with a sugar-loaded lager. "She's threatening me with a rowing machine, a bloody bicycle that doesn't go anywhere and something called a Biceps Building Weight Frame that sounds as if it was the star turn of the Spanish Inquisition."

She didn't reply. Her teeth were lasering through her Ryvita with deadly precision.

He gazed out of the window, for some reason unwilling to meet her gaze. Over the years he was aware their relationship had changed; well, how could it not? He was no longer her boss, her employer; although he had never laid on the heavy hand, he had once been in charge. But after that trip to Caernarvon, over eight years ago now – after that last glimpse of Nick in the dock – when he had shown her his vulnerable side, things had started to change. And now, with their sessions in the Red Room – but no, they were compartmentalised in an entirely different area. He refused to be embarrassed. They provided a need, a welcome respite, and obviously gave her a strange satisfaction too. They were two lonely souls finding solace where they could.

Lonely? Was he lonely? God yes, he realised. More so as the years passed. Perhaps Leo was a godsend. Perhaps she would be the saving of him.

"I think," he said suddenly, "I'll call on Will. See how he's getting on."

"Don't pressure him, Laurence."

"Oh no. I don't, Deborah."

"I know you don't. But he's such a strange boy. And he

idolises you. He'd do anything for you."

"Yes."

"And with the viewing coming up, he might think…" She sighed, absently polishing the lenses of her glasses against her blouse. "Well, we can always put in a few of Dermot's to make up."

He drove the Jag to Wapping, wondering if he should have put off the viewing for another month or two. But with Will back in his studio, he had to strike while the iron was hot. For the first few weeks Will painted day and night, producing one or, at the most, two masterpieces, and then began physically to fall apart. In two years he had painted only nine finished canvases, all of which had sold immediately, the majority to Denver. He needed a viewing at the gallery to alert the press to Will's full genius. The boy was gaining a reputation based mainly on hearsay, and would soon fall from favour if no physical proof could be furnished.

He parked the car and rang the bell a couple of times, thirty seconds apart. After a long time – two or three minutes – a faint voice said, "Yes?"

"It's me. Laurence."

"Oh! Yes!" The buzzer sounded; the door was opened to him.

He knew what he would find when he got into the loft. At the flat, Deborah told him that Will was tidy to the point of obsession; he would spend hours making sure everything was in its rightful place. She described Will making a pot of tea as more intricate than the Japanese Tea Ceremony - the measuring of the water, the boiling of the kettle, the careful filling of the teapot (no teabags for Will) – and the boy's drawn, earnest face, tense with the vital necessity of doing everything right. But when he was painting he took on a completely different persona. It was a different Will who confronted him now, his colour hectic, his hair uncombed. He wore a filthy paint-splattered shirt, tattered jeans and was barefoot. He eyes looked spaced-out, as if he was high on drugs – which was strange, because when he painted he didn't take his medication, Laurence knew.

The room looked as if it had been hit by a hurricane. Rags, tubes of paint, bottles of turps, knives and brushes were everywhere. Half-finished canvases looked as if they had been hurled around. Only the easel in the middle of the floor, on which sat another canvas, was a calm oasis in the middle of chaos.

Laurence stood at the window looking down on the river, getting his breath back after the eight flights of stairs, itching to go over to the easel or to look through the canvases on the floor. But he would never do this without invitation.

"I'll p-put the kettle on," Will said. His voice sounded rusty, as if he hadn't used it for a while. "I wasn't exp-pecting…"

"Don't worry, Will, I hadn't made arrangements."

"Oh. I thought I m-might have forgotten…"

Damn. He should have rung. "No, I'm sorry. I should have thought."

But the boy just stood where he was, gazing round as if suddenly woken from a trance. Laurence walked over to the kitchen area. As usual, he would have to clear up the mess and take the rubbish downstairs. He would never tell Deborah about this; she never came to the loft and thought Will perfectly capable of seeing to himself.

"Are you looking after yourself properly?" He was filling a black plastic sack with opened tins still half-full of beans and dried custard and other mouldy substances that didn't bear too much inspection. Most of these were on the floor, some had made it to the waste bin, others lined the worktops.

"Oh yes."

"You look very thin. Are you taking your pills?"

There was no answer. Will lowered his head and shifted from foot to foot. "I c-can't," he said at last.

"I think you should."

"No, I c-c-can't." He looked desperate.

"But the doctor said…"

"I c-can't p-p-paint if I t-take the p-p-p…"

"All right, all right." Laurence yearned to put his arms round the boy, but the counter was between them. "Don't worry, Will,

it's all right." But of course it wasn't. "I just think perhaps –
we're not looking after you as well as we should."

"Oh no! I'm f-fine. I'll be f-finished soon."

"But is it worth it? Is anything worth what you're putting
yourself through?" The beseeching look in Will's eyes pulled
something in his gut. "Surely not even Michelangelo's David is
worth destroying oneself for. Humanity could live perfectly well
without it." He finished lamely, "All I'm saying is, Will, you don't
have to do it. We'd look after you anyway."

The boy said desolately, "I've g-got to. It's my l-life."

Laurence went behind the counter and took the lad in his
arms. The curly head reached just beneath his chin. His body was
skin and bone. Why did he still think of Will as a boy, when he
was at least twenty-two? "Come back to us soon. Deborah
misses you."

They could have stood there all day, but after a few minutes
Laurence unhooked the locked fingers from around his waist
and pushed Will away from him. "Well," he said brightly, "can I
have a look at what's been going on? Am I allowed?"

Nodding eagerly, Will led him over to the easel. Upon it was
a bright blue canvas, dotted with white shapes and wavy lines,
with a few black ticks signifying birds. It was a happy picture.

Laurence said, "It's a river scene."

Will smiled.

"It's good, Will. Anything else?"

Will began picking up the strewn canvases and piling them
against the wall. "I've done a few not very good, but there's one
I w-wanted to show you because I think…" A shadow fell over
his face and he shook his head hard. "Oh n-n-no, I c-c-can't…"

Laurence pretended not to notice the boy's obvious distress.
There was a few half-finished canvases covered in Will's
trademark bright colours and dots, some almost completed,
others abandoned after a few slashes of the brush. "Some of
these are well worth working on. What's wrong with them?" He
didn't get an answer; perhaps there wasn't one. Will just stood
mute and distraught.

"You know," he said carefully, "we have a viewing at the

gallery in a couple of weeks. Do you remember me telling you?"

"Yes."

"I need a few more of yours, Will. We've still got the two already sold, and I'm putting Wheels One in there as well, and this one... any chance of you finishing another in that time?"

Will stood mute.

"If not, don't worry. I'm sure Dermot has a few we can hang."

Will nodded.

"See what you feel like, eh?" Laurence himself felt like a fat Victorian industrialist whipping an impoverished workforce to up production. But the boy was popular, damn it; people were beginning to queue up for Murchisons. Especially that fellow of Deborah's, from Denver. If he could crack the American market... "Anyway, enough of work. Let me take you out for lunch." His sandwiches, crackers and cheese had been digested hours ago. He could manage a good three-course meal, he needed it.

But Will shook his head. "I c-can't. I've g-got to g-get on."

"Listen, forget what I said. There's no hurry."

"N-no, I c-can't. I've g-got to g-get..."

"All right. You know best." He knew better than to try persuasion; Will only dug in his heels and became agitated. It was the lesser of two evils to leave him to confront his own demons, he supposed. But as he left the loft and descended the eight flights of stairs he couldn't shake off a faint but insistent depression.

******

"Is the star of the show putting in an appearance?" Dermot Timberlake stood in the middle of the gallery, puffing on his pipe.

Laurence was casting a last glance over the walls; the lighting was fine, the hangings well spaced. He'd been a little worried that they wouldn't have enough to make it worth the invitations, but Dermot had come up trumps and so, evidently, had Will. Two new Murchisons graced the walls, as well as the happy river scene. Obviously Will had had two up his sleeve he'd forgotten about.

"I hope so," he said absent-mindedly. "I've sent a taxi."

"Thanks," Dermot said dryly. "I was hoping you'd say the star's already here." But the sting was taken out of these words by his placid puffing. Laurence didn't bother to reply. He had left the hangings to Deborah, having been busy himself recording another two programmes of *Meet the Experts* in Coventry, arriving back in London just an hour ago. It was damned annoying that Deborah herself had been called away unexpectedly, leaving Rosemary in charge.

"So who's turning up?" Dermot asked.

"Oh, the usual suspects. Hacks from the *Times* and *Observer*, Maudie Madison from the *Review*, some bloke from the BBC Ralph knows, a plethora of lesser mortals from the fringes…"

"Any news from the Yanks?"

"They don't even bother to come over. They just ship money." The two Murchisons destined for Denver, together with the recently completed picture, had made a high five-figure sum, but Laurence wasn't going to tell Dermot that. "Deborah did try to interest them in your back catalogue but they're after new artists, apparently."

"Oh, I'm not bothered about that," Dermot said mildly. "Glad to be out of the rat race, frankly. I paint what I like, when I like. Suits me."

"Good." This new mood of Dermot's was surprising, but a relief to Laurence, who had only just got Freddy back on side. Freddy had boycotted his parties for over a year, bad-mouthing Laurence at every opportunity. But now he had found himself another young catamite and peace was restored. "Between you and me," he had said, "I was glad to get shot of the little bugger. Beginning to make a godawful mess. Paint and rags everywhere but no sign of a painting." Laurence had offered him a small one as a consolation prize but Freddy had haughtily refused. "Don't need your charity, Bassett. Got one of my own, anyway. Should be worth something soon if you don't cock up, old boy." He'd got Wheels Two, obviously, the one Laurence would give his eye teeth for to hang beside Wheels One in his library.

But for the moment, just tonight to be precise, Wheels One was hanging next to the two paintings already earmarked for Denver, all sporting the little red dot on the bottom right-hand side of the frames. He must also remember to add one to the frame of the newly-completed Murchison – *Thames Docks with Boats and Birds* – which would make up the third picture already paid for by the Venn Pegasus Agency. Unfortunately that left only two Murchisons for sale, the two new ones he hadn't had a chance to study in detail but which seemed to be a complete departure from Will's usual hectic colourful style.

"By the way," Dermot said, "where's the lovely Miss Routledge?"

"Unfortunately she was called away. She got a phonecall this afternoon about some old aunt of hers about to pop her clogs in hospital." Laurence had been in the middle of recording when Deborah's call came through. His first thought, when told, was damn, he'd have to take charge of the evening with only the backup of Rosemary. Then felt ashamed of himself.

By eight o'clock the viewing was in full swing and most of the invitees had turned up, except the star of the show. At first Laurence wasn't worried, knowing that a taxi at the door meant a summons that Will would have to obey. But halfway through the evening (which Laurence had indicated on the invitations would end at ten o'clock sharp), he began to feel one of his panics coming on. The photographers were becoming restless. The journos were beginning to ask searching questions. Laurence took refuge in the company of Ralph's bloke, who turned out to be the new commissioning editor for the arts at the Beeb.

"Weinstock has shown me the pilot of that programme of yours," he said, gulping at a glass of champagne. "It could be revived, under a different name. You still interested in fronting it?"

"Well, yes."

"Nothing guaranteed, obviously. But we live in hope."

"We certainly do."

And at that moment Will arrived. He had obviously been caught by surprise; he was still wearing his threadbare jeans and paint-splattered shirt but at least had thrust his feet into battered trainers. For a second, Laurence was mortified; would these people think he kept the lad short of money? – when, in reality, he'd set up a trust fund and paid all his bills. And how ill he looked, thin and pale and trembling with remorse.

"I'm s-sorry, Mr B-Bassett, I f-f-forgot."

"That's all right, Will." Laurence threw an arm round his shoulders and firmly steered him into the gallery. Flash bulbs exploded in their faces, and Will froze. "Courage, lad! Your photo will be in all the papers tomorrow." And what a photo, he thought – the proverbial artist starving in a garret, fleeced by the evil Svengali, Bassett, leering at the camera. No doubt the media hyenas would make a meal of this.

For the remainder of the evening Laurence kept Will at his side and fended off intrusive questions. Most of the guests flocked round them while Dermot stood aloof, puffing away, wearing his placid smile. Will, though struck mute, tried to keep an expression of eager helpfulness on his face, nodding and shaking his head when required. The press seemed enamoured of him, especially the women. Maudie Madison tried to make out he was her discovery; Laurence heard her saying, "It was actually me who got him his first sale, I just knew he was destined for higher things." And then someone asked him why he was holding the viewing at the end of August, surely the dead heart of the year, and he replied, forgetting Maudie, that it was precisely because of the dearth of news that the media were desperate to fill their pages. Why had he kept Will under wraps for so long, someone else asked, and Laurence replied that the boy was still young and easily overwhelmed. No more questions, please.

And just as it seemed Will was relaxing a little, and even enjoying himself, something went wrong. He had just been photographed beside *Boats and Birds* when his eyes were drawn to the other two pictures alongside, and Laurence saw panic settle. It was just a shifting in the depths at first, a sudden shaft of recognition that transferred itself swiftly to his whole being. He began to tremble. Laurence gathered the boy into himself.

"What is it, Will? What's happened?"

The boy was staring at the paintings, his eyes darting from one to the other. He swallowed and tried to speak but the words stuck. He shook his head violently.

"Anything wrong?" Dermot had strolled over, sucking on that damn pipe. "What's the matter with him?"

"I don't know. What is it, Will?"

"Looks like he's had a seizure. He epileptic or something?"

Laurence looked around. Most of the guests had left; only a few remained, drinking the last of the champagne and nibbling at left-over canapés. Leaving Will with Dermot, he hurried over and told them the gallery had closed; the viewing had finished. He waited barely patiently as they tossed their drinks down their throats and congratulated him on his find. He kept himself between them and Will, and hurried them off into the night.

"Now, Will. Tell me what's wrong."

Will was gazing beseechingly at Dermot. "I c-c-can't…"

"Can't what, old fellow? Come on, speak up." Dermot smiled encouragingly.

But Will seemed to have lost all power of speech. He pointed to one picture, also a river scene but obviously painted at night, with towering black spider-webs of cranes set at crazy angles, some almost toppling from a grey-black sky into the thick grey depths where no boats were bobbing. A sad picture, but still with that odd pulling power of the best Murchisons. *Study in Grey* #1, read the caption. Will now had his arms across himself, as if holding himself together.

"I think he's trying to tell you," Dermot smiled, "that that's his."

"Well, of course it is."

"What about the other one?"

Will shook his head violently. Laurence stepped up to it and, feeling in his pocket for the glasses he had to wear more frequently these days, studied it at close quarters. It was a variation on a theme; the grey river picture done once more on a smaller canvas but with subtle alterations: cranes with boats at anchor and birds perching. *Study in Grey #2.*

But there were differences, mainly in the brushwork. Will painted with a loaded brush; he hardly ever let it run dry, but knew exactly when to stop to reload. Consequently his swirls were almost uniform, almost the same thickness. Sometimes there were tiny variations in colour; he would mix a little chromium red with the cobalt blue and the next swirl would just be a shade down. Laurence had never seen him paint with tones of grey, but their effect would be the same. But No 2, compared now to No 1, lacked those minute differences in texture.

Also the draughtsmanship – something lacking there. The spiderwebs were cruder, less worked out. Everything in Will's paintings somehow belonged, they could never be anything other than they were, or placed differently. And Will's paintings had a hectic exuberance that this one lacked. Even when plunged in despair, Will painted like a demon.

Laurence had been hoodwinked. "Ah," he said, taking off his glasses.

Dermot took his pipe from his mouth and stabbed the stem triumphantly at Laurence. "I told you I'd prove it."

"Yours?"

"Guilty as charged. And furthermore," he stabbed the pipe stem towards the painting, "it's been sold."

It was true. On its frame was the small red dot that signified a sale. Oh God, Laurence thought, if only Deborah were here.

But how had the mix-up occurred? Dermot, of course, must have brought his paintings, including the fake Murchison, to the gallery this morning, and Deborah would have sorted them for hanging, obviously including the fake with the Murchison originals. Even if she'd been wearing her glasses, she would not have been looking out for telltale variations in colour and texture. And Deborah, as far as he knew, had never watched Will paint.

Or, of course, she had left the hangings to Rosemary, and not seen them at all.

Laurence hurried to the sales book that little Rosemary had been in charge of. Maudie's name was beside No 2. Because it was only a small painting, its price had been fixed at £500.

"I'll have to get in touch with her. This is going to be so embarrassing…"

"Then why bother?" Dermot shrugged. "If she's willing to pay, surely it doesn't matter who painted it."

"It's attributed to Will Murchison."

"But," Dermot said, "it's unsigned."

And so it was. Even in the book Rosemary had omitted to write the name of the artist beside it. *Study in Grey #2* was just listed under Murchison, but there was space to write another name underneath. Could he write *Dermot Timberlake, after Will Murchison?* Oh, of course not.

Laurence held his head in his hands and groaned.

"I painted it," Dermot said, "and Maudie's bought it. So you owe me the proceeds, less your exorbitant commission if you must."

Laurence wrote the cheque for the full amount right away. He wanted Dermot out of the gallery so he could think in peace. And Will - oh God, he'd forgotten Will.

The boy stood without moving, staring into space, obviously seeing nothing. He looked catatonic. Not even his eyes moved. Laurence couldn't even see him breathing.

"Come on, Will," he said, "I'll take you home."

Fortunately the boy was obedient to instruction; it was as if his body could move independently of his brain. He allowed Laurence to steer him out of the gallery towards the car. He sat down in the passenger seat, facing ahead. All the way to Hampstead Laurence kept his eye on him but he was like a zombie, his body corporal but his mind absent. There was nothing behind his eyes.

Laurence pulled up outside his house but Will didn't move. "We're here," he said. "We're home, Will."

But it wasn't Will's home. He didn't move.

"You want to go to Wapping?" He couldn't take him to Deborah's, who wouldn't be there. The aunt lived somewhere in depths of Devon. Oh God. Oh God, God, God.

He started the car again and drove through the bright

teeming streets of the West End then the dark dead streets of the East End and still there was no movement beside him. The building was in darkness. But Will would have the key; he would have made sure he'd have the key. Yes, it was in his pocket, and Laurence unlocked the door to the building before helping Will out of the car, although he didn't need help after that, he stood on the pavement quite independently but so insubstantial, so ethereal he was almost transparent. He climbed the eight flights of stairs as though he didn't touch the ground, while Laurence lagged behind, stopping halfway up to gulp air, gaining the top floor at least a minute later. Will was waiting patiently outside the door.

As soon as it was unlocked he went in and stood for a while in the middle of the room, turning his head slowly through a hundred and eighty degrees like an animal checking its territory. Laurence found himself holding his breath. He didn't switch on the light.

After what seemed aeons of time, Will moved towards the easel. He put out his hands and explored the frame all over with the tips of his fingers and the delicate touch of someone blind. Then, after a few more aeons, he moved to the stack of canvases. He didn't touch them, but stood merely looking down at them as if they were things he had never seen before in his life. And then, further aeons later, he moved towards the window and stood staring out into the darkness.

Hours later – or it may have been minutes, time for Laurence had also slowed down to a snail's pace – he found himself by Will's side, also looking out into the black void. The boy's profile was calm. He almost seemed to be smiling.

How long they stood there, Laurence would never know. He would never know, either, how he had persuaded Will to leave the window, to get undressed and lie down under the covers of the unmade bed in the little partitioned-off bedroom. Probably he had needed no persuasion. He moved like an automaton – no, like a small obedient child wanting to please. And, after tucking him up nice and safe, Laurence had removed his own top clothing and, after only a second's hesitation, climbed in beside him and pressed the thin, fragile, almost hollow body against his for the rest of the night.

4.   April 1987

Leo has kept watch at her window for the last couple of nights and is here again in her room, writing in her Diary with one eye on the street light. He will have to come before Gemma returns to Moscow, she knows that with complete certainty. She had thrown him a bombshell of her own and he is not the sort to ignore it.

She's been reading the back editions of her Diary – and it's not a Diary, strictly, just a shelf full of A4-size ruled exercise books with dates on the front. Twelve exercise books per year, the entries becoming neater as the years rolled on but her spelling still eccentric, especially at times of stress. The one labelled *January 1986* is open in front of her.

Thurs 28th Jan 11.27pm

Well, wot a homecoming!! Sorry I've left you unritten in for a few days, but things have been frort to say the least! It appears that the Man has been arrested – he was picked up almost as soon as their plane landed at Heathrow. Gemma had to make her way back here in a taxi, and her mother and Daddy were waiting for her. The charges are unlawful burial and VIOLATING A CORPS. Yuk!! It was that skeleton they dug up last September on the farm in Wales, the bones all over the place. The mother told Daddy that the body was that of an unknown drug addict who'd died of a heroin overdose – she and the Man had found it in the woods and she'd sworn a statement to say they'd buried it together. Why couldn't they have just told the police?? – that would have saved an awful lot of bother.

The Man has been releesed on bale (which Huwie told me Daddy had put up) but he's not here any more. He's apparently pleeding gilty, saying he'd done the dredful deed alone and denying any involvement of the mother. What a pair they are!!!

Anyway, Huwie has been doing sterling work holding everyone together but the house is full of gloom and I'm worried Daddy is going to be miserable again, like he was a few months after I came to live here. I told Huwie not to worry, I would take over the good work. He's gone back to his flat today, leeving Yours Trooly in charge.

Which had left her to deal with the next crisis, when Gemma realised she was pregnant.

By that time, though, Gemma had been offered the job at the BBC, her dream job, one that entailed flying all over the world. Who wouldn't have chosen that over boring motherhood? Of course she wouldn't have told the Man about the baby. She would have known his reaction, as Leo herself realises now; he would have wanted her to keep it, not abort it.

She can't call him the Man any more. Can she bring herself to write Nicholas? Nick? Naming him somehow negates his crime, makes him human. She pictures his capable hands on the steering wheel – those quick, fleeting smiles – that boyish profile under those riotous curls – all these intimate details have rendered him more human, less dangerous. And yet – he killed Daddy. He must have. That's the only explanation she can cling to. She turns to the latest edition of the Diary and takes up her pen.

But if I succeed in prooving he killed Daddy, she writes, *I'll expose Daddy as a peedofile. There. I've ritten the horrible word. I can't beleeve Daddy would do anything like that. The Man – Nick – would only have been 14. But what other explanation can there be? Mummy said he chased boys and the Man – Nick – said he'd hated Daddy once. But Daddy told me it wasn't troo. I remember that. He was telling me off for something – no, not telling me off, Daddy never did that, he was explaning something and he told me it was all the folt of the tabloid press. The media hyenas, that's what he called them. Do I beleeve Mummy and the media hyenas, or Daddy?*
I want to beleeve Daddy.
And the only way I can do that is to ask Him. The Man. Nick.

When she lifts her eyes from her writing she catches a movement at the end of the drive. And yes, there on the gate is the fluttering piece of string. Good. Gemma is out, she hasn't said where but Leo will bet anything she's with Huwie, the two seem to be inseparable.

She closes her Diary and replaces it on the shelf with the others. She waits as long as she can – five or ten minutes – to make sure he's not still around, but she knows he won't be, he'll be walking quickly back to the tube station, hands in pockets, kicking out at objects in his path. Then she flies out of her room leaving the light on, switching all the lights on as she goes down the stairs, landing light, hall light, the light in the dining room on the left, the sitting room on the right... it had still been daylight when she went up to her room and now the house lies around her in darkness, the back of the house, kitchen, lounge, conservatory – library... all in darkness and silence. What will she do when Gemma goes back to Russia in two days? She can't keep all the lights on all the time.

She flies along the dark path to the oak tree. She should have brought a torch; the street light doesn't throw any illumination this side of the drive. She unties the string from the gate, then bends down, searching with her fingers in the cracks of its roots. They touch wet earth, slimy leaves, and then – ah! a piece of paper – no, an empty cigarette carton, tossed over the hedge. She thrusts her hand further into cold dank secret places among twisted roots and rotting vegetation and imagines what it would be like to dig holes among trees to bury chopped up chunks of human flesh and bone in the dead of night, and finds she is shivering uncontrollably and tears are pouring down her face. Well, that's not unusual. She's spent hours shivering and crying up in her room, she might as well do it here.

There's nothing there. Perhaps she's wrong. Perhaps the string on the gate means something else; they've already decided the venue, perhaps it means they'll meet the next day. Or not. Only Gemma and Nick know what it means. Gemma and Nick, Gemma and Huwie, Gemma and someone else who might have meant something to Leo back in the past, BB, Before Bombshell. And now she, Leonora, must go back into the empty house with all its lights blazing, to nothing and nobody...

She puts her hand on the trunk of the tree to steady herself as she gets up from her knees, and there it is – a piece of paper, stuck in a crack. She knows immediately it's the message. And no sooner has she pulled it out, and thrust it into her jeans pocket, and turned from the secret dark places back to the light and safety of the house than something drops on her shoulder and a voice says, "Leo?"

It's Him, the Man, Nick, he's discovered her snooping about and now there's no safety anywhere and she opens her mouth and screams.

"Leo! It's me, it's Tony."

She collapses against him, sobbing. All the pent-up terror of the last two months pours out of her and she clings to him, drowning.

"Oh, Leo," he says, stroking her hair, "oh Leo, I should have known, I should have come earlier…"

After a while, how long she doesn't know, she grows calmer. She gulps a few times, swallows, wipes a hand over her wet face and tries to smile. The hand on her shoulder grips her more tightly and they walk together up the drive and into the house.

It's so wonderful to see him. Tony Masterson, photographer extraordinaire, Gemma's former boyfriend. Well, they'd been out a few times when Gemma had first arrived in London and he'd come round after the posh boyfriend's death to try to comfort her. He'd disappeared for a while after the Invasion, knowing he wasn't needed. Then he'd come back on the scene, but only when Gemma was in London which wasn't often. Before Bombshell, Leo had hopes that a spark could be ignited between them; After Bombshell, there was no chance. But she'd stupidly imagined she was in love with him, and had been going to make a play for him while Gemma was in Russia. Until It happened, after which all other thoughts had flown out of her head.

They sit in the kitchen drinking hot chocolate. After her storm of tears, Leo feels strangely empty, at peace. She knows she doesn't have to pretend with Tony, she doesn't have to make sure her hair is brushed or her teeth cleaned. He's seen her at her lowest ebb and is still here. He actually made the chocolate.

"I've been hanging round for a while," he says, "trying to get up courage to call. I thought nobody was in, the house was in darkness, then all of a sudden it was lit up like a Christmas tree. I wondered if Gemma…"

"She's out," Leo says quickly.

"Yes, I know."

"You'll have to come back tomorrow, she's off to Russia after that."

"I know."

They drink their chocolate in companionable silence. So what if he's only here because he wants to see Gemma? Leo can live with that.

"I can't imagine what it must be like for you," he says. "I know how you felt about your father. He was a lovely man."

"Yes."

"I just can't believe he'd do it. He wasn't the type."

"No," Leo smiles, "he was an awful coward. He couldn't stand the sight of blood." The scene in the library that morning is before her eyes. "He wouldn't have done it," she says slowly, "because he knew I'd find him. He wouldn't have done that to me."

There is silence for a moment, then Tony says, "Depression is a terrible thing. My mother suffered from it. When she was down in the black hole, she said, she couldn't think of anyone but herself. No one else existed. You don't think of consequences…"

Leo nods. "I know, I've thought all those things. But Daddy wasn't depressed. I don't think he was. He was just sad."

He puts down his mug and takes her hands in his. She looks down at them – at his nice clean photographer's hands with their long artistic fingers. She wraps hers round them. "I'm glad you came," she says. "I can't talk like this to anyone else. They all think I'm paranoid, or something."

"I think you're very brave." They smile at each other. "So," he says, "what are you saying? It wasn't suicide?"

"I was convinced it wasn't, but…"

"Murder?" The word makes her flinch, but she's glad he's said it. "Did he have enemies, Leo? Did someone hate him enough to kill him?"

"I thought they did, but…"

"I can't believe it, but you never know, do you? What goes on in other people's lives, even people you think you know well.

And the world he moved in – well, you must know how cutthroat it is, the fashion industry is just as bad. I know at least one designer who'd happily knock off the competition for the sake of a few frocks."

"So you don't think I'm paranoid?"

"No, not at all. Is there some mad artist he cheated, or television celebrity he slighted? I bet there's a few people out there who think they'd have a motive to get even."

"Oh, Tony. You don't know how good it is to hear you say that." She can even laugh. "I must be mad, to be relieved that Daddy could have been murdered! That someone hated him enough to… oh, anyway. We'll never know now. And it doesn't really matter, does it? Daddy's dead."

"I'm glad I've cheered you up." They drink the rest of their chocolate in silence. And then he says, "Leo, I…" just as she says, "Gemma…" and they both stop and laugh. "Go on," he says.

"I just wanted to say that Gemma will be pleased to see you. You must come tomorrow, it's her last day here."

And he says, "I didn't come to see Gemma. In fact I'm glad she's not here. I came because we miss you, Leo. The shoots aren't the same without you."

"Oh."

"When are you coming back?"

"Oh," she says, "soon."

"But that's not all, either. I miss you. And not just at the bloody shoots."

"Oh."

"Didn't you realise, Leo?"

"What?"

"When Gem and I got together after she came back from Australia. She didn't want me and I didn't want her. She was using me as a stand-in for someone else, and I was using her so I could keep close to you."

"Oh."

He leans over the table and kisses the tip of her nose. She lifts her swollen, tear-streaked face and he kisses her bare,

136

unglossed mouth, pushes his tongue between her uncleaned teeth. Then draws back, uncertain.

"I don't think," she says, "that Gemma will be home tonight."

"Oh."

"The house is awfully dark and empty."

He thinks for a moment. "It's a good job then," he says, "that I've got nothing else on tonight."

"Good," she says. "Then you might as well stay."

"Okay," he says. "I might as well."

Waking late the next morning, Leo fears it is all a dream. She can't bring herself to turn her head on the pillow for a good five seconds, then when she does the relief is instantaneous. He's still there – lovely, uncomplicated Tony, flat on his back and snoring slightly. She studies his face. He's not drop-dead handsome, just rather boringly pleasant with nice regular features and medium brown straightish nondescript hair. She can't remember the colour of his eyes, but they're probably neither blue nor brown but something in between. And that is very okay with her.

She can't remember much about what happened last night either, but again that is perfectly fine. She only knows she feels a hundred times lighter, happier, altogether more *together* than she's felt for a long time.

After sitting beside him for a while just studying his sleeping face, she gets up to go to the bathroom and then spends a few minutes studying her own face in the mirror. Yes, Huwie is right – it looks softer under its uncombed frizz of hair; she's moussed and gelled and waxed it for so many years she'd forgotten she first started doing that because of its frizziness. And those gallons of tears she's poured down her cheeks have obviously plumped them up and given her eyes prominence like a short-sighted giraffe's. It's a *pretty* face staring back at her. A kind of odd, screwball prettiness.

In the mirror, behind her face, Tony comes in. He slides his arms round her waist and rests his chin on her shoulder. They both stare into the mirror.

"Hello dormouse," he says.

"Dormouse?"

"You look like a dormouse. All little and bleary. With big soft eyes."

She leans back against him. They are skin to skin; no clothes to come between them. "And you're a – oh, a nice shaggy pony."

"Shaggy?"

"You need a shave. Your chin's all scratchy."

"God, shaggy and scratchy. That puts me in my place. I thought I was strong and smooth and totally macho."

"I'd rather shaggy and scratchy." She turns towards him and kisses him. The kiss turns into something else. He picks her up and carries her back to bed.

Only later, when she's lying in the bath and he's downstairs cooking breakfast (it's Saturday, no Mrs Wainwright, hurrah!), does she remember the message. She hasn't even read it. Her jeans lie discarded in the bedroom in a unisex heap, his jeans, her jeans, his sweater, her sweater, his shirt, her bra, his socks, her socks, his pants, her pants... She lies back in the bubbles and looks at her toes, little islands in the foam. Does it matter any more? Her pursuit of the Man is at an end.

Although – if it *is* an assignation, he'll be waiting. Waiting for Gemma, who won't come. Well, she wouldn't have gone anyway, would she? She wouldn't have been back to find the string on the gate (which isn't there now) until probably tonight, when it will be too late. So he would have waited in vain anyway. Sitting in the café in Euston station, or somewhere else, waiting...

Her lazy bath is spoiled. She gets out, dries herself, pads through to the bedroom just wearing a towel. His pile of clothes have vanished, and hers look raked and abandoned, diminished. She picks up her jeans and feels in the pocket, brings out the scrap of paper.

We must talk. I'll be on the Heath, by the pond, on Saturday. I'll be there about ten. I'll wait till it gets dark as you might not get this straight away. Please try to get there Gem, I need to see you before you go. NW.

She screws it up and thrusts it back into the pocket. She

dresses quickly and skips downstairs to the kitchen, from where a heavenly smell of bacon and eggs is wafting along the hall.

"A fry-up! Daddy loved these! I tried to put him on a diet once – grapefruit and prunes. He lasted about a week."

"I bet you were a right little bossy boots." He sits down opposite her.

"I still am, so watch it." She looks at her wrist. It's half past eleven.

They eat in silence. Then he says, "Anything you want to do today?"

"Not particularly." She glances out of the window. "It's quite a nice day. How about a walk?"

"If you like."

"We could go to the Heath."

"Fine."

But first they have to finish breakfast and wash up, and put the plates away, and kiss, and chase each other round the house, and kiss again, and it could easily have led to something else but Leo looks at her watch and sees it's half past twelve.

"It's clouding over," she says. "We'd better go now before it rains."

"We could stay here." He is nuzzling into her neck, his chin still scratchy.

And they could, but what if it *does* rain? There's not much shelter around the ponds, and which pond does he mean? He'll sit on a bench in the rain, not wanting to miss her. And she won't come.

"No, come on," she says, dragging him towards the door. "Lazy bones."

"Okay, bossy boots."

They put on their coats and take off for the Heath. Passing the gate, Leo is almost tempted to replace the string and the message and pretend she has never seen either, but how can she do this when Tony's arm encircles her waist and her hand nestles snug in his pocket? And anyway, it was always her plan to intercept the message and go to meet the Man herself and demand an explanation from him as to why he had hated Daddy

139

and possibly even make him confess to having pulled the trigger…

It begins to rain when they arrive at the Heath. "It's only a shower," Leo says. "Shall we just walk round the big pond and go home? We might as well now we're here."

Tony doesn't reply, just gives her a look. He must think she's mad. She says brightly, "I love walking in the rain, don't you?"

"Not much."

"Well, I do." She urges him on as the rain buffets them harder, coming down in slanting stair rods, stinging their faces.

The Heath is almost deserted. Just a couple with a dog (they're under an umbrella), and a bloke swathed in waterproofs on a bike. Of course nobody is swimming, not even the ducks. They stand by the edge of the biggest pond watching the rain drilling holes in its surface. Tony's arm has dropped from her waist. He stands, water dripping from his hair and nose, getting soaked. At least she's wearing a cagoule.

She can't suggest walking any further. If the Man – Nick – has any sense he'd have taken shelter anyway, so there's no chance she'd have seen him. She's about to say they might as well turn back when Tony hisses, "Don't look now Leo, but there's that bloke over there."

"What bloke?"

"The guy who took Gemma to Australia. The mad axeman."

"Where?" She peers in the direction he's just been looking, over by a clump of trees on the left.

"I said don't look! Oh Christ he's coming over."

Leo watches the lone figure approach. He's wearing the leather jacket and his hair, nice and springy, is still fairly dry. It must have been his day for the public baths; he is clean-shaven.

"Hi," he says, looking at her, ignoring Tony.

"Hello."

"Nice weather for a walk."

"It was dry when we left."

He stares at her, his eyes slightly narrowed. Then he says, "I was hoping to meet Gem."

"Oh, she's not home. She didn't even come home last night.

140

But she'll be back sometime tonight because she's got her packing to do."

He says nothing, just continues to stare.

"Shall I tell her to call you?"

"No," he says, "don't bother." He turns to walk away, and she breaks away from Tony and runs after him.

"Listen," she says urgently, "if you wanted to talk to Gemma about the baby, please don't. She made me promise not to tell anyone. Especially you."

"Then why," he says evenly, "did you think I'd know about it?"

"I don't know. I just thought – well, she *might* have told you, but was testing my integrity. Or something. I thought it was another reason you'd have for…"

"What?"

Killing my father, she almost says. You'd blame him, not Gemma. You'd blame him for her opting for career over motherhood. She'd been seduced by the world my father moved in, so she murdered your baby to stay in it. So you murdered him.

Instead she says, "Oh, I don't know. It's all so confusing."

His dark brown eyes are fixed on her, almost as if he is reading her mind. But the expression on his face is sad; sad and resigned. There's a desolation in those eyes that pulls at her heart. His hair is getting wetter now. He puts his hand up and rakes his fingers through it in a defeated gesture.

"I probably wouldn't have said anything," he says at last. "I just wanted to see her before she goes off."

"Can I give her a message?"

"No." Then he hesitates and says, "Just tell her I'll get in touch somehow. I won't be around when she gets back."

"Where are you going?"

He shrugs. "I'll have to find work elsewhere. It's not easy."

"Have you found any digs yet?"

"No point in looking. I won't get another job round here and I can't afford the rent. Anyway, I hate London. I'll probably go down to Sussex."

Sussex. To the Mad Mother, of course. "Can I come and see you before you go?" she hears herself asking. "We could take another car on a test drive."

He smiles and shrugs. "Please yourself. Can't guarantee a fast one, though." And after another second or two spent contemplating her, he turns and walks away with his quick, self-contained strides.

She is aware that Tony is at her elbow, also watching him recede. "I just had a thought," he says. "Maybe he could have had a grudge against your father. He's got the form."

"Oh no," she says. "I don't think so." And she doesn't. As Nick disappears round a bend in the path and the rain stops as suddenly as it had begun and the sun lights up the Heath, she thinks with a savageness that surprises her, *If she breaks Huwie's heart as she's broken so many others, I'll scratch her eyes out.*

5. October 1979

Before she left for the gallery every morning, Deborah looked in on Will to make sure he was all right. He was always still in bed, although awake, and waiting for her to come in, lay a hand on his forehead to check his temperature, then bend down and give him a kiss on the cheek.

"I've left your breakfast," she always said, "and your pills. Now don't forget to take them. Promise me."

"I promise," he always said, and she knew he meant it. He was childlike in everything but this – he never told lies.

It had been a long haul to get him back from the brink. He had remained mute and frighteningly somehow *not there* – for days it seemed that no one inhabited his body. She had taken a week, then two weeks, off work to nurse him. The doctor prescribed more medication. If he was off it too long, he warned Deborah, any trauma could be devastating. What exactly had caused his catatonia?

Of course she had asked Laurence this. A bloody trick of Dermot's, apparently; he'd taken one of Will's paintings and copied the style of it. Nothing like Will's best, but good enough to fool Laurence from a distance. It was almost, Laurence said, as if Dermot had stolen Will's identity.

But these weeks were the best of Deborah's life. All through the long years of nursing her mother she had resented the role, thinking herself not cut out for patience and fortitude. But nursing Will was altogether different. It was like rearing a child in fast forward, from helpless infant to almost independence in days, not years. He was still not fully independent and if she were honest she would admit she never wanted him to be; she wished he could stay forever with the mind of a – what? – eight-year-old? When she had felt happy about leaving him, he managed to look after himself fairly well. He showered and dressed and fed himself from the tins she left out. What else he did all day was a mystery. He didn't paint, nor seemed to want to. She had a feeling that as soon as she shut the door behind her he reverted to his passive state in front of the television, only stirring at one o'clock to have his lunch (a tin of baked beans, spaghetti or macaroni cheese) and to make himself a drink. She cooked an evening meal when she arrived home. He ate everything on his plate.

She kept Laurence informed as to how things were progressing. He, too, was having problems at home keeping his daughter under some kind of control, so they had plenty of notes to compare. Lunch times were spent in mutual commiseration.

"At least I'm off the diet," he said, tucking into his cheese roll and goose liver paté. "She couldn't bear to see me so dejected. We've compromised, anyway; I'm allowed two rashers and one egg at weekends. No fried bread, apparently that's lethal."

"Will likes a poached egg on toast."

"Ah. I hope it's an exact square of bread and the egg's perfectly round and placed dead centre."

"Oh yes. He's trained me well."

"*Study in Square and Circle Number* – how many days has it been? At least twenty-eight. I can see it now, alongside Mondrian."

"I don't think," Deborah said slowly, "he'll ever paint again."

Laurence was silent. He put down his half-finished roll and sat staring at it.

"It's as if – he's lost all desire, all inclination – all his talent."

"Oh, but it's happened before. Not like this, but – well, once he's back on his feet he can stop taking the pills…"

"No he can't, Laurence. The doctor said he must never stop taking the medication. And that's what blocks his creativity. We either have Will, or we have his paintings." She gazed back at him, ready to interpret his reaction.

"Oh, we have Will, of course." But he began crumbling the roll between his fingers, his mind still working at the problem. She knew him so well; his intentions were good, his actions less so. "But it's a bugger, isn't it? The Yanks will take everything he paints. He's just on the cusp…" He glanced at her quickly, saw her face, looked down again. "Ah well, so be it. What are we going to do with him?"

"I'll look after him. In a funny way I've missed having

144

someone to fuss over." She kept her eyes fixed on him and saw that muscle move at the corner of his mouth, that little twitch of the cheek. How long had it been since their last session in the Red Room? And how long would it be until he'd come again? That brat of a daughter had thrown everything out of kilter. Now Laurence was a full-time father he had become distanced from her.

"Are you willing to do it for ever, Deborah?"

And she said steadily, "If I have to." And meant it. She herself was now, she realised, a full-time mother.

******

"I don't mind taking another picture, but I can't afford more than five hundred pounds."

"No, that's fine. It's a bigger one – the happy one, I expect you remember. Much more suited to your personality, Maudie."

"Well, all right. I did prefer that one, way out of my price range of course, but I thought it was already sold? Well, that's very philanthropic of you, Laurence." Then she added, "Though I must say it's not like you to have got into a muddle."

"Blame old age and the bloody BBC. Mind on other things, I'm afraid."

"I did wonder why it wasn't signed like the others, but it was obviously a Murchison. Possibly unfinished?"

"Yes. I suspect I also need new glasses." Laurence replaced the receiver and heaved a sigh of relief. He'd told Maudie that her painting had been mistakenly included in the hanging; to have told her it was wrongly attributed would have put his reputation on the line, and now Maudie was editor of the *Arts Review* that was tantamount to cutting his own throat. No, better to take a loss – to give her *Boats and Birds* with no doubt about its authenticity. He had substituted *Study in Grey #1* in the shipment to Denver and then, after a quick calculation, included #2. *Boats and Birds,* a bigger, obviously happier, picture was priced higher than the first *Study in Grey,* which was not immediately as saleable, and the two grey studies obviously belonged together.

145

The Timberlake, unsigned and unattributed, would more than make up the value, and he couldn't afford to adjust the price already paid. The lease of the Wapping flat had taken a big chunk out of his finances and obviously wasn't going to be financially viable for some time – if ever.

He'd thought about sending Wheels One instead and destroying the fake, but only for a split second. He couldn't part with it; he had only to look at it to remember his faults, his shortcomings. It was his Mea Culpa. And Deborah had told him that this Dave Symons was not an art expert; he probably relied on people such as Maudie to point him in the right direction. Chances were that his client was also a dilettante, a dabbler, but if not – well, he could always use the same excuse, that an unfinished painting had been wrongly included, and ship off another as soon as Will was in full production again.

He was having to spend more time in the gallery now Deborah was looking after Will. He didn't begrudge this, but how long it could go on he didn't know. He had his own private life to worry about; now Leo had started college the house was filling up with strange androgynous creatures, all wearing makeup and alarming garments. Girls looked like boys with cropped hair and large boots, and boys looked like girls with long ringlets and frills. His library had become his refuge. Even Mrs W had taken fright and was beginning to talk of retirement.

"Me and Bernard aren't getting any younger, Mr B. It's time we were thinking about where we want to end up before we end up, if you know what I mean."

"Dear Mrs W, there's plenty of time yet! You're not much older than me, surely!"

Mrs W beamed. "I'll be sixty-three next birthday, and Bernard…" her face creased with worry, "…is getting twinges. Well, he's had twinges for a long while but they're getting worse. And he's having trouble with his piles. He shouldn't be doing so much heavy work, Mr B."

"I'll advertise for a strapping young lad to help him."

"Now that's very kind, but it doesn't solve the problem, does it? I've always wanted a nice little house on the south coast. Near

146

the sea. Near our Eileen."

This conversation had taken place a few days ago. Nothing had been said since, but Laurence felt unsettled. He couldn't imagine the Hampstead house without the Wetherbys. How would he ever replace them? Another worry to add to his mounting anxieties. About now he would be slipping a little note in Deborah's ledger and looking forward to the soothing ministrations of Miss Routledge but that line of escape was closed to him while Will was on the premises.

He could only think of her as Miss Routledge in the Red Room. She took on a different persona, thank God. She seemed to know exactly what he yearned for; when to be nanny, when nurse, when he needed someone more severe – police constable, army captain. He never asked where she got her uniforms from – probably a fancy dress shop or mail order – because that would destroy the illusion. In the Red Room he could revert to childhood or adolescence. Sometimes, though, he had other fantasies that he also couldn't put into words. Sometimes he yearned – needed – something more severe than a reprimand and a less tender, more perfunctory bringing to climax. He needed punishment. For what? Hadn't he confessed, and gained a kind of absolution? But mere words weren't enough. Perhaps they had it right in the old days – some crimes could be purged only by pain, by physical torment.

He sometimes thought Leo was the cross he had to bear, when she was in one of her tantrums or flights of fancy. But when she was loving and pliable she was his darling and his heart was all hers. She would perch on his knee and wind her arms round his neck and kiss his face all over. "Am I your most favourite thing in all the world?" she would ask, and he would say yes, knowing that Huwie would forgive him; he had made his peace with his son years ago.

"Your really, really most favourite?"

"Yes."

"Your most precious thing?"

"My most precious, precious thing. My precious princess."

"Your most precious princess?"

147

He paused for only a nanosecond; she would pounce on any hesitation. "Yes. My one and only precious princess." And gave only a fleeting thought to Deirdre. And Gemma.

******

It seemed to Will that the flat was the only home he had ever known. If he tried to think back to a time before the flat, his mind was blank. He knew there had been a time before the flat, but he didn't like to think back because he got that feeling again, the feeling that the ground was slipping away from his feet and underneath was a black bottomless hole. He knew he'd been ill, and was what Miss Routledge called 'convalescing', which meant eating what she left for him and swallowing the two little round pills. He did other things, too; he watched television, which was beginning to make sense, and had begun to tidy up the flat, turning on the machine that cleaned the carpets and walking up and down with it, and flicking the feather duster over the shelves. He always made his bed in the morning. He liked things to be neat and in their places.

So he was getting better, he thought. He had begun by exploring the flat first – all the cupboards and drawers in the kitchen, every inch of the big sitting room and Miss Routledge's bedroom (he already knew his own like the back of his hand), but he couldn't get into the room at the end of the corridor because it was always locked. Then he had begun to venture outside, down the stairs past the other flats whose doors were always closed. At first, as soon as he got to the bottom of the stairs he turned and went up again and his heart would be beating fast when he got back to the flat. But he made himself do it every day so he got used to it, and when he'd done it a few times he made up his mind to go along the hall to the front door.

Today. If he could, he would open it and look out into the street. Would that be a Sign? He was waiting for a Sign but he might not recognise it and didn't understand what it was for anyway. Perhaps when it happened he would know. He just knew that one day he would do something, or see something, and everything would make sense.

He got down the first flight of stairs and was about to start on the second when one of the doors to the other flats opened. He stopped, frozen. He kept his eyes facing forward so he didn't have to see what was there.

"Hello!" It was a man's voice. "You new here?"

If he didn't move a muscle the voice might go away. He held himself rigid.

"Are you lost or something? Who did you want to see?" The voice sounded more impatient. "These are private flats, you know."

He made his breathing slow, almost stop.

"Anything wrong? Shall I call someone?"

He must get back to the flat. He must get past the voice and run up the stairs and bolt himself into the flat. He started very slowly, moving past the open door sideways, keeping his face to the front, and then when he got to the stairs he took them two at a time without a pause. He heard the voice say something like, "Bloody hell!" but by that time he was inside the flat and he closed the door and bolted it on the inside and sat on the floor with his back to it until Miss Routledge came home.

She must have known what had happened because she was home earlier than usual and had to ring the bell because he'd bolted the door, and when he knew it was her he let her in and she hugged him and told him it was all right, the man downstairs had phoned her because he thought someone had got into her flat but she'd put everything right. She was proud of him, she said, for going outside and getting down the stairs.

He didn't want to go outside the flat ever again but he knew he would have to. He would have to make himself do it again to make her proud of him.

6. May 1987

Huw has lifted the telephone and put it back at least half a dozen times. He must do it, of course; no putting it off. But how to do it? Should he take Pudge out to a restaurant and tell her during the dessert? No, too cruel. Invite her round here to his flat and tell her straight out? Again, not his style. Take her off for a weekend – somewhere far away where he won't be constrained by familiar surroundings... oh hell. But he can't tell her over the phone, that's for sure. Face to face, watching total incomprehension cloud her face, that jolly, good-hearted face that has come to mean something to him, of course it has; he's still fond of her, he can tell her that, and over these last months she's been an absolute brick...

Oh hell, hell, hell. But perhaps he needn't tell her straight away, just when Gemma has gone back to Russia. She'll be away at least a month, so there's no rush. He can take it as it comes – surely during this next month an opportunity will arise – he can possibly orchestrate an argument, a good old-fashioned shouting match that can end in him demanding the ring back... But Pudge never argues. She always lets him have his own way, agrees with him on all points. That's part of her infuriating niceness. And partly, he knows, why he has allowed her so thoroughly to take him over. He's a coward, like his father.

But the last few days have been so fantastic. He can't believe, even now, that Gemma reciprocates his feelings. But she must do; last night and the night before had been wonderful. More than wonderful. Much, much more than wonderful.

In spite of his string of broken romances, Huw is not what could be described as an experienced lover. Only two girls had made it into his bed, and only one – Pudge again – had come back for more. He had wondered, after that first embarrassing liaison, if he'd inherited his father's proclivities, but he knew he hadn't; he'd just been extremely bad at knowing what was wanted. The girl had just lain there expecting him to know what to do, when all he wanted to do was get the act over with. A kiss, a quick nuzzle at her nipples and bang – all over in ten seconds.

She had still lain there when he rolled off ready to go to sleep, and then said, "Is that it?" and got up and walked out in a huff. Well, it had been pleasant for him and he'd imagined it had been for her, but obviously not.

Pudge had taken him in hand – literally – and educated him in the finer points of female arousal. *Educated* was the only word for it; she was like a hearty biology teacher explaining the various bits and bobs of anatomy. Embarrassment was unknown to Pudge. She had stripped them both in front of the mirror and then proceeded to put her instructions into practice. It had been rather nice, admittedly, allowing her to take the upper hand; he had lain beneath her obediently while she threw her leg over as if mounting a horse and had joggled up and down enthusiastically, big breasts flying everywhere like two large zeppelins. Since then they had tried various positions and he had at last got the hang of it. The secret was, apparently, to take things slowly. Women liked what Pudge called foreplay; the twiddling, rubbing and nuzzling was what turned them on, got them ready for the final gallop to the finishing post.

Armed with this knowledge, he had been confident of coming up to scratch with any other girl who might pass by, but Pudge had exacted her due reward which he couldn't begrudge her. That damn engagement ring, the price he had paid for experience, had also put a stop to the practice of it.

Until Gemma. If she hadn't been going off for a month they might have taken things more gradually. Of course they hadn't needed to get to know each other socially, which was a bonus. But the transition from half-siblings to lovers had been made so swiftly that he could almost believe it had been a dream, all in his imagination, were it not for the crumpled sheets on his tumbled bed that he's now sitting on, his mind going over the events of the last couple of days.

Their conversations had almost been better than the sex. No, not better, but just as intimate. More intimate, even, than those they'd had after the arrest of Big Brother. Then, he had done nothing more than listen to her, a willing pair of ears, but now he could also contribute. He told her about his early life in Swansea, his unhappiness, his low self-esteem. She told him about life in Suffolk with her mother, her unhappiness, her lack of confidence. It wasn't until she'd gone to Cambridge and met Sebastian that she felt she had found her niche.

Sebastian, the boyfriend who'd been killed in a car accident. For some reason the mention of this boyfriend had aroused Huw's jealousy – foolishly, as the poor guy was dead. But after their first fling under the sheets, when Gemma had revealed herself in all her wondrous naked beauty, a Venus more perfect, more erotic, more sensual than Pudge, on whom his expert foreplay of nuzzling and stroking had worked mutual wonders, he had asked casually, when they lay sated, her dark head on his chest, "How do I measure up to your other boyfriends, Gem?" and held his breath for her answer.

"Other boyfriends! How many do you think I've had?"

"Judging by your performance," he'd grinned, "quite a few."

"And judging by yours," she'd retorted, "you've had hundreds."

A thousand blessings on Pudge and her flying zeppelins! He said modestly, "Oh no, not hundreds. Dozens, perhaps. How about you?"

"Two."

"No!" Yes! Yes! he thought. Oh yes, I've cracked it. "Only two? I suppose this Sebastian was one."

"Yes."

"And was he – any good?" Oh, he was being tasteless, the poor guy couldn't answer back. And if he'd been as good – or better – he was now a spent threat anyway. But still.

"He was wonderful." She propped herself up on one elbow, her hair tickling his face. She looked sad, but was smiling.

"Oh."

"Almost as good as you."

"Ah. What about the other one?"

She collapsed against him. He couldn't see her face. "It was only the once. It was lovely, but it won't happen again."

"So he's still around."

"Yes."

"So why…?"

She stopped his mouth with a kiss. That was the start of their second fling.

Their third and fourth flings took place last night. She should have gone back to Hampstead to pack, but her flight wasn't until this afternoon and most of her stuff was ready anyway, so she had stayed with him for another night. He had driven her over in the morning, gathered her things, and driven her on to Heathrow. He had stayed until she'd gone through to Departures, then lingered on until her flight had taken off. He'd stood by the big plate glass windows watching each plane take to the sky, wondering which one was bearing her away from him.

He doesn't know how he will get through the next month.

He doesn't know how he's going to tell Pudge their engagement is over.

He doesn't know how he's going to tell Leo what the Coroner's verdict will be.

*****

For the past week, Leo has lived in a bubble of happiness. Tony had actually taken time off work – he was between assignments – and they had spent the time mostly indoors, mostly, if truth be told, in bed. Sometimes not even making love, but talking and cuddling and getting to know each other in the most intimate way possible. Sometimes she even had to make a conscious effort to think of Daddy, when BT – Before Tony - he had been the only thing on her mind. But now she could speak her thoughts out loud, any time they struck her, without feeling stupid or morbid. She had never been able to do that before, not even with Huwie. Especially with Huwie.

The Wainwrights have gone. Without giving any notice, they had just stopped coming. Well, good riddance. It meant Tony could stay without any explanation, he can share her bed without any disapproving looks and barbed comment.

They had been in bed when Huwie and Gemma had come back to collect Gemma's luggage. It was about midday, and they were just thinking of getting up and dressed when the front door opened and merry voices filled the hall. Leo had entirely

154

forgotten that Gemma was going back to Russia, that her plane was leaving Heathrow about four-thirty, and that she had promised to see her off. There was a mad scramble to get into their clothes and brush their hair and look fairly presentable, and they'd strolled downstairs and into the kitchen where Gemma was making coffee. Huwie was seated at the table watching her.

There was an uncomfortable few seconds when Gemma saw Tony, but she said hello in a neutral but friendly way, and glanced at Leo; and in that glance had obviously got the whole picture. And in her turn Leo had studied her brother and then the girl who until so recently had been her sister and knew what the score there was, too.

They all sat round the table drinking coffee and talking of inconsequential things, and Leo was wracking her brains as to how she could impart Nick's message without giving away the fact that she'd intercepted his note when Tony remarked, "Oh, by the way, Gem, we met your friend on the Heath – that bloke – Woollidge. He seemed to be waiting for you."

Gemma's eyes darted to Leo, who kept her face blank. "Oh. What did he say?"

Leo shrugged. "Just that he was probably going to Sussex. I think he'll try to get a job down there."

Gemma said, "Oh." For a moment her face looked nakedly dejected, desolate, and she fixed eyes on Leo full of a desperate pleading. I know he's your brother, that look said, but please don't tell him about the abortion. And Leo turned her face away, deliberately not answering that look with a reassuring smile or shake of the head. Of course she would never tell Huwie, but it was good for the moment to feel her power, to make Gemma stew for a while. Tables had been satisfactorily turned, she felt.

Thank goodness nothing was said about her going to Heathrow; Huwie had stowed Gemma's cases in the boot of his car, turned to her at the door before they left and said, "You okay, sis? Now I'm back at work I won't be able to come here so much," and she had said, "Don't worry about me, I'll be fine," and he had looked a bit shifty (a Daddy look) and said, "Leo, there's something I've got to tell you," and she had said, "Oh

155

keep it till later, you'll miss the plane," and off they went.

Of course all good things have to come to an end. Tony has had to go off to the wilds of Scotland for at least three days, leaving her alone in the house. But that is all right; he'll be back, he promised, he'll stay with her for as long as it takes for her to make up her mind what to do. And her thoughts, too, are turning to work. So they miss her, do they? Well, they can wait a bit longer. But soon – soon, she'll be able to decide all sorts of things. She feels as if she is coming out of a long period of hibernation and the world, though totally different, is still reassuringly the same.

She's made up her mind to do one last thing before shutting the door on the past and going forward into the future. She's driving along the Archway Road, more confident now, knowing exactly where she's going. She turns off up side streets, finds the industrial estate, draws up outside the garage. Gets out confidently and walks into the dark interior smelling of grease and oil; the clang of metal on metal comes from underneath a car from which a pair of overalled legs protrude.

She says, "Hello."

The legs slide out, followed by the upper body of a fat middle-aged man with a shaved head.

"What can I do you for?" he says, looking her all over.

"Oh," she says. "Where's Nick?" And the name slides out of her mouth quite naturally, with no bother at all.

The man gets to his feet, still looking at her in that uncomfortable way. "He's gone," he said.

"Where?"

"Don't know. Didn't say."

"Sussex, do you think?"

"Search me, darling. Don't say much, our Nick."

"Oh. Well, thanks, anyway." She turns, walks out of the garage, gets back in the car, while he's still standing, watching her. The bloody three-point turn takes six points, and she kangaroo-hops off up the road. The drive back to Hampstead seems to take twice as long, with a lot more angry hoots behind her.

7. November 1979

The gallery was gearing up for Christmas, always a busy time, and Laurence was left on his own most of the day to cope with it all. Well, there was little Rosemary, of course (and not so little any more, she had married last year and was now three months pregnant. He would soon have to think about advertising for another assistant and training her up – all that effort gone to waste!), but she couldn't be left on her own all day. His home life was similarly chaotic. He spent most of his evenings now shut up in his library while his house was taken over by creatures from the planet Zarg. He would have to put his foot down soon; he was letting Leo get away with murder.

Deborah was doing her best, but with Will having taken another turn for the worse she was finding it hard to give much attention to the business. He'd apparently got himself lost in the streets, had punched a man who'd tried to help, and was hauled to the local lock-up. It had taken the combined efforts of Deborah, the doctor and two representatives from social services to get him reinstated at Hurlingham Mansions but she was having trouble with him now taking his pills. The man, he kept saying, was a sign. A sign for what, Deborah asked, but he couldn't say. She had to stay with him now to make sure he took his medication, because he'd been putting the pills in his mouth and spitting them out again when she wasn't looking.

Oh God, how had he got into this mess? Of course he wanted Will to take his medication, to get back to normal, and then Deborah could take her rightful place in the gallery. There would be no more paintings, though. And just when he could have sold them by the dozen... oh, best not to think about it.

That commissioner friend of Ralph's (the one who had mooted the possibility of resurrecting *Whither Art* - Christopher? Christian? - 'call me Chris', he had said) - had been in touch to say it was still on the back burner but he hoped to bring it forward at the next policy meeting, and Laurence had told him with sincerity that it was fine by him for it to stay simmering for a while longer. He could do without any more complications.

The art world was in a similar state of chaos, he was pleased to see. The Keeper of the Queen's Pictures, no less, had been exposed as the Fourth Man in the Fifties spy ring. Now it was Anthony Blunt as well as Burgess, McLean and Philby, the dark deeds of whose youth had brought the whole arcane world of high art into disrepute. It wasn't a good time to be involved in the arts all round, Laurence thought, what with this forger also getting his comeuppance soon.

He had just finished reading the newspaper after his lonely lunch (not-so-little Rosemary could manage by herself for half an hour, at least) when his intercom buzzed.

"There's a man to see you," Rosemary said in those flat vowels affected by youngsters these days, "do you want me to send him up?"

"Who is he? Have you asked?"

"It's a Mr – Simmons. No, sorry," she said, as a man's voice corrected her, "Symons. From the Venn Pegasus Agency." She pronounced it, after a slight hesitation, *PegAYsus,* but the name rang bells. That was Deborah's bloke, wasn't it? The one from Denver?

"Oh, yes. Send him up, Rosemary."

He stood by the door, holding it welcomingly open. As soon as the man had mounted the stairs, he held out his hand. "Laurence Bassett. So pleased to meet you. My assistant, Miss Routledge, has always dealt with you before, I've not had the pleasure…"

But he realised he had.

After a brief handshake, the man sauntered into his office, his thumbs hooked into his pockets, sunglasses pushed up on the crown of his head like another pair of eyes staring at the ceiling. He wasn't wearing a turtle-neck sweater now, but a sharp grey suit under an expensive black wool coat. He swaggered over to the window, looked down, then turned to Laurence and smiled.

"You know why I'm here, I guess?" His accent was a curious mixture of American and London's East End.

And suddenly Laurence had that sensation of the ground sloping away from his feet and had to put a hand down on the

158

corner of his desk to steady himself.

"Take a seat, Mr Symons," - gratefully sliding down into the reassuring arms of his high leather chair.

"Dave." The man drew the ladderback chair towards the desk, dragging it across the carpet, and sat with legs carelessly apart. He had unbuttoned his coat and now threw it open, revealing the light grey suit, dark grey shirt and fat white silk tie.

Laurence said nothing, just sat smiling encouragingly at the man. Dave. Was that a friendly request, or something more sinister? The Mafia, Laurence suddenly thought, treated their victims like soul buddies until the payoff.

"You look kinda worried, Larry. Let me enlarge. That last shipment – that help you at all?"

"Ah. Let me think. As I said, Miss Routledge usually deals... Yes, there were a couple of Witt lithographs, I believe, and a Gibbons etching I thought you'd like, and four Murch..."

"Got it, Larry. Four Murchisons."

"Yes."

"Three fabulous. No gripes there. But one unsigned."

"Oh."

"Pretty puzzling, that. All our others have got the mark, know what I mean? That little W Murchison in the right-hand corner, with the date? Never varies. And you always sign an attribution. But that didn't happen in this case."

"Oh."

"Any explanation there, Larry?" The man – Dave – was smiling pleasantly with his mouth, but it didn't quite reach his eyes.

"No, I can't – can't quite recall..."

"I understand. You're a busy man. Can't be expected to remember everything. That broad of yours, Deborah, she's a sharp one, though. Bet she'd remember."

"No, I actually saw to that shipment myself. She had nothing to do with it."

Dave's smile widened. "Interesting."

Laurence's brain seemed to be working independently of his stomach, which was heaving. What excuse had he used on

Maudie? He would have to embroider it a little more to satisfy Dave Symons. He said evenly, "Yes, I remember now. There was a little misunderstanding about sales at the time – Rosemary, the junior, forgot to write down a sale in the book, and we inadvertently sold a picture twice. I thought the two grey studies would more than make up the difference." Dave was still smiling, so he plunged on. "I found the second one in Will's studio, obviously a companion piece. They went so well together, I thought, to make up the value, I'd send both. Perhaps I omitted to ask him if he'd finished it, I was slightly rushed at the time…"

Dave was nodding sagely. "No need to go into details, Larry, I'm not what you'd call an expert, just a courier. It's my client who's the connoisseur.' (He pronounced it *connoysewer*). 'And he was just a bit puzzled…"

"Oh?" Laurence feigned surprise quite well, he thought. "Why?"

Dave worked his mouth before speaking; it seemed he'd wedged some chewing gum in his cheek and was now masticating it slowly. "Well," he said, "the thing is this. This unsigned painting is a bit – how shall I put it – *cruder* than the other one. Not so well executed. And it doesn't appear to be unfinished. So my client says, anyway. He got a second opinion, and it confirms what he thought."

"And what is that?" Oh God, Laurence thought, now it's coming. They've seen through the fake. He's going to say it's by another artist entirely. And then what excuse do I have…?

"It's an earlier work, apparently. A – what do you say – juvenile piece."

"Ah."

"Which throws up an interesting dilemma."

"Oh?"

"It's titled Study in Grey Number 2. If it's an earlier picture, done when he was younger, surely it should be Number 1?"

"Oh yes. I see your point." Laurence leaned forward and held his head in his hands, hoping he looked as though he were thinking. What he was really doing, of course, was breathing deeply, letting relief pour through his entire body. Taking an extra deep breath, he raised his head, nodding sagely. "It sounds like another mix-up, I'm afraid. Possibly the labels were wrongly attributed."

"Quite a few little mix-ups all round."

"Unfortunately yes."

"Again, Larry, I sympathise. We all make mistakes, don't we? But when we do, we have to put things right, you with me?"

"Oh, entirely."

"My client wants the attribution. And the signature."

"Obviously."

"No hurry. I'll bring the picture next time I'm over."

"Fine. I look forward to it."

"Good doing business with you." The man – Dave – got to his feet, shrugged back into his coat, held out his hand. Laurence took it. He preceded Dave to the door, held it open, watched the short, swaggering figure disappear down the stairs.

After another few seconds, he closed the door, lurched to his desk, opened the bottom drawer and poured himself a good treble whisky to calm his still churning gut.

Then he lifted the telephone receiver and dialled the Baron's Court number.

******

Miss Routledge had gone out after a telephone call; was that a Sign? She'd gone out before, but this time she said she might be away for a while, and trusted him to take his pills. When she came back and saw them still on the table she would make him take them, so should he hide them? But if she asked if he'd taken them, he couldn't lie. Ah, but he *would* have taken them, wouldn't he, if he moved them somewhere else. She might ask him if he'd *swallowed* them, and that was different. He'd be caught then.

Things were becoming very complicated, which could be another Sign. When he'd gone out into the street – yesterday? The day before? Last week? – he didn't know – he'd thought things had become clearer. It had been nice being in the open

161

air. Everything looked sharp and clear, the light was different, colours were brighter. Being indoors so long – how long had it been? - had dulled his senses. It was like someone had switched on a light in his brain and he'd been like a child again, seeing everything as if for the first time. He smiled and said hello to everyone he met. Some people were nice and smiled back, some even said hello too. But others looked at him as if he were stupid, or worse.

The air smelt different, too. There were traffic smells, dog smells, wee smells sometimes, but nice smells too – bread, and fish and chips, and coffee. But if he looked up in the air, he knew it would smell even better up there. It was a nice day, cold but bright, and the sky that clear metal-blue that looked hard enough to touch. Something stirred in his brain. He wanted to make that blue on his palette, cerulean blue mixed with a little titanium white and a tiny stroke – just the tiniest brush-stroke – of lemon yellow. And then the tiniest touch of Prussian blue to deepen it at the corners, so the eye was drawn inwards and upwards and you could gaze and gaze and lose yourself so much you didn't exist any more...

But he did exist, because someone grabbed his arm and pulled him roughly backwards and a voice said, "Christ, son, watch what you're doing! You were nearly under that bus!" and he had shaken the hand off and gone on walking, quickly, to get away.

After that he felt frightened and didn't smile or say hello any more. He had to say *It's all right, it's all right* to himself over and over again but it wasn't all right because he didn't know where he was. Everything looked different. And when he looked up the sky was different, there were angry grey clouds and it was getting darker. Was that a Sign?

And then someone had come up and shaken him, and made him look at him – a big man who got him by the shoulders and was saying, "You all right, mate, what's the matter with you?" – and he'd been so scared and confused he'd doubled up his fist and smashed it into the man's stomach so he could get away but it didn't do much good, the man still had hold of him. "You little bastard, you're going to come with me," he said, and got him in some kind of armlock and marched him off somewhere where he was given tea and two biscuits (a Rich Tea finger that he liked and one with currants in that he didn't) and was told to sit still, which he did, until Miss Routledge came. She had sewn his name and address and telephone number into his ski jacket, he showed them that when they asked him.

And that must have been a Sign. He couldn't make her understand that all these Signs meant he could stop taking the pills and go back to painting. Instead she made him take the pills and, when she had to leave him, she locked the front door behind her so he couldn't get out. It wouldn't be for long, she said, only until the pills started working again, but he couldn't go on taking the pills because of the Signs. He couldn't explain this to her. He couldn't even explain it to himself properly.

But he couldn't just sit still and watch television, like he used to. He had too much energy; he paced up and down the hall, up and down, up and down, like a big white bear behind bars he'd once seen somewhere long ago. He'd already explored all the rooms; he knew every one of them by heart, what all the cupboards contained, everything in every drawer; he'd counted all the spoons and knives and forks in the kitchen, all the towels in the bathroom, even all the lady's knickers in Miss Routledge's underwear drawer. He'd folded everything away tidily, and labelled things, and washed things that looked not clean enough. There was nothing he hadn't done, nowhere he hadn't gone, in the flat.

Except – that door that was always locked. He hadn't opened that, had he? And hadn't he just rearranged the keys in the kitchen drawer by shape and size, starting with the little ones for the windows, and ending with the big ones for the doors? He knew, just by looking at the shape and size of the key, and the shape and size of the lock, which ones fitted what.

There would be a lot he could do in the room that must be beyond that door because he'd never been in there. He could spend a day, two days, just looking at things, memorising things, then cleaning things that looked dirty, tidying away things that

163

didn't belong where they were. He was good at that. Miss Routledge would be pleased with him when he'd finished.

So he took the right key from the drawer, and went along the hall, and fitted the key into the lock and turned the key once round anti-clockwise and pushed the knob and the door opened. For a while he couldn't see anything, it was dark inside like there were no windows, and he had to inch his hand along the wall to find the light switch. And even when he turned the switch it still wasn't very bright. It was a dim red light, everything seemed to be red, everything swathed in red from ceiling to floor.

He went further into the room, his eyes blinking. He had never seen a room like this before. It was a bedroom because there was a bed over by the wall, again all in red, with dark red curtains all round it, and there was also another bed in the opposite corner which wasn't red but metal, like a hospital bed although with no covers, just a flat metal surface with dark brown leather straps at each corner. Over this hung a low light, with a short cord hanging down. Which, when pulled, flooded the whole bed in a brilliant stark white light that made him jump back in alarm because the light lit only the table (it looked like a table, lit up), and the rest of the room was still bathed in that dim redness.

He could feel his heart racing. There was something not nice about that table, he didn't like the look of it at all. He pulled the cord and the light went out, which was better. He liked the redness best, he'd got used to it now. The other bed looked safe and cosy; he could climb in there and pull the curtains round him and feel warm and looked-after, like he did in his own bed when Miss Routledge brought him his milk. He wouldn't look at the metal table any more, he'd keep his face turned away.

Now that his eyes had adjusted to the gloom, he saw a wardrobe in the other corner, a large, very ornate wardrobe also painted red so that it matched the walls and couldn't be seen very easily. He pulled open the doors and looked inside. There were a lot of clothes hanging up, looking like a queue of people waiting for something. He'd never seen Miss Routledge wear any of them – they weren't the sort of thing she would wear anyway, they looked more like uniforms. He'd seen people wearing things like that at the place the man had taken him to, where they'd given him tea and biscuits. They'd been friendly enough to him but the uniforms made them look scary and he hadn't looked at them at all, but kept his face turned down to the ground. He felt the same now, staring at these clothes in the wardrobe.

So he looked down, and there were rows and rows of shoes but not shoes he'd ever seen anybody wear – they had very high heels and were more strap than shoe. And, at the back, there were a row of boots ranging from little boots to long high black leather boots done up with chains, and the sight of them made his heart race again. And in the corner...

He shut the door quickly and leant against it, holding the things in so they couldn't get out. He wished he had a key to lock the door to the wardrobe, like there was a key to lock the door to the room. No wonder Miss Routledge kept the room locked; if all these terrible things got out...

He would have to make a dash to the door and lock it behind him, to keep himself safe. He must never look at the door again. If he went around with his face turned down to the ground he might be safe but he must never ever look at the door again. He must get out of the room and shut the door and fit the key in the lock and turn it once round clockwise and take it out and go into the kitchen and open the drawer and put the key back in its proper place and shut the drawer and he must never ever look up from the ground to see the door or the sky or anything else ever again

"Have you taken your pills, Will?"

A good Sign. "Yes." He'd taken them into his room and placed them with the others under the bed.

"You've been all right while I've been gone?"

Not a good Sign. He remained silent.

She came into the sitting room where he was looking at the television. He could raise his eyes as high as the television, but no higher. He turned his head to see her skirt. Her legs. Her shoes. Her usual shoes with heels but solid, black solid no-

165

nonsense shoes. Her hand, wearing a black glove. Carrying a shopping bag.

"I'll make us some supper." She put the bag down while she took off her coat and gloves. The bag was red with gold writing. The writing just said *Fantasia* but he didn't like the look of it. He could just see some red tissue paper inside. Then he looked quickly away back towards the television as she picked it up and went into the hall. His hearing was keen. She went into the kitchen and opened the drawer. She called, "Thanks, Will! I see you've tidied up!" She closed the drawer. She was going out into the hall and up the corridor. She was unlocking the door at the end.

He kept his eyes fixed on the television, slowing his heart down to almost nothing so he didn't have to breathe.

But she was coming out and locking the door behind her. She was going back into the kitchen. He heard sounds of chopping and running water and saucepans clattering. He let his heart beat again.

She brought his supper in on a tray. He liked eating in front of the television and he had to eat everything she made him and this was his favourite, soup and bread and hot baked beans on toast. And a cup of tea in a proper cup and saucer, not a plastic beaker like he'd been given by that lady in uniform which he hadn't been able to drink because there was something nasty in it, a brown sodden lump on a bit of string. Not a good Sign.

When he'd eaten everything and she'd taken it away and come back again she said, "Mr Bassett's coming tonight, Will. I want you to say hello to him and then go to bed. Will you do that?"

"Yes."

"He might still be here in the morning."

"Yes."

"Is that all right?"

He said carefully, "Is he sleeping here?"

"Yes."

"Is he sleeping in your room?"

He heard her draw in her breath but he couldn't look up.

166

"Not in my room, Will."

If Mr Bassett wasn't sleeping in Miss Routledge's room there was only one room left. He said, "No. He m-mustn't."

"Mustn't what, Will?"

"He m-mustn't sleep anywhere else."

"What do you mean?"

"He m-must sleep in your room. Nowhere else."

There was silence. He knew she was looking at him, but he couldn't raise his face. "Will, look at me."

"I c-c-can't."

"Will," she said slowly. "Tell me. Has Mr Bassett…" He could hear her swallowing. "Has Mr Bassett," she said again, "ever got into your bed?"

He couldn't answer. His memory was bad. He couldn't remember anything before he came to the flat. No, he had a vision of somewhere big and light where he could mix his paints, the colours bright and pure on his palette. Where the air was clean and pure and he lived in the sky.

"Has he, Will?"

He couldn't answer. He couldn't lift his face. He could only nod his head because he couldn't tell lies and he knew, although he couldn't remember, that it *had* happened, that Mr Bassett had once got in beside him and held him tight and kept him safe and that it had been nice.

PART THREE

1987 and 1980

1.   May 1987

"We'd love to see you, pet! Bernard and I were just saying, when will we get up to see Leo and Huwie! We've been thinking about you, my darling. Not a day passes but we talk about it all, how dreadful it was... and Dee too, of course."

Dee? Dee? Dee-dee. Her infant name for the Mad Mother.

"Oh, Mrs W! I'm sorry I haven't been in touch. Things have been – oh, awful..."

"I'm sure they have, pet. If it wasn't for Bernard's trouble, we'd have been up to see you ourselves. But I'm so glad you're coming down! I'll bake your favourites – still iced fingers and brownies? They're Dee's favourites too."

Replacing the receiver, Leo basks for a moment in the almost-forgotten joy of being cherished and pampered that she'd revelled in when she first came to live with Daddy. Daddy might have been a grump sometimes but Mrs Wetherby had always taken her side and spoiled her. What, she wonders, is Bernard's trouble? She's sure she's never heard anything about this before.

She's set herself a whole day to drive down to West Wittering and back again. She leaves at seven-thirty in the morning to miss the rush hour and breaks her journey at the services on the A3. Hesitant in traffic, Leo feels much more liberated on the open stretches of semi-motorway and urges her little Triumph to nearly sixty. Daddy had driven her this way a couple of times when the Wetherbys had first moved to West Wittering ('the Ws of WW,' he'd laughed), so she vaguely knows the route. The house is a comfortable three-bedroom detached with an annexe which had originally been earmarked for Bernard's potential hobbies of picture framing and model boat building, but after the Mad Mother had gone bonkers Daddy had paid for it to be converted into a separate one-bedroom dwelling where the Wetherbys could keep an eye on her. Leo has suspicions that her father, too, had paid for a good share of the house.

She makes record time down to Sussex and is turning into the drive of *Journey's End* (written in curly script on a wooden plaque set into the gatepost, with a little girl tucked up in bed cupped in the tail of the *y*) at just turned ten. Mrs W has obviously been looking out for her and rushes out in flowery pinny. They meet in an ecstatic hug. But Mrs W is smaller and thinner than Leo remembers. When had she last seen her? Nearly a year ago, although she had telephoned religiously every week. Her hair, too, is sparser and completely white. She must be well into her seventies.

And Bernard – well, it's clear what his trouble is. He's obviously dying, hooked up to an oxygen cylinder beside the wheelchair he's sitting in. If Mrs W is thin, Mr W is skeletal. But he holds out a shaking stick hand to her and she sits beside him, bare bones pressed between her fleshy palms, tears pricking her eyes.

Mr W had given her rides on his sit-on lawn mower, holding her between his ample knees, big hands over hers on the handlebars. Mr W had allowed her into his sanctuary, the garden shed, and showed her the little seedlings snug in their trays and told her which were weeds and which flowers in the borders. Mr W had known the names of all the birds that came into the garden. Mr W had dubbed her his Jill of all trades when he had to mend the gutters or creosote the fences. After Daddy, Mr W was her most favourite person in all the world. As well as Mrs W, of course. And Huwie.

"Lung cancer," Mrs W tells her in the kitchen, when they are preparing lunch. "And him having given up smoking twenty years ago."

"Did Daddy know?"

"No, pet. If he had, he'd have whisked him off to a private hospital and paid for his treatment, and we didn't want that. Your father has done enough for us, bless him."

Breaking off from chopping spring onions into the salad bowl, Leo hugs Mrs W who is making the dressing, and they both have a weep, and then continue their chores. It is solitary and companionable, sad and happy at the same time, and Leo has reverted to her fourteen-year-old self when the kitchen had been her refuge when Daddy had been a grump about her clothes and hair and the company she kept. Not that he'd done

172

anything about them, in fact she suspected his grumbles were more to do with the trouble he foresaw with Mummy rather than any worries about her.

And just as the salad is ready, and Mrs W is bringing out the cold chicken and ham, the back door opens and something spins in like a whirlwind in a flurry of bare limbs, white shift and masses of black hair.

"Darling Barbie, look what I've found! Just the thing for your salad – nasturtium flowers! Don't they look pretty! Oh! It's Leonora!"

It's Dee-dee, Deirdre, Drusilla – the Mad Mother. Looking particularly mad, too, with bare feet and a couple of nasturtium flowers stuck in that wild riot of hair which now, Leo can see, is streaked with grey – quite a lot of grey. But the face beneath is smooth, hardly wrinkled – well, they say the mad don't age, they have no worries – and her eyes, those large green eyes that Leo remembers so well, are still clear and glittery like jewels. She had forgotten how small she is, almost as short as her, but with bigger boobs and wider hips which the shift barely covers. It's quite a warm day, but hardly warm enough for this get-up.

"Hello," she says.

She is scooped up in arms that still flourish a little bunch of wild flowers. "Oh, Leonora, I'm so sorry! I couldn't believe – we couldn't believe – I just cried for days. Why on earth did he do it? He was my first love, you know. My very first."

Yes, I know, Leo thinks silently. You shared a very special moment that he remembered with joy and fondness. And how many other lives have been affected by that moment? And Gemma isn't even the result of it.

She has to say something. She says, "How are you?"

"Oh, I'm fine. Aren't I, Barbie?" She turns to Mrs W, who beams and nods. "Well, I have good days and bad days, but don't we all. I'm very happy here. I'll get back to painting soon… I've still got all my paints, it's a shame to waste them. I think I put it off though because I don't know if – I sometimes think I've lost the knack…"

"Now don't say that, Dee," Mrs W chides gently. "You won't

know till you try. A talent like yours isn't easily lost, that's what I say."

"Isn't she a darling?" The Mad Mother – Dee – flings her arms around Mrs W and kisses her warmly on the cheek. "Now, can I help? Have you done everything? Shall I lay the table?" – and she's off into the sitting room to charm Mr W.

Mrs W looks at Leo. "She's just like a child," she says, her voice sad but proud.

Leo says, "What exactly happened? To make her – you know."

"It didn't happen all at once," Mrs W whispers. "I think it was an accumulation of things. I think she was hit hard by the death of that boyfriend of Gemma's, but that seemed a bit of a delayed shock. Then the discovery of that body they found on the Welsh farm – that must have brought memories back. She insists she helped Nick bury it, but he won't have it. Says it was all his own doing. But the thing that sent her over the edge – well, we'll never know. Your father said something upset her when they identified the body, but she wouldn't say what. And then, of course, Nick was arrested…"

It seems strange to hear the name Nick on Mrs W's lips. She says it easily, as if she knows him well. Did they have much to do with each other during the Invasion? Of course Mrs W would have cooked his meals, changed his bed (he'd slept on a camp bed beside Gemma) and they'd probably exchanged a few words – more than he did with her. And of course he would have visited the Mad Mother from time to time. But the way Mrs W says his name speaks volumes – there's a smile on her lips and a tender look in her eyes. But then Mrs W finds good in everybody.

"He should be in soon," she says as an afterthought.

"Oh? So he's here?"

"Yes. That job of his in London came to an end, so he thought he'd try to find something round here. I told him a few likely places, so I hope it's good news." She picks up the salad bowl and the plate of chicken and Leo follows behind her into the dining room with the ham and bread.

174

The table has been laid with cloth and cutlery, and the little bunch of wildflowers has been arranged in a blue ceramic pot as a centrepiece. "There," says Mrs W, "you see, she hasn't lost her touch." And the flowers do look carelessly but artfully placed for maximum impact of colour and foliage.

Back in the kitchen to fetch cheese and crackers, Leo says, "Why did he stay in London? He said he hated it."

"He wanted to make sure Gemma was all right," Mrs W says, filling the cheese board with a wheel of Edam and a nice Brie. "It was obviously a terrible shock for her when he was arrested. And he felt bad about not staying in Hampstead until the case came to court."

"Why didn't he stay?"

"Oh, I don't know, pet. He didn't want to be a nuisance, I suppose. Your father said he could live there, but you know Nick. You can't make him do anything he doesn't want." Mrs W smiles indulgently. "He stayed with a friend somewhere in Gloucestershire, I think. Anyway, when he came out of prison he wanted to make it up to poor Gemma, so he was looking after the business for someone he met in there. It was somewhere fairly near Hampstead. That's what he's told us, but of course we weren't in London ourselves then." Then she lowered her voice and leaned towards Leo. "Poor Dee has missed him. They fight like cat and dog, but she can't live without him."

When they return to the dining room, Dee has wheeled Mr W in and is sitting beside him, holding a beaker to his lips. Grudgingly, Leo has to admit that dear Mr W looks as happy as he is able; he grips Dee's hand tightly and fixes his eyes on her gratefully when she replaces the oxygen mask. "Like a daughter to us," Mrs W whispers. "I won't say anything against Eileen, but she hasn't half the patience of our dear Dee."

Lunch is a rather stilted affair, despite the brave attempts of Mrs W to keep conversation going. Dee sees to all Mr W's needs and it's clear she's a frequent guest at their table. But Leo resents her presence, although she realises she had come here to see her too. Did she also hope to see Nick? – because, when lunch is almost finished, the front door opens and he comes into the room and Leo's heart leaps into her mouth.

He registers no surprise to see her, but of course Mrs W must have told him she was coming. He hardly registers her at all, but looks first at Mrs W, then towards Dee.

"Any luck?" asks Mrs W, beaming at him.

"Yes, I think so. One looks promising. They just need help for the summer, but it's a start." He answers her but still looks at Dee, who is wiping Mr W's mouth with a napkin.

"Wychways Farm?"

"Yes."

"Ah, I knew they'd find you something. Sit down, dear, and finish up the chicken. Have you had enough, Bernard? Would you like to lie down?" And Mrs W wheels Mr W out, leaving the three of them round the table.

Nick makes no attempt to finish the chicken. He's sat down and is leaning forward on his elbows, his steady gaze fixed on Dee who is deliberately gazing the other way, out of the window.

"Are you pleased for me, Dee?" he asks at last.

She shrugs. "If you are."

"But do you want me to stay?"

She turns to him, fixes him with those unsettling green eyes. "It doesn't matter what I want, does it? You always please yourself."

He doesn't answer, but bites the side of a thumbnail while he studies her. Eventually he sits back and helps himself to a chicken leg. There is an uncomfortable silence that Leo doesn't know how to break. But after he's torn some meat from the bone in his fingers and eaten it, he says quietly, "I can always go back to Cirencester."

"Yes." There's a defiant, hectic look in the Mad Mother's eyes.

Another silence. Nick gnaws at the chicken bone, seemingly concentrating on the task in hand but there's a watchful quality in the way he does it, and an enclosed holding-together intensity on the other side of the table. Leo feels superfluous, invisible.

He throws the bone down on the plate. "Okay." He pushes his chair back and stands.

The Mad Mother gets up too, and flings herself at him. "No, don't leave me, Nick!" She winds her arms round his neck and buries her face in his chest. After a slight pause, he holds her to him, one hand in her hair. The expression on his face is one of exasperation mixed with relief.

And they stand like t hat until Mrs W appears in the doorway. A significant look passes between her and Nick, and Mrs W smiles.

"All right, Dee." He pushes her away from him, gently. "I'll stay. We'll try and get you painting again." And he turns away out of the room and Leo hears the front door close behind him. She realises he hasn't even acknowledged her presence.

Driving up the A3, skimming around the Hog's Back, stuffed with cake and coffee and having said what she fears is her final farewell to Mr W, Leo recalls that little scene in all its intricate detail and wonders what it all means. There is definitely something between Nick and Dee, but it's obviously not conventional love. And Nick loves Gemma, doesn't he? Oh, it's all so confusing. She can't wait to get back to Hampstead, back to the arms of her lovely, uncomplicated Tony.

2.   March/April 1980

Laurence shifted the flat package further up under his arm. He'd parked the Jag in the car park, at least a hundred yards from the entrance, and was now walking stiffly up the long sweeping drive towards the mock Gothic frontage. Set in twenty acres of Hertfordshire countryside, the nearer gardens overflowing with drifts of daffodils and narcissi, this was obviously one of the better psychiatric hospitals, housed in an elegant 18th-century mansion. Prime real estate, he couldn't help thinking. How lucky to live in a country where the less fortunate were taken care of and allowed to live in such surroundings! At a price, of course.

But he didn't begrudge a penny of it. Will certainly seemed to be happy here and was back to his old self. His old self without the talent, but everything came at a price. Perhaps he could soon be released back to the comforts of Hurlingham Mansions. Deborah certainly hoped so.

Comforts? At that, Laurence had to smile to himself. Hardly comfort now, not to start with, at least. He had to pay for his comforts. She exacted a fine revenge, did Deborah, but then of course he deserved it. Did she blame him for Will's second rapid descent into that catatonic state it has taken months to lift him out of? Why? Because it had happened after that night he'd stayed while Will was there, the night after the first visit of Dave Symons which had put the fear of God up him?

He'd availed himself of the facilities of the Red Room again last night, after another visit from Dave Symons, and obviously had to spend the rest of the night swaddled in the soft depths of the four-poster bed while Miss Routledge administered balm to his wounds. How could such gentle hands wield such exquisite torture? Strapped face down on the table he could see only the tops of her legs in their fine black silk stockings and suspenders attached to a red satin basque, although he'd never seen that properly. The blinding white light illuminated the table but nothing much beyond that. Her figure was shrouded in gloom, in the dull redness. She wore a black mask, he thought; he had a fleeting impression of a black hood with two eyeholes fixed on

178

him as she buckled him down like a large white terrified sacrifice. Terrified? – oh yes, but also, oh God, bloody excited.

And he deserved it, didn't he? That, and more. If she knew he were here now, on this particular mission, his punishment would be even more extreme. As it should be. But what other choice did he have?

"Will?" The girl behind the reception desk smiled at him. She wore a cheerful dress and cardigan with a name badge: Sharon. No uniforms here. "I think you'll find him in the leisure room, Mr Bassett. He likes watching the old films on TV in the afternoon."

"Thank you, Sharon." He walked as casually as he was able along the marble hall to the large bright room at the end, passing a lady wearing a ball gown, eye patch and slippers. "Good afternoon, madam," he said courteously, and she inclined her head regally at him. He had grown to love these oddball characters; it would be quite fun to work here, he thought.

There were a few more in the leisure room that he recognised: the old bloke with the terrible wig who stood at the window staring out, the chain-smoker who demanded of all newcomers what the time was every five minutes, and the young girl, probably even younger than Will, sitting on the floor nursing a doll. What horrors had they witnessed, to have affected them like this? The young girl, who somehow reminded him of Deirdre although she was blonde and much fatter, was a self-harmer; her pasty arms were a mass of scars and bruises.

And there sat Will at the end of a three-seater settee, knees drawn up to his chin, his head resting on them and his fingers locked around them, gazing unblinking at the television set. He looked healthier than Laurence had last seen him, a month ago; he'd put on weight and his hair looked clean and brushed.

Before he could make his way over, the chain-smoker accosted him. "Hello mate, got the time?"

Laurence glanced at his watch. "Two thirty-three." He had to be exactly right or the bloke would ask him again in two minutes, not five.

"Thanks mate." The bloke ambled back to his chair, lifted his fag from the ashtray and began blowing smoke rings at the ceiling.

Will was smiling up at him. "Hello, Mr Bassett."

"Hello, Will. Everything all right?"

"Yes."

He drew three small packets out from his coat pocket. "Here are your liquorice allsorts and dolly mixture. Thought you might like to try these, too. Fruit drops."

He should have known better. Will pounced on the first two packets but left the third. "Thank you, Mr Bassett." He could buy these from the shop on the premises, of course, but it had become a ritual with Laurence and he knew better than to break it. He went over to the girl, knelt down beside her (with an involuntary grimace) and held out the packet of fruit drops. Instead of accepting them, as he'd expected, she'd raised her arms and brought the doll down on his head. He moved hastily away as, springing to her feet, she kicked out at him, then screamed at the top of her voice. A couple of male nurses hurried in who proceeded to hustle her away.

"Sorry," Laurence apologised. "I'm sorry, but I didn't do anything..."

"Don't worry, sir. All in a day's work."

"But I don't want you to think..." He watched as she was manhandled off, still screeching. Will sit sat watching television as if nothing had happened.

After a minute, Laurence settled himself back carefully on the settee. He felt shaken and somehow guilt-ridden. The girl's screams still rang in his ears. He said, "When are you coming back to us, Will?"

"I don't know."

"Have they said anything...?"

The boy stared at him, then shook his head.

"I'll have a word before I leave. You'd like to come back, wouldn't you? Back to Baron's Court, back to Miss Routledge?"

The boy stared, then looked down. Laurence knew this was what he did when he didn't want to answer.

"She wants you back, Will. She misses you."

Still no answer. Will gripped his knees even tighter.

"Well, all right. Perhaps it's not time yet." They stared at the television together. Out of the corner of his eye, Laurence saw the smoker stir. He called over, "Two thirty-eight," and the bloke slumped back, satisfied.

Ten minutes later, at two forty-eight, Laurence said carefully, "Will, I'd like you to do something for me."

"All right."

"Look, I've got a marker pen here. Do you remember when you used to sign your name? And the date? Do you think you can do that for me now?"

"I think so."

Laurence laid the flat parcel, which Dave Symons had given to him yesterday and would pick up tomorrow, across his knees. It was wrapped in brown paper, and Laurence had untaped the bottom right hand corner. He drew apart the paper, hoping against hope that Will wouldn't recognise the grey paint underneath.

"Just there, Will. Just your name, W Murchison, and the date. Just to see if you remember." He held out the black felt marker towards the locked fingers.

Will didn't move for a few seconds. Then he unhooked his fingers, stretched his legs, and held out his hand for the pen.

"That's a good lad. Just there, I think. W Murchison."

The boy obediently and painstakingly wrote the letters, a little bigger and untidier than usual but that was all right, he would have been younger, wouldn't he, if he'd signed it? Now for the tricky part.

"And the date, Will. Do you know the date?"

The boy shook his head.

"Just the month and the year. It's March, isn't it?"

The boy nodded.

"Then write March, and then the year." He took a deep breath. "Seventy-five."

Will was laboriously writing *M-a-r-c-h*, then stopped.

"What's wrong, Will?"

"Do I write letters or numbers?"

181

"Oh," – on an outward breath, "just numbers. A seven, then a five." And watched while the boy wrote them next to the *March*. "Good lad. That's very good, Will." He wrapped the brown paper over the corner of the picture, laid the parcel down on his knees, leant against the back of the settee. The smoker was stubbing out his fag and preparing to rise. Laurence called out, "Two fifty-three," and the bloke nodded, sat back and lit another cigarette.

******

"Oh," Hilary said on the other end of the line, "I suppose Laurence isn't in?"

"No, he's not," Deborah said smoothly. "Can I give him a message?"

"Will it get to him?"

"Of course." She wouldn't rise to Hilary's bait. "All messages left with me are relayed to Mr Bassett."

"Oh, come off it, Debs. You guard him like bloody Cerberus. Or do I mean Medusa?"

"If you have anything to say," Deborah said, "you can either say it to me or call back when Mr Bassett is here. Or shall I get him to call you?"

"No, I know what he's like. Listen, tell him to look at page 4 of the *Standard*. I think he'll know what I mean." Hilary hung up.

Deborah left Rosemary in charge while she went out to buy the newspaper. She would have sent the girl but, in her seventh month, Rosemary was now unwilling to stir as much as a finger. They ought to be training up a new assistant to take her place, but things had been left to slide somewhat since Will's incarceration.

Oh, how she missed him! The flat seemed so bereft without him. And their little rituals – the morning cup of tea, the hand on the forehead, the farewell kiss on the cheek; the coming home at night to him on the sofa in front of the television, making supper for two, tucking him up in bed. The sessions in the Red Room with Laurence helped to make up for it, but nothing could replace that maternal tug, that pull at the heartstrings when Will looked up and smiled his open, guileless smile and spoke without stammering. She visited him in the hospital twice a week and was confident he would be discharged very soon; he was making good progress. Then the sessions in the Red Room would have to come to an end. She would not repeat the mistake of having Laurence in the flat when Will was back there.

She was conscious that her feelings for Laurence had undergone a change. Not a huge, cataclysmic change, merely a shift in her perception of him. She could no longer trust his word. He had lied to her in the Savoy Grill. She had been so sure she was his confidante, and now she realised she had been taken in and was ashamed of herself for being so blind. Blind to his faults, which were probably so deeply embedded in his nature that he didn't even acknowledge them. He would deny having shared Will's bed as he'd denied laying a finger (or anything else) on Nicholas Woollidge. He was the worst kind of liar, the kind that even denied their lies and thought themselves honest.

She didn't look at page 4 until she was safely upstairs, sitting in the high leather chair behind the mahogany desk. Then she spread the newspaper over the desk and perched her glasses on the end of her nose.

There was a photograph of a well-known politician shaking the hand of a balding, well-built man in a smart Savile Row-style suit who she didn't recognise. But somehow, even from the flat surface of the paper, he exuded power. He wasn't especially tall, but his biceps filled out the sleeves of the suit. The little finger of his left hand, held by his side, sported a chunky diamond ring. He wore sunglasses. He was, she guessed, in his late fifties.

...*the Minister for Trade,* read the caption, *welcomes wealthy tycoon Dominic King to the Fourth Trade Convention in Blackpool.*

Irish-born Mr King, she read on, *now based in Denver, has international business interests ranging from publishing to armaments and has come to attend the conference on arms sales to Africa and the Middle East... He is also gaining a reputation as a patron of the arts, having amassed a sizable collection of work from new artists all over the world...*

She sat back and took off her glasses. How on earth did

Hilary come into this? What did she know about Denver-based businessmen who were patrons of the arts? But hang on – perhaps that wasn't her area of interest at all.

Irish-born Mr King, whose business interests include armaments. And hadn't Hilary rung Laurence shortly after his return from Caernarvon, in North Wales, after Nicholas Woollidge had been sentenced for possession of offensive weapons? Weapons thought to be destined for the IRA? And hadn't her news, whatever it was, made Laurence sink further into gloom – and wasn't that the night he decided to buy his Hampstead house, a place he could bring his children and give parties…?

Oh Laurence, she thought. What have you done? How have you got mixed up in this? This is bigger than both of us. If Dominic King was involved in illegal arms dealing and was buying works of art as a way of money laundering, how much did Laurence know about it? Could she ever trust him ever again?

No wonder he was so keen on the 'corrective therapy' she practised in the Red Room. At first she'd held back, not wanting to hurt him too much; a little spanking with the fine horsehair switch followed by a slow walk up his spine in her highest heels, after the table had been cranked down to floor level. But he soon demanded the full treatment; a taste of the assortment of canes in the wardrobe, all the panoply of footwear from slipper to boot. This preferment of his for punishment over pleasure lowered him in her estimation. She was seeing another side of him, one that enjoyed cruelty and pain. And wasn't he enforcing a kind of punishment on her, by requiring her to inflict cruelty and pain? And in the process, making her realise that this was also part of her nature? Oh yes, she enjoyed their sessions too, she couldn't deny that. Sometimes she couldn't wait to get back to her bedroom for her own gratification. He had unlocked her sexuality, which she had kept at bay for so many years, and now she realised just what she had missed. She would have preferred, on the whole, to have been left in ignorance.

******

The invitation arrived in the morning's post at the gallery. Laurence knew it was something more grand even than a BBC black tie do – the envelope was expensive cream vellum, the writing fine italic script in Indian ink. The stiff cream card inside requested the pleasure of the company of Laurence Bassett, Esquire, at a cocktail party to be held at No 11 Downing Street.

"Christ." He stared down at the small square card as if mesmerised.

"Will you go?" Deborah, he could see, was similarly struck.

"God, no. Can I decline? Deborah, it's not me, is it?"

She said, "Isn't it?" in a tone of voice he'd never heard before.

"What the hell – what's it all about, do you think?"

"It's in honour of captains of industry, apparently. People who put lots of money into the economy." Her voice was neutral. "You must have caught the eye of someone very high up in the business world."

"Me? I put sod-all... I'm just a sprat in a world of sharks, Deborah. This must be a mistake."

She refused to help. She turned back to the study of her account books. After a moment of helpless bafflement, both at the invitation and her dismissal of it, he climbed the stairs to his office and spent all morning trying to frame a polite excuse for non-attendance.

His next invitation was less easy to refuse. This one came by telephone, a few days later.

"Bassett? Swainton. Need your help, old chap."

"Always at your service, Freddy."

"Don't piss me about, you old tosser. Lunch. Twelve o'clock. Tomorrow."

"Right."

"Le Gavroche okay?"

"It'll do. Are you paying?"

"You're not, that's all you need to know. You old skinflint."

"See you there, Freddy."

185

This was much more up his street. He would look forward to lunch with Freddy. But when he told Deborah, the tight pursing of her lips alerted him to her disapproval.

"You know I can't leave the gallery, Laurence. It's Rosemary's ante-natal day."

"So…?"

"Will's being discharged."

"Ah." Damn and blast! He'd forgotten he'd agreed to pick him up and drive him back to Baron's Court. "Oh well, I can put Freddy off. Will's much more important."

Which he was, of course. But Freddy was implacable. This lunch couldn't be postponed; didn't he know how long the waiting list was for the Gav? – besides which, his host was due to leave the country the day after. Goddammit, Bassett, that little wanker can spend another day in the loony bin, can't he? Or can't you wait to get him back in your clutches?

He would send a taxi to pick Will up and deposit him safely at Hurlingham Mansions. Will was used to taxis. He still had the account at the taxi firm, although he'd had to give up the lease on the Wapping flat. But if Will was never going to paint again…

No more Murchisons, no more sessions in the Red Room. Deborah would be lost to him in every way; she would become another boring domestically-fixated female who would put Will before everything. Even Gali-Leo's. And he would be stuck with the bills, of course. Oh God.

So now he was responsible for Will, and Leo. And Huwie, who had decided to leave Swansea when he left school next year and live in London. What had happened to his former carefree bachelor life? Thank God, he thought, as another scenario flashed across his mind – thank God he'd never found Deirdre. And his other offspring, Gemma. He already had more than enough to cope with, thank you very much.

"Glad you could fit us in, you old tosspot!" Freddy was already ensconced in the restaurant, napkin spread over his lap in readiness. Laurence was escorted to his chair by the maitre d', who pulled it out and slid it back expertly as he seated himself.

The third chair was empty.

"Gone to the bog," Freddy said, seeing Laurence's eyes flick over to it.

"Who is it? You were very mysterious on the phone…"

Freddy tapped a long bony index finger on the side of his nose. "You're in demand, old boy. I've been wooed like the proverbial maiden aunt, now it's your turn. You can't say no to this chappie, he's a bloody smooth operator. Ever seen *The Godfather?* Well, all I can say…" His voice trailed off, his eyes fixed on a spot behind Laurence's left ear.

"Mr Bassett."

At the voice, Laurence stood and turned. He found himself face to face with a person whose presence gave him a physical blow in the gut. There was nothing overly remarkable about the austerely handsome face and the bullet-shaped head which, unlike Laurence's, was bald except for silver wings slicked back above small, well-shaped ears. He was only of average height, but muscular; Laurence, the younger by a good few years, was all too conscious of his rounded shoulders and bloated belly. The grip of the hand was like a vice. But the eyes - pale slate-grey eyes beneath finely drawn black brows - were a pair of snakes ready to strike.

"Dominic King." The hand released his. Laurence involuntarily flexed his fingers.

"I'm very glad to meet you, Mr King. I don't think I've had the pleasure…?"

"Dominic, please. Sit down, Laurence."

He sat. Dominic King moved round to his chair and seated himself, first brushing his hand over the seat and dismissing the waiter who was ready to spring into action. They waited – Laurence, Freddy and the hovering waiter – while he shifted to get comfortable, shot his cuffs and leaned over the table with his fingers steepled in front of him. The waiter, a good-looking blond youth who had obviously tickled Freddy's fancy – the old goat was almost slavering - moved forward with the menus. Turning his face in profile, his long straight nose and decisive chin lifted to full advantage, Dominic King halted his progress with an outstretched palm.

"The wine, please."

"The Chateau La…"

"Please." The word wasn't a pleasantry but an order.

He leaned forward again. Laurence found he was holding his breath and knew Freddy was doing likewise. He knew, now, how Will felt when words wouldn't unlock themselves from his tongue; he couldn't have framed a sentence if his life depended on it.

"I'm glad," Dominic King spoke in calm, measured tones, "you found it possible to accept this invitation. Your overseas engagement must have been very brief." He paused. "Laurence." He smiled, a slow, glacial smile.

"Ah. Yes."

"You must be a very busy man."

"Well…"

"And so am I. So we shall get straight down to business."

But first they had to wait while the wine was poured, and Dominic approved it, after due consideration and a curt nod of the head, as fit for drinking. And then the menus had to be proffered, and waved away; Dominic ordered for the three of them. Laurence was pleased to see that even Freddy was cowed but, paradoxically, would have loved the old roué to be back on form. If even Freddy found it politic to curb his usual blithe blasphemies, this lunch was going to be an almost impossible ordeal.

Laurence said, when the salmon and prawn terrine was almost consumed and the wine had gone some way to unlocking his tongue, "What line of business are you in," - he set down his glass - "Dominic?"

The well-shaped eyebrows arched. The long thin lips almost stretched themselves into a smile. "I have fingers," he said, "in many pies. But I'm here today to talk about art."

"I see."

Dominic patted the corners of his mouth with his napkin. "You've already met my agent. He's introduced me to some interesting works. Through your good offices, mainly." He

188

turned his gaze, without moving his head, on Freddy. "Frederick here has been very helpful. He's offered to sell me one of his most prized possessions."

"And at a bloody fair price, may I say."

"It's worth every cent." The pale eyes moved back to Laurence. "I'm willing to pay top bucks to get what I want."

Their plates were removed and the main course set down before he elaborated. During this time Laurence's brain was racing. This was David Symons' client, obviously. Dominic King – where had he heard that name before? In the newspapers, probably. King was a common enough surname. But a King who was based in Denver... His brain buzzed. Oh, Hilary, he thought, what did you dig up...?

"Murchison," he suddenly heard. "Will Murchison."

"Ah yes. He's..."

"Very good. You've sent over quite a few of his, Laurence. I'm impressed. The lad has talent."

"Unfortunately he also has mental problems." Laurence glanced at his watch. The taxi should be picking Will up about now.

"Is that so?" Dominic was giving his attention to his comfit of duck. Laurence picked up his knife and fork, his appetite already ruined.

"Nutty as a squirrel's fart, isn't that right, Larry?" Freddy put in, already halfway through his plateful.

"Well, no. He's fine now. The problem is..."

"There's no problem, Laurence." Dominic smiled thinly. "And if there is, there's always a solution. It depends where you want to look for it." Laurence remained silent while Dominic took a few leisurely forkfuls, masticated slowly and swallowed. "That's the first rule of business. There are never any problems, only different ways of solving them." The prongs of the fork were stabbed towards him. "Remember that."

"Right."

"So if you think there's a problem, we must work out the right solution to it." He was working methodically through his meal. Laurence's first mouthful was still unswallowed. A leisurely appreciation of the wine followed before Dominic continued. "So tell me the problem."

Laurence swallowed. "It's one that can't be put right, I'm afraid. It's just that – when Will is – well, ill – he can't paint. I'm afraid he's never going to be prolific."

Dominic sat back, dabbed the napkin at his mouth. "No problem there, Larry."

"No?" The use of the diminutive of his name made Laurence even more uneasy.

"No. That's precisely why I want to buy up the whole Murchison canon." Again that thin smile. "Come on, Larry. The second rule of business, eh? The rarer the product, the pricier it becomes. I've tracked down most of the privately sold paintings and made offers nobody has yet refused." His glance rested on Freddy. "I think Frederick will confirm that I offered more than a fair price for his picture. What was it called again, Freddy?"

"Oh, some bollocks about a clobbered mind with closed circles."

"Closed Circuits of the Cluttered Mind," Dominic corrected, "Number Two." His glance came back to Laurence. "Do you know of that one?"

"Yes. I wanted to buy it myself."

"I know. My agent was also interested, but Freddy here wouldn't sell. So I only got one picture, but that was enough to convince me that here was an artist who would go far." There followed another leisurely appreciation of wine while their plates were cleared, Laurence's hardly touched. Then, after Dominic had placed the glass back on the table, he raised his eyes with their cobra-like stare. "Number Two," he repeated. "To me that signifies that there must be a Number One somewhere."

"Oh, not necessarily. As far as I remember the picture, there were two main wheels. Or circles," Laurence amended hurriedly.

"So the Number Two refers to its content? Not the quantity of pictures?"

"Yes, I would think so." He smiled. "I've certainly never heard of a Closed Circuits of the Cluttered Mind, Number One."

"Ah. So," Dominic said, leaning back in his chair, "not like the Studies in Grey, then."

Laurence was silent.

"Thanks for the attribution and the signature, by the way."

Laurence inclined his head.

"Ups the price by quite a few thousand bucks, obviously."

Laurence nodded.

"So how many more do you think young Murchison will produce?"

Laurence cleared his throat. "I think it unlikely there'll be many more. If any."

"I see. So what about his back catalogue?"

"I – don't know. I'll have to ask him."

"I don't mind if they're juvenilia. Like the second Grey Study."

"Yes."

"Just so long as they're signed and attributed."

"Yes. Of course."

"Dessert?"

"No thanks. Not for me."

"You haven't eaten much, Larry. You feeling okay?" Dominic didn't wait for a reply. He said to the waiter, "Three coffees. And dessert for Mr Swainton. Choose whatever you want, Freddy."

"I most certainly will, squire." Freddy was back on form. He had obviously cottoned on that Laurence was uncomfortable, and this had given him courage. He raised a long finger to the blond waiter who came over and, as Freddy's finger cocked towards his ear, bent towards him. "What can you tempt me with, you saucy young gigolo? How about a fruit-filled nut-stuffed knickerbocker glory?"

"I'm sorry, sir…"

"No, of course this establishment offers nothing so vulgar. Ah well," Freddy sighed, "I suppose I must content myself with the delights of your cheese board," – the waiter straightened as if stung, and Laurence saw Freddy's other hand return to his lap from the boy's nether regions - "if there's nothing else on offer."

Freddy and he waited for their taxi on the pavement outside.

Dominic King had been driven off in a black Daimler with tinted windows. Freddy remarked, "Seems a pleasant enough cove but he scares the piss out of me. You too, it looked like."

"What?"

"You also seemed to be having the urine fairly painfully extracted."

Laurence laughed. "Oh come on, Freddy…"

"Looked like you'd caught sight of your old granny's fanny, dear boy. Just what's he got on you?"

"Don't know what you're talking about."

"I've always thought you played the bluff old queen for more than it's worth. What are you hiding, you old reprobate?"

Laurence was saved from replying by the young waiter hurrying up to him. "Mr Bassett?"

"How come you get all the luck, Larry?" Freddy's nostrils were flaring like a stallion's.

"Phonecall for you, sir."

"Take the cab if it comes," Laurence said, "I'll just take the call."

"A likely story," Freddy sniffed. He stood disconsolately on the pavement, scanning the street for the taxi, as Laurence went back into the restaurant and picked up the phone. It was Deborah, who had closed the gallery early and was back at Hurlingham Mansions.

"Will hasn't arrived." She sounded distraught.

"The taxi was probably late. Phone the firm."

"I have. He should be here by now. I wish you'd gone yourself, Laurence."

"So do I." He paused. "Don't worry. I'll find out what's happened."

But he suddenly found himself physically incapable of doing anything other than ordering a double scotch on the rocks to try to blur the hideous clarity of those pale, cruel eyes.

******

The driver said, "Here we are," but Will didn't move.

"I said, here we are, mate." The driver turned to face him and opened the glass window that could be slid across to keep them separate. Will preferred the glass to be shut.

He shook his head, keeping his face forward.

"Hurlingham Mansions, Baron's Court. We're here." When Will didn't answer, the driver sighed. "You sure they discharged you? Shall I take you back?"

"W-wapping."

"Sorry?"

"I w-want to go to W-wapping."

"That's the other side of London! You sure, mate?"

Will nodded. With a shake of his head, the driver drove on. Will leaned forward and slid the glass partition shut.

He had spent the journey looking out, up into the sky. He'd been doing this a lot lately. He knew he'd spent a long time looking down at the ground, and when he began to look up he was told he was getting better. He must be really better now because he only wanted to look right up, above people's heads.

He quite liked the hospital. He felt quite safe. He liked Miss Routledge's visits, and Mr Bassett's too, although he didn't come so often. He didn't much like the other people there, although there was one lady who looked like a duchess who was nice to him. But he'd been given a lot of pills and he didn't like that, although he'd taken them because they were pleased with him when he took them and he thought it best to do as he was told or he might be sent away from the hospital like he was sent away from somewhere else a long time ago and he'd had to find his own way to somewhere else which hadn't turned out to be very pleasant.

But he'd stopped swallowing the pills a while ago, although he'd pretended he was still taking them when they asked. He'd forgotten about the Signs, but when one came along he knew what it was. And this must have been a Sign, because he'd had to sign something himself – Mr Bassett had made him write his name and that had unblocked something in his head, like a rusty key being turned in a lock, and a few memories had started to come back. Was that when he began looking up into the air? –

because a vision had floated into his mind that wouldn't go away. The vision was of a large bright place, and bright colours, and the feeling of living in the sky. It had been a good feeling, although mixed with other feelings not so good – sometimes he knew he'd felt scared, a grey kind of feeling - but mostly it was blue and yellow, a splash of red, the happy colours.

They had told him that Mr Bassett was coming to pick him up but in the end it was a taxi. That was all right, he liked taxis, he felt safe in taxis, although sometimes they had taken him places he hadn't wanted to go. He didn't have to get out, though, if he didn't want to. How had he known that? He'd always got out before, but this time he knew he didn't have to. Had someone told him?

...the someone sitting beside him in the taxi. It was nice he wasn't alone any more. And now he remembered the streets they were passing through, although the last time he'd done this it had been dark and Mr Bassett had been driving his big silver car. So when the driver stopped and turned round in his seat and slid the glass window open and said, "Okay, we're in Wapping. Where now?", he could tell him quite precisely and in great detail. In too great detail, apparently, because the glass window was shut quite rudely and the taxi took off again.

It was nice sitting in the back of the taxi with the someone else and being driven along the streets he knew quite well. He knew where he was now, and when the building came into view he tapped on the window and pointed, and the driver drove the taxi to the kerb and stopped.

"You sure this is where you want to be?" The driver wound down his side window, after Will had got out, to say this.

"Yes. Thank you."

He waited until the taxi had gone before he rang the bell. And when the man who looked after the building opened the door he asked for the key, as he was being told to do.

"Sorry, mate. It's been let."

Will went on smiling politely.

"I can't let you in." When Will still stood smiling, he said, "The lease was up. It ain't yours no more."

But it *was* his. He remembered. "My p-paintings are up there."

"They were all cleared out, mate." The man was looking at him closely. "Sorry, but you'd better see the bloke who paid your rent. Nothing to do with me." And the door was closed.

"It's not mine," Will said.

It is. It's still yours. Go up.

"I can't. I haven't got the key."

You don't need a key. See the steps over there? They go up.

"That's the fire escape."

Yes. It'll take you up.

And it did. The steps were on the outside of the building and the rungs had holes in them so he could see through them, right down to the ground. It was quite hard to keep looking up when he wanted to look down, but if he looked down it meant he wasn't better. So he kept his face turned upwards and his feet climbed the rungs and his hands gripped the rails both sides, so hard he could feel the cold metal eating into his flesh. It was a long way, and quite scary.

He remembered there had been eight flights of stairs inside, ten steps on each stair, eighty steps in all, but there were more than eighty steps on the outside because the fire escape didn't go straight up but went horizontal sometimes along the sides of the building so it took him a long time to reach the top. His feet clattered on the steps because they were made of iron even though he wore trainers, and sometimes he felt them swaying a bit which was scary, especially when he was halfway up a run of steps and it seemed like he was climbing into the sky.

You're all right. You're nearly there. Keep going.

"Yes. I'm nearly there." It was hard to say this, not because of the stammering (he wasn't stammering) but because he had no breath to speak properly.

You're there.

"Yes." It wasn't what he'd expected. He thought the top of the building would be flat, but it wasn't. It had little bumps and round openings and cables and pipes and more metal railings. He didn't like the look of it.

Go on. Walk on. It gets better.

He picked his way over the various obstacles, looking down. He had to look down if he didn't want to trip. There were puddles of dirty water, and feathers, and dead animals. He didn't look too closely, but there was a dead bird and something like looked like a rat. But as he walked it did get better, and suddenly he was out on a flat bit that stretched away into the sky.

There. You're here. It's nice, isn't it?

"Yes. It's nice."

Well done, Will.

"Thanks." He liked praise. "I like the smell of the air. And the wind. A nice clean wind. Thanks for bringing me here."

You're welcome.

"Shall I go on?"

If you want.

"I do. I will." And he walked on, to the middle and then to the end of the flat bit.

Don't look down. Look up. Into the sky.

"Yes. I'm looking. It's nice."

It's better up here, isn't it? You don't want to go down there any more, do you?

"No. I want to stay here."

You can. You can stay up here forever if you want.

"In the sky." He laughed.

Yes. Go on.

On. He must go on. If he wanted to stay up here, he must go on. So he took a deep breath and stepped, smiling, out into the clean, pure air

3. June 1987

On the other end of the line Huwie's voice says, slightly crossly (has she woken him up?), "Picture? What picture?"

"The Murchison. You said you'd taken it to be cleaned."

"I said I'd *take* it to be cleaned. I took it off the wall when – well, you know. The room was seen to."

"Then where did you put it?"

"Oh, I can't remember – the hall, probably. I leant it up against the wall so I'd remember to take it."

"But you didn't."

"No. It had gone – I thought you'd..." But his voice trails off. She wouldn't have touched it, obviously.

"Then we've lost it." Leo has never liked the picture but Daddy had told her it was the family heirloom, probably worth more than the house. She hadn't believed him, but then she doesn't know much about art.

It was only yesterday that she remembered the Murchison. Tony had mentioned something about the big red eye on the library wall being the only painting he'd taken much notice of, and Leo had suddenly realised they hadn't got it back. She'd realised she didn't even know where it had gone.

"Don't be so dramatic," says Huwie's voice in her ear, while another voice seems to be whispering in his. "It's there somewhere. Perhaps Mrs Wainwright moved it. Ask her."

"I can't. They've gone."

There is a silence. Then more whispering. Then, "Oh bloody hell, Leo...!" He puts the phone down.

He arrives on the doorstep forty minutes later. "Is anything else missing?" He pushes past her and sprints into the lounge.

"Pudge was there, wasn't she." She stands by the door, watching him scanning the walls and shelves.

"For God's sake, Leo, this is important!"

"You're just like Daddy. A big fat coward."

"I've never taken much notice of what's in here. He changed things round a lot, didn't he? Brought things from the gallery and took them back. The only thing that didn't change was the

Murchison…"

"It's just not fair, Huw."

He stops and frowns at her. Then his expression changes almost imperceptibly to one of contrition. "Oh, I know. You're right. And I will tell her. Honestly. It's just…"

She turns away. Huwie's face has reminded her so much of Daddy it's like a knife in her stomach. As she's holding back the tears she feels herself enfolded in his arms and leans her head against his lovely Daddy-like chest.

He says, after a moment, "When did the Wainwrights leave?"

"A couple of weeks ago."

"And you didn't think to check…?"

"Why should I? And anyway, if they'd taken the picture they would have left months ago, wouldn't they?"

"No, that's what's so clever. Don't you see? They've probably been squirreling away a lot of stuff without us even noticing. We can't go to the police now without looking bloody fools. And there's no proof…"

"Oh, I don't care anyway."

"And that's exactly what they counted on. Oh, bugger." He's still holding her, though. "The Murchison is worth a bomb. But they can't sell it, can they? It's probably destined for some private collection… Oh, bloody hell." He squeezes her more tightly. "So how are you, sis? Where's Tony?"

"I'm fine. Tony's working. He'll be back tomorrow."

"Do we know where the Wainwrights live?"

"No."

"Damn." He says, his chin joggling against her head, "They won't still be around though, will they? They'll be long gone. I always thought there was something funny about those two."

"Funny?"

"Funny strange. Creepy."

"Creepily funnily strange. Odd."

"Oddly creepily funnily strange. Weird."

"Weirdly oddly creepily funnily strange. Pax." She burrows deeper into his chest. They'd played these silly word games when they were young, driving Mummy and Uncle Alun crazy. A way of getting back at the Groosome Toosome. Oh, it's lovely to be Leo and Huwie again, the two of them against the world! So what if he's weak and cowardly and easily led? He's her baby brother and she loves him to bits.

They make an inventory of the room. Daddy had used the lounge as an extension of the gallery, bringing paintings home for a while and taking them back again. So she hadn't really noticed what were on the walls from one week to the next. She only knows that two Timberlakes had hung there before It happened, and they're not there now, having been replaced by a couple of others that seem familiar because paintings that had hung around Gali-Leo's and couldn't be shifted were recycled on to the walls of the lounge fairly frequently. She can't remember exactly when the Timberlakes had vanished, but they're probably back at the gallery. The few sculptures, too, are old friends. There is nothing new, nothing obviously worth anything much.

"It looks like we've been had," Huwie says, after they've finished.

"Why?"

"Well, they've taken the best things and left the tat. Or things we would have noticed missing. They relied on us being unobservant, and we've played right into their hands."

"Do we tell the police?"

"Tell them what? We don't even know what's missing, apart from the Murchison."

She says slowly, "What about that head? That horrible bat-winged thing he kept in his desk drawer?" That had never been in the lounge, but kept under lock and key. She now knows why.

"It wasn't there when – you know."

"You went through the drawers?"

"I had to. The police wanted to know if Dad left a note."

"A note?"

"Apparently most suicides do. Leo…" He hesitates, looks away from her as if he has something to hide. He *is* hiding something; she can read him like a book.

"What?" Why does he think she needs shielding? She's more adult than he is. At least she would never keep anyone

199

deliberately in the dark like he's doing Pudge.

"Oh – nothing. There wasn't one, not in the drawers. And the head wasn't there either. But I don't think they'd have taken that. It wasn't very saleable, was it? It was too - intimate." He looks at her and shrugs. They both know what they're talking about. They've never openly discussed Daddy's reputation and won't start now. "Perhaps," he says, "he gave it back to her. Gemma's mother. She made it, after all."

She says, after a pause, "We know someone who might be able to help us."

"Who?" He laughs. "Oh, you mean Old Pokerface."

"Miss Rottweiler."

"Deborah Dusty Drawers."

Leo says slowly, "I'll pay her a visit. I always meant to, but kept putting it off. And she doesn't want to see us, does she? She hasn't come here since Daddy's funeral." She pauses, to let Huwie remonstrate if he wants, but he doesn't. Of course he'll leave it up to her since she's volunteered. "I'll go tomorrow."

"Thanks, sis." He sounds relieved. "And I will tell Pudge, I promise. Just – well, just not yet, okay?"

After he's left, she goes along the hall to the library. Taking a deep breath, she enters, taking purposeful strides up to the desk, keeping her face averted from the wall. The drawers are unlocked, their contents neatly sorted. The bat-winged head isn't there.

The filing cabinet, then. It's a wide mahogany one that matches the desk, two deep drawers that usually contain only one or two files brought back from the office. The top one is empty. The bottom one is locked.

Oh, she shouldn't be snooping on Daddy, it isn't fair, but she goes back to the desk and sorts out the keys, fits them to the desk drawers. One is left over that doesn't match, but yes, it fits the bottom drawer of the filing cabinet.

Pausing just a fraction before turning it in the lock, she pulls the drawer open. It's empty. And yet something strikes her as strange; this drawer seems to be shallower than the top one, although on the outside they are both the same depth. She taps the bottom with her fingers, and it rocks slightly. It's a dividing shelf which she lifts carefully out - and there is the bat-winged head scowling up at her. She's never looked at it properly; it has always frightened her, made her feel – what? Unloved? Insecure? Because Daddy had obviously treasured it above her? No, of course not. And it's not scowling, really. The face isn't hostile, just unfriendly, stern – suspicious? Frightened? Is that fear in his eyes, as well as accusation?

No wonder Daddy had studied it so often. She is aware she's been staring at it for a long time herself, her gaze held by that uncompromising glare. She becomes aware, too, that she's sitting in Daddy's chair, gripping the armrests so tightly her knuckles have turned white. Because next to the bat-winged head is another sculpture, one even more hideous, and both rest on the canvas surface of a painting that she knows she will have to take out and study - and knows, too, that she is going to regret doing it.

4.   April 1980

The gallery had been closed for a week as a mark of respect. Even this merely excited more media interest. Journalists and photographers camped outside the doors for days. Rarely had the arts been so much in the news – the treachery of Blunt, the forgeries of Keating and now the untimely death of Will Murchison.

A mark of respect, yes – but also expedience. Rosemary had left, Deborah was walled up in Baron's Court. Laurence found himself going through the motions – giving interviews, making the necessary arrangements with police, Coroner and funeral parlour – without even his brain being actively engaged.

He had first heard the news on the radio, which he'd switched on moments after he'd arrived home. About to pour himself a coffee, he heard the words, "...chison, a rising young talent in the art world, found in an alleyway in East London. Extensive injuries on the body point to his having jumped off the roof of a nearby eight-storey building..." The next minute, the phone began to ring.

He had left the house immediately, not even stopping to put on a coat. His brain had ceased working. He passed along the streets like a dead man among people who were walking ghosts. They jostled against him, shouldered him out of their way but he felt nothing. He crossed roads clogged with traffic without even looking. He stepped into the path of an oncoming bus but it stopped just in time amid a cacophony of horns and shouts that reached him only through aeons of space. He was walking through a Brugel landscape - no, a Bosch depiction of hell. People were grotesques. Their conversation was the dialogue of the damned, each face wore a rictus of dread.

He walked, one foot in front of the other, head down so no one would see him. Great dry shudders convulsed his dead walking body but he couldn't stop. He walked. He walked for miles. He walked until the streets emptied, until the ghosts thinned out, disappeared. Until the night darkened and grew cold.

He found himself in Baron's Court.

He walked up the three steps and rang the top bell. He said, "It's me."

The door opened and he walked into a long dark corridor, up the long dark stairs. Up from the darkness to a pool of light at the top. A voice said, "Come in."

He went in. The light was extinguished. It took place in the dark. His punishment. His atonement. The last, worst flagellation of his flesh, the final purification of his soul.

After that, he was on his own.

Leo said, "Daddy, please don't be sad." She wound her arms round his neck, kissed his face. He could only stroke her hair and stare at the picture, high on the wall.

"Daddy, why won't you look at me?" That great red eyeball, that wheel that went nowhere. "I hate that horrible picture! Take it down!"

No, he would never take it down. It would stare back at him for the rest of his days. His Mea Culpa.

But what had he done? Only failed to pick Will up, that was all. If he'd picked him up, dropped him off at Hurlingham Mansions, would the result have been different? Yes, of course it would. Deborah would have looked after him. She would never have let him go back to Wapping. He would have been a prisoner in Baron's Court, a prisoner of the pills. He could have chosen Baron's Court, and safety.

But Will had outsmarted them all. Brave lad. Bravo, lad.

He, Laurence, would never have had the courage.

The media hyenas made a meal of it. A photograph of Laurence leering at the camera, his arm around a thin, haggard, wide-eyed Will, made front page news. In the background, all too visible, was Wheels One.

When the gallery opened again, and Miss Routledge back in charge – Miss Routledge in her black suit, black stockings, black no-nonsense shoes, heavy glasses always on her nose now, not dangling on a chain – he had a visit from Mrs Dawson. Mrs Murchison, as never was. Diane Jane Erica Hallam, formerly of Hackney.

She was a small, faded little woman, probably once very pretty, accompanied by a tall, weasel-faced man who stood, hand clamped firmly on her shoulder as she perched herself on the very edge of the ladderback chair in front of his desk. She spoke in a wispy, apologetic voice, only occasionally looking across at him. The man never took his eyes from Laurence's face.

"We're really grateful to you for looking after Will," she'd said; and, "...he was always difficult, when I was on my own it was almost impossible to cope," and, "...the social wasn't much help, he wasn't bad enough to be taken in," and, "...we didn't want to do what we did but there really wasn't any other way..." and then the man, cutting in with a thick Geordie accent: "We heard he was making some money out of his painting, is that reet, mon?"

He told them about the trust fund and explained how they should go about making their claim. Mr Dawson asked how much it was worth. Diane Jane Erica's eyes filled with tears; Mr Dawson's weasel face cracked into an unaccustomed smile. "Bloody hell, Di," he said, "who'd have thought he'd be worth that mooch?", and the pair of them made an exit.

The next, and last, time he saw them was at the funeral.

He slipped a note into the account book. It had taken him all night to compose, and still it didn't express what he felt. Nothing, of course, could. He couldn't bring himself to look her straight in the eyes. He couldn't bear to see her closed, chiselled profile as she sat at her desk downstairs. He didn't know which was worse: her silent icy containment in the gallery or the sound of her naked grief as he passed the ladies toilet on his way to the gents when they closed for lunch. She didn't bring his tray up any more.

She never mentioned the note.

He loaded the eight unfinished canvases, the ones he'd cleared out of the loft when the lease expired, into the boot of his Jag and drove to Dermot's little country cottage in Woodstock. Dermot had given up city life, saying he was fed up with the rat race. Dermot hadn't been a rat for some time, Laurence thought and, drawing up outside a little square bungalow on a small plot of untended land, catching sight of the Augustus John-like figure in his brown corduroy jacket and red neckerchief hanging over the fence puffing at his pipe, he knew why.

Inside, the bungalow was small, cramped and full of finished and unfinished canvases. "Come to choose the best?" Dermot asked, smiling. "No, don't bother to think up excuses. Even without the rising star of the firmament, I know I'm washed up. I was sorry to hear about it, by the way." He filled a battered kettle from a tap in the kitchen area of the front room. "Poor bugger. Can't help thinking I might have had something to do with – you know."

"I don't think so. He'd got over that."

"It was something else then? Pushed him over the edge?" Dermot gave a wry grimace. "Sorry. Wrong turn of phrase."

"We'll never know. The Coroner's verdict will be the usual balance of mind disturbed."

"Right." Dermot dropped teabags in two mugs. "I'd like to offer something a bit more exciting but the cocktail bar's non-existent."

Drinking his tea, Laurence said, "Do you want to know what happened to your Study in Grey?"

"Not particularly."

"It's in America. It sold for ten thousand dollars."

"Christ."

"It would easily be worth treble that now. I got Will to sign and backdate it."

"Bloody hell, Laurence!"

Laurence said steadily, "You can turn me in if you want. I deserve it."

"So how do I explain painting the damn thing?" Dermot put down his mug. "Ten thousand bucks, and you paid me a miserable five hundred pounds."

"I'll make up the difference. The thing is, Dermot – I've got eight more canvases in the car. And a punter willing to buy. Megabucks."

Dermot stared at him.

"What do you think?"

"It's certainly do-able. Question is, do we want to do it?"

"Do you, Dermot?"

"No name, no pack drill?"

"That's right. Juvenilia. Unsigned."

"Attributed?"

"That's up to me. Entirely my judgement."

"Can't go wrong, can it?"

"No." It couldn't. Dominic King would be entirely satisfied. The collection, now set for astronomical heights, wouldn't go out of his ownership, would rarely, if ever, be publicly exhibited. The knowledge that he had the entire Murchison canon – except Wheels One, which he didn't know about, and Maudie's happy picture, which he probably did – would give him enormous kudos in the art world.

"Why are you doing this?" Dermot asked.

He had asked himself that all the way to Woodstock. He had never consciously broken the law before; hidden receipts from the Inland Revenue, told little white lies to prospective clients about shaky provenance; that was all in a day's work. But never consciously flouted the law. So why was he doing it now? It wasn't only that, deep down, he wondered if he'd really done his best for Timberlake; if he could have done a better job of representing him. During the Seventies he might have been too wound up in his own career to bother enough about Dermot's. Did Timberlake blame him for his slide from the heights of success down to relative obscurity, to life in this ugly bungalow in the backwoods? But that had not been his fault; surely not. No, this unaccustomed rashness had something to do with

206

Dominic King. Getting one over on Dominic King. Playing a dangerous game, just for the hell of it.

"Just because I can." He felt strangely, wildly reckless. "There's money to be made. You need it. I can get it. Other bastards do it all the time and get away with it, why not us?"

"Then you're on, Larry."

They shook hands. This was the second handshake, he thought, that would change his life. The first one, fifteen years ago, exchanged with Nicholas Woollidge in the Matron's office of the Swansea children's home, had started his fall from grace and his elevation to wealth. Where this one would lead, he didn't know. And didn't, he realised, even care.

PART FOUR

1985 to 1987

1.   September 1985

On the morning the parcel arrived, Deborah Routledge was at her usual place behind the desk downstairs in Gali-Leo's, getting to grips with the monthly accounts on the new computer. She merely looked up as the courier struggled in through the door with a large lumpy rectangular package which he propped against the desk, and signed the chitty he gave her. And then she forgot it until about half an hour later, when Laurence came in. Normally she opened all correspondence, unless of course it was marked Confidential, even if personally addressed to him. But the accounts had taken all her attention and she remembered the parcel only when Laurence bent down and read the label.

"Are we expecting anything?"

"Pardon?"

"Looks like a picture. Strange it's come through the post." He knelt down and tore the paper off a corner. "More than one, it looks like. Give me a hand, Deborah."

She rose and came round to the front of the desk. Together they stripped the paper and, when completed, she straightened to go back to her chair. He grabbed her hand.

"Laurence…"

"I'm on my knees. I asked for your hand."

Smiling, she shook her head and withdrew her hand from his and took her place behind the desk. He clambered clumsily to his feet, groaning. "Bloody arthritics. I could do with a massage."

"There are plenty of masseuses advertised in the local telephone box."

"Ah, but they don't have your touch, Deborah."

"No one has that." She wetted the tip of her pencil with her tongue and went on with her calculations. A few minutes later, aware that he hadn't gone upstairs, or even moved, aware too of a different quality in the air around her, she lifted her eyes from the columns of figures and saw him standing stock still, his face ashen.

"Laurence! What's the matter?" Oh God, was her first thought, he's having a heart attack. He was a big man and ate all the wrong foods; he drank to excess; he took no exercise; he drove everywhere in his new silver-grey Jag. He was a prime candidate, according to all the medical articles she'd read. This, she now realised, had been her worst nightmare for years.

Rising so hurriedly the chair tipped backwards and crashed against the wall, she flew to him. But he wasn't about to keel over, although he'd put out a hand and was steadying himself against the desk. He grasped her arm, pulled her round against him.

"It's her," he said.

"Who?"

"Deirdre."

The name was familiar, even though he hadn't mentioned it in years. She followed the direction of his eyes down to the painting propped up against the desk, one of three canvases that the parcel had contained along with a small square cardboard box with an envelope sellotaped to it.

She peered at it. If this was an example of the work of the mysterious Deirdre, the hugely talented artist Laurence had fathered a daughter on twenty years ago, she didn't know why he had made all that fuss. Pitted with some kind of mould, it was merely quite a competent painting of a girl with tumbling black hair in a red dress that almost seemed to be falling off her.

"Well," she said, her voice back to normal now her fears had abated, "if you were worried you'd ruined a world-shattering talent, I think I can safely say…"

"No," he said, "the girl's Deirdre. I painted the picture." He lifted it up in both hands. "It's crap, isn't it." He gave a sound between a snort and a hiccup.

She was staring at the one now uncovered. Now this – this *was* a work of near-genius. Two little girls, hand in hand, one dark and one fair. Both about four or five, both laughing, both dressed in party dresses; but somehow the different characters shone through, the fair-haired girl timid and slightly vacuous, the dark-haired one stubborn and wilful and frightened and deeply unhappy. How could all that be shown by a few strokes of a brush? – and yet it was all there, so naked, so unsentimental, that

212

she felt a lump come to her throat. Oh, stupid, stupid! – all those years she had kept her feelings bottled up and now – oh, now she could cry at the drop of a hat.

"How the hell…" Laurence was tearing the envelope off the box. She heard the crackle of the sellotape, the opening of the paper, but her eyes were still fastened on the picture. "Oh, good Lord Almighty." He slumped against the desk; she felt it shift under his weight.

She moved the picture aside and looked at the third. This was of the same dark-haired girl standing next to a pig, as big as she was. Their expressions were so similar it could have been comical, but again there was that depth to the child's face – this time frowning, belligerent – that caused her to snatch her breath. The pig had been given a personality – inquisitive, almost bolshie – and the girl likewise, but also oh, again, so heartrendingly fearful and sad that Deborah had to look away, and take a few deep breaths, before she could bring her attention back to Laurence, slumped over the letter.

"Who sent them?" Her voice sounded reedy and thin.

He waved the paper at her. "I don't believe it. Deborah, this is almost beyond…" And then he was staring down at the paintings and was bereft of all speech.

She couldn't read the letter, but she could, and did, open the box. Swathed in bubblewrap was a small, perfect sculpture, only a little bigger than a fist - a bat with serrated wings outstretched but no body; it was all face, and a face of such fierce but vulnerable hostility that she wrapped it up again quickly and placed it back in the box before Laurence could see it. It wasn't the child's face but a man's – a boy's – Nicholas Woollidge's, the face of the photograph in the newspaper but older, the face Will might have had if he'd been given insight and intelligence instead of instinct and grace.

How long they both stood speechless she didn't know; it seemed hours before she cleared her throat and said, "Go upstairs and I'll bring you a coffee," knowing that the first thing he'd do would be to pour himself a stiff scotch, and she couldn't blame him.

She found out later where the parcel had come from. She read the letter: *...they might be worth something, but then I'm only a humble physicist... might need cleaning, especially the gypsy girl... the mother of a girlfriend of mine, I thought you might be interested... she could do with the money, this house is almost falling to bits...* It was signed 'Sebastian', with 'Montfort' in brackets.

She found out later still that Sebastian Montfort was the son of Sir Denis Montfort, QC, who in his less exalted days had handled Laurence's divorce; they'd been students at Cambridge together. The girlfriend was Gemma, the dark-haired child in the paintings. The artist was Deirdre Thomas, whom Laurence had known in Swansea, and who was now calling herself Drusilla Belling and mouldering away in a tumbledown cottage in Suffolk.

******

She had spent her own incarceration five years ago amid the genteel clutter of her shabby flat. She had watched television endlessly, sitting on the settee eating cold baked beans out of tins. She watched repeats of early Seventies situation comedies, remembering watching them the first time round: *Open All Hours, Dad's Army, Whatever Happened to the Likely Lads?* Arkwright's stutter, which had made them both laugh, now made her weep. Mainwaring's 'stupid boy!', Fraser's 'doomed, doomed!', likewise. The Geordie accents of Terry and Bob, ditto – although Will's was never so pronounced. Will had spent most of his life at home with his mother. (She still watched these sitcoms; she had treated herself to a video recorder, made herself master the switches and knobs, and watched recorded repeats.)

She had thought the anguish would never pass. And it never had, although as the months, years, passed, she managed to contain it – in public, at least. Brought the shutters down. Constructed a sheet of ice around herself. She should never have opened herself up in the first place. Stupid, stupid – by allowing emotions to enter, you were inviting nothing but grief.

The room at the end of the corridor was kept locked. She hid the key at the back of the drawer, knowing she would never use it again.

She had, of course, forgiven him. Eventually. Like Freddy.

Not entirely, though. She kept his note in the key drawer. Sometimes she sat all evening at the kitchen table with the note in front of her, just looking at the words, full of loops and squiggles. Usually large and florid, he had consciously made his handwriting smaller and less ostentatious. She could study a phrase for hours: ...*Deborah, I know I'm asking for the impossible. Forgiveness. Your forgiveness... I will never, ever forgive myself.... All I can say is that I'm so very very sorry*...

Just words. Easily written. And she knew him well enough to know that he *had* forgiven himself; had justified his actions in his mind, had come to the conclusion that he had done nothing very much wrong at all. Merely had put a lunch date before Will. He had sent a taxi, hadn't he?

And of course he had atoned. He had submitted to her punishment (she had used the thick leather tawse) with barely a whimper; had spent most of the night strapped down on the table while she lay in the soft comfort of the cotton sheets under the silk duvet and listened to his weeping. She had relented in the early hours when he had fallen asleep, released him and covered him with a soft cashmere blanket. He had risen the next morning, uncomplaining, and gone off to formally identify the body. Will's poor broken body laid out on a slab.

...*I haven't been a good man. It's not enough for intentions to be good, I know that now. If I could make amends I would, but there's nothing anyone can do now*...

A whole paragraph of self-pity. She had felt no pity for months. Pity, or something like it, had crept up on her almost without her knowledge. Why else had she stayed on at the gallery, the keeper of his secrets? Making slight adjustments in the accounts, shipping off works of art to the Venn Pegasus Agency in the names of various clients who she knew were bogus, who didn't exist, or who existed only in the person of

215

Dominic King? Tightening the noose around his neck, a noose of his own making. Those teardrops on his doodle pad – the faces were all his.

She would remain his faithful servant. It was all she had left.

…but I hope …we can look forward to a future. Perhaps together?… Deborah, I need your help. I need you. Help me.

Emotional blackmail. She had no emotions. Blackmail, then. But that was all the future held anyway. She could make him suffer on her terms. Make him believe there was a future… And possibly there could be. In time. Perhaps.

Oh Laurence. A weak, wicked man. Weakness *was* wicked. But endearing. Lovable, even.

As always, when she reached these thoughts, she folded the note around the key to the third bedroom and shut it away in the drawer.

They had never replaced Rosemary. Neither of them had mentioned it. The gallery was run as efficiently as usual by the pair of them; by her, mainly. No need to involve a third party in its affairs. And if, sometimes, they had to close in normal business hours, it didn't really matter. Money arrived every month, even if nothing had been shipped that month. A retainer fee, Laurence called it.

The discovery of Will's back list (eight unsigned paintings Laurence told her his mother had sent him, having found out how valuable they would become) had surprised her. The three she had seen seemed unusually competent for a teenager, unusually disciplined. They were variations on a theme, entitled *Study in Blue & Green, Nos 1-3*, and featured his trademark swirls and dots in very precise patterns. She'd have thought that Will, in his younger days, would have been more erratic. More experimental. But who could say what had gone on in that head of his? Perhaps he became more undisciplined as he got older. Trust Will to do things his way.

His fame had rocketed in the last five years. His was a strange reputation, based almost entirely on prints and photographs of the originals, most of which were in the sole ownership of one

216

mysterious collector based, it was rumoured, in the United States. Will Murchison's mental problems had elevated his artistic abilities to godlike proportions. The manner of his death had given his work an almost mythological status.

To Deborah, though, he remained the son she never had, and she had never stopped grieving for him.

******

The daughter whom Laurence had never seen arrived Friday lunchtime at Gali-Leo's together with the boyfriend. Laurence, Deborah was fairly sure, was not expecting her; he was expecting Sebastian to bring Drusilla Belling, née Deirdre Thomas. He was up in his office, no doubt pacing the room, hiding behind the curtains whenever a taxi drew up. One had just left, bearing off Cyril Lyttleton with one of the three unsigned Murchisons Laurence had kept back from Denver – "Why should they get all the goodies," he'd said, "and leave us with nothing?" – but Deborah thought he was playing a dangerous game. The whole future of the gallery now rested on the goodwill of the Venn Pegasus Agency and its shadowy client.

Maudie Madison had phoned and told Laurence that she'd been approached about *Boats and Birds* and been offered an astronomical sum for a painting that had cost her £500. What should she do? And Deborah had been in the office to hear him tell Maudie to hold on to it; it would be worth even more outside the United States, the only signed Murchison on the loose. When he'd put down the phone, she'd murmured, "Is that wise?"

"What are you getting at, Deborah?"

"I thought you'd agreed to sell the entire canon to VPA."

"Who on earth told you that?"

"Freddy."

"Well, he's wrong." He passed a hand over his hair, then rubbed the side of his nose with his thumb. "Just because he can be bought with a few miserable dollars and lunch at the Gav…" He stopped, coughed. He had never told her what had happened at that lunch, the lunch that had cost Will's life. But Freddy had filled her in on a few details. She had studied his face carefully. It held an expression she had been seeing more frequently lately: anger, obstinacy - greed... He had changed over the years, as she herself had. They couldn't pretend they were the same people any more.

Laurence had kept one of the unsigned Murchisons which he had just sold to Cyril. Apparently he needed a sizeable chunk of money to purchase a house on the south coast for his housekeeper and her husband, who were well over retirement age. Cyril had been after a Murchison for years. She and Dermot Timberlake had been given the others. Hers was *Study in Blue and Green #1*. On the back Laurence had written on a Gali-Leo's label: *Will Murchison, unsigned, circa 1974,* with his signature. She had hung it above her bed and spent long hours looking at it. Even though she couldn't find Will in it, even a younger Will, there was something about it that mesmerised her. Although ostensibly complete in itself, it seemed somehow unfinished.

She knew, though, she could never sell it. It was the only thing she had left to remind her of Will.

Just after Cyril left, the doorbell bleeped again. And in they came – a tall young man of about twenty-three followed by – well, a girl who could only be Gemma. The unhappy little girl in the pictures had blossomed into a striking young woman whose dark beauty contrasted perfectly with Sebastian Montfort's louche blond good looks. He could be one of the golden-haired Adonises who graced his parties, she thought, as she pressed the button on the intercom and informed Laurence they'd arrived.

As she watched them mount the stairs she wondered at his reaction. Would it be heart attack time again? She brought the pills out of her drawer, just in case. But there was no sound of distress from above, and when they eventually came downstairs Laurence was leading the way, his face alight with joy. She raised her eyebrows at him, and he shook his head. She didn't know, then. He hadn't told her. Would he tell her over lunch? Knowing him as she did, he would not be able to keep himself from telling her she was his daughter. And as he ushered them out the back into the car park, she wondered what his other brat of a daughter Leonora would have to say about that.

******

Life had a strange way of getting its own back, Laurence thought. You might think you'd travelled on, put distance between you and the past, and then – wham! – it reared up and hit you right between the eyes. You could never escape. The past travelled with you, it was there beside you, in front of you, you could never outrun it.

"I'm your father," he had told Gemma, after ascertaining that there was no other fellow in her mother's life, no other man she'd called father all these years. Of course the poor girl had been stunned; Sebastian, too. Poor Sebastian, who'd made contact, obviously, not only because of the paintings he'd discovered mouldering away in a Suffolk attic but because he wanted Laurence's help to find him a job in television, fronting popular science programmes. Science, Laurence might have told him, was almost as unpopular as the arts on the telly – although *Whither Art?,* so long on the shelf, had now been resurrected as *Art Meets Life,* Laurence informing the nation's housewives on how their various domestic chores had been portrayed over the centuries by the Old Masters, leading up to how their now 'labour-saving' gadgets had been artfully designed to fuse practicality with aesthetics.

"You have a sister," he'd informed Huwie over the phone, and left Huwie to tell his other sister of her existence. What a coward he was! And Huwie was not noted for his tact; he would have blundered feet first into the revelation, not prepared Leo for it in bite-sized stages. Well, he couldn't blame Huwie; he hadn't exactly prepared Gemma, had he? Just blundered feet-first into the revelation…

Fri 13 Sept (!!! – apt or wot!!!) 10.17pm
BOMBSHELL. Daddy has thrown us a Bombshell. Who would have thort a phonecall could change your whole life? Huwie took it. I could tell he

was shocked, but then he larfed. Larfed!! Would you larf if you'd been told you had a sister you never even knew about?? I WILL NEVER FORGIVE HIM, EVER. He told me I was his only preshus princess. He lied. He's a big fat liar. Oh, I could SCREEEEM!!!

Was that wot all the fuss was about in Swansea? Not about boys at all, but Her, the girl who came every Friday for lessons? Huwie asked if I remember her but I don't, not really. I wasn't even 3. He said Daddy said I called her Dee-dee. And she was only 15!!!

Anyway. Her name's Gemma and she's not like us at all. She's quite shy and wears awful clothes. I'll take her in hand. It might not be so bad if we can be frends. But she's a bit of a bloostocking, she's studying politics and economics at Cambridge. Daddy sat all night just looking at her, smiling. He's never looked at me like that. I'll try to be frends but inside I'm SEEEETHING. It's not fair. Huwie would say I'm being childish but it's different for him, he's a man. I could tell he liked her. If she comes between me and Huwie I'll scratch her eyes out. I meen it.

This is the first day of the rest of my life and nothing will ever be the same again

A few days after he had made that momentous announcement to Gemma, Nick had turned up on the doorstep, giving Laurence one of the most profound shocks of his life. He hadn't changed, just grown taller and broader; the same hair, the same face, the same expression of guarded watchfulness. He had only come to see Gemma, he said, to make sure she was happy. He'd refused to talk about the past, refused to put Laurence's mind at rest about his guilts and omissions. Laurence had lived for twenty years blaming himself for his part in Nick's past, wanting to explain, to avert Nick's hatred; to be told, in no uncertain terms, that Nick himself was totally indifferent.

"Forget it," he'd said. "I forgot it years ago."

Mon 16 Sept 8.39pm

A very strange day. It started well – Daddy gave us some money to buy clothes so we went shopping. We croozed all the shops, tried on everything, Gemma of course looking fantastic in it all, even the crap. Then we stopped off at Freida's and got her hair cut. She wasn't too keen, but in the end

Giorgi perswaded her. And he was right! – she looks fantastic. It's taken years off her, makes her look 14 instead of the 40 she looked in that county crap. Couldn't wait to get back to show Daddy.

But as soon as we went into the lounge I knew something was wrong. Daddy wasn't alone. There was a man with him, they were talking, they were face to face over the cocktale bar but I could tell right away he wasn't frendly, there was a terrible tenshun in the air (I think I'm sykick or something, atmospheers just get to me) – and in that split second I knew Daddy was terribly unhappy. But Gemma ran up to the Man and throo her arms round him, and I could tell there was something between them. He's older than her but he's got one of those faces that never age, that have always been 30 even at 13. And he had the most wonderful dark curly hair and brown eyes. Him and Gemma just looked so good together.

She took him off into the garden and he didn't come back. And Daddy went off to his library and ½ hour later I went in there and he was just sitting drinking his wisky and staring at that awful eyeball painting. I know he's in one of his glooms that will take days for him to get out of.

Gemma didn't say anything when she came back in. She was in a bit of a strange mood at first, but she radiated happyness. She's next door in her room and I can still feel the heet through the wall. It's something more than love. I think I'm jelous. Will I ever feel this way about anybody? On second thorts it doesn't really matter, becoz I don't think I want to.

Some things, of course, were best told head-on, without prevarication. A shock was a shock, however well-prepared one was. And Laurence, having delivered his own thunderbolt, couldn't blame Gemma for the shock she'd given him this morning, head-on, on her twentieth birthday. "I was at least three weeks premature," she'd said, off-the-cuff, apropos of nothing, and failed to see him reeling from the revelation. For, of course, she should have been late; first babies usually arrived late, and she should have been a week or so overdue.

After Gemma and Leo had gone off on another shopping expedition, Laurence had driven his Jag to Suffolk to call on Deirdre; a strange, almost surreal visit. He had made up his mind to ask her who Gemma's real father was, what exactly had happened when she'd run off to London; to set the record straight once and for all. But once in that dilapidated cottage, sitting in a room strangely divested of all personality (there were no paintings, no drawings, no sculptures, no junk of any sort), his resolve had deserted him. He had been seduced again by that helpless enchantment he remembered all those years ago in Swansea. Deirdre herself had hardly changed; he recognised immediately the young girl behind the grown woman's more guarded gaze. She was still his little Beggar Maid. And she had said nothing either. They had both been conspirators, shielding themselves from the truth simply by omission. And if she was happy to keep it so, then so was he.

Returning from that visit, buoyed up - and, as he'd allowed himself to believe, forgiven – he had switched over to Radio 4 to hear the six o'clock news on the car radio. And had listened to an account of human bones being dug up on a Welsh farm, the site of a commune in the late Sixties, the body apparently having been dismembered and buried in the woods fifteen years ago.

The past had reared up again; he had relived his journey to Caernarvon in March 1971, that glimpse of Nick in the dock as he'd been sentenced to three years for possession of offensive weapons. Relived, too, his meeting with Nick's pregnant ex-girlfriend from whom he had found out that Deirdre – now calling herself Dee – had also been at the commune with her four-year-old daughter Gemma. From whom he had also found out that the person she blamed for the weapons was the leader of the hippies, an Irish drug taker and free love promoter who called himself King.

Patrick King, he'd found out from Hilary. Younger brother of Dominic King, a well-respected businessman recently relocated to Denver and fast moving up the corporate ladder, whose fingers would one day stretch out to infiltrate many pies. Including armaments. And art.

Oh yes, the past certainly travelled with him. The wheel had picked up debris that was still riding the years, that would, one day, engulf him. Wheels and circles, circles and wheels. Will, in his innocence, had been wiser than them all.

A few days ago he had booked a table for eight at Langan's to celebrate Gemma's birthday, when his life had seemed relatively straightforward. He had sat with his family and their various consorts in the opulent surroundings of the restaurant, a fond father footing the not inconsiderable bill.

There was Gemma, alight with happiness, seeming to radiate a glow that reached out even to him, seated opposite. Was he looking at her with new eyes, now he knew she wasn't his? No, he didn't think so. There was an ache in his loins, a sadness lodged in his heart, but he still felt proud and paternal. He didn't think she would guess the truth by any word or deed from him. Surely it was kinder to keep her in ignorance? – at least for a while. Some day he would tell her, when the time was right. But that wasn't yet.

He hadn't told her about the bones. She obviously hadn't heard the six o'clock news. There might be something in the paper tomorrow, which he would keep from her. Unless the body turned out to be someone important, there would probably be nothing more heard about it.

Next to her, on her right, was Huwie. No, he couldn't go on calling him Huwie - on Huw's right, and Laurence's left, was his latest girl – Charlotte or Charmian or some such (all his girls were top drawer – where on earth did he find them?). Huwie – Huw - had hardly spoken to her all evening, his attention being focused on Gemma. Poor Charlie had hardly eaten anything, but then she was probably on some diet or other (there was nothing of her, a beanpole of a girl).

On Gemma's left was Tony Masterson, who had rather commandeered her after that last party Laurence had thrown to introduce her to his friends. He had since carried her off almost every night to some theatre show or music gig, and was now valiantly trying to keep up his end of the conversation. Laurence recognised the tack Huw was taking. His son, after a late start, was fast gaining a reputation as a latter-day Casanova. Poor Charlie wouldn't last long.

On Tony's left sat Leo, who had hardly said a word all evening. She was attacking her pasta as if it were a mortal enemy, shooting black looks at Tony. And on Leo's left was poor Sandeep, grave and courteous, his dark eyes resting on Leo with a sad patience. Laurence had hopes that Leo had at last found a chap who would calm her down, but he was beginning to think Sandeep would go the way of all others. He knew his daughter so well. She baited her traps for men who provided a challenge, but when she'd hooked them she lost interest. Tony was a friend from work, but since he'd been dating Gemma (and was 'dating' the right word? – they were only enjoying each other's company, surely), Leo had jettisoned poor Sandy from her affections. Was she now discovering feelings for Tony, or was she merely jealous of his interest in Gemma?

Oh God. The table was a mass of seething undercurrents. He glanced to his right, at Deborah, bringing them full circle. He would like to believe that Deborah was still his rock, his anchor, but could he be certain of this? She had changed, of course, as he had. She hadn't forgiven him, he knew, for a long while after Will's death, but then he hadn't expected her to. At least she had kept working for him. By a campaign of attrition he had worn down her defences; by putting on an act of remorse and contrition he had slowly but surely won her back to his side (and was it an act? – of course not, oh God, he *had* been remorseful and contrite, he prayed every night for forgiveness, he had castigated himself for years, lashing himself mentally since she had refused him the physical solace of the Red Room – how much more could she expect?)

… *I haven't been a good man,* he had written in his note. *I've thought through my entire life and it doesn't add up to much… It's not enough for intentions to be good, I know that now.* Just ink on paper; mere words couldn't convey the weight of sincerity (and the more he'd tried, the less they conveyed). But he had been sincere. …*I hope these feelings will pass and we can look forward to a future,* he had gone on. *Perhaps together? Who knows. I only know I need someone to keep me on the straight and narrow… Deborah, I need your help. I need you. Help me.* Every word written from the heart. He hadn't known he was going to write them, but once written he knew he had meant every word. A future with Deborah was his only hope of salvation. He would work on her. He would persuade her. Eventually.

"This is my best birthday ever," Gemma had said, reaching across for him. "Thank you, Laurence." She couldn't call him Dad, like Huw, or Daddy, like Leo; Laurence would have to suffice. He had smiled at her, hoping he looked proud and paternal. Inside, he was bleeding. "And it's all thanks to Sebastian."

Sebastian. Poor Sebastian, whose hopes of a media career had suffered a setback. Laurence had asked him to stay on in London with Gemma, but of course he'd refused and gone back to his parents in Berkshire. He, Laurence, would make it up to him; invite him down later and talk to him about a career in television. Even physics might prove riveting viewing if Sebastian were its presenter; the boy was certainly telegenic, and that was all the criteria needed these days to make it big on the box.

Mon 23 Sept 10.13pm (Autumnal Equinox)

Gemma's birthday. 20 years and 9 months ago (give or take a few days) Daddy did the Deed. I wonder where it happened? Did Mummy know? - she can't have, because she thought he liked boys. She had grounds for divorce right there, but she didn't set the divorce in motion until March 65; the cort case was finally settled in September, probably around Gemma's birth. I remember it was a good time for us, becoz Mummy came in for a lot of Daddy's inheritance and we moved from Swansea to the Gower, into a nice big house with a proper garden. I remember that becoz Huwie was stung by a bee when he put his nose to a flower and had to be taken to hospital. He's never thort much of nature since. It was fate too becoz Uncle Alun lived next door, he was married then but he got divorced about 4 years later and him and Mummy got married. And then 2 years later along came the Groosome Toosome…

Anyway. Gemma's birthday. We went out shopping again and bought bag loads of stuff. Daddy wasn't in when we got back. He'd gone out in the Jag. He didn't get back till about 7pm and he went strait into the library. I thought he'd got over the glooms but when I went in he was sitting there, drinking his whisky. He wasn't looking at the picture, tho. He was looking at a horrible object on his desk, a bird or a bat or something, and as soon as

225

I went in he put it in a draw and locked it.

But he didn't look sad, he looked a bit shaken. He took my hand and pulled me down on his lap like he did when I was little and hugged me and called me his preshus princess. Not his one and only, but still. And it was lovely, just me and him like we were before, and I made him larf – not a roaring big larf but a small rooful one, but still. Gemma doesn't make him larf. I saw him looking at her tonite and he looked sad and rooful and gilty. Gilty? – well, he was probably remembering what happened 20 years and 9 months give or take a few days ago and I might be meen and spiteful but I'm glad he feels gilty about that becoz it changed all our lives and I would rather it hadn't happened even tho we might still be living in Swansea but Gemma and the Groosomes would never have been born.

PS The meel was horrible. Not only is she charming the pants off Huwie (who can't see he's being made to look a fool), she's 2-timing Tony. Why can't he see it? She's already got a boyfrend. WHAT DO THESE MEN SEE IN HER?? She's nothing but a ball braker. And nobody can see it but me.

PPS I suppose I must tell Sandy it's over. I think he knows anyway. I won't be like her, keeping 2 or 3 in toe. At least Huwie only has them 1 at a time. And it looks like Charlie will soon be given the push.

Wot is it with us Bassetts??? It must be in the jeens.

******

Laurence was in Shepherd's Bush, having coffee with Hilary in the BBC canteen, when the call came through. He saw Ralph waving at him from the door, hand held to his ear miming a telephone receiver. Laurence took the call in Ralph's office and was surprised to hear the voice of his old Cambridge colleague, Denis Montfort. Sir Denis, as he now was.

"Denis! Nice to hear…"

"Is Gemma with you?" He sounded curt.

"Gemma? Well, yes. Not here now, obviously, I'm at…"

"I tried the house, then the gallery. I was told…" There was a sound of a sob, a high pitched wail, in the background. When Denis spoke again, his voice had an unaccustomed catch. He cleared his throat. "I need to speak to Gemma."

"If she's not at home, she's probably out with Leo. They're getting on famously. Spending all my money..."

"Please. Laurence. This is difficult..." Again the background wail. "Louisa, please..." More sobs, then Denis's voice again, barely audible. "It's Sebastian, Larry. Accident. Car... couldn't take a bend, straight over a hillside, driving too fast... stupid, stupid... God Larry, he's dead. My boy's dead."

Laurence said without thinking, "But he can't be! I only saw him a couple of weeks ago..."

"Happened night before last. He was in the Lake District, staying at a friend's..."

"But he was going back to Berk..."

"No, he went to Cumbria. Larry, I've got to go, Louisa's in a terrible state. We all are. Can you tell Gemma?" The phone clicked.

Laurence was left staring at the receiver. Sebastian? Car accident? Lake District? Sebastian, dead?

He caught a taxi home and waited, pacing the lounge, for the girls to return. When they bundled in, a pair of laughing mermaids, his face must have given him away. Leo said, "Daddy, what is it?" and he could only stand, gazing at Gemma and watching the blood drain from her face.

She fainted. He lifted her up and carried her upstairs, laid her on her bed. He felt as helpless as a kitten. He sat beside her, staring across at Leo who hovered in the doorway, helpless too. He told her to ring the doctor.

It was Will all over again.

For the next few days the house was wrapped in a suffocating blanket of silence. They crept round on tiptoe, almost as if there had been a death in the house. Mrs W made fortifying soups and stews which they ate without tasting, and Gemma's tray came down untouched. The doctor had put her under sedation, and for the first couple of days she slept, waking only to weep. Sometimes she sat up and screamed that it was her fault, she was to blame. She should never have stayed on in London. They should have gone back to Berkshire together, to Roothings, if she had done that he would never have gone to his friend Nigel's holiday cottage in the Lake District.

Huwie and Leo took turns at her bedside. Tony Masterson arrived, offering to help. They sat beside Gemma, doing their best to talk her through her grief. They helped a little. As soon as they left, she went back to weeping.

Laurence attended the funeral alone. It was terrible; Louisa Montfort was inconsolable, Sir Denis stiff, ramrod-straight, iron-faced. Their elder boy, Julian (a carbon copy of Denis; Sebastian resembled his pretty, fine-boned mother) seemed still in a state of shock. Mourners overflowed the church. There were banks of flowers, wreaths and sheaths and cliffs of flowers. To make it worse, it was a beautiful warm golden day.

"I feel terrible," Nigel Pettit told Laurence at the gathering afterwards. "I didn't even know he was there. He had a key – I told him he could use it, you know, if he wanted somewhere to…" His voice trailed off. Laurence didn't press him, but could have finished the sentence for him. To conduct a clandestine affair? So soon after leaving Gemma in London? Well, yes. Laurence had no illusions about young Sebastian's fidelity. Out of sight, out of mind. He probably had a couple of other girls on the side while he was with Gemma at Cambridge. There were quite a few long-legged, red-eyed beauties among the mainly youthful mourners.

He wanted to slip away as soon as he decently could, but Denis caught him at the door. He'd drunk more than was good for him. "Thanks for coming, Larry. Means a lot. Can always count on old friends, eh?" Laurence had smiled, nodded, taken a few steps backwards. Denis had hung an arm round his shoulders. "Just want to tell you," he said, bringing his face close, "they've got it all wrong. My boy wasn't on drugs. Never took drugs. Never drank to excess. Good driver, fast yes, but never careless. No accident, Larry. I'm going to prove it was no accident."

Delivering Denis into the care of Julian Montfort, Laurence left Roothings and caught the train back. He decided to walk from the station, even though his rheumatics were playing up badly. He had found it painful to climb stairs for months, and now his knees complained when he walked further than a few hundred yards. He'd been putting off the X-ray his doctor had advised.

There was nothing like a funeral to concentrate the mind on the passage of time, he thought as he hobbled along. No more had been said about the Wetherbys' retirement; he had employed a boy to help Bernard in the garden and the subject had been laid to rest. But Bernard was looking his age now, and Barbara, bless her, was finding things difficult. Laurence had telephoned a few estate agents on the south coast to start the ball rolling and had made sure he could pay the deposit in ready cash.

After a great deal of soul searching, he had sold *Study in Blue & Green #3* to Cyril, who had been after a Murchison for years. He had never been comfortable with the picture, which had never been hung on the wall in the library or anywhere else; he had kept it in the wardrobe with his portrait of Deirdre. It was a reminder of his recklessness, his moment of madness, that same foolhardy impulse that had caused him to include the fake Study in Grey in the shipment to Denver. Sometimes actions couldn't be explained logically; the brain had an agenda of its own which put the body in danger. That rush of adrenaline that came from such an action was reason in itself; a throwback, perhaps, to the days when victory favoured the brave. He, Laurence Bassett, wasn't brave, but he had sailed close to the wind on several occasions and got away with it.

And besides, Cyril wasn't an art connoisseur; he didn't move in those circles. He would hang the painting on a wall in his house purely for the pleasure of owning it. He might not even bother to insure it but if he did, it would surely be taken at face value – and the attribution by an acknowledged expert to be genuine. There was nothing to worry about there.

Plunged in these thoughts, he merely registered the incongruity of the Ford Escort parked further up the road among the gleaming Audis and Alfa Romeos of his neighbours. He'd forgotten it as soon as he turned in his drive but immediately Mrs W hurried up to him in the hall, relief written all over her face, he knew.

"I hope you don't mind," she whispered. "Gemma was so pleased to see him. I've made up a bed…"

The house seemed suddenly alien; not his at all. He was a stranger in his own home. But somehow it didn't matter; it didn't matter at all. All that mattered was that Nick was once again under his roof.

It wasn't that he took over. In fact they hardly saw him. And when they did, he rarely spoke. But even his absence spoke volumes. At breakfast, which Nick came down to, Leo glowered at him from under black brows. Huwie went to stay with a friend (or, more likely, his latest girl) after a couple of days. Tony Masterson vanished. Only Mrs W, dear Barbara, took it all in her stride. She fussed around Nick and Gemma like a mother hen, taking meals up on trays and cheerfully seeing to his washing.

"He's doing her world of good," she confided. "They sat out in the conservatory this morning and she even had a bite to eat. Whoever he is, Mr B, we must thank our lucky stars he's come."

Laurence and Leo haunted the house like a couple of ghosts. "Who does he think he is?" Leo demanded. "He looks at me as if I'm something nasty he's trodden in. And he's not grateful, is he? Daddy, why don't you tell him to go? He frightens me."

Leo? Frightened? Well, possibly. He had got so used to his fiery, volatile daughter that his memory of the tortured, wary child, her face bleak with misery, had been superseded. He hugged her close, kissed the top of her head. The past is within us as well as around us, he thought. We carry our young selves inside us even when we're old.

He wouldn't tell Nick to go, even to reassure Leonora. The week or so Nick was in his house Laurence would remember as a special time. He treasured the days, stored up the hours like gold coins. When they came face to face in the hall, or on the landing, Laurence would return Nick's deep, searching gaze with one of his own, not flinching; sometimes it would be Nick who looked away first. They were still joined by that collusion, sealed in the Matron's office in Swansea; that handshake that had bound them together down the years. They had conspired to procure Deirdre an abortion; even though their plan had gone wrong, it had still been a conspiracy. And the child they would have got rid of without a second thought (another man's child, he now knew, not his at all) was now at the centre of their lives.

Forget it, Nick had said. *I forgot it years ago.* Forgot what? Not the conspiracy, surely. His hatred of Laurence, perhaps. The hatred that had blazed from his face in the police cell – that might have waned over the years. Was there still hatred in that cold steady gaze? – no, Laurence thought not. He had been forgiven, then. But kept at arm's length. Nick was still implacably hostile.

Laurence could live with that. Hostility, not hatred. It was liveable with.

One evening he passed Gemma's bedroom door. It was slightly open and he stopped, glanced in. Gemma was sitting up, arms round Nick's waist, face buried in the curve of his throat where neck met collarbone. His chin was resting on the top of her head. He was gazing at the window, his face for once unguarded. His expression drilled Laurence to the floor. It was sad, desolate. Yearning. Then his eyes flicked towards Laurence. For a moment they gazed at each other in silent acknowledgement. In that split second Laurence experienced the full bonding he had ached for; a sharing of guilt down the years. His heart, his whole being (his soul?) had lightened. He felt giddy with relief.

Then Nick smiled. A genuine smile, a genuinely happy smile such as Laurence had longed, but never expected, to see. A forgiving, forgetting smile. Almost without thinking, he pushed open the door to enter.

Nick said, "Fuck off." But he was still smiling.

Deirdre rang every day about five. She didn't have a phone in her cottage, but she rang from the vicarage in the village. Nick took the calls, giving her daily bulletins. He put the phone down before Laurence could ask to speak to her. Once Laurence had got there first and Deirdre had managed to say, "I don't care what he says, I'm getting the next train down...", before Nick had taken the receiver from him and calmly told her not to bother. "Gem's not up to seeing anyone at the moment," he said. "She's still fragile. She probably needs to get away for a while." And then, after listening a few seconds, "I brought her passport with me. I got the visas today. It's all arranged." He replaced the receiver without saying goodbye.

A few days later Laurence came back from recording another two shows at the BBC to find them gone. Mrs W hurried out from the kitchen as soon as his key turned in the lock.

"They left this morning," she said. "Cases all packed and in the hall and the taxi at the door at ten. He's taken her to Australia, Mr B. He didn't want to worry you, he said. Did I do right, letting them go? Only he seemed so capable..."

"That's all right, Mrs W. He'll look after her. It's probably for the best." Which it was, of course. But the house seemed bereft of its centre. He felt an impostor, a ghost, suddenly without substance. When Leo came in they clung together for a long while, two ephemeral lost souls trying to rediscover their bearings.

1. November 1985

"I don't want to sell," Maudie said, "but I don't think I can afford to hold out much longer. It's certainly getting very hard to refuse."

"I can ask Mr Bassett's advice."

"Oh, I know what he'll say. But it's the insurance, Deborah. I really don't want the responsibility…"

"In that case, Miss Madison," Deborah said pointedly, "I would advise you to sell. Gali-Leo's will act as intermediary. And I do know our client is willing to pay all costs."

"Well…" Deborah heard Maudie's sigh of capitulation down the line, "you'd better tell them I'll sell for the revised offer plus costs. I'm going to miss it, I've got very fond of it, but frankly it's beginning to be more of a pain than a pleasure."

Deborah replaced the receiver and smiled across at Dave Symons. "I thought she could be softened up."

"Well done." He eased himself out of the chair and wandered across to the window. "So now I can tell my client we've tracked them all down."

She studied his back in its expensive suiting. His stoop had become more pronounced over the years. He had been a regular visitor to the gallery, calling in at least twice a year, but she had never felt completely at ease with him. Or perhaps it was merely her conscience that made her uneasy. Had he got wind of the three unsigned Murchisons? Surely not. Laurence would have told the Venn Pegasus Agency that there had only been five juvenile paintings, not eight. But she wouldn't put it past Dave to have tracked down Will's mother to ask her about Will's early work. She was beginning to think that owning all the Murchison canon had become a fixation with Dominic King.

It was strange how, after first seeing his photograph in the paper, King's name kept cropping up everywhere. He was now one of the wealthiest men in America and was seen frequently in the company of Middle Eastern potentates and African dictators. She wondered how Laurence had met him; they had nothing at all in common, except an interest in art - and that tenuous link, the commune in Wales where the IRA arms cache had been found.

She had rung Hilary Frost with a request, purporting to be from Laurence, for further information about Dominic King. What could she tell her about Mr King that might help her define his taste in art? She only knew, Hilary said, what most people knew about him, namely not much. Then, obviously realising her reputation was at stake, she mentioned a younger brother named Patrick, a hippie drop-out who'd been found dead of a heroin overdose in the Thames at the end of September 1970.

Nicholas Woollidge had been arrested for possession of offensive weapons in September 1970. He had been the only person left at the farm; everyone else had disappeared, and nobody had come forward since to offer any information either in mitigation or accusation. The locals had never known the names of the commune dwellers and even the present owner of the farm, son of Elwyn Hughes, a neighbouring farmer, could offer little assistance. The farm, he said, had been owned by Bronwen Thomas who had left it to Nicholas Woollidge in her Will. His father had been made Trustee, but had promised Bronwen to let Nicholas run it as he wished, without interference. Her granddaughter, Deirdre, had been seen in the town around this time but had since vanished completely.

There was one account, in the transcript of the hearing she had unearthed, that was interesting. After sentence had been passed, there had been a disturbance in the public gallery. A pregnant girl had stood up and stated categorically that the accused was innocent. She had been taken away and questioned, and had later retracted her statement. She said she had spoken in the heat of the moment, obviously upset that the father of her unborn child had just been given a three-year prison sentence.

And now bones had been dug up on the same farm, bones that had been in the ground for fifteen years. Which would bring it back to 1970. Something had obviously happened in that year that had been effectively covered up.

But she would never know what. She only knew that there was a link between the guns that were found and Dominic King; and somehow Laurence had got involved. And if she wanted to protect Laurence, she had to play ball with King's agent, David Symons.

Who now turned from the window and studied her. "All accounted for," he repeated, "except one."

"Oh?"

"There's one still on the loose."

She said slowly, "An uncatalogued Murchison? Why do you say that?"

"Oh come on, Deborah." Dave grinned. "You know what I'm talking about."

Well yes, she did. But did he know that? Perhaps he was just testing her. "No, I'm sorry. I can't think…"

He slipped a hand inside his jacket and brought out his wallet. Flipping it open, he slid out a small folded piece of newsprint. "Piece of luck spotting this. Would you believe it, the newspaper was wrapped around a clock I bought at auction a coupla months ago. Unwrapped it, and wham! – lookee here." He flicked it over to her.

She unfolded the small piece of paper, knowing exactly what she would see and bracing herself for the shock. Yes, there he was as she remembered him – Will, thin and gaunt and hollow-cheeked, his hair a halo of disordered curls, his eyes oddly unfocused as they became when he hadn't taken his medication for some time. Beside him, Laurence, bursting with health and vigour. And behind them, unmistakeably, Wheels One.

"Good Lord." She could say this in all sincerity. Her voice shook with the effort of keeping back the tears.

"Undisputedly a Murchison, wouldn't you say?"

"Yes, indeed."

"So you must have known about it, Deborah."

"I didn't attend the viewing." She lifted her face, looked him straight in the eyes. "I had the night off. The picture must have been hung without my knowledge."

"So where do you think it is now?"

"I really couldn't say. If it was sold, it would be recorded in the ledger."

"Then I suggest we take a peek at the ledger, huh?"

She made a play of opening the safe, bringing out the accounts book for 1979 and opening it up to find August's sales figures. She knew it wouldn't be there, but she had to feign surprise. She was becoming as adept at deceit, and getting away with it, as Laurence.

"Well, it wasn't sold on the night of the viewing. And it wasn't in the gallery the next day, of that I'm completely certain."

"So it was on loan."

"Yes. That happens quite frequently."

Dave frowned. "And no record of who loaned it, huh?"

"No. Again, that's not surprising. The owner was probably there that night and took it away with him. Or her."

Dave shrugged. "So we've got to find out exactly who was at this viewing, eh, Deborah? Who would be able to tell us that?"

She was silent.

"Your boss man was there that night, I take it?"

She nodded.

"Then he'd know, wouldn't he? Ask him, Deborah. I'm sure he can be made to remember the guest list. I'm not an unreasonable man, I'll give him a few months to come up with the names. But my client will be very unhappy if I tell him there's an important Murchison on the loose that nobody knows about."

She promised she would jog Laurence's memory and was glad when Dave made his exit half an hour later, after a leisurely coffee and a saunter round the gallery. His visits made her nervous. There was always an air of unfinished business about them, as if he knew something she didn't.

His story about the clock was obviously a fabrication. He, or his client, must have known about the viewing, if not at the time, then fairly soon afterwards. It had been in all the arts sections of the newspapers. Did he know the owner of Wheels One was Laurence himself? Or did he merely suspect? And how to tell Laurence to be careful, not to cross Dominic King, when

Laurence now seemed further away from her than he had ever been?

It was all the fault of Nicholas Woollidge. He had been staying at the Hampstead house for just over a week, and had now taken Gemma off to New South Wales, since when Laurence had been plunged into a trough of despair. No, she couldn't blame this entirely on Nicholas; it was Sebastian Montfort's death that had precipitated it, obviously. Deborah couldn't believe that the young, good-looking fellow who had accompanied Gemma on that fateful day had been killed, and yet there was a certain inevitability about it; it seemed that anyone who had swum into the orbit of Deirdre Thomas and Nicholas Woollidge had somehow come to grief. Was there a link between the death of Patrick King and the body dug up on the farm? Could it just be coincidence?

She held her aching head in her hands. What was the point of these thoughts? Why did she spend her time searching the past for clues to events she would never uncover? Is this what her life had become – a sad, lonely existence made bearable by trying to piece together bits of other people's lives? And why? Just to get closer to Laurence, to understand him, to help him get over whatever it was that caused his bouts of depression? But didn't she already know? Hadn't he told her years ago, the night she had taken him to meet Will?

There was one way she could get closer to him. *But I hope these feelings will pass,* he had written, *and we can look forward to a future. Perhaps together? Who knows. I only know I need someone to keep me on the straight and narrow... Deborah, I need your help. I need you. Help me.*

The first time she had read these words she had disbelieved them. Only words, she thought, easily written. She had underestimated him. Now she knew they'd been written from the heart and her stony reception had devastated him. She hadn't even acknowledged the note, had never mentioned it. No wonder he had turned obstinate and greedy. She had made him like that. He had turned Will's memory into money because it was the only road left open to him.

But he had kept trying, hadn't he? Little allusions, jokey references, asking for her hand while on his knees… was he still living in hope? Did he still need her help? *Deborah, I need you. Help me.*

They were both growing old. The past was past. They could look forward to a future. Perhaps together? Yes, she thought. Next time he asks, I will say yes.

******

Mon 18 Nov 7.58pm

Didn't go to work today. Neither did Daddy. Another day he stayed home, saying now the Wetherbys are leaving he's got to get to grips with the housekeeping. Wot a laugh! Daddy, with a hoover! He wouldn't know one end from the other. Anyway, that wasn't the reeson becoz he stayed in the library nearly all morning until the doorbell rang. And it was just fate I was coming out of the lounge becoz I got to the door first and there she was. Gemma's mother.

I knew it was her tho I pretended I didn't. I don't know how I knew becoz I hadn't seen her since I was 2½. She doesn't look much like Gemma either, tho they share the same coloring. She's smaller with masses of black hair and these catty green eyes that make her look witchy. Gemma doesn't look much like Daddy either, come to that. She must have her own set of jeens or something. She's certainly got a nature of her own — underneeth that girly self-effacing exterior lies a will of iron. Even when she was prostate with greef there was something hard about her — and it wasn't so much greef as gilt, she was prostate with gilt about staying in London rather than going back with poor Sebastian. And she loved all the attenshun, I could tell. Huwie and Tony couldn't see they were being used. And then when He came…!!!

Well, I won't go on about Him. He's taken up enough pages of you, deer Diary. I'm just glad the pair of them have gone, I'm only sad Daddy's taking it so badly. Does he miss Gemma? Or Him?

Anyway. There she was, on the doorstep, asking me if I remembered her and how I used to clime all over her and pull her hair and call her Dee-dee. As if I'd remember that! But then Daddy came up the hall and said, all rite, Leo, off you go to your room while I take Deirdre into the lounge, like I was some servant or something. Anyway I didn't, I stayed in the hall with my ear to

238

the keyhole tho I couldn't hear much. They talked for a long time and I just cort a few words – 'commune' and 'hippies' and 'drugs' and such. Bones came into it, too. Huwie said something about bones being found a few months ago but I didn't take much notice. I didn't realise he ment they were found on the same farm as the guns. Gemma must have told him more than me about that time of her life before Suffolk. He probably asked her about it but I'm not interested, why should I be???

Anyway. I was just giving up and going into the kitchen to make coffee when there was this almity screem. More like a shreek. And then this maniacal larf, like a madwoman. I didn't have to put my ear to the keyhole, I could hear everything. Daddy said, wot's the matter, and she just went on larfing. Then she stopped and said wot happened to the king, or something. Wot did he do with the king? And Daddy said he'd been found in the river at Grenidge.

I didn't stay to hear more. I knew she'd be leaving soon, so I crept up the stairs to the landing. And then they came out and walked to the front door. Daddy was trying to make her stay but she wouldn't. She'd carmed down by then but she had this mad look in her eyes, I could see that from upstairs. Stay with me, Daddy said, and she said something about cats. And then he said, I love you, Deirdre. And she said something about a fate worse than death. And then he told her to go on painting and he would be her agent. And then she said nothing changes – we can't change, nothing changes – and then she was off down the drive like a demented harpie (or hippie, ha ha!!!) And Daddy went into the library and didn't come out for hours.

******

Sitting at his desk far into the night, Laurence made up his mind to get rid of the business. What had put this thought in his mind he couldn't say; only that, once there, he realised it had been in the back of his mind for months – even years. He spent most of the evening writing letters and composing a glowing testimonial for Miss Routledge. Then tore them all up.

Gali-Leo's was no longer his, anyway. It belonged to Deborah. She was running it almost single-handedly even now. By giving her free rein, he would, he hoped, make up for all the years he had kept her guessing as to his intentions. That was cruel, he realised now. No wonder she had never given any sign of capitulation.

Since Will's death he had worked on her. At first he needed her forgiveness. He had paid, he'd thought, for his earlier transgressions by physical pain and atonement, but now that wasn't enough (and hadn't he gained some satisfaction too, some perverse sexual pleasure, which had rather defeated the object?) The years since Will's death had been a kind of exercise in attrition, a slow, laborious, painstaking wearing down of her hatred. No, not hatred; not the hatred Nick had felt for him, not that. In a way, what she'd felt for him was something more terrible. Pity, possibly, and disappointment, and a depth of desolation he couldn't hope to get to the bottom of. Grief, obviously. They had shared that.

If guilt bound him to Nick, then grief bound him to Deborah. And she had worked through it in her own way, subjugating herself to the business. Gali-Leo's was now her life.

And he wasn't so blind that he didn't realise what had happened in the intervening years; how far the business was in debt to the Venn Pegasus Agency. Had that been part of her revenge on him? But he had colluded in that too. The unsigned Murchisons – the forgeries, he must call them that – now resided in the collection of Dominic King. He had thought he had got his own back, that he'd been cleverer than King, but now he doubted that. King must have realised Grey 2 was a forgery and that the five unsigned Murchisons were also fakes. That was what he held over Laurence's head; what he held over the business.

Dermot, of course, was safe. Dermot was now a wreck of a man, drink-sodden, living on past glories. He was trolleyed out sometimes on talk shows, along with actors and footballers and other huge talents gone to waste. They had recently come face to face in the corridors of the BBC, after Dermot had been a minor guest on *Parkinson*. Laurence had been friendly, genuinely glad to see him; since Dermot had delivered the eight unsigned Murchisons (and he had donated one back – Dermot had been loath to part with them, he could see), they hadn't met up again.

But Dermot, along with his addiction to alcohol, had also grown a large chip on his shoulder. Why, Laurence couldn't think; he had split the proceeds of the sale equally down the middle. If Dermot had chosen to spend the entire fortune on drink, that was his problem.

"Proud of me, Larry?" Dermot had shouted, hanging a heavy arm round his shoulders. "Kept our little secret, eh? Nearly gave it away but – oops! – don't think anyone noticed. Gets my goat, though. Always referred to as Murchison's biggest influence – Dermot Timberlake, Muse of Murchison. Can't shake the little bugger. If only they knew, eh, Larry? If only they knew!"

Laurence had extricated himself, murmured apologies to the floor crew who had come up behind them, and hurried away to their sympathetic smiles. Dermot was safe, and so was he. No one took any notice of a professional drunk.

But he wanted to distance himself from the business, from the whole sordid mess. He would shake off the dust of corruption (he'd never really been a businessman; he should have remained in the ivory tower of academia) and turn back to those more innocent days. Now Deirdre was back in his life, he could work on her, he could get her painting again. His reputation, in his own eyes at least, would be reinstated. He would start his great project, a series of populist books on the Old Masters seen from the viewpoint of an enthusiastic amateur. And he would give all the rest of his attention to Leo and Huwie and Gemma and Deirdre. And Nick? Well, obviously Nick was his own man, but he had hopes that the hatchet had been buried.

Oh God – a rather unfortunate turn of phrase, in the circumstances. And the real story of what had happened fifteen years ago on the farm in North Wales would never be revealed. To him, at least. He would have to live with that.

He pulled the writing pad towards him. The second letter he would write to Deborah, even harder than the first. *The future looks bleak,* he had written in that first note, *...but I hope these feelings will pass and we can look forward to a future. Perhaps together? Who knows. I only know I need someone to keep me on the straight and narrow...* But she had shown no indication since that she had received it, or read it, or had lived in hope. Just, sometimes, a softening of the eyes, a smile of genuine affection; that's all he had to go on. But they'd been through so much together. She must, surely, still feel something for him.

So this letter must be a final nail in the coffin of hope. By concentrating on his thoughts for the business, by setting out in words what he planned for the future of the business, she would read between the lines. *I will be withdrawing from an active role,* he wrote, and *I know I'm leaving Gali-Leo's in a safe pair of hands,* and *We don't change, Deborah. Nothing changes. I thought I could, with your help, but I can't. I'm still the same weak, worldly man unworthy of you. You have always deserved better.*

At two o'clock in the morning he sealed the note in an envelope and walked along dark empty silent streets to drop it into the nearest letterbox.

2. January/February 1986

Laurence was awoken about six by the phone ringing. The extension was beside his bed and, half asleep and groping, he knocked over something that fell with a crash to the floor. It couldn't be the Teasmade, a large heavy contraption Leo had bought him a few years ago. Snapping on the lamp, he saw it was the bat-winged head.

Thank God it was undamaged. He sat it back on the cabinet and lifted the receiver. Deirdre's voice whispered, "Laurence? Can you come and fetch me? I need to be in London."

"What, now?"

"As soon as you can. They're coming back."

He didn't need to ask who she meant. "Today?"

"Yes. I need to be there."

He rolled over and swung his legs out of bed. He'd told her he'd be on the road as soon as he could. Driving up, he had all the time in the world to wonder why Gemma hadn't phoned to tell him they were on their way. The only explanation was that she'd been told not to.

Deirdre had given him the address of the vicarage where she was staying the night. He drove past the cottage, screened behind wild hedges and looking even more desolate than he remembered in September. Sebastian had told him there was a whole attic full of paintings; he slowed down as he passed, looking at the threadbare thatch, wondering what sort of condition they'd be in, what marvels were rotting under that roof. The two Sebastian had sent him were still in his possession in the safe at Gali-Leo's. He had tried to persuade her to let him hang them at the gallery, but she'd refused. She hadn't asked for them back.

The vicarage was a building of sturdy Edwardian red brick set in half an acre of tidy vegetable allotments on the other side of the village. He walked up the flagged path and rang the bell on a dark blue door of patrician proportions. It was opened by the vicar himself, a tall ascetic-looking individual with flyaway sparse sandy hair, rimless glasses, a wide smile above an immaculately white but unobtrusive dog collar.

"You must be Laurence. Adrian Rice-Wallace, vicar of this parish. And quite a few parishes beyond." His hand was warmly shaken and he was ushered into the long echoing spaces of an empty hall. "Very glad to meet you. So you're a friend of Drusilla's? Funny thing, but I think I know you. Have we met somewhere before?"

"Oh, I very much doubt it."

"Ah. Well. Drusilla's upstairs, getting her things together. I thought it best for her to spend the night here. I'm rather…"

But what he was rather was never known. Deirdre herself appeared at the top of the stairs, wearing a shapeless shift and baggy cardigan. It wouldn't have taken her long to get her things together, judging by the lone carrier bag she held in one hand. She looked thinner and paler than when he'd seen her last, in November.

"Will you stop for a cup of tea?" The vicar, Laurence thought, wanted to detain them a while longer, but Deirdre walked past the pair of them, opened the front door and went down the path. Laurence smiled his apologies, and hurried after her.

Her silence on the way back was unnerving. There was a hectic, coiled intensity about her, in the way she twisted her hands in her lap and stared unseeing out of the window. He tried to keep up some sort of conversation but in the end lapsed into silence himself.

As soon as she stepped into the hall of the Hampstead house, she said, "I've done a terrible thing."

"Surely not, Deirdre."

"I told him to come back."

"They would have had to have come back sooner or later."

"He's coming back because I told him to." Those green eyes stared into his. "He'll go to prison, won't he."

He felt way of out his depth. There was something going on here he knew he would never get to the bottom of. But he must take the plunge. "Did you make your written statement to the police? What did you say?" He remembered her hysteria, there in the lounge, when he had revealed the identity of the body. She had obviously expected it to be someone else. But she wouldn't explain. She had run away from him, down the drive, exactly as she'd run away from him in Swansea, and then in London, from the Tate...

She still didn't explain. She left his side and wandered into the lounge. He hadn't tidied up for weeks, but of course she wouldn't notice. The Wetherbys had moved down to Sussex a month ago and he hadn't done anything about advertising for a new couple. What was the point? Huwie was back at Southampton Poly and Leo was in the Bahamas and wouldn't be back for another three weeks. He was still rattling round the Hampstead house like a lost soul.

Deirdre had poured herself a brandy by the time he followed her into the lounge. "Your written statement, Deirdre," he repeated. "You'd told the police verbally that you and Nick found the body and decided to bury it. That you helped him bury it. But you didn't, did you? Because you didn't know who it was until I told you."

She shrugged. "It doesn't matter."

"But did you swear a written statement?" As he had done, he realised. He'd sworn a statement that Nick had stolen the abortion money all those years ago in Swansea.

"Yes."

"So what did it say?"

She sipped her brandy, then wandered over to the window. He watched her impatiently. Was she play-acting her little-girl-lost routine, or was it genuine?

"I told them," she said, parrot-fashion, "that we buried the body between us. That he was a heroin addict. Nick was selling the place, he didn't want any trouble..."

"Yes, I know," he said shortly. "You told me that before. But that was before you knew who it was. You said the police wanted you to make a written statement..."

"That was my written statement."

"Ah." So she had lied under oath, just like he had. To protect Nick, though, not to accuse him. "Why do you want to share the blame, Deirdre? If it wasn't true?"

"Oh, but it is true. In a way. I was responsible." She tossed off the last of the brandy. "I left Nick to clear up the mess in the field." And laughed.

"So he buried the body alone? He cut it up and buried it? Why?"

"He couldn't dig a whole grave, could he? Elwyn would have noticed it. Elwyn was buying the farm," she explained, obviously seeing his bafflement. "So it had to look like rabbits, or something. Lots of little holes instead of one big one. Nick's not stupid, you know."

"Yes, I know."

"Well then. Even I worked that one out." She threw herself down on one of the two-seater sofas, the one facing the patio. Her voice rose from its depths. "Anyway, it doesn't matter. He'll deny I was involved. He'll take all the blame. As usual." She sounded bitter, though, not grateful. "Well, if I'm lucky I might get done for perjury or something. Isn't that what they call it, lying under oath?"

"Or perverting the course of justice. Except you aren't perverting, are you? He'll tell the truth and be punished. But it sounds like you also want to be punished."

"Oh, I've tried, believe me. I was given fourteen days for aggravated trespass but got thrown out after two. Why does nobody believe I'm wicked?"

Laurence, having poured himself a stiff scotch, took a large mouthful. He and Deirdre were the same, he thought. Seeking atonement for past sins. Whatever hers were.

He tried to frame a question that she would answer, but he didn't get the chance. Just then the front door was thrown open and they heard footsteps in the hall. The next minute Gemma had burst in upon them.

She didn't see her mother, sunk in the sofa with its back towards them. She threw herself at Laurence. "Oh, it's so good to be home!" She looked tanned and healthier, though still thin,

246

and tired. Jetlag, obviously. He crushed her to him. The question on his lips – where was Nick? – was asked by Deirdre.

Gemma pulled away and gazed down at her mother. A complicated set of emotions chased over her face – surprise, irritation, guilt (guilt?) – before she settled for a smile of strained greeting. She still clung to Laurence, however.

"Oh, he – he told me to get a taxi. He was held up at the airport."

Deirdre flashed a glance towards Laurence. "Who by?"

Gemma swallowed. Now he was looking at her closely, Laurence saw that her eyes were red and puffy and there were streaks of tears down her cheeks. "Just as we were leaving customs. Two men came up to us." She gave a gulp. "They said they wanted to question him. He'd already told me on the plane coming back that it might happen. He told me he wouldn't be long, that he'd probably be home tomorrow." She said bleakly, "Who were they, Laurence? Do you know?"

He could only take another mouthful of whisky and gaze despairingly at Deirdre. Who said flatly, "The police, Gem."

"I thought they were. What did they want to question him about? He wouldn't tell me."

"Oh, plenty of time to explain all that." Deirdre said this with a light laugh that didn't fool Laurence. "So did you have a good time? Do you feel better?" And then, almost as if she had just remembered the circumstances, "I wanted to come to see you, Gem, only he wouldn't let me."

Gemma's stony stare chilled Laurence. This was the first time he had seen mother and daughter together and the omens weren't good. Gemma had told him they weren't alike and didn't see eye to eye, but he hadn't realised how much antipathy Gemma held for her mother. "I didn't expect you to," she said.

"But I did want to, believe me."

"All right."

"And I – I was so sorry about - Sebastian." She had a little difficulty getting the name out.

"Yes."

There was an awkward pause. Then Deirdre said, "So how did you like the land of Oz? You look very brown. Did you do a lot of sunbathing? The weather's been foul here, I bet you soaked up all that lovely sun…" But there was a subtext beneath the words, Laurence thought. With a sudden flash of enlightenment, he realised she was jealous. Jealous of Gemma's prolonged holiday with Nick.

As he was, too. He suddenly realised it. His long period of depression – what Leo called his glooms – was on account of Nick's being with Gemma. Or Gemma being with Nick. Thousands of miles away. On their own.

He poured himself another whisky, Deirdre another brandy. Gemma accepted a glass of white wine. They drank to Nick's homecoming, hopefully tomorrow. Three people, he thought, united by love. And guilt. And jealousy.

In the event, Nick didn't get back until the day after. He had been formally charged with the rather quaint offence of cheating the Coroner and mutilation of a corpse. By pleading guilty and exonerating Deirdre of all involvement he was allowed out on bail, which Laurence willingly put up. He'd thought, by doing this, that Nick would have to reside in Hampstead until the case was heard, but Nick had already made arrangements to stay with a friend in Cirencester. As long as he reported daily to the local police station, the bail conditions were satisfied.

Laurence drove him back to Hampstead to see Gemma and Deirdre before he left for Gloucestershire. It was a strange and rather stilted reunion. Gemma had flown to him and he held her close for a few moments before gently pushing her away and going over to Deirdre, hovering by the patio doors. A long, eloquent look had passed between them. It was Deirdre who turned away first, a shadow of rage and bitterness passing over her face. She wasn't going to be allowed her atonement, Laurence realised.

Gemma pleaded with him to stay in Hampstead, but he was adamant. Why, thought Laurence, was he going to Gloucestershire, not Suffolk? It was almost as if he were punishing the three of them. Or perhaps just two of them, and Gemma was the loser. He spent a long time talking to Gemma in the sitting room while Laurence and Deirdre sat in silence in the lounge. When Nick and Gemma rejoined them her face was streaked with tears but she looked calm, resigned.

He wouldn't accept Laurence's offer of a lift, and left on foot for the station five minutes later.

The next day Laurence drove Deirdre back to Suffolk. She remained as silent as she had coming down but it was a different quality of silence. Not nervy intensity but a seething rage so deep and unfathomable that Laurence was reluctant to leave her alone. He wanted to take her back to the vicarage, but she made him stop at the cottage and said goodbye with such cold finality that he had no option but to drive all the way back to London, a terrible weight in his chest.

At the weekend Huwie arrived from Southampton and remained in the house for a couple of weeks. He and Gemma were inseparable. Sometimes Laurence heard them talking in the early hours of the morning, either in her bedroom or downstairs. Neither of them said anything to Laurence, but he knew in his bones that something was going on. Oh, nothing sexual, not that – something in fact much more intimate, a sharing of histories, a discussion of private thoughts and feelings. Huw was discovering things about Gemma that she had told nobody before, things that had happened in her past which she'd been too young to understand. The discovery of the body had stirred memories buried too deep to be easily excavated, but Huw was patiently drawing them out, laying fears to rest. Laurence was proud of his son. It was only later, seeing Huw's radiant face, that misgivings began to stir. Oh Huwie, he thought, don't fall in love. She's not your sister, but I can't tell you that. Not yet.

He was glad when Huw returned to Southampton, to other girls who might wipe the slate clean.

Then Leo arrived back from the States.

******

249

Wed 12 Feb 9.16pm

Well. Again, sorry for the long silence. Again, things have been frort. They were bad enough when I first got back but they got a hundred times worse.

Thank goodness Huwie had gone when she realised. He wouldn't have known wot to do. She (Gemma, of corse) came into my bedroom a few days after I got back and sat on my bed looking sheepish. Leo, she said, I think I'm in trouble. O, I said, join the club. I've just got my credit card statement. No, she said, I mean real trouble. Trouble with a capital T.

And I still didn't get it. All rite, I know she'd been Down Under in the back of beyond for nearly 3 months all alone on a cattle ranch or whatever with Him, but I just didn't think of the obvious. Somehow I didn't think their relationship was like that. I thort he was the mother's boyfrend. I thort he was like some uncle or brother. But he's still a Man, isn't he? And I suppose she's a Woman, even tho she was supposed to be prostate with greef about Sebastian.

Her period was late, she said. How late, I said. 3 weeks, she said. O, I said, perhaps it's just the change of air or something. No, she said, it's not that. And I said, You don't meen you...? And she said yes. We did. Just the once.

Just the once, I said. Yes, she said, altho we shared a bed from then on. But he didn't do it again, tho I wanted him to. We just cuddled. But it happened by a pool in the rocks after we'd been swimming.

O, I said.

It just happened, she said.

O, I said.

I wanted to, and he wanted to, and it just happened.

Well, I said. These things do.

But I think it was something else too, she said. He wanted to free me somehow.

Free you, I said.

From greef. From gilt, probably. It was like I was carved from ice, like nothing could touch me. But afterwards it was like I'd thord. I began to see things again clearly.

O, I said.

It was like — like I'd woken up.

O.

That's why he did it, Leo. And why he didn't do it again.

Well, wot could I say? I said nothing.
So it wasn't wrong, was it? It can't be.
But you're up the spout, I said.
Yes, she said. Wot shall I do?
Well, wot could I say? I said, do you want it? And she said no, of course
not. I can't have it, can I? And I said, then you'll have to get rid of it. And
she said, will you help me, Leo? To get rid of it?
So that's wot we did. I won't go into detales, but the Trouble is over. I went
to the clinic with her and stayed there till the Deed was done, and brort her
home again. She was distrort and tearful and begged me not to tell anyone.
But I wonder if He told her to do it. I wouldn't put it past Him.
Anyway, it's all over now. And no one need be any the wiser.

Thurs 20 Feb 6.03pm

One of Daddy's cronies at the Beeb has offered her a job. She told me today.
She said she doesn't want to go back to Cambridge to finish her degree. It
would be too painful without Sebastian. But this cronie of Daddy's has
offered her a research job in the news dept, just wot she always wanted.
Does she think I'm green or something? She must have known about it
before and that's why she got rid of the Trouble. I helped her kill a poor little
defenceless feetus just becoz of a job. If she'd been honest I might still have
done it, but I feel as if I've been had.
She shouldn't have a job behind the seens, she should be an actress. She'd
win an Oskar.

******

A shadow slid along the walls of the gallery. The afternoon was
already grey; this was a deepening of the outside gloom, almost
as if dusk had already fallen. Deborah looked up to see a large
black Daimler with tinted windows blotting out what little light
there was.

She had been expecting this moment; well, not this, exactly,
but the return of David Symons. She should be prepared, but her
heart still began pumping faster and her mouth dried as it always
did when he visited. He had never arrived in a Daimler before
and, even as the back door opened and a pair of expensively-

251

tailored legs swung themselves out, she knew it wasn't him. She watched as the short but powerful figure, square shouldered, bullet-headed, gave instructions to the driver and then turned to the door, shooting his cuffs, settling his tie, flexing his fists. Behind him the car slid away and the gloom lightened.

He walked in, shut the door behind him, turned the sign to Closed and pulled the blind. He did this all in one fluid movement and as if he owned the place; which he almost did, Deborah thought. Then he turned and studied her. He wore tinted glasses which were adjusting to the light so that his pale grey eyes, slightly magnified, came slowly into focus. He was of course older than his photograph in the paper; he had lost the little hair he'd had and the shape of his head was even more definitive. But he approached the desk with an even gait and the hand he held out was rock steady, his grip that of a man half his age.

"Miss Routledge."

She smiled. "Mr King."

"Ah," he said. "You know me." He sat himself down on the hard-backed chair in front of the desk and placed his hands over his knees. "I suppose Mr Bassett is unavailable."

"I'm afraid Mr Bassett rarely comes to the gallery these days."

"He's left it in your very capable hands."

She smiled.

"He must be a very wealthy man," Mr King said, "to give up his business."

"He hasn't given it up completely. He's made me a working partner. One day, I think he intends to sell."

"Ah." Mr King sat back. "I think that might be rather a foolish move."

"If he does," she said smoothly, "I would buy him out, of course."

They studied each other for a long moment. Deborah returned the cobra-like stare, determined not to waver.

Then Mr King got to his feet, clasped his hands behind his back and made a slow circuit of the gallery, studying each painting intently. "Since the unfortunate demise of young

Murchison," he said, scrutinising a Roald Niffenberger, "I find I'm not as excited by new art as I was. The craftsmanship is lacking. Schools don't seem to be teaching the basics any more. Drawing. Perspective. Light and shade. Do you not agree, Miss Routledge?"

"I do, Mr King."

"These seem shallow in comparison to the Murchisons. I'm after portraits, Deborah. Figurative stuff." He swung round. "May I call you Deborah?"

"Please."

"Feel free to call me Dominic."

She inclined her head and watched him complete his circuit, which took him at least twenty minutes. There was nothing that seemed to excite his attention for more than a moment, although each painting was given the same intent scrutiny. She rose and, without asking, poured coffee into two china cups and added cream. He was already back and seated at the desk by the time she brought them to him.

"As I suspected. Nothing to touch our young Will." He stirred his coffee and drank in spare, leisurely sips. When at last he had finished, he placed the empty cup and saucer back on the desk top, stretched back in the chair, shot his cuffs and placed his hands on his knees.

"The unaccounted for Murchison. Any enlightenment, Deborah?" She was aware he was watching her for any sign of discomfort. Before she could frame a reply, he said suddenly, "I'll give you a moment to recollect. What I'd like to know first is if there is any up and coming talent you might have heard about that concentrates on the basics."

"Portraiture?" She sipped the last of her coffee, then passed her tongue round her dry lips. "Well, as you say – Dominic – it's hard to find good quality these days. But there is someone…"

She was favoured with his wintry smile. "I bow to your expert judgement, Deborah."

"We do have a couple of examples, as a matter of fact."

"Excellent."

Opening up the safe in Laurence's office, she took out the Bellings. She didn't even try to analyse why she had told Dominic King of their existence; she would do that, inevitably, later on. Besides, if they were to be kept under wraps, either in Cork Street, Hampstead or Denver, she might as well make money out of them. Like the Murchisons, they would never be made public.

He spent some time studying them. She found she could read his expression, even though he kept his face blank; there was a sharper intensity in those pale eyes, as if the irises had contracted. The contour of his jaw had also snapped into straighter lines. The snake had found its prey.

"Interesting." He lifted his gaze and studied her face with the same razor-like contemplation. "These are unsigned. Who is the artist?"

"A very reclusive woman. I doubt if she would like her name to be known."

"Oh come now, Deborah. This is between friends."

"She calls herself Drusilla Belling. It's not her real name."

"I see." He studied the paintings again for another long moment. She could almost see, feel, the cogs beginning to turn in that square robot-like head. "Has she done many more?"

"I don't know. I know nothing much about her. I only know these were done about fifteen years ago."

"So it's Laurence who's the expert here? He would know how to get into contact?" He took her silence as assent. Again that wintry smile. "Oh, Deborah. If only all women were as loyal as you. Larry is a very lucky man."

Loyal. Was it loyalty that kept her silence? It might have been, once. Now it was more complicated than that.

After another long pause, he said, "And the missing Murchison, Deborah. I think we both know where that can be found." He sighed. "I won't ask you the address. I know it's in Hampstead. I can make my own enquiries. I won't compromise you in any way. That's the least I can do after all your many kindnesses to my agent. And myself, of course." He stood, still holding the paintings, taking one last look. Then, relinquishing them with reluctance and placing them carefully on the desk, he said, "Keep them for me. Keep them safe. I need the signature. Tell Laurence I shall be offering the same deal as the Murchisons. I want them all, Deborah. Every last one."

That shadow, deeper now, slid over the walls. She didn't need to raise her eyes. She sat unmoving as Dominic King took his leave, turning the sign back to Open and raising the blind. They didn't shake hands. She sat, her gaze fixed on the little girl and the pig until the shadow had passed on.

She had to tell Laurence about the visit; an expurgated account. She told him about showing Dominic King the two Bellings, but not about his guessing the Murchison was in Hampstead. She would keep some secrets of her own.

As she knew he would be, he was angry. Although he kept his anger under control, she knew by the twitch at the corner of his mouth that she should have kept her nose out of his business. Since he had renewed his acquaintance with Deirdre his attitude towards her had changed. There was that letter, of course; that formal, stilted letter, one business partner to another, though 'partner' was not the right term. She was not a partner, in any sense of the word. Gali-Leo's was still his, and she was still an employee. Nominally she was in charge; in every other respect she was still an underling.

And as a good employee should, she reminded him they needed the money. The Murchison money had dried up. The art scene had moved on. Old Masters were commanding astronomical sums in the sales rooms and youngsters seemed more interested in the visual arts of film and video than painting. Gali-Leo's was representing art, and artists, whose time had gone. Even exceptional portraiture like the two Bellings was not in demand.

He knew that, of course. That was why he agreed to King's demands. He could do nothing else. They were both compromised, both flies caught in the web of international intrigue. Even if he had decided to cast her aside, dash all her hopes, just keep her on in the service of the gallery, they were still bound together by circumstance. That had been enough for her in the past.

It would not be enough for the future. But she would bide her time. Time was all she had left.

3. March 1986

Wed 5 March 7.12pm

Sebastian's inquest. Gemma wanted to go so I said I would too as Daddy wouldn't know wot to do if she throo a wobbly. She didn't but got a lot of attenshum becoz of how pale she was, but that was becoz of the aborshun. Well, obviously it was about Sebastian too, I mustn't be spiteful. It was horrible, his mother was there, and the father and brother too and his mother never stopped crying. Gemma went over and said she was sorry she hadn't gone to the funeral but her thorts had been with them and she must have said all the rite things becoz his mother throo her arms round her and sobbed on her sholder. Daddy sat next to Sir Denis in the cortroom and Gemma sat next to Lady Montfort so I had to sit next to the brother. It was all very awkward.

It went on longer than I thort it would. Apparently Sir Denis doesn't beleeve his death was an accident so there had to be witnesses called. The police said the body was full of drugs but was burnt quite badly so finding the cause of death wasn't easy. (Poor Lady Montfort throo a wobbly here.) But the body had been cut by glass, and a large piece had lodged in his jugular probably from the windscreen, which was the probable cause of death. The car had burst into flames becoz there was a petrol can in the boot that had obviously been punctured in the crash. Sir Denis said Sebastian never carried a can of petrol, he wouldn't even have thort of it, but the Coroner said he was driving at nite so it was feesible, being in the wilds of Cumbria. Nigel Pettit was called and said it was feesible that Sebastian stayed at his cottage but he wouldn't have known becoz the cottage had been let out the week before and he hadn't got round to having it cleaned but there was nothing of Sebastian's there, no clothes or stuff, altho a few things had been in the car. If the cottage had been let a week before then he couldn't have been there, so where was he before that? That's the mistry. That's wot Sir Denis is going to find out.

The verdict would have been accidental death except that Sir Denis objected so it's been left open. That's wot they called it, an open verdict. That meens, I think, that it can be looked into again if there's any more evidence found and Sir Denis told Daddy he'll leeve no stone unturned to find it.

******

It was Will all over again.

He was going up the same drive towards the same Gothic mansion with the same daffodils nodding in the borders, only six years later. He had a package for her, but it was still in the boot of the Jag. He was walking just as stiffly but now it was because of pain in his knees, not welts on his backside.

There were other differences. A glossy new board on the perimeter fence announced that Capel Park Manor was now a nursing home in the private sector with no mention of psychiatrics. His silver-grey Jag was parked only twenty yards away, where once were rolling green lawns. And, when he arrived in the hall, he was greeted by a receptionist wearing a smart floral uniform and dogtag bearing her photograph and the name Caroline Beecham.

"Deirdre?" she said, puzzled. "Oh, you must mean Dee. I didn't realise her name was Deirdre."

So Drusilla Belling was no more, he thought.

She wasn't in the lounge watching television. Nor were the man in the ill-fitting toupee, the chain-smoker, the silent girl. The duchess was not in the corridor. He wondered where they had gone. Care in the community, that was the thing now. They were probably wandering the streets, accosting people in the tube. Did they think that progress, he wondered.

He stood by the long doors giving on to the gardens, watching her. She was kneeling by the flowerbeds, fingering the frilled trumpets of daffodils and the tight buds of grape hyacinths, but in her hand was a little bouquet of wilting weeds, fragile flowers he didn't know the names of.

"Deirdre," he said softly.

Although she didn't turn, he knew she'd heard. But she was going to make him wait. It was several seconds before she rose to her feet and faced him.

She was wearing one of her smocked shifts with long floaty sleeves. On her feet was a pair of wooden clogs like Leo had once favoured. Her hair had been cut and stood out around her face like a dark halo.

"Laurence."

(She'd said that before, in the same flat tone of voice, when the police had smashed open her front door and he had stepped through into the sitting room. The same sad, flat tone with a hint of accusation. But also, perhaps, forgiveness. For what else could he have done?)

"I'm sorry, Deirdre." He'd said that before, too. And he didn't know why he said it now, because he wasn't sorry. He was glad to see her being taken care of, and looking well. Still thin, but calm. Serene. Those green eyes were fixed on him now without that terrible hectic glare.

("I'm sorry, Drusilla." The vicar – Adrian something – had said that too, as they had watched the paramedics give her an injection to calm her before leading her off into the ambulance. He and Laurence had exchanged looks. Both reluctant conspirators, helpless in the face of the unknown.)

And of course she wouldn't let him get away with it. "Why are you sorry, Laurence?"

"I don't know. I'm sorry for everything, I suppose."

"Ah." She smiled her familiar, impish smile, threaded the wilting bouquet through his top buttonhole and tucked a hand through his arm. "As you should be. We should all be sorry for everything. Even things we're really glad about."

"That's too deep for me." They began to walk slowly along the flowerbeds. Her hand on his arm was light as thistledown. He covered it with his large clumsy one. "So," he said, "they're taking care of you, are they?"

"Oh yes. I'm being very well taken care of." A very slight hint of sarcasm, which he would ignore.

"Good."

"Your money is well spent, Laurence."

"Ah." There was no other answer to that. They walked on in silence, a companionable silence with unspoken and, on her part, unfathomable depths beneath its surface. It didn't matter.

Nothing mattered now but that he was here, with Deirdre, and he was forgiven.

(Adrian something – or something-something, a double-barrelled surname – had telephoned him to say that something must be done about Drusilla. She was alone in the cottage, he said, no one had seen her for weeks, she couldn't be eating and didn't seem to be sleeping either. Lights were on at all hours. Passing the cottage, people heard her muttering, talking, sometimes laughing – a loud, maniacal laugh – but she wouldn't answer the door. The back door was locked, which it never had been before. What should be done?)

He must have groaned, because she led him to a bench under a sycamore and made him sit down. "Rheumatics," he said ruefully, rubbing his knees. "Quack says I'll need replacements. Seems they can manufacture joints out of titanium these days."

"You need new knees," she said, smiling, "and I need a new brain."

"Oh, come now, Deir…"

"I'm joking. You mustn't take me so seriously."

He must take the plunge. "I do take you seriously. I take your painting seriously. So should you." She didn't reply. But the moment would pass and might never come again. "You have a great talent. Please don't waste it."

She sighed, and stared ahead of her, her face closed.

"Don't give up on it. Please. You owe it…"

"To whom?" She turned the full glare of those eyes on him. "To me? To you? To the world…!"

"Yes. If you put it like that, yes. Talent belongs to the world, surely."

"Well, the world can't have it." She sounded like a spoiled child. She looked like a mulish little girl, perched on the edge of the bench, ankles crossed, fists in her lap.

"Why not?"

"I've burned all my daubs. They've all gone up in smoke."

"Why, Deirdre?"

She shrugged, swung her legs.

"For God's sake, why?" Anger, not at her (or not entirely) but at the sheer waste, the blind unthinking selfish bloody stupidity of it, made his voice shake. And the obstinate child still sat swinging her legs, hands grasping the wooden slats either side of her, staring ahead.

(When Adrian something-something had left, after they'd shaken hands and reassured each other that nothing else could have been done, they'd had no choice, this was a case best left to professionals, he'd climbed the stairs to the attic. A painful exercise. Even more painful, when he'd discovered the attic to be empty. Just a rocking chair, a chest of drawers, an old mangle, a tin bath. Nothing else at all.)

He was not ordinarily an angry man. Anger was an emotion he had rarely felt, but recently – was it age? – he had recognised it rising in him more frequently. He felt it now, coursing hotly through every vein in his body. He thought of the package in the boot, its precious contents now even more precious, and looked away from her, afraid of the violence he knew he was capable of. He wanted to think it was because of the world's loss but it wasn't, of course. It was *his* loss. His, and Dominic King's.

He said, "Why?" again, wearily, and glanced back at her. She was sitting slumped against the bench like a limp rag doll, and her face was bathed in tears.

"Oh, God." He gathered her up in his arms, clasped her thin frame to him, smoothed the damp tendrils of hair away from her eyes. He kissed the top of her head, then again, and again. Sobs wracked her body and he felt a tide of grief well up inside him, at her distress but also at the waste, the total bloody waste of it all.

How long they sat there, he didn't know. He knew he should get help, that perhaps she was having a relapse, that it was all his fault, but he couldn't move. Eventually she grew quiet. They still sat there.

"I don't know why I did it," she said at last, against his chest. "I was angry. He shouldn't have done it. I wanted to punish him for doing it."

He didn't need to ask who she was talking about. Sebastian, of course. Sebastian had sent him the paintings. But surely she'd punished herself, not him. Sebastian wouldn't have cared less about the loss of the paintings, Sebastian had been in the Lake District conducting a clandestine affair in Nigel Pettit's holiday cottage.

Or was she talking about Nick? What would Nick have done that she wanted to punish? But, again, destroying her paintings would not have been punishment for him. And besides, wasn't he going to be punished soon enough anyway, by the full weight of the law?

Or perhaps she was talking about him, Laurence. Why should she want to punish him? Well, obviously for telling Gemma he was her father, and not telling her when he discovered he wasn't. For, of course, she would have known he would find out about Gemma's birthday, and put two and two together. That was the obvious explanation, now he thought about it. But he didn't think she was referring to him.

His head throbbed now, as well as his knees. He went on stroking her hair, kissing the top of her head. And then she said, suddenly pulling away from him, "There's one left. One I didn't burn."

"That's good, Deirdre."

"But I've forgotten…" She was suddenly agitated. She stood, fists clenching the sides of her dress. "It wasn't in the house, was it? Can you remember?"

"There were no paintings in the house." None in the sitting room and none in the attic. He'd also looked in the scullery, the kitchen, the bedrooms. The only paintings left of hers were in the package he had brought with him.

"I put it away somewhere. It *was* in the house, I kept it there until I – I couldn't look at it any more. He tried to make me do it, you see. But it was an accident…" She was pacing up and down, pumping her fists at her side. "It was an accident,

Laurence. You must believe that. Say you believe me." She had stopped in front of him now and was gazing imploringly at him.

He said despairingly, "I believe you, Deirdre." Oh God, he thought, now what was happening in that brain of hers? She had looked sane enough, he'd allowed himself to think all would be well, and now – now those eyes were glittering dangerously again, as hectic as when he and Adrian something-something and the police had entered the sitting room...

"Let's go back inside." He stood up and encircled her narrow shoulders with his arm, feeling the coiled tightness in that thin frame. It was Will all over again.

They got her back to her room, a rather nice room decorated in restful shades of duck-egg blue and lavender looking out over the garden. A jolly West Indian in Mao-Tse Tung-style tunic and trousers administered a couple of pills and tucked her up in bed. She raised her eyebrows at him, signalling that he should leave. He nodded, and she went out. Turning back to Deirdre, lying against the pillows like a small girl about to be told a bedtime story, he said, "I must go. I'll see you again soon."

"Yes."

"Don't worry about anything. Just get well."

"Yes."

"Goodbye, Deirdre."

"Goodbye, Laurence." As he turned to go, she caught hold of his hand. "I've remembered," she whispered, "what I did with the painting."

"Good."

"I can't leave it where it is. Will you get it for me?"

He brought his face level with the bed, his ear against her mouth. He would rather not know about any paintings, he would rather report back to Dominic King that the two portraits he'd already bought were the only Bellings in existence, but would he be believed? He knew (or hoped he knew her well enough to know) that Deborah would not have told Dominic about Wheels One, but Dominic seemed to have a sixth sense about such things. And the small matter of the two unsigned paintings was

263

not such a problem, after all. He couldn't ask Deirdre to sign them, as he'd asked Will. She wouldn't be as acquiescent as poor Will. But if Drusilla Belling no longer existed, who would know her signature? If Dermot Timberlake could get away with forging Murchisons, surely Laurence Bassett could forge a couple of signatures?

Walking stiffly back along to the car park, he wondered when he could make the drive back to Suffolk, to rescue the painting she'd told him was wedged in the trunk of a hollow tree in the middle of what she called the Enchanted Wood.

******

Fri 28 March 12.16pm

Something rather spooky has happened. Had to rite it down strait away, if I leave it any longer I might forget how it was.

Daddy has gone out, he took the car this morning so he must be out most of the day as he didn't take a taxi. As usual he didn't say where he was going, just dropped a kiss on my head at brekfast. He's back to grapefroot and proons by the way, since the Ws left. I told him I'm not cooking leethal saturated lumps of animal fat for him or anyone. Gemma wouldn't know how to cook anything and just has a bowl of moosli before she goes off to the Beeb. We don't say much to each other but I think it's all off with her and Tony. She's very quiet and I wonder if as well as Sebastian she's brooding about the Trouble but it's too late now. She's probably worried about her mother too but Daddy says she's getting on all rite. He went to see her the other day after they took her to the loony bin. (He says I shouldn't call it that, there are no such things these days.) I suppose she's worried about Him as well, tho I haven't seen anything of Him thank goodness.

Anyway. The spooky bit.

I wasn't working today, thort I might put the hoover round and tidy up a bit as the place is getting out of hand. I suppose I was upstairs hoovering so didn't hear the bell. But when I came down, shock horror — there was a man peering in at the patio doors! At first I thort it was Him but it wasn't. I just dropped the hoover and screemed. He disappeared and then the doorbell rang. I didn't know wether to anser it but I went along the hall, there was a shadow on the glass and I knew it was him and I was shaking all over.

Anyway, I thort he couldn't be a potenshul theef becoz he wouldn't be ringing the bell so I opened the door just a crack and said, Wot do you want?

He said, is Mr Bassett in.

I said no, go away.

He said, he's expecting my call, can I wait?

I said no again but he pushed the door open and said, Mr Bassett will be angry with you if you don't let me in young lady and my employer will be too. We both don't want to lose our jobs do we? HE THORT I WAS THE O PAIR!!!

I said, I beg your pardon I'm his daughter and he looked at my apron and turban and the duster in my pockit and said O, can't you afford domestix and I said We're between housekeepers at the moment and he said Well then I won't hold you up from your chores I'll wait inside and pushed his way in.

I followed him into the sitting room and dining room and kitchen and then I said, wot are you looking for becoz it was obvious he was looking for something and it wasn't Daddy. He said, wot other rooms are there and I said mind your own bizniz, there's the front door, goodby. But he must have seen the inner hall becoz he took off along it to the lounge and conservatory and then opened the door to Daddy's library.

I said, that's private, if you don't go I'm calling the police and he shut the door and smiled and said, don't worry I'm off now thanx very much. And he sauntered off down the hall, opened the front door and went.

Well. My hart was hammering 19 to the dozen and I couldn't do much for a few seconds or so and then I got angry and ran after him down the drive and there was this great big black car with black windows and it just drove off when I got to the gates. So I've come strait upstairs to rite it all down.

He was only a short man and he walked with a stoop and he wore sunglasses so I don't know exactly wot he looked like, but he was SPOOKY.

I'm still shaking all over. Wot did he want? I don't think he even wanted to see Daddy, I think he was making sure Daddy wasn't in, no cars were in the drive and no one ansered the bell when he first rang it and he was looking in the windows to see if he could see something and I was stupid and let him in.

Wot shall I tell Daddy? He's got a bit better lately but this mite send him down to the dumps again.
So I don't think I'll say anything. Not yet, anyway.

4.   April 1986

The case made quite a splash in the media. Deborah followed it avidly, buying two or three newspapers and watching the news bulletins on television. It was all speculation, of course; the perpetrator of the grisly deed kept silent. The case of the IRA arms cache was re-aired; most commentators agreed that the guilty plea then had been a cover-up, that the accused had been the fall guy. He would hardly have wanted a full-scale police investigation on a farm where he had recently dismembered and buried a corpse. It had obviously been a case of choosing the lesser of two evils.

The victim was a mystery man too. Nobody had missed him. Nobody had reported him missing. Nobody, even now, turned up to claim acquaintance, apart from a couple who had been at the commune but had left a long time before the events of September 1970 and who could hardly remember him anyway. That left commentators free to speculate wildly about motives, reliving, in some cases, their own hippie youth and the drug and free love culture that, some bemoaned, had led to today's fractured society.

She wondered if Laurence would attend court for the sentencing, as he had done fifteen years ago. She waited for a phonecall at Gali-Leo's. There had been a time when he would have opened his heart to her, when she had been his trusted confidante. No longer, it seemed. The phone remained silent.

Except for a call in the early afternoon. Not, as she had expected, from David Symons. It was Dominic King who said, "Deborah?"

"Yes."

"What's the news?"

"The paintings can be picked up from here or shipped to Denver whenever you say."

"Are they signed?"

"Yes." Laurence had brought the paintings back, both with a small *D Belling* in childish letters in the right hand corner. He hadn't fooled her.

"Good. Ship them to Denver." Then he paused. "I shall be in London next month. Will you allow me to take you out to dinner? You deserve my gratitude."

"I shall look forward to it." She hesitated, then added, "Dominic."

She put the phone down and listened to the racing of her heart. Then studied her face in the mirror. Her cheeks were flushed and there was a sheen in her eyes which might merely be the light glancing off the lenses of her spectacles, but she didn't think so. She had been speaking to Dominic King, one of the richest and most influential men in the USA, who had called her Deborah. He'd called her Deborah before, of course, when he had sat opposite her and drank the coffee she'd made, and congratulated her on her loyalty. She remembered his hands with their long aesthete's fingers, nails buffed and manicured; somehow she knew he would be expert in whatever he did with them. He had a fastidious temperament contained within a powerful body; she was drawn to men like him. Like Laurence. But Laurence's body was soft and rapidly going to fat. Dominic King, on the other hand, though older, had kept his at the peak of perfection.

He would be in London next month. He had invited her out to dinner. Thank goodness she was used to waiting.

The doorbell rang at Hurlingham Mansions at eleven o'clock that night.

He was wearing his dark blue business suit but his shirt was not so spotlessly white and his shoes lacked their usual high polish. He looked in need of mothering, but she was not his mother.

"Eighteen months," he said. "The court took note of his good conduct since the crime and his excellent references. His solicitor thinks he'll be out in ten."

"How did he take it?" They were seated at the kitchen table. She had turned on the coffee percolator but had poured him a scotch.

"Impassively, as usual. No – I think there was relief, and resignation. Could have been much worse. Oh God." He tossed off the whisky in one gulp.

"You're not to blame, Laurence."

"No. In some ways I wish I was. I wish I knew…" He left the sentence hanging, drumming his fingertips on the table top. Then he stood up and paced the room. His bulk filled all available space. His physical presence filled her throat like a strangulation. He paused by the window, his back to her. "Deborah…"

"It's too late, Laurence."

"No, I want…"

"I threw the key away."

"No." He turned back to her. "I want companionship. Just a little human companionship."

A companion. That was what she had become.

"Is that too much to ask?" His eyes were holding hers, full of entreaty.

"Probably."

He dropped back on the chair. "I know I don't deserve it. I think I've hurt you – have I? I've been too involved in my own affairs for too long. I'm a selfish man, Deborah. You deserve better."

"Yes."

He was silent, staring down at his hands spread flat on the table. She watched him, studied him. Her feelings – what were her feelings? Did she have any? After Will, she had wrapped up her feelings and put them away. She had been thawing, a little, but his letter had put an end to that. *We can't change. Nothing changes.* Well, it could, and it had. And he had changed, too. He couldn't deny that.

"You're right," he said at last. "It's too late."

She would give him one last chance. She made him wait a little longer, then got up and stood over him. "What exactly are the duties of a companion?"

269

His face creased into its rueful smile. "Oh, nothing arduous. No exertion of energy. Just your presence, Deborah. To be with me."

"When?"

"Now."

"Where?"

He grasped her hand. "In your bed." And then, holding it tightly, afraid she might snatch it away, "I'm asking for nothing, only your presence. Beside me. Your body beside mine. I haven't had that since…"

Since Will. She saw his face change, remembering. She should have withdrawn her hand but she didn't.

She woke in the early hours, aware that the front door had clicked to. She lay unmoving, her eyes closed. Then opened them and turned her face to the right. The pillow next to hers still retained the indentation of his head; the sheets were warm to her touch.

He had been as good as his word. He had wanted nothing from her but her presence.

******

So the case was over and Nick had gone. He, Laurence, would have to face a year, possibly more, of his absence. He had faced years of his absence before, but this was different; Nick had been in his house for over a week, they had met on equal terms, he had been allowed to believe he was forgiven – or was he? Laurence chose to interpret that smile as one of forgiveness. The smile, and the "fuck off" – did that signify that Nick had forgiven him for past sins? No, it was all probably in his own mind. Nick had forgotten it years ago.

He walked back from Baron's Court in the early hours of the morning, retracing his same steps after Will's death. He had left Deborah asleep. He had lain beside her, afraid of what he might feel; she lay next to him in a nightdress done up to the chin while he had stripped down to his boxer shorts. Had he hoped her

270

hand would stray across the divide? Only six inches or so separated them, but it might as well have been a chasm. Did she itch to touch him, or were their sessions in the Red Room, her first tentative sweet and fumbling explorations (before she had grown more expert, and he had spoiled them with his fantasies) buried in the past? She was lying awake, like him, hardly daring to breathe too loudly, aware of the beating of her heart, just as he was listening to his. He wondered what she would do if he put out a hand and touched her breast; he had almost done so, then didn't. Rejection would crucify him. At last the rhythm of her breathing told him she had fallen asleep. He had risen, thankfully, dressed and let himself out of the flat.

Walking along the deserted streets, he found his mind wandering, raking over the past, projecting into the future. Nothing there to give him much comfort. If anybody had asked him to define himself, he would have said he was basically a good man, a man who wanted to do good, to live in a world where goodness was prized. But wasn't that true of almost everyone? So why was it so hard to achieve?

Because, he thought, we're all, every one of us, on our own. No matter how many people surround us, we're alone. Even our nearest and dearest – our own children, flesh of our flesh – are unknowable. We stumble through life unaware of what is being thought, only inches away, in other people's skulls. Good intentions are subverted by ignorance. Faced with this knowledge, what can the good do but compromise – or go mad?

Oh Deirdre, he thought. You were never far from my thoughts for over twenty years, but I knew nothing of your life, or how you were living. A whole new scenario has opened up about which I know nothing. My sweet little Beggar Maid, drawn into a web of God knows what.

He had driven to Suffolk in the Jag, stopping off in Newmarket for a good lunch and a walk round the town. He had taken the long way round, bypassing motorways, cruising the back lanes at a speed the car disapproved of, judging by its sullen performance. He should have borrowed the Triumph – God

271

knew it needed a good run – but he would have had to tell Leo why, and where he was going, and this he was loath to do. He hadn't analysed his reluctance then, but he did so now, knowing that, since his revelation about being Gemma's father, he had rather neglected his legitimate daughter. He had presumed on her goodwill, taking her apparent acceptance of her half-sister at face value, rejoicing at their shopping trips as he dished out the money. But what had been going on in Leo's head even as he did this? Because, of course, her life had been turned upside down. Not only by the revelation, but by the events since – Sebastian's death, Nick's stay at the house (which she had hated, he knew), the discovery of the bones, Deirdre's mental breakdown; all these events following on from his revelation, over which Leo had had no control. She had been drawn along in their wake, a helpless yet gallant little trouper, his plucky pugnacious one and only precious princess.

He didn't stop at the cottage. He drove into the car park of the Lamb and Plough, the village local, and ordered a pint, then another, and another. He was the only customer in the place. A far cry from a tourist's idea of an English country pub, it had dark brown varnished anaglypta on the walls, ceilings brown with ancient cigarette smoke, floors worn brown boards. The few tables and chairs were thrown together in front of a large pool table that dominated half the space. The landlord, a surly-looking individual, glowered at him from behind the bar as if he shouldn't be there. After half an hour of this suspicious surveillance, Laurence had risen from the discomfort of his hard wooden chair and heaved his buttocks over a rickety stool at the counter.

"Have something yourself," he said, offering a fiver.

The landlord – Edward Frobisher, according to the name over the door - put down the glass he'd been wiping with a cloth for the past five minutes, sniffed, and grudgingly accepted the note. "Don't mind if I do, squire. Gin and tonic, if that's all right."

"A good choice. Very pleasant at this time of day."

"Closing soon. Open twelve to two-thirty lunchtimes."

"Do you do lunch?"

"Nope."

"Ah." No one in their right minds, Laurence thought, would choose to eat in these gloomy surroundings. "Keep the change," he said, as Frobisher opened the till. "Have another later on."

His philanthropy only served to deepen the landlord's suspicion. "Usually them that want something are free with their cash. You'll get nothing out of me, squire."

"There's nothing I want from you," Laurence said smoothly, "other than your excellent company."

"I seen you before. With vicar."

"Yes."

"You were at her cottage on bend." He rubbed the side of his face with the cloth. "She were taken away."

"For a rest. A holiday."

Frobisher nodded. "Strange one, her. Never mixed. Quite pleasant, but never mixed. Artist. Keep themselves to themselves, I've heard."

Laurence indicated the wall at the back of Frobisher's head. "I couldn't help noticing those painted plates. They're very good." Dinner-plate size, they hung one each side of the landlord's prominent ears. One showed a flock of sheep dominated by a huge curly-horned ram at the back. The faces of the sheep were individualised, human; one was obviously Deirdre, another the pregnant girl who had denounced the verdict of the court fifteen years ago. But the focus of the painting was the ram, its beard long and flowing, its glassy black eyes with their horizontal green slits fixing those of the beholder with a sardonic – demonic, even - stare. The other – a lone reaper in a field of wheat – was even more disturbing. Laurence had to clear his throat before he could ask, "Are they hers?"

"Yup."

The reaper was Nick, of course. Holding a scythe.

"I don't suppose you'd ever sell them."

"Nope."

"Only I'm in the art business myself. I could offer…"

"Nope."

273

"I can quite see why. But take care of them, please. They could be worth quite a lot in a few years."

Frobisher went on polishing glasses. Laurence supped his pint. After two or three minutes, Frobisher said, "In the art business, eh. Thought you might be the law."

Laurence laughed. "God, no."

"Customs and excise. VAT man."

"No, no."

"Trouble with poachers round here. Big estate, owns half the county, but still wants to hang on to rabbits like the little bleeders don't breed like…"

"Rabbits?"

Frobisher stretched his lips in what might be a smile. "Citizen's duty to keep 'em down, I say."

Laurence nodded sagely. "Indeed. I do agree."

"Have another pint, squire."

After another couple, supped convivially when Frobisher had closed the doors, names had been exchanged. "Call me Ned," invited Frobisher and Laurence said, "Edward Smith. Call me Ed, Ned," resurrecting the ghost who had sat in the Caernarvon court and spoken with the pregnant girl.

"You remind me of someone. Someone on telly…."

Laurence laughed. "Oh, I'm always being taken for some antique quiz show host. Everyone has a double, so they say." He was fairly confident Ned would not have been a viewer of *Art Meets Life,* now consigned to the shelves for programmes deemed unlikely to be given a second airing. Now he felt emboldened to indicate the reaper. "I might be mistaken, but that chap also reminds me of someone."

Frobisher drew a long pull of his pint, wiped a hand across his mouth and brought his face closer. "The mad axeman, that's him."

"The mad… ah, yes. He's been in the papers."

"Worked on the estate. Nice bloke. Wouldn't have thought it in a million years."

"Was he a regular?"

"Came in here most Friday or Saturday nights for a game of pool. Not many could beat him. Not much of a drinker, couple of pints at most." He brought his face even closer. "I could tell you a funny thing or three, if you've a mind to hear 'em."

And another fiver, Laurence thought, drawing it out. "No more for me, thanks, but you have another gin and tonic."

Frobisher grinned. "The other fellow came in here, too. With him."

"Other fellow?"

"The posh one. The one killed in the car crash. Wouldn't have thought much of it except it was in the papers, father one of them high-up lawyers causing a fuss." When Laurence was silent, he said, "He were staying at the cottage. Boyfriend of the daughter. Came in here one night for a game of pool."

"Yes, I know. I'm a friend..."

"Ah, but, squire, he was still here when he shouldn't have been, if you get my drift."

Laurence gazed down at his pint.

"Had a thing going with the mother. The artist."

Laurence sat back, his mouth suddenly dry.

"Funny thing, that. Our Nick gets done for chopping up a body, boyfriend gets fried, mother goes barmy. Just struck me what a funny coincidence. Not," Frobisher said, finishing his pint with a satisfied gargle, "that I'd say a word to the filth. This is in confidence, mind." He indicated Laurence's empty glass. "One more for the road?"

"No. Thanks. I must be off."

Back in the Jag, Ned's offer of a brace of pheasants politely refused, Laurence sat with his hands on the steering wheel, staring ahead, for quite a few minutes before putting the car in gear and pulling away.

It was only a short drive to the cottage, but probably a fifteen-minute walk. Situated on the curve of a long bend a mile or so outside the village, it could easily be overlooked, screened as it was by overgrown hedgerows and a couple of tall trees. Would the car be noticed outside the house? Well, of course it would. But word would already have gone round. Even now,

Ned would be spreading the gossip about the man in the Jag, last seen with the vicar, drinking in his pub.

Gossip? Was that what his revelation amounted to? But there was no point in Ned making it up. So Deirdre and Sebastian had been having a bit of a fling while Gemma was in London? How long would he have been there? When had he gone to Nigel Pettit's holiday cottage in the Lake District? He remembered Nigel's statement at the inquest, that the cottage had been let the week before the accident. So when had Sebastian left Suffolk…? Laurence should have asked Ned, but he didn't want to seem too interested. And of course he'd say nothing to Gemma.

He must concentrate on the job in hand. Deirdre had told him to go down the side of the house and make for the trees on the left hand side of the meadow. But it wasn't a meadow any longer; the ground behind the small back garden of the cottage had been ploughed and planted with a crop already two feet high. He had to skirt round the perimeter, wading through knee-high waves of wheat, to reach the line of birch and hornbeam that stretched away into the distance.

It was quite dark immediately he stepped under the canopy. He had jotted down her instructions, and read them again now to remind himself. A long, lithe shape passed his feet and melted into the undergrowth; there was a colony of feral cats, she had told him, that would now have to fend for themselves. And mind where you tread, she had instructed, there could be traps.

So it was slow progress, what with the undergrowth, potential lethal devices and his aching knees; keeping his head down to watch for obstacles, he hit it more than once on low branches and got himself entangled in the thorny embrace of a briar. There were sudden sunny patches that blinded him, before he plunged back again into gloom. And possibly a wild goose chase anyway, he thought, at the end of it all.

That must be the huge fallen branch she had described, and there the tall trunk with the knot hole marked with a cross; he must be getting close. And yes, he could now hear that strange keening on the air, a whispering, that marked the spot. A slight crosswind, she said, striking a certain configuration of leaf and bough that was heard quite clearly at night or when the air was weighted but motionless. This was the little glade at the centre of the Enchanted Wood.

And there was the hollow tree. He stood for a while getting his breath back before he approached. It was an ancient oak, gnarled and venerable, its base a fretwork of root and cavernous orifices, a living shelter studied with lichen, fungi, clinging ivy. How many species of insect and small mammal called this place home? It was the planet in microcosm, and Laurence felt himself drawn towards it like a fly to a web though the tree was no spider but a huge benign presence; at least he thought so. He had no feeling of dread as he stuck his face into the largest cavern, thrust his hand inside with groping fingers outstretched.

At first they encountered mossy moistnesses, sticky threads, sharp splintered bark that got under his nails. But then – ah – they grasped an object, something small, lying on top of – yes – a textured, shiny surface that had sharp corners, a fairly large canvas that needed two hands to grip and pull out and prop up against the trunk. Without looking at it, he delved back inside the tree and drew out the object, a sculpture, the same size as the bat-winged head. But this one had legs. Eight legs.

Eight crouching legs and a body that was a face. He had never liked spiders, he couldn't deal with the leggy ones sometimes found squatting in the bath, he had called on the services of Bernard who had scooped them up and thrown them out the window with cheerful nonchalance; but this one stuck to his hand, filled his palm with the weight and presence of one of those hideous arachnids found in the rainforest, hairy-legged and furry bodied, commanding an appalled respect even as it repelled. But the face – the face was angelic, eyes lifted heavenwards, expression calm and forgiving, mouth smiling a blessing. A Victorian depiction of Jesus.

It was some time before he could draw his eyes away and look at the painting. At first he saw nothing but two white, and two red, dots; the light under the tree was diffused and the painting sat in shadow. Comparisons with Sebastian's parcel came to mind; he stared at this painting as he had first stared at

277

the gypsy girl, uncomprehending. Then it swam into view: the two white dots became pinpoints of light in a pair of eyes, staring out from a set of features gradually coalescing into a face. A narrow, gaunt face with a high forehead, and long black hair merging into a black beard and moustache, and a full, almost feminine mouth, lips parted in a beneficent smile that became a leer of contempt even as he gazed at it. The two red dots were just above the hairline parallel to the glassy black eyes (these without the green stripe) - the glistening tips of two horns, not huge and curly like the ram's but squat, speckled. The whole painting was speckled with some kind of mould (had it been in the tree so long?) but these cut-off, bleeding stumps, and the glittering black eyes, seemed fresh and alive with a kind of benevolent evil.

Was it his imagination, or had the keening become louder, the shadows denser? – no, surely it was merely the effect of those four or five unaccustomed pints downed at an ungodly hour – but he found it nearly impossible to tuck the sculpture in his pocket and heft the painting under his arm (face staring outwards) and make his way back through the trees and the briars and the lurking perils in the undergrowth; but, breathing great gulps of relief, he somehow managed to regain the wide expanse of cornfield, rippling in the balmy breeze under a blessedly infinite sky.

5. May 1986

Where would she like to go, he had asked her on the phone. He had made suggestions: the Dorchester, Connaught Rooms, Le Gavroche? – no, Deborah said hastily, she wouldn't feel comfortable there. Perhaps the Savoy Grill...? A good choice, he said, he'd order a table right away.

He was coming to pick her up at nine o'clock (he was obviously a late diner). At half past five she had a bath and washed her hair. At six o'clock she varnished her nails with a colourless gloss. Between six-fifteen and eight-thirty she wandered around in her slip, wondering what to wear. She tried on the contents of her wardrobe; she didn't want to look too dressed up, but not too casual either. She still had a good figure which she could show off to full advantage. But her natural reticence was, perhaps, what had attracted him to her (was he attracted?). What kind of women was he used to taking out?

She realised she knew nothing about him. Why hadn't he married? Men like him were usually on their third or fourth wives by the time they reached their sixties. Perhaps no woman had measured up to his obvious standards. He was one of the world's most eligible bachelors, she had read in a recent tabloid, sometimes seen with beautiful women but whose private life remained a mystery. He had no entry in Who's Who.

Oh, she was like a teenager on her first date. And it was, she realised, almost her first date. She'd been out with a couple of boys at university but always in a crowd, never alone. Once she'd been to the cinema and suffered what she assumed was called 'heavy petting' – a hand had ventured into her bra and a wet tongue in her ear – but she'd found the experience so off-putting she hadn't gone there again. Did first dates always bring on these palpitations of the heart, this constriction of the throat? How foolish, a fifty-two-year-old woman suffering the afflictions of youth!

When the sleek black car drew up outside, she was dressed in a smart but not too formal navy blue suit in soft linen, skirt just below the knee, with a butter-yellow silk shirt open to the cleavage (she had bought a padded and underwired bra which certainly made the best of her rather small, though still fairly pert, breasts), and short sleeves that would show off her forearms when she took off her jacket. She was as proud of her arms as she was of her legs; her limbs were the best things about her. She had invested in contact lenses a month ago, and was now expert in applying them to her short-sighted but still pretty violet irises. Her face in the mirror looked a stranger's, soft-focused, her hair loosely curled about her shoulders. She remembered taking all this time to dress ten years ago, first experimenting to one of Laurence's parties and then, wearing the same creation, to the Savoy Grill. Her preparations had had the desired effect then. What did she hope to gain now?

The bell sounded. She pressed the button. An unfamiliar voice said, "Mr King for Miss Routledge," and she said, "I'll be down in two minutes."

A chauffeur in a smart uniform stood on the step and escorted her to the car, opened the back door and remained standing as she eased herself gracefully inside. No sooner had her feet in their strappy stilettos left the pavement than the door was closed almost silently behind her.

A glass of champagne was being offered to her. She accepted it, noticing the flash of a diamond in the darkness. The car moved smoothly forward, not even disturbing the liquid in her glass. Another glass chinked against hers. A voice from beside her said, "To us. Deborah."

She settled back into soft leather, aware of his presence against the same upholstery only inches away. As the car cruised under sodium lights his silhouette loomed and showed his face in profile. She kept hers facing forwards. Her nose was too long, her jawline too square, but she couldn't help that; he would have to accept her as she was. She felt comfortable. She felt – oh, calm and relaxed and in control of herself. She was holding nothing back. She would offer him the Deborah Routledge without the self-protective layers she had built up over the years. Even Laurence didn't know the real Deborah Routledge. Who exactly was she?

Perhaps she would find out tonight.

******

Fri 9 May 4.52pm

It gets spookier. I got home early today, filming suspended becoz of the wether, and there was this strange woman in the kitchen. Hallo, she said, you must be Leonora. I said yes, who are you. She said I'm Mrs Wainrite the new housekeeper. Your father's just hired me and my husband.

So I went into the library. Daddy was riting on his computer as usual, two fingers bashing the keyborde and swearing. Who's this Mrs Wainrite, I said, you didn't tell me you were hiring anyone. And he said this is my house Leonora, I can hire whoever I want. I said I don't like her, she's spooky. He said why. I said she's not Mrs W, and burst into tears.

He sat me on his lap then and we both had a silly 5 mins, him snivelling more than me. O Daddy I said, tell her to go. I can do the housework, I'm good at hoovering and sqwerting a bit of pollish about and he said O Leo wot about the garden and it's not fair on you and this house is too big and everything's getting on top of me and the money's not coming in any more and everything's all my folt and I said O Daddy we'll be alrite it'll be just us again tell everyone else to go and I ment Gemma too becoz if anything it's all her folt, hers and the Man's and the Mad Mother's, tho I didn't say this to Daddy of corse. But I said if there's no money we can't afford a housekeeper and he said O I just ment money is tite at the moment, there's enuff for home help, besides they come from an agency and it's all taken care of.

And then he said, Leonora you know I love you don't you, I don't offen say it but I do, you're everything to me, you and Huw.

Me and Huw. He didn't say Gemma. I think his not saying Gemma made me cry even more. I'm crying now, riting it.

Tears of happyness. Becoz he didn't include Gemma.

******

His house had become a prison; comfortable, well-appointed, but a prison nonetheless. The library was his cell. Here he spent most of the day, ostensibly working on his magnum opus, but more usually gazing at Wheels One, or out the window at the garden or sometimes, opening the bottom drawer of his filing cabinet, at the two heads, which now seemed to belong together. The painting he kept face down.

Today he was staring out the window at Mr Wainwright sitting on the mower, going round in long lazy circles. When Mr W had done this, Laurence would usually stroll out and watch for a while, then fetch a couple of lagers and a plate of Mrs W's sandwiches to the gazebo where, deep in two deckchairs, they would remark on the weather, discuss the merits or otherwise of weedkiller, pass comment on the cricket and, after half an hour or so, get round to putting the world to rights. Laurence would fulminate on the state of current affairs while Mr W had a more magnanimous attitude: "Leave it to the politicians, Mr B, and let's get on with the important things in life." To Bernard, the garden was his world and he was quite satisfied with his lot.

What was Mr Wainwright's first name? Laurence was sure he'd asked, and was told, but he couldn't for the life of him remember. Nor that of his wife. Had the agency supplied names? And what the hell was the agency called, anyway? He'd had a phonecall one morning when he'd been rather distracted (he'd made a start with Leonardo, and realised he'd bitten off more than he could chew) and before he knew it he'd agreed to interview a couple who, he was assured, would ideally fit the vacancy on offer. Had Leo advertised for home help? He thought not; she would have told him and besides, she didn't want the Ws replaced. Neither did he.

He had hated to see them go, but at least the problem of Deirdre was solved. When she came out of Capel Park Manor (which, all being well, would be in about a fortnight), it had been decided that she would convalesce with the Wetherbys until she felt strong enough to return to Suffolk. Barbara was delighted to have her but Laurence hoped there was no coercion involved; he had gifted them a sizeable chunk of the purchase price of their house before Deirdre's breakdown, and it had been Barbara's idea to look after her, not his at all. The money he would save on the nursing home had already been spent on the conversion of the Ws' annexe into a one-bedroom self-contained house for

Deirdre, and after that he would send money for her keep. He had also paid a deposit on a flat in the Barbican to set Huw on the road to independence. Cyril's money had been put to good use. Laurence had ceased to think of the Blue & Greens as forgeries, anyway; they had become, in his mind, authenticated Murchison juvenilia.

Lack of ready money had been his trump card when the Wainwrights turned up for their interview, which he had completely forgotten about. He had opened the front door to find two people planted there like a couple of unsuccessful hybrids: a man whose large head seemed to have been grafted on the trunk of a dwarf conifer and a woman whose tall ungainliness and sour expression seemed the result of an unfortunate experiment with poison ivy and deadly nightshade. Oh no, he was being unkind; it was just that the juxtaposition was unnerving, the man reaching only to the woman's shoulder and both glowering at him with identical expressions of distaste.

Who had interviewed whom? Still in a state of bemusement, he had sat behind his desk listening to their catalogue of skills and previous placements and could find no excuse for declining their services. Apart from the money situation. He had opened his mouth to say that their obvious expertise should naturally be financially well rewarded and unfortunately at the moment he would find this impossible, when Mrs Wainwright had scuppered this last forlorn hope.

"And," she'd said, handbag barricading her meagre bosoms, "our salary will be paid by our agency for the first two weeks. That is a measure of its confidence in your satisfaction with the standard of our work, I'm sure you'll agree." She had risen to her full height. Her husband rose too, to his. They were like ventriloquist and dummy, although it was the ventriloquist who had done all the talking. To this day, Laurence had never seen Mr Wainwright so much as open his mouth, apart from making an unpleasant whistling sound between his teeth as he carried out his chores. And he had no complaints as to their work. The two weeks passed. When he received the contract from the agency, he would politely decline their services, and all would go back to normal. But no contract came and the third week passed. No invoice, no communication of any kind. The Wainwrights still arrived on the stroke of eight o'clock (from where, he didn't know), carried out their duties to their own agenda and left on the stroke of three-thirty. Mrs Wainwright cooked breakfast and provided lunch, but an evening meal wasn't included. Terms and conditions had been decided by the employees but as Laurence wasn't their employer, he couldn't complain. He did what he had always done: kept his head down, tried not to stir up trouble, and let things run their own course.

The first month passed with no mention of wages. Mr Wainwright spent all day out in the garden, which suited Laurence; Mrs Wainwright went grim-faced through her chores but the house was sparkling and the meals she cooked adequate (not like Barbara's, but hers had been prepared with love). There were also house rules: no outdoor shoes allowed beyond the threshold, all rubbish to be placed in the bins provided, clothes hung up in wardrobes unless they were for the wash, in which case they were to be deposited, neatly folded with pockets emptied, in the laundry. It was, Laurence sometimes thought, like living in a hotel.

Leo, he knew, hated these arrangements. Gemma took them in her stride, but then she was rarely home these days. He worried about Gemma but didn't know how to broach the subjects of Sebastian, Deirdre or Nick with her; she had built a wall around herself, like a glass barrier which, if he tried to breach it, might smash to smithereens and expose her once again to the full onslaught of grief. Her friendship with Leo seemed to have cooled. Her friendship with Huw, though…

Oh, he was worrying unduly. His son knew how to look after himself. If, sometimes, Laurence caught Huw gazing at Gemma with that desolate yearning he had seen on Nick's face in the bedroom, he dismissed it as his imagination; Huw had plenty of other girls, he wasn't likely to fall in love with his own sister. He had more sense than that. But of course love knew no boundaries, as well he knew. There was no guarantee that common sense could prevail, once those feelings were unleashed. Love and longing and lust; there was no cure, no sticking-plaster solution. One day, he thought, I'll tell them the truth. When Gemma is stronger, I'll tell her the truth.

He said, "Deborah."

A caught breath, then silence on the other end of the line. Then the voice that she used to clients said, "Laurence."

"How are you?"

"Fine."

"How's business?"

"A little slow. But fine." A pause, then, "How are you?"

"Oh, fine."

"Why don't you come in sometime?"

"I will. Yes."

"How's the magnum opus?"

"Oh – not fine. Not fine at all." He paused, then said, "I think I need some wine and plums. Are they still on offer?" And held his breath.

She was holding hers, obviously. Then, "I threw the key away, Laurence."

"Surely you can find it again."

A long pause. "I don't know…"

"Look for it, Deborah. Please."

"I'll try."

"Please."

"I will try, Laurence." Her voice betrayed the trace of a tremble.

He dropped the handset on his desk, and held his head in his hands.

She held the receiver for a little longer before replacing it.

It was a good job she was used to waiting. It would be another month or so before Dominic King would be back in the country.

******

285

"I dislike travelling," he'd said, "unless there is a specific reason for doing so."

They had finished their meal and were lingering over the coffee and liqueurs. Their conversation had been enjoyable; they had ranged over subjects such as art, about which he was fairly knowledgeable, but bowed to her greater expertise; business, about which, although fairly knowledgeable, she obviously bowed to his; and current affairs (although some areas were studiedly avoided, Third World politics and guerrilla warfare among them). They discovered a mutual appreciation of music and theatre and good wine. He was erudite but not arrogant; he listened attentively and without any obvious condescension. After a rather formal start to the evening, she began to enjoy herself. She tried a few light-hearted remarks about their fellow diners and, although he smiled dutifully, she thought humour was not one of his strong points.

Did he find her attractive? She had caught him looking at her legs in their sheer silk stockings when he helped her from the car (waving the commissionaire away); his eyes had briefly strayed to her cleavage when she had removed her jacket in the foyer; at the table, she had cupped her smooth white upper arms in her long perfectly manicured fingers while she gave full attention to his opinion that the Post-Impressionists were probably over-valued – "Do you not agree, Deborah?" he'd asked, quite prepared, she felt, to be contradicted.

Did she find him attractive? Well, there was something – powerful, wealthy men exuded sex appeal, she supposed – but it wasn't that. There was something buried deep, something he might even have forgotten, that she sensed, something that had kept him alone and single over his sixty-four years.

Throughout the meal she had been conscious of his hands and the restrained but expressive way he used them. Waiters bowed and scraped to a lifted finger, an outstretched palm. He steepled them, elbows on the table, when he wanted to make a point. He laid them flat on its surface, leaning forward slightly, when concentrating. He flicked subconsciously at his chair seat before sitting, at his cuffs, at the tablecloth; he disliked crumbs, specks of dust, disorder of any kind. He was the kind of man who had risen from poverty without trace and constructed his own world about him, one in which he could operate without revisiting the past. His past, she thought, was a closed book.

He didn't mention Drusilla Belling. Neither did she.

When they eventually rose from the table (at around midnight), she became aware of a fluttering in her stomach. The car cruised back to Baron's Court and they shared another glass of champagne. The fluttering became a wave of panic - or excitement, she didn't know which. When they eventually drew up outside Hurlingham Mansions, and the chauffeur remained in his seat, she experienced a feeling almost of dread. Was this to be the end?

She made a move, almost imperceptibly. His hand covered hers on the leather seat.

"I hope you enjoyed the evening."

"It was lovely. Yes."

"We must do it again."

"Oh – yes."

The chauffeur got out, opened the door opposite hers. She felt the upholstery shift as his weight was removed.

Her door opened. His hand was on her elbow, helping her out.

They walked up the steps to the front entrance, his hand still lightly holding her arm. They reached the door.

This was the moment she'd been dreading. What was the etiquette? In her day, an invitation for coffee could be misconstrued. Besides, in this situation it didn't seem viable. And yet...

"I'll see you to the elevator." He opened the door for her, handed her into the lobby. He pressed the button, then turned back to her. "Thank you for a very nice evening."

She smiled. Her face felt stiff. Very nice? Was that all it was?

"Deborah." The lift was descending; she could see the lights winking. "A Biblical name."

"Rebekkah's servant, I believe." She added pedantically, "Rebekkah, wife of Isaac."

The lift had arrived. Its old-fashioned mechanism whirred. "I think you're doing yourself a disservice." The wrought-iron gates clanked. His hand was ready to open them. "The Deborah I'm thinking of was rather more interesting." The hand drew away from the gates and lifted one of hers which he brought to his lips. She felt his mouth on her knuckles.

Women, she had read, were always swooning in Victorian novels. A strange word. One she had never thought about before. But now – she felt as if she would swoon. It was not a faint, not as final as that, but a gradual melting, starting at her hand and travelling down, down as far as the pit of her stomach, and down further, to that particular point between her legs that she had discovered long ago, after their sessions in the Red Room, and which she had done her best to forget after Will...

Her eyes were closed. Her lips – oh God, was her mouth ready, it must be, she could almost feel his mouth leaving her hand (and leaving, too, an imprint of moisture) and coming towards hers, and hesitating, and thinking better of it...

"I dislike travelling, unless there's a specific reason for doing so. I'll be in touch, Deborah. Perhaps in a month or so. I will be in touch."

She stood beside the lift and watched him walk away, through the door, down the steps. The chauffeur, standing beside the car, waited until he'd settled himself inside, then got in the driver's seat. A few seconds later, the long black car had vanished into the night.

6.   July 1986

Wisteria had always been Barbara's favourite climber and Journey's End would have been covered in swags of its melting blue cascades, hiding its rather staid Seventies exterior, a couple of months earlier. Now the front garden overflowed with hydrangeas and hollyhocks and other old-fashioned flowers he didn't know the names of, a testament to Bernard's skills. Although he'd made this journey a few times in the recent past, Laurence was struck again, as he parked the car in the double driveway and walked up to the front door, by the contrast between this and his own bleak house in Hampstead; now the Wainwrights were in semi-residence it seemed to have absorbed their dour charmlessness. And still no mention of wages. Still he kept his head down, his curiosity at bay.

He was welcomed with effusive warmth from Barbara, although Bernard was nowhere to be seen. Neither was Deirdre. He waited until he was enthroned like a king in the best armchair with a cup of tea and a plate of homemade cakes before he felt he could broach either subject.

"Dee's coming along beautifully," Barbara said, before he could even ask. "She'll be here in a minute. She's picking some flowers at the end of the back garden in your honour."

"You've been very good to her."

"Oh, nonsense. She's been like a breath of fresh air to us pair of old codgers."

"When you offered to look after her," he said carefully, "I never thought it would be such a long arrangement…"

She brushed the remark away. "She can stay as long as she likes, Mr B. She's no trouble at all. In fact I think Bernard would go…" She pressed her lips together and said no more, just passed another strawberry tart on to his plate.

He munched his way through the cakes and accepted another cup of tea. The subject of Deirdre's keep would have to keep a bit longer, he thought. He wondered what was happening about the Suffolk cottage. Nick had bought it, but whose name was on the deeds? Would it be left to go to wrack and ruin? Property prices in East Anglia were going through the roof, even if the roof was in a shocking state of disrepair. Did Nick realise that these yuppies, as they were called, young puppies working in stocks and shares and rolling in money, would pay top whack for a thatched and picturesque country retreat ripe for refurbishment within striking distance of London? Oh, it was none of his business. He would go on forking out for Deirdre's keep as long as it took, of course he would, but still...

"And how's Bernard?" he said, through a mouthful of crumbs.

"Oh, he's fine. He had an appointment this morning, he should be back any minute. He rarely lets me go with him. Every time we go to Chichester, he says, it costs him a fortune in clothes and toys. Not for me," she chuckled, "for Eileen's two."

"They're a bit old for toys...."

She wagged her head at him. "Eileen's two *grandchildren*. Dougie and his wife have just had a boy, and Nessa had Gracie last year."

Oh God, where had the time gone? He stirred his tea, feeling the depression descend, when he thought he'd left it behind in Hampstead. Barbara only had one child and was already a great-grandmother. He had two, both of whom showed no signs of settling down, let alone carrying on the line. Were the Bassett genes destined for oblivion?

"Oh, Laurence," Barbara said, "you do look sad. How are things really?"

There had been a subtle shift in their relations since her retirement. Now he felt, not her employer (although he had never been that), but possibly a younger brother, an unfamiliar feeling but one he could very well get used to. He had been an only child. He was glad Leo had a sibling; of course, he was only thinking of Huw. It was strange how soon, although he still loved Gemma as a daughter, he had ceased thinking of her as *his* daughter.

He smiled. "Not good, Barbara. I feel I've aged ten years in the last few months."

"You've had a lot of shocks."

"Yes, I expect that's it."

She hesitated, then said, "I've had a letter from Nick."

"Ah."

"He sounds all right, but then he would, wouldn't he? It's what he doesn't say that worries me. He doesn't write to Dee, and I know she's fretting."

"Does she visit him?"

"Oh no. No, he doesn't want visitors. We've all been told not to."

He placed his empty plate and cup back on the tray on the occasional table drawn up beside his knees. "If that's what he wants..." The terrible blank despair was overtaking him. He took off his glasses and polished the lenses.

"I just feel so helpless," Barbara sighed. "Does he write to Gemma?"

"I don't know. She's never said." Mrs Wainwright had taken it upon herself to distribute the post in the mornings. Sometimes he had the feeling she censored what little he received, although nothing, as far as he knew, had gone missing. Or was he getting paranoid in his old age?

"He says he hopes she's not brooding. She's got to get on with her life, he says."

"Oh, she is." Gemma had been badly affected by Sebastian's inquest back in March, but she'd insisted on going. It had been a tough day for everyone; he'd had to be strong for Denis and Louisa, but had been pretty cut up himself. The details of the accident were horrific. Much better, he'd thought, to reach a proper conclusion and come to terms with it. But Denis had insisted on an open verdict, leaving the wound still unhealed.

But he was proud of the way Gemma was getting on with her life. She'd made an excellent impression at the BBC and was now entrusted with the big overseas stories. She was overseas herself much of the time, and had probably given Mrs Wainwright instructions to forward her post. Perhaps the atmosphere in the house had got to her, too. It had certainly got to Leo.

And Deborah? What exactly had happened to Deborah?

"Oh," said Barbara suddenly, "here's Dee!"

He hadn't seen Deirdre since her discharge from Capel Park. He had wanted to give her time to settle in at Journey's End. He'd spoken on the telephone to her a couple of times, when he'd phoned Barbara. She sounded happy. She hadn't asked him any questions and he hadn't volunteered any information. He was aware he'd been putting off this meeting until he knew he couldn't do it any longer.

"Hello, Laurence." And there she was on the threshold, his little Beggar Maid, restored to him. Hiding behind a big bunch of gladioli. Her face, when she lowered the blowsy blooms, was smiling. "I picked these for you."

"My favourite." They weren't, of course, and she knew it. They were showy, opulent. Shallow.

She came towards him. He stood, feeling stupidly nervous. She put the flowers down on the table, stood on tiptoe and threw her arms round his neck. His arms went round her waist; he could almost have clasped his hands behind his own back, so slender was she. But not thin; not that terrible skeletal thinness he remembered. In fact he could feel the full roundness of her breasts pressing against his chest.

"Ah," Barbara said, "I think that's Bernard," and left the room.

It took a few minutes before he could disengage himself; not that he wanted to, but her face was buried in his shoulder and her hands were groping in his hair and they couldn't stay like that for much longer. She was pressed up against him and something was happening in his groin that hadn't happened for months - years – and he unclasped her hands and tried to hold her away from him but her head was lifting and she was pressing her mouth against his, and then kissing him all over his face.

"My God," he said, when he could, "that's a welcome."

"Oh, Laurence! I'm so happy! Thank you for sending me here!" She picked up the sheaf of flowers and pirouetted round the room. She looked fourteen, not nearing forty. "Don't I look better? Don't you think so?"

"You look wonderful, Deirdre."

"And you look terrible." She stood still, head on one side, assessing him. "You're getting fat."

"No, I am fat."

"You need exercise. It's that horrible great car of yours. You need a bike." Then she said, "And how is Deborah?"

The name, in her mouth, made him start. And then he remembered, back in September, the day he'd heard about the discovery of the bones, he'd told her about Deborah. About how – oh God – he was thinking of marriage.

"She's very well," he said.

"Still a companion?"

He didn't answer. She stared at him, then lowered her head. "Ah. I see."

"I don't think," he said, "I'm cut out for marriage."

"No. Nor me." Nor Nick, she could have said, but didn't. She put the flowers down again and fell gracefully into the sofa, patting the place beside her. It was a two-seater sofa. By the time he'd settled his buttocks in, she was pressing against him, her mouth against his ear, her hand on his knee. "I'm sorry for giving you such a fright. And poor Adrian. I don't know what came over me. I've thought about it since. I've worked it all out."

"Good."

"It was an accident. *They* were accidents. Not anybody's fault."

He didn't know what she was talking about, but let that go. He was only conscious of the hand on his knee, making little circular motions, little patting movements, as if he needed to be reassured.

He had wanted to talk to her about the paintings. Why had she never mentioned them? - the two of Gemma that had been shipped off to Denver (at nearly double the price he'd made on any of Will's – the market had gone mad), and the other one that still resided in his bottom drawer. Did she want it back? That, and the two heads? One he couldn't live without?

"Are you painting again, Deirdre?" was what he said.

The hand fell still. She pushed herself away from him and stared ahead.

"I'm not asking for selfish reasons. I just want you to paint again. For you. For yourself."

"I can't." Her tone was flat.

"I'm sure you can. Mrs W can buy whatever you need. Money's no object." The Denver money had been invested, ready to be transferred to her when she was back in Suffolk, or wherever else she wanted to go. That wasn't what she meant, of course, he knew that.

"No, I can't. It isn't possible."

"Why not?"

She turned those green cat's eyes on him. "I can't paint when he's not around." She paused, looked down at her lap, gave a small laugh. "I never painted in London. I did my best work in Wales, after he came back. And again in Suffolk, after he came back. When he's not here I can only draw, just silly drawings."

He hadn't thought of that. He was silent.

"So I am being punished, Laurence. He is punishing me."

"Oh, Deirdre…"

"No, I'm glad. It's what I wanted." But her eyes sparkled with tears.

When Barbara came back into the room with Bernard, they were still sitting side by side, not touching, staring ahead. Laurence caught Barbara's puzzled look before her usual brisk cheerfulness took over. He stood up and shook hands with Bernard who looked well, although a little thinner.

"She's working you too hard. You're supposed to be retired."

"Oh no. Not with those little buggers still alive and kicking, even down here." Bernard called all his enemies 'those little buggers' – weeds, squirrels, bugs – waging a one-man war against them. Laurence laughed. On an impulse he threw his arm round Bernard's shoulders, something he had never done before. To his surprise, Bernard's arm went round him, and they embraced briefly before pulling apart.

Despite his reputation (or because of it?), Laurence had been careful in the past not to show affection in public, especially to men. Women threw themselves at him, kissed him, clung to him, but he rarely reciprocated. The only woman he'd allowed close to him was Leo, and now Deirdre. But with men he kept his distance, only shaking hands, maybe allowing himself a brief pat on the shoulder. He was surprised how good it felt, how *manly*, to clasp a man against him. And Bernard was a man, in every sense of the word, even though, as he pulled away and Barbara came up and took his hand and patted it affectionately, Laurence was sure he'd seen tears in both their eyes.

He left Journey's End after a good lunch and good conversation. He left without asking Deirdre about the painting, which she had obviously forgotten. He was a little worried about Bernard – "That's a nasty cough you've got there, you ought to get it seen to," and Bernard had promised he would – but on the whole the arrangements seemed to have suited both Deirdre and the Wetherbys. His conscience was clear. He drove back to Hampstead with his depression thankfully lifted, the sheaf of gladioli beside him on the passenger seat.

******

Sat 19 July 4.29pm

Just had a surprise and had to rite it down strait away. Gemma came into my room. She nocked on the door and came in and said Can I talk to you so of corse I said yes. We haven't had a girly seshun since the aborshun. Well, she's away a lot of the time and so am I altho I don't stay away long becoz of Daddy.

It's Tony, she said, he wants to go out with me again. He foned me up at work. He said he hadn't called before becoz he thort he mite be introoding. He said he's missed me and I've missed him too but I don't know if it's rite, Leo, wot should I do?

I hadn't said a word all this time.

Wot should I do, Leo, she repeated, as if I hadn't herd.

I said, why don't you think it's rite? becoz that's all I could think of to say.

Becoz of Sebastian, she said. Becoz of the baby. Becoz of – o, everything.

But you went out with him when Sebastian was still alive, I said. That's worse, isn't it?

And she looked at me and said why, as if she really didn't know.

I said, well, becoz you already had a boyfrend.

295

Yes, she said, he knew that. So I was safe.

Safe? I said.

He didn't try anything. You know. Becoz he knew about Sebastian.

So you don't want him to try anything?

No.

O.

He's a good frend, I like him, but that's all. If I go out with him now, Leo, he mite think we can – well, you know.

No, wot?

Be more than frends. You know.

Yes, I did know.

Do you think I'm awful, she said. Only…

Wot, I said after a long paws.

Only there is someone else.

Well, I know that, don't I? Someone else who's banged up. She can't have him so she'll have the next available. Does she think I'd come down in the last shower? So I didn't say anything.

Someone else, she repeeted, I can't have.

I still didn't say anything becoz my brain was working 10 to the dozen.

I'm so miserable Leo, she said, I had to talk to you.

And I said, you should go out with him. With Tony. It's all rite. Just so long as you tell him you're just good frends.

Poor Tony, I thort, he's such a pushover he'd agree to it. And he'd be safe that way. If he was going out with her on that basis then he couldn't meet anyone else who mite be more dangerous. And I could keep an eye on them.

She sprang up then and kissed me on the cheek and said O Leo, thanx, and then she went off.

I know now why I always get fed up with boyfrends when I've spent ages hooking them. I've only just fallen in. I thort love should nock you off your feet but it doesn't, it creeps up on you. Like it's crept up on me.

******

"Deborah," he said, pressing the button to summon the lift, which he called the elevator. "The servant of Rebekkah, wife of Isaac."

296

"Oh, someone more interesting than that." She had done her homework.

He smiled. He'd smiled a lot more this evening. When her summons had come, she had been prepared. His arrival had been heralded in the business pages of the broadsheets. She had decided what to wear as soon as she read about it. She'd had her hair cut. After just a brief hesitation, she had also opted for a facial which, contrary to expectation, she had enjoyed. He'd kept her waiting only three days.

She had let him choose the restaurant, only stipulating that Le Gavroche was out of the question. They had dined in the discreet opulence of the Café Royal.

Over their first course, the conversation had ranged over the same subjects as before but on a more intimate level. He asked about her personal tastes in art, about which she was fairly definite; literature, about which she was fairly expert on the novels of Trollope and George Elliott; and opera, about which she knew next to nothing. Over the main course he asked about her life. She told him about the convent and her thwarted ambitions. Over dessert (she had a crème brulée, he kept to the cheese board), she told him about mother. About all the years of looking after an invalid, not a good patient even when she had been too ill to complain. He had listened with genuine empathy. He punctuated her account with sympathetic yet probing questions. Had it been a labour of love, he had asked, even after so many years? Had she ever felt driven to despair? About the futility, the waste? Had she ever been tempted... but he didn't finish the question, and she chose not to have heard.

Over coffee, his hand had brushed hers for a fraction of a second as he reached for his napkin.

On the journey back to Hurlingham Mansions she had trouble keeping her champagne glass steady. A second date was different to the first. After one invitation to dinner, she thought, options were still open. Having accepted a second, though, she was sending signals. Perhaps. Or did he still think of her as a business partner? What was the etiquette now?

She had spring cleaned the flat just in case. She had even thought of redecorating but there hadn't been time. She had bought new sheets for her bed, expensive Egyptian cotton. Not crimson, but purest white. Spreading them on, smoothing them out, was almost an erotic act in itself.

She took *Study in Blue & Green #1* down from the wall and stowed it safely away in the wardrobe.

She had gone to the library to do her research. She found her in the Old Testament Book of Judges. Deborah: leader and lawgiver, warrior, scourge of the unbelievers. Austere and morally upright.

"And have you judged me?" The lift had arrived, whirring and clanking like a mechanical locust.

Was he testing her? She ran her tongue round her dry lips. "Not yet."

He drew her hand up to his mouth. "Then I must wait a little longer. We need to be sure, Deborah. I need you to be sure." Still keeping hold of her hand, he brought his mouth to her cheek. Did his tongue flick over it, just for a brief second? She steadied herself against the doors, fingers round the bars, as she swooned.

Back in her dark, lonely flat, she sat on the pristine white sheets with fists clenched. He was as used to waiting as she was. Was he as frightened as her? He could go back to his other women - he had other women, she was sure of that. And equally she was sure he knew she would wait for his next call. And she was equally sure he *would* call.

It was just a matter of waiting.

"Deborah."

"Laurence."

"How are you?"

"Fine."

"How's business?"

"Oh – steady."

A pause, then, "The key. Have you found it?"

"Not yet. I'm looking."

"Look harder. Please."

"I – I don't…"

"Please. Please, Deborah." The pleading in his voice brought tears to her eyes. She could picture him sitting in his library, Wheels One on the wall, that bat-winged head under his hand. A blank computer screen in front of him.

"I'm still looking, Laurence." She put the phone down.

7.   August/September 1986

"No photographs," Hilary said. "Apparently he didn't like his photo taken. Not keen on publicity. But I finally came across something you might find interesting." She sat at her console in the offices of Independent News Broadcasting where she was spooling a film whose images strobed on the screen in front of them. At a stab of her finger, they froze.

Laurence stared over her shoulder. The screen was filled with police in old-fashioned helmets holding back a screaming crowd, many with faces contorted, mouths open and waving placards declaring *Homes not Bombs!*, *Youth Unite!* and *Down with all Fashist Pigs!!*

"The late unlamented Sixties." It was a newsreel in black-and-white. Hilary's finger stabbed again and the figures leapt into life. The police struggled; one lost his helmet, another was forced to his knees by the press of protesters surging forward. The camera panned round to show a flight of stone steps leading to an open doorway. Another two policemen appeared there, obviously hauling someone between them who wasn't co-operating. A hand was placed briefly over the camera, which wobbled violently. When it steadied, the police had made it down the steps with their captive, whose face loomed into the camera. Close-up of a pair a nostrils and a mouth obviously uttering a string of obscenities.

"Notting Hill," Hilary said. "Nineteen-sixty-eight. A group of anarchists or whatever took over a flat, started the first big squat. Big publicity, apparently a lot of rock stars became involved. When the bailiffs were sent in, this happened."

"Must have passed me by."

Hilary heaved a sigh. "Oh you, Laurence! You don't belong in the real world." Where had he heard those words before? Quite recently, too.

He continued watching the screen. The camera had focused on a group standing in the road beside a police van. It lingered over a couple of girls in mini-skirts, then swooped into close-up

300

on an earnest bearded fellow in black horn-rimmed glasses who was talking to someone with a microphone.

"Is there sound?"

"Not good quality." Hilary turned a knob and the fellow was ranting, "...property-owning classes are today's fascist oppressors... (a burst of static) ...taking back what belongs to the proletariat... (more static) ...power to the revolution!" – this accompanied by an arm upraised with closed fist.

"That, you may be interested to know," Hilary said, "is Alan Paterson." At his frown, she explained patiently, "Lecturer in sociology at the University of St Andrews. Him and his wife were the only people to admit to having been at your commune in Wales."

"Ah." Laurence peered at the screen with more interest. "Can you reel back a bit? Those two girls..." Yes, there they were, a small girl with a heart-shaped face – not Deirdre – and a taller girl with long blonde hair who could well be the pregnant girl at Caernarvon... Francine Everett. "Well done, Hilary."

"Not finished yet." She fast-forwarded; Alan Paterson harangued the reporter and his fist punched the air in double-quick time. The film slowed; the camera panned round again to the steps, where more police were manhandling more unco-operative captives. "There," said Hilary, and pointed.

Behind them, in the doorway, stood a figure in a long white robe. The camera stopped, as if transfixed. The figure walked forward and came down the steps, holding his palms outstretched almost in blessing. He kept his head turned from the camera. His hair was long, hanging a good six inches below his shoulders. There seemed to be a cheer from the crowd, although Hilary had turned the sound down again and it might just be static. As he reached the bottom step, the camera swooped round to the front and there, for a split second, was his face. That long narrow face, high forehead, black beard, mesmerising black eyes under lowering but well-shaped brows. He looked searchingly into the camera; smiled a calm, knowing smile, lifted his chin slightly and turned away. The next shot was of the unco-operative captives being bundled into the van which took off at speed, its siren blaring.

Hilary rewound the film and punched the button at the precise point the camera panned to the face. "Patrick King," she said.

Yes. It was the face of the ram. The face of the spider. The face in the picture that still resided face-down in the secret bottom drawer in his library. The younger brother, by a good few years, of Dominic King, and whose body had been found in the Thames at Greenwich in September 1970.

Laurence straightened. "Well done," he said again. "Thanks, Hilary."

"You're welcome."

"I owe you."

"When are you having another party? I haven't been invited to one for yonks."

"I haven't thrown one for yonks." He clapped her on the shoulder. "But you've given me an idea. The invitation will be in the post."

******

When Laurence broached the subject of Gemma's birthday on the phone to Deirdre, he was surprised at her reaction. Athough, on reflection, he shouldn't have been.

"We've never made much of birthdays. I'll send a card."

"But it's her twenty-first…"

"Oh, keep up, Laurence, it's eighteen that's the big one now. And we didn't do anything for that, she didn't expect it."

"I just thought it might be nice…"

"For me to be there? What are you planning?"

"A party."

"And I'd be the spectre at the feast." Then she added in a softer tone, "But thanks for thinking of me. Kisses all over."

What was it about him and women on phones? He was left holding the receiver to his ear while the line echoed through the ether. Deborah had done it to him, too, when she'd declined his invitation. And he hadn't even mentioned the damn key.

Should he keep the party a surprise? He thought Gemma would appreciate that. But women were becoming an unknown species to him. He decided ask an expert on the subject.

"Sounds great," Huw said. "She'll love it."

"Are you sure? Perhaps she'd prefer to look forward to it, prepare herself – you know, do all the things women do…"

"Such as?"

"Well - diets and sunbeds and - waxing…"

"Oh Dad." If Huw had been the sort to hug him, he would have done so, Laurence thought. As it was, he just stood smiling. "They do that anyway. They don't need an excuse." For a moment they both stood smiling at each other before Huw roused himself to deal with practicalities. "I suppose you want to hold it here."

"Yes, why not?"

"No, it's good. The place is big enough. How many were you thinking of inviting?"

"Oh God, I don't know. That's a point. There'll have to be her work colleagues – that's easy enough. Yours and Leo's friends. Gemma's friends…" He stopped. He knew none of her friends. People she had met at Cambridge – but that might be awkward. No Deirdre. No Nick. He hadn't thought this through, obviously. He said glumly, "Perhaps dinner at Leith's might be a better idea."

"No, it's cool. Don't worry Dad, I'll see to it."

"You?" He couldn't keep the disbelief out of his voice. Huw had never volunteered for anything before.

"Yes, me." Huw grinned. "Now *that's* a surprise."

He decided to pay another visit to the gallery. Now Huw had hijacked the preparations for the party, he had time on his hands. He should be getting on with Titian (he'd given up on Leonardo) but that old monster was defeating him too. He couldn't get the tone right – too erudite and he'd turn his public off, too facile and he'd be accused of dumbing-down. Perhaps he would write it under a pseudonym. Perhaps good old Ed Smith would hit the right note.

On his last visit to Gali-Leo's, in the middle of August, he realised things had changed. There had been new pictures on the walls, of course; he expected that. And Deborah had moved the furniture round; the counter was now along the left-hand side, her desk at the back. She'd employed a college girl on vacation as receptionist who, dragging her gaze from the pages of a paperback book the size of a brick, didn't recognise him. "Mr Bassett," he'd said to her enquiry and, at her blank look, "Laurence Bassett. I own this place." Too young, obviously, to watch morning repeats of old quiz shows. She remained obstinately unfazed. "She's upstairs, if you want to go up," she shrugged, and returned to the latest Judith Krantz.

Deborah was sitting in his leather chair behind his desk speaking to someone on the phone. She was perfectly entitled to do that. He drew up one of the chairs used by clients - a comfortable ladderback with upholstered seat in green velvet, perfectly serviceable – and waited until she'd finished her conversation. He occupied the time looking round his old office, drumming his fingers on his knees. His filing cabinet was still there, next to a work station with computer, printer and fax which, even as he looked at it, sprang into life with a series of bleeps and whistles.

"Laurence." She had put the phone down.

"Hello Deborah." He had the idea she wasn't pleased to see him.

"You should have told me you were coming. I'm very busy…"

"Oh, just passing. Thought I'd call in."

"I'll get Zara to make us some coffee."

"No, don't bother. I'm not staying long." After a pause, he said, "You've had your hair cut."

"Yes. I thought I was due for a change."

"It suits you." It did, too. He was so used to Miss Routledge with her hair swept severely back from her face, it had taken him a while to register the soft fringe, the curls licking her cheeks. Was the colour slightly different? "And no glasses."

"Contact lenses. Marvellous things."

"You didn't tell me."

"You didn't ask."

He spread his hands on both knees. "Ah, Deborah…"

She rose quickly and, opening the cabinet in the wall, poured him a scotch. He took it gratefully. He seemed to be getting through at least half a bottle most days.

As he drank, she talked about business. About the need to change, to get networked. To harness the awesome power of technology. Businesses that didn't embrace a global future, she said, were doomed to extinction. As he listened to these words issuing from her scarlet, glossy mouth he looked from her red stiletto shoes (one of which hung from the tips of her toes and which she was tapping against her foot as she spoke), up her long silky legs to the tomato-red suit, navy and red blouse and gold chains slung across her bosom (which seemed to fill out the blouse more than he remembered). Her jacket made her shoulders seem almost deformed; they looked wider and at least three inches higher than they should be.

"And that," she said, obviously winding up her speech, "is what I believe to be the future of Gali-Leo's."

He gulped his whisky and nodded.

"You agree?"

"I leave it in your capable hands, Deborah."

"So," she said, steepling her fingers with their long scarlet nails, "can we look forward to any more Bellings?"

The name was a shock. He swallowed. "I don't think so. Not for a while."

"You're in touch with her?"

"With Deirdre? Yes."

"So she's not producing any more paintings?"

"No. Not yet."

"You think she will? In the future?"

"I hope so."

"Oh, Laurence." It was a sigh of exasperation. "You really must get connected to the real world. I don't know how you've kept this place going so long. No wonder it nearly went down the tubes."

He said, "Did it?" and finished the last of the scotch.

He'd left soon after. He left her in his leather chair making another phone call. He bid goodday to Zara, who never lifted her eyes from the brick but wiggled the fingers of her right hand in what he presumed was a wave. He walked through the streets of Fitzrovia, which he thought he knew well, and realised the world had changed.

New York? She hadn't, as far as he knew, ever left the country before. There was a gallery opening in New York, she'd told him when she declined his invitation, and she felt she should be there. A link between New York and London galleries could be advantageous. Her voice had throbbed with excitement.

"So how long are you going for?" He was again seated on the green velvet seat of the ladderback chair, nearly a month later.

"Three days at the most."

"And the gallery…?"

"Unless you want to come in," she said, "we'll have to close."

"Can we do that?"

She regarded him levelly. "It's been done before. Do you think I've been here six days a week, eight till seven, for the past nine months? Even with part time help?" Her eyes, without the glasses, were a deep shade of violet. He hadn't noticed them before. The outfit, and the fingernails, were the colour of damsons. She added, "I do have a life, Laurence."

He'd thought Gali-Leo's was her life. He didn't say so. He drank the scotch and soda she'd poured for him.

"Is this anything to do with the viper?" he said eventually.

"Viper?"

"VPA. Acronyms seem to be everywhere these days." The snake-like stare of Dominic King was before his eyes.

"It's involved, yes." She swung round in his leather chair and tore a sheet of paper from the mouth of the fax machine. She ran her eyes down it but didn't offer it to him to read. She folded it up and tucked it under the blotter. "I am rather busy, Laurence."

"That's good." He tossed off his whisky and lumbered to his feet.

"And the key," she said, as he made for the door. "I can't find it."

He turned. "Is it worth going on looking?"

She had the grace to lower her eyes. "I don't think so. I think it might be lost forever."

As soon as the door closed behind him, she slid the fax out from beneath the blotter and reread it, this time more carefully. Dave Symons had listed her flights and timetable; she would be met at the airport by a VPA representative. At the bottom, another hand had written: *I look forward to seeing you, Deborah. I hope I have been judged favorably.*

Their last meeting had been at the end of August. Again, his arrival had been heralded by the *Financial Times* – 'Once again USA-based businessman Dominic King is back on these shores. For a man who is said to hate travelling, he seems to be spending a good deal of time this side of the Atlantic. Government sources deny any covert reasons for his recent visits…' This time he made her wait only two days.

"I've reserved a box at Covent Garden," he told her over the phone. "It's *Così fan tutte* – a good introduction to opera. I shall pick you up at six-thirty sharp."

They had dined in an intimate bistro-style restaurant a stone's throw from the Opera House. This time she had opted for an ankle-length skirt and beaded top with silk shawl the same colour as her eyes. They dispensed with the usual subjects of art, business and current affairs. He took her hand almost immediately and asked about her life. How she spent her days, what she did in her leisure time, her favourite holiday spots. He seemed amused when she told him she had only ever ventured as far as Edinburgh. She hadn't even crossed the Irish Sea to Dublin.

"Let's see how you get on with opera," he said. "Then if you'll allow me I'll introduce you to some of my favourite bolt holes around the world. Why do you smile, Deborah? Do you still doubt me?"

"I've never doubted you."

"No. You doubt yourself. A very cautious judge." And before she could frame any sort of reply, he had lifted an imperious finger and ordered a new bottle of Chateau Margaux.

He was always doing that, she thought; skirting a subject which might lead to more intimate revelations than he was prepared to hear. Or to speak of. What was he afraid of? The certainty that there was something he never acknowledged was growing in her mind together with the equal certainty that she would discover what it was; she could bide her time as well as he. This was their third assignation; the first could have been impulse, the second more deliberate, but a third denoted something deeper than mere interest. A box at Covent Garden spoke volumes about his motivation. She was sure he had never taken any of his other women (the ones he had sex with) to the opera. (Was he thinking of having sex with her? If not, why was he bothering?)

Outside the Opera House was a tangle of photographers and people with microphones. She hadn't realised it was a first night, and that Dominic King was only one famous face among many. In fact most of the flashbulbs exploded behind them and it was only when they reached the top of the steps that one went off in their faces. Dominic reacted angrily, shielding her with his shoulder and giving the unfortunate paparazzo the full vent of his glare. "They won't use it," he muttered, "when they realise who I am they'll also know I'll sue." But he'd been photographed lots of times squiring various high-profile women; what was so different now?

It was a new sensation to be treated like royalty. They were shown to their box by a uniformed flunky who brought a chilled bottle of Perrier water in an ice bucket with two glasses, which he proceeded to pour as if it were the finest champagne. Dominic lifted his to hers and they drank, smiling at each other over the rims. Then the orchestra began to tune up and the magical evening unfurled.

Afterwards, she couldn't have described the music, the scenery or the plot. Her eyes had drunk in the spectacle, her ears the singing; she was entranced. The plot was ridiculous but that didn't matter. She was transfixed. Transformed. As she gazed at the stage, she had even forgotten his presence at her side and, at the end of the performance, as they descended the steps towards the car, his hand at her elbow, her feet seemed to float two inches above the ground.

He didn't ask her if she had enjoyed the evening. They didn't speak on the return journey to Baron's Court. She couldn't have held a glass of champagne; she was weightless, composed entirely of air, wrapped in enchantment.

He summoned the lift. When it arrived she found herself with him and he was closing the doors from the inside. They travelled up to the third floor. He took the key from her hand and unlocked the door to the flat, holding it open for her to enter.

Once inside, with the door closed behind them, the real world took shape - in the form of huge hideous pieces of furniture, of peeling wallpaper and threadbare carpets. Even when he switched on the lights, especially then, the place seemed dark and forbidding. She led him through to the lounge, pulling the cords of the two floor- length swathed and tasselled lamps which only illuminated a pool of butterscotch light around their plinths; the grand piano lurked like a cornered beast and the cabinets containing mother's collection of Victorian china loomed like two immense sentinels each side of the fireplace. She decided not to draw the heavy brocade curtains; the windows were the only elegant features of the room.

She motioned him to sit down on the sofa, keeping her eyes on the floor. "I'll make coffee," she said, and escaped to the kitchen.

Under the merciless glare of the striplight the kitchen showed itself in its true colours: old-fashioned, functional. She plugged in the kettle and stood staring at it, her fists clenched on the scored, musty-smelling work surface. How had she lived all her life in this place? There was nothing of her in here at all. And now he knew all about her. She couldn't hide any longer.

She mustn't cry; tears would dislodge her contact lenses and then he'd know another of her secrets. Oh, for the magic world of the opera! But that was all make-believe. This was reality; this was where she belonged.

"Deborah." He was behind her; his hands had encircled her shoulders. In their firm grip she was turned round to face him, although she kept her own face averted. He was a few inches shorter than her, although of course she still wore her three-inch heels; without them, they would be on a level.

He knelt at her feet and removed the shoes. "Cinderella," he said, "in reverse." When he stood, in a fluid movement that showed no sign of discomfort, they were nose to nose. He slid the shawl down her arms with the tips of his fingers. His mouth was next to hers. It touched hers for a second only. Then he drew back as if he'd changed his mind.

Her lips, where his had been, tingled. She drew in a long sharp breath. "Dominic…"

"No," he said. "Not if you don't want to."

But perhaps it was him. Perhaps *he* didn't want to. "I – I don't…"

"Then coffee will be perfectly acceptable."

"No, I mean I don't – I don't know what…"

He waited.

"I don't know what you want." She drew in a deep breath and looked him straight in the eyes. "What you want of me."

"I want all of you, Deborah."

The breath left her body.

"I want you body and soul."

The room swam.

"I think you know the kind of man I am. I possess things. Everything I want I possess entirely. I want you. Entirely."

There wasn't enough air in the room. She was gasping like a fish.

"So I need you to be sure. I need to be sure. I won't embark on this lightly. I don't think you will either." He took a step back from her. "I'll leave you to think about it."

He didn't stay for coffee. He left her stranded in the kitchen with only enough wits left to hear the door close behind him.

She had thought of nothing else. That was his intention, obviously.

No, that wasn't quite right. She had thought of the business. She had to think of something else, or she would spend all day sitting in the office in Laurence's leather chair, gazing vacantly into space. *I want all of you.*

She'd reorganised the showroom downstairs, hanging new pictures, moving the furniture. *I want you body and soul.*

She'd ordered new equipment and learned how to use it. Getting connected to the real world, the new global business economy, plugging herself in to the technological future. *Everything I want I possess.*

She was her own woman. She would dress like her own woman, in ballbreaker business suits with shoulder pads, she would be seen as successful, intelligent, focused, feminist – post-feminist…. *I want to possess you. Entirely.*

When the invitation arrived to go to New York, she accepted.

******

Huw had done a good job, Laurence had to admit. He hadn't known his son had it in him. The lounge had been entirely stripped and decorated with flowers and balloons, but all in the best possible taste. It had a silver theme with purple trimmings. The buffet was being taken care of by trendy caterers – Mrs Wainwright obviously not up to the task, even if she'd agreed. Nor would Barbara have been, he had to concede, when he saw the tables laid with smoked salmon terrines, prawn cocottes, delicate lemon-scented crab *en filo,* salades Caesar and Nicoise and Waldorf, with roquette and lollo rosso and baby nettle; everything but lettuce. There were vats of chicken korma, chilli

311

con carne, wild rice with porcini mushrooms ready to be heated; mounds of white grapes, mangoes and kiwi fruit. Crates of wine, beer and spirits were stacked behind the bar.

"Don't worry, Dad," Huw said, "I've paid the bill."

He remonstrated, but not for long. The guest list ran to at least seventy.

He wondered where Huw had found them. The people who jostled into his lounge weren't those on his usual circuit; he'd invited the occasional actor or singer in his time but never these semi-famous faces from serials and soaps, and certainly not the young aristos, scions of landed families whose upper-class accents drowned out every other conversation. He was sure Gemma had never met any of them but knew, too, that she would relish this company. Leo was bringing her back about half past eight from the final fitting of the dress that was Laurence's present, and which Leo no doubt would have persuaded her to keep on in order to show him what he'd paid for.

Thank goodness, was his first thought, that Deirdre and Deborah had declined his invitations. Hilary had turned up with a friend, almost a clone of herself, and they'd immediately made themselves at home in the television camp.

At twenty to nine the signal was given that Leo's car had turned into the drive. The lights were doused. Even the raucous aristos kept quiet until the lounge door was thrown open, the lights suddenly blazed and Gemma stood framed, wide-eyed, mouth agape, wearing a heart-stopping creation in antique cream silk, draped to show her figure to perfection.

Laurence stood behind the bar (he'd opted to play bartender – he felt entirely out of place anywhere else) and watched as her expression changed from profound shock to intense pleasure; watched as Huw came forward and escorted her round the room, making the introductions. He noted how Huw's hand rested on her arm even when he was speaking to other people; noted how his face flushed with annoyance when she spoke to other men. Tony Masterson had not been invited. He had appeared back on the scene recently but Laurence had the feeling that he and Gemma were just good friends. Leo also contrived to be around when he was expected. His offspring were not having much luck in the romance stakes, Laurence thought.

Although there was one jolly girl who seemed to be making a play for his son. Laurence had noticed her early on, hanging around Huw. Later in the evening, when the live band had arrived and the party had moved out to the marquee on the lawn (it was a beautiful autumn night, thank goodness), she commandeered Huw whenever Gemma was dancing with someone else. One of the cut-glass voice brigade, she at least seemed hard-working and capable; throughout the evening she gathered up empty glasses, swept litter into bin bags and topped up the buffet.

"You don't have to do it," he said when she brought a tray full of empties back to the bar. "Guests aren't expected to be waitresses."

"Oh, I'm not a guest." She beamed at him; she had a sunny, open face and freckles over the bridge of her nose. "I'm helping Huw."

"Yes, but…"

"I'm the party planner." Seeing his obvious bafflement, she explained, "It's a part-time business of mine. Planning parties."

"Good Lord. I never knew they were a business."

"Oh yes. People don't have time these days to plan things properly. And they don't know enough – well, exciting people. That's where we come in. We plan the party right down to the knives and forks." She turned her beam on Huw, who had come up behind her. "It's a great success, isn't it? I told you."

Huw said, "Sorry, I meant to introduce you. Pudge, this is my father. Dad, this is Prudence Ursula Denby-Jessop."

"Nice to meet you, Pudge." It was, too. He liked her immediately. But as he watched her capture his son in a cheerful armlock and waltz him back to the marquee, he wondered if Huw had at last met his match.

At one o'clock he decided to leave them to it. He'd enjoyed his stint as bartender, and prided himself on keeping the guests amused while demonstrating his prowess with the cocktail shaker. One rather fetching blonde in blue and silver had perched on a stool and seemed to find his company congenial; it had been rather nice flirting with a female who obviously hadn't heard of his reputation. She was American; she had an excuse. But she had eventually drifted away, and after that he felt his part in the proceedings was over.

The party was still in full swing and his garden was beginning to look like a scene from one of those Government awareness films depicting the aftermath of a nuclear disaster. He picked his way between mainly prone bodies, averting his eyes from those that obviously weren't, and entered the marquee. He would say goodnight to Gemma and slide off to bed.

She was dancing with a group of young aristos over by the band. How their ears coped with the din he couldn't think. He stood, arm upraised, trying to catch her attention.

Her face in profile looked different. Somehow, among this press of people, she'd become a stranger. He loved her like a daughter but she wasn't; now he gazed at her with eyes that recognised this fact. That smooth forehead, straight nose, well-shaped eyebrows, strong chin; where had he seen them before? She turned in his direction, her head on its long neck perfectly poised; seeing him, her face lit up in a smile. A calm, knowing smile, with that lift of the chin as she turned away to say a few words to her friends before coming over to him to bid him goodnight.

The ground swayed and tipped, but he had righted himself before she was at his elbow, kissing his cheek.

******

"I'm sorry. It's not been possible for me to get away."

"Oh," she said.

"Enjoy the opening."

"I will."

"Did you have a good flight?"

"Excellent."

"First class is usually – first class. You get what you pay for in this life, Deborah. And when you don't – somebody else has to pay for it."

There was no reply to that.

"Don't you think so?"

"I don't know what you mean."

"Good girl." A pause, then, "I'll call again. Perhaps it might be possible… I'll call you again tomorrow."

She sat in her hotel room, the lights of Manhattan outside the window, and blinked back the tears. She didn't know why she was crying. Disappointment that he wasn't here? Annoyance at herself for being disappointed? Or was it the terrible knowledge that she'd let herself down and become one of those females she'd always despised, who sat by phones waiting for calls, who dressed to please men, who jumped at their every command…

She was by the phone when he called again the next morning, just before she was due to leave for the opening of the gallery on Fifth Avenue.

He said without preamble, "I've made arrangements for you to come over to Denver when you've finished there." And before she could protest, "Don't worry about Gali-Leo's, I'll see to it." And rang off.

No, she wouldn't go to Denver. She would fly back to London in three days, as she'd promised Laurence. She would get her life back under her control.

9.   October 1986

"Miss Routledge is still in the States," the girl behind the desk at Gali-Leo's told him. She was tall and slim and had an American accent.

"Still in New York?"

"No. She's in Denver."

"And how long," Laurence asked, "will she be staying in Denver?"

The girl shrugged her elegant shoulders. "I have no idea, Mr Bassett." She stared into his face; hers was exquisitely made up and perfectly blank.

"Did she hire you before she left?"

"No. I'm employed by an agency."

"And what agency might that be?"

"VP Associates."

"I see. Is that a branch of the Venn Peg…"

"The VP stands for Vital Personnel. They have a branch in Piccadilly."

"And they presumably pay your wages."

"Of course. The agency specialises in placing the right people in the right positions. I'm fully qualified to run this business. I have an arts degree from Bryn Mawr and have just completed my MBA…"

"Yes, yes. I'm sure you'll do brilliantly."

"Do you want to go upstairs, Mr Bassett?"

"No. No, no. I was just passing and thought I'd call in."

******

She had arrived at the head of the British Airways queue at Kennedy with her passport and ticket to London Heathrow ready to be presented when the tannoy made an announcement. As usual, the disembodied voice was distorted and drowned out by the buzz of a busy airport but something about its message made her take notice.

316

"Excuse me," she said to the girl behind the counter, "did it say Routledge?"

"Pardon me, ma'am?"

"I'm Miss Routledge. Miss Deborah Routledge."

The girl looked puzzled.

"I thought the tannoy…" She picked up the passport and ticket she'd laid down and hurried away.

She found the information desk at last. "Excuse me, but…"

A voice beside her said, "Miss Deborah Routledge?"

She turned to see a tall black man in a grey uniform who saluted and took her cases from her. "This way, miss," he said, carrying them off.

She followed. She could do nothing else.

They went through passport control to the VIP departure lounge, along a corridor that led out on to the apron where a long black car stood waiting. She was helped inside and her luggage stowed in the boot. The car glided off across the tarmac for a couple of hundred yards or so, then stopped. The driver came round to her side, opened the door. She swung her legs out, straightened, stood looking up at the snout of a Learjet as her luggage was taken from the car and transferred to the aircraft. She presumed it was a Learjet; she had only read about them and had probably seen a photograph of one at some time. She moved as if in a dream, up the steps, through the door and into a sumptuously furnished cabin like something out of *Ideal Home*.

A beautiful girl in a smart charcoal grey uniform brought her a cocktail as she settled herself in one of the two armchairs. The plane taxied off and took to the air like a bird, without noise or fuss, and soon reached its cruising speed which seemed no speed at all.

I didn't want to do this, she thought. This wasn't what I wanted. But how could I have refused? I had no choice in the matter.

Oh, but you did. You could have ignored the announcement.

But I didn't know what it was. It could have been important. It could have been something to do with the business – with Laurence…

Oh, don't kid yourself, Deborah. You knew very well what it was. You know what you've done. You've got to go through with it now.

Outside the airport in Denver was another black Daimler. He wasn't inside. There was no glass of champagne.

She was driven through streets of tall wide buildings and rolling open spaces. There was a feeling of spaciousness, of views of the Rockies even 'downtown', as the driver informed her as they cruised along. After the cramped, dirty streets of London and the pulsating sidewalks of New York, everything sparkled, everything looked clean and cared for. They left the city behind and drove through rolling plains, along a straight road that led towards the mountains.

She felt as if destiny had taken over. Destiny had brought her to America, had guided her through the opening of the gallery on Fifth Avenue at which she thought she'd made quite a hit. It was her accent, of course, her English reserve, her self-deprecation. She was treated like royalty yet again; she was becoming used to all the attention. It was addictive.

Watching the majestic scenery roll past the window she thought of her stay in New York; the first-night cocktail party, Broadway show, the tour of the city in the company of the gallery director and his wife. She could get used to this style of life. When the car turned off the road and stopped before large wrought iron gates which opened at a command of the chauffeur, she no longer felt any lurch of fear. Even sweeping up the long straight drive past security men in uniform holding dogs and with gunbelts slung round their hips didn't dent her poise. The car came to rest in a large courtyard outside the marble portico of an imposing white mansion of classical proportions. Again she had the impression of order, of cleanliness. Even the flowers, arranged in huge tubs beneath the shuttered windows, looked as if someone had buffed and polished each individual petal.

Stepping from the car, resisting the temptation to look behind to check her luggage (she had learned these things were done with impeccable efficiency), she ascended the flight of stone steps to the open front door where a man dressed in the frock coat of a butler was already waiting.

She was shown into a wide atrium with a mosaic floor, a winding staircase down one wall and two full-length statues either side of the door, Greek or possibly Roman and, at a brief glance, almost flawless. Both male. Both nude. A young girl in a black dress and white apron led her up the stairs to a large airy room furnished plainly but well, with two high-winged armchairs each side of a fireplace, a wall of books and a writing desk under a full-length window overlooking a stretch of perfect green lawn.

The girl opened a door in the wall opposite the fireplace. "The bedroom, ma'am."

Deborah stood on the threshold gazing into another bland but tasteful room with its king-size bed and fitted wardrobes. Another door obviously led to the bathroom.

Behind her, she heard her cases being brought in and set down. Turning, prepared to thank whoever had brought them up, she caught a look being exchanged between the butler, who had obviously supervised the action, and the little maid. "Where's Mr King?" she said sharply.

The maid jumped. "He's not here, ma'am."

"When will he be back?"

The butler said smoothly, "We expect him any minute, madam." His accent was English. The girl's was broad Irish.

"I'm not used to being kept waiting," she said. "Tell Mr King I've gone back to Denver. I shall book into a hotel tonight and fly back to London tomorrow."

She made it down the stairs and across the atrium. He was standing in the front doorway between the statues. Despite his diminutive stature next to theirs, he wasn't overpowered.

"My apologies, Deborah. I meant to be here to welcome you."

She took a deep breath. She was on the verge of tears, but of rage, not relief. "I didn't want to come here, Dominic. I was on my way back to London. I can't stay."

"Please…"

"Do you bring them all here?"

"Who?"

"Your other women."

"Ah. Deborah." He came towards her, his hand outstretched to take her arm, then evidently thought better of it and let it fall to his side. "Come into the drawing room. I need to speak to you. Please."

She had no choice; the black Daimler had disappeared, the drive was empty.

The drawing room was furnished in the same unadorned simplicity as the rest of the house she had seen. He stood beside a large open hearth and motioned her to sit on one of the four cream sofas set around a low marble-topped table. Unwillingly, she complied.

"My other women," he repeated. "Yes, I have had other women. I'm a man of large appetites, Deborah. I've had a great many women in my time."

Of course she had known this; it came as no surprise.

"I have been a user of women. They've been necessary to me like air or water. When I was young I picked up prostitutes from the street. They taught me a lot. They taught me the art of – discrimination. A word that has unfortunately been devalued, that has taken on a negative meaning. I'm using it in its positive sense. Now I use call girls, high class hookers. There's nothing wrong with paying for sex, Deborah. It's a much purer, less messy, arrangement."

She sat on the edge of the sofa, arms across her breasts, holding herself in.

"Other men find women they want to marry, to spend their lives with. I never wanted that. I never believed I could find a woman who would satisfy all my needs. Who would be my equal intellectually as well as physically. I believed I had found that in you, Deborah."

"You kidnapped me."

"I couldn't let you go."

"Why didn't you come to New York?"

He sighed. "Business, Deborah. Always business. You must realise sometimes business takes precedence over pleasure. I thought you of all people would realise that."

"Duty has always taken precedence in my life."

"Duty. Business. Two sides of the same coin."

"I can't stay, Dominic."

He clenched and unclenched his fist, laid along the mantelpiece. "So you've made up your mind. I can't pretend I'm not disappointed. But strangely I also feel – relieved." When she remained silent, he went on, "I've never been in love before, you see. I believe that's what it's called, this terrible yearning, this despair. It's an affliction, one I could do without, frankly. While there was still hope I could suffer it, but now – now I will have to try to smother it, snuff it out." On these words his face contorted, a brief, tic-like spasm, but he got it back under control. "But I don't know if that will be possible."

"Oh, it is. Eventually."

They were silent for a while. Her resolve was slipping, but she still didn't know if she could trust him. Was he really in love with her? Or was it just an elaborate ploy, a game he was playing? Was she in love with him? Was this love, this terrible longing, this despair? Surely love should make you happy?

"I find it hard," he said at last, "to bare my soul."

"Yet you want to possess mine."

"Yes. Is that selfish of me, Deborah?"

"I think so, yes."

"A very stern judge." He pushed himself from the wall and sat down beside her. "So what should I do?"

"Confession is good for the soul, I believe."

"But if I confess, I shall lose you."

"If you don't, I'll catch the next plane back to London."

He put his head in his hands. "I come from a Catholic family," he said at last. "Yet this is my first real confession.

You're the first person to have heard it. And when you hear what I've done, you'll catch that plane anyway."

"Don't judge me, Dominic. I may surprise you."

He lifted his head. There were tears in his eyes. Real tears, she thought, genuine tears. He was not the sort of man to weep lightly. She took his hand in hers, which he gripped in a fist of iron.

"I've done things in my life I'm not proud of," he said. "You must know that. When I started out in business I did things – sometimes terrible things. I had to succeed, whatever the cost. I had no ethics, Deborah. Yes, I've dealt illegally – drugs, guns – if I hadn't, someone else would. I made my first million in the black market. But not now. Now I give generously to charity. That doesn't excuse me, but I hope it goes some way to make amends."

She waited. Her hand was still clenched in his.

"There were thirteen of us," he said. "I was the eldest. There was me and Siobhan and Liam and Mairead and Niamh and then Michael. A year between us. Then Sinead. Mother had a hard time with her. She nearly died. They both nearly died. Sinead was the joy of her life. She was a beauty, inside and out. An angel come to earth. Mother didn't want any more after her. She begged Father to allow her to 'have the operation'," – he said this in a thick Irish brogue - "but he was a good Catholic, he was put on this earth to breed God's brats, so they went on. Two sets of twins, an idiot who was put away in an asylum at nine and then Patrick. By the time he was born, she was worn out. She took to her bed. Sinead became mother. The others had moved out, the girls had got married, Michael and Liam had gone back to Ireland – we lived in a three-bed basement in London, sharing with rats and cockroaches – but I stayed on. I was making money, Deborah, the only money that was coming in, blood money but what else could I do? Father was drinking it away as fast as it came in. Sinead was wearing herself out with the housework and looking after the young ones. We survived somehow. And then she was killed."

322

He paused, removed his glasses, rubbed his forehead. His eyes looked wet and naked. Then he replaced the glasses and said, "It wasn't the first death. The idiot died at fourteen, Michael blew himself up with a bomb and Liam got shot by the Prots. But Sinead's death was the worst. Mother never got over it."

"How did she die?"

"Oh, it was stupid. A bloody stupid death. She'd got the kids ready for school, given them their sandwiches and satchels, then had to run for the bus. She worked as a waitress in a hotel, the only job she could get with the right hours – sometimes she worked till gone midnight – and the bus was already at the stop and she had to run, and somehow she tripped over and fell. Fell right under the wheels."

She said nothing, just gripped his hand tighter.

"That was the end of us, really. Patrick was hit hard, too. She was the only mother he'd known. He blamed himself, he was the one who'd played her up, made her late for work."

"It was nobody's fault."

"It was probably mine. I'd promised to help her but I overslept. I'd been working thirty-six hours non-stop."

"It wasn't your fault, Dominic."

"Mother blamed me. She couldn't say it, but I knew. The way she looked at me, I knew. I was the eldest. I should have been there."

"These things happen…"

"She hadn't got out of bed for ten years. Her legs had gone. By that time she was mute too. Sinead fed her mash with a spoon. Sometimes it took hours. She'd spit everything out. She was trying to die, Deborah. I knew that. I saw it in her eyes. She wouldn't take anything from me. She spat it out at me."

Mother did that to me, Deborah thought. In the end.

"She wanted to die," he repeated.

"Probably," she said.

"We shouldn't have to go on living. Not like that."

"No."

"But you went on, Deborah. You carried on."

"I couldn't do anything else. Until she went to the hospice."

"Did she want to go to the hospice?"

"I don't think so. She wanted to die at home."

"Ah."

"I felt I'd sent her off to die among strangers."

He was silent.

She said, "How did you do it?"

"With a pillow. It was easy. Five minutes. I held it over her face for five minutes but she probably went before two."

They sat on the sofa, clutching hands. She didn't look at him because her own eyes were clouded with tears and she daren't turn her head because of her contact lenses. She blinked fiercely. Beside her, she could feel the uneven rise and fall of his chest. When she had her eyes under control, she turned and placed her hands either side of his face and turned it towards her. She carefully removed his glasses. She kissed his eyes, then his temples, then the tip of his nose, then his cheeks, both sides. Then his mouth.

It was a strange feeling, kissing his mouth. Skin was unyielding, but this – this was soft, pliable, the gateway to the body, or one of the gateways… she explored his lips with the tip of her tongue, then the inside of his mouth, raw and fleshy, warm and wet, the tongue surprisingly more sensitive than the tips of the fingers…

She had never kissed Laurence. This was her first kiss. It might be his, too.

******

Wed 8 Oct 11.53pm
Nothing to do tonite except wotch the telly. Tony and Gemma have gone out, they invited me too but I didn't want to trail along seeing them holding hands and larfing at stupid in-jokes like they do. Huwie never comes round these days either, he seems to have found himself a girl who wants to stay around, I don't know why. She's got some stupid name too. Fudge or Podge or something.

Anyway, was in the lounge wotching telly and Daddy comes in and sits down. He never wotches it, or hasn't recently, but he looked so down in the dumps I asked him wot was the matter and he said O Leo I'm wasting my time I can't rite anything and I don't know wot to do. I said why don't you go to the gallery and he said it's not his any more, there's some girl running it who's got more kwalificashuns that he ever had so I said where's Miss Routledge and he said she's still in the States.

I said wot's she doing there and he said I wish I knew, Leo.

Anyway, there was one of those art shows on at 10.30 on BBC2 so I turned it over thinking he mite like it but it was one of those late nite review shows about theatre and books as well as painting so I was going to turn it over again when he said no leave it Leo and stared at the screen. These two arty-farty types were chuntering on about books and one said, I hear you're riting a book, an awtobiografy is that rite Dermot, and there he was, Daddy's old artist who I thort had drunk himself stupid years ago but was sitting there large as life and sober as a judge. He'd even shaved off that horrible beerd.

Yes, he said, that's rite I am.

Wot made you want to rite it, the other bloke asked.

Well, said Dermot, I think I've got a lot to say that people mite like to know about.

How you stopped drinking for starters, larfed the bloke.

Yes, said Dermot, and how I started too.

And about your life as an artist, said the bloke.

Yes, said Dermot, I can lift the lid on the whole bloody mess.

Ah, said the bloke, so you will reveel a few sordid detales about wot goes on in the high relms of art.

You bet, said Dermot, wot I've got to say will bring it down to the gutter.

I look forward to that, said the bloke. When will it be published?

When it's finished, said Dermot, until then nobody can see it. But it won't be long, I'm on the last few chapters.

Christ, said Daddy.

Yes, I said, you see, he can do it, he can rite a book, why can't you? I was joking, I didn't meen he couldn't rite one, I ment why wasn't he when that old soak can do it, but I don't think he took it like that, he got up and went out without saying a word and when I followed him to the library he'd locked the door.

Daddy, I said, I didn't meen it like that, open the door, but he wouldn't.

He's got the grumps again and it's all my folt.

******

So Deborah was in Denver. With Dominic King, obviously. He hadn't seen the picture in the paper of the opening night at Covent Garden, but Hilary had. A famous playwright and his wife had been the target of the photograph but King had been caught in the background with an elegant woman on his arm. Laurence wouldn't have recognised Deborah, but Hilary did.

"Bloody hell, Laurence! Talk about ugly ducklings!"

She had never had her hair cut for him. She would never have swapped her glasses for contact lenses even if he'd asked her. But then he had never taken her to the opera.

His life was slipping out of control.

He had spent most of his time in his library, staring at the picture of the horned man. Sometimes it smiled benignly at him, sometimes it leered with an expression of supreme contempt. Sometimes he could see Gemma in those steady black eyes, sometimes she was completely absent.

But Deirdre had obviously known him. At the commune, of course, but before then. In London. She'd got pregnant in London. And not long after she'd run away, after that sweet encounter in his studio in Swansea, when she had asked him to run off with her. If only he had. If they had eloped together, he would not now be sitting in a big house in Hampstead as his life collapsed around him.

Had Patrick King lived in London in January 1965? He would set Hilary on the trail.

He had driven to Woodstock the day after he'd seen Dermot on *Wednesday Review*. He had trouble finding it; the bungalow was almost drowned by creeper, the path obliterated by weeds. As he picked his way through high grass and tangled undergrowth, a window had opened. Dermot's face was framed in it. Without the beard he looked gaunt but younger, more ordinary.

"Thought word would get round to you."

Laurence stopped in his tracks. "Why are you doing this, Dermot?"

"Conscience, old boy. Want to set the record straight before I bow out."

"You look the picture of health."

"Looks can be deceiving. Liver's shot to buggery. Next drink I have could be the last."

"I thought we agreed…"

"There was no agreement. Possibly a gentleman's agreement, but I'm no gentleman. But don't worry, Larry. I'm the one who'll get the flak. With any luck I'll get off on grounds of ill health, like Keating."

"My name's on the attributions."

Dermot shrugged. "I painted the buggers. It's only your reputation that'll suffer, old chap, and that's nothing to write home about, is it? Anyway, I thought you'd got out of the rat race yourself."

"Those pictures made a lot of money for both of us."

"More fool whoever bought them. Couldn't have been an expert, eh? Wouldn't have got past an observant A-level student."

"What do you mean?"

"You kept one, didn't you?" Dermot laughed. "Take a closer look. My signature's all over them."

"I sold it. I needed the money."

"And at a hefty profit, I daresay. Wait there, old boy." Dermot disappeared from the window. When he appeared again, he hefted a canvas over the sill. "Go on, take it. I don't want it. More trouble than the damn thing's worth. Kept me awake at nights, staring at the bottom of a bottle."

Laurence took the canvas and propped it by his feet. "I'll sell it and give you the money."

"Don't need the money, old love. Won't need it, when the book comes out."

"It'll ruin me."

"It's ruined me." The window closed. The face vanished.

Wheels One stared down at him from above. The horned man leered up at him from inside the cabinet. Now he had another painting propped against the wall, *Study in Blue & Green #2,* a companion to Nos 1 and 3, which Deborah and Cyril Lyttleton possessed. Nos 4 to 8 were in Dominic King's collection in Denver. They were all variations on a theme; Dermot had obviously thought Will would have been as obsessive in his youth as he'd become later. But probably not; he got worse as he got older. Will's mental condition had been a bit of a puzzle. A schizoid disorder had been the eventual diagnosis, with a mild degree of something like autism. But people couldn't be labelled so easily. We're all mad to some extent anyway, Laurence thought.

He would be driven mad, studying the painting. Small swirls of blue alternating with larger swirls of green. Yellow and brown dots. Will's trademarks, yet without his passion. Laurence couldn't read anything in it. But he'd attributed the eight of them as juvenilia and they were good enough for an art expert, let alone an A-level student, to be satisfied. Drink must have befuddled Dermot's brain. There was no signature that he could see.

******

They had become experts in kissing.

He had also taken her on trips, sometimes in the Daimler, sometimes by helicopter, to the Rockies, the Colorado River, the Grand Canyon. They had visited art galleries on Santa Fe Drive and strolled through the many parks of the city. They dined in the best restaurants. They held hands while they talked. And they kissed.

Oh, they were experts in waiting. Perhaps they had waited too long.

She knew they couldn't go on like this, and yet didn't want to break the spell. Alone in her king-size bed every night, she ached for his body next to hers, but also dreaded it. Failure and disappointment – was that what he feared, too? Her failure to live up to his expectations – and how could she, when she had no experience to fall back on? – and perhaps her disappointment, after all these long celibate years. His disappointment, too, after all these months of hooking her like a fish. He'd had so many women. She was bound to be a disappointment.

At least they'd progressed from just kissing. Sometimes, while their mouths were occupied, his hands strayed to her breasts. She allowed his fingers to burrow inside one cup of her bra. They fondled the nipple which became firm and erect; she knew that feeling from the sessions in the Red Room. But to have his fingers – and then, oh God, his mouth, his tongue, licking it with a kind of passionate reverence – this was a new sensation entirely. If she hadn't been lying along the sofa while he knelt on the floor beside her, she would have swooned completely.

She thought, I'm not the dried up old maid I thought I'd become. I do have the right feelings. If he wants me now, I think I can do it. I think I can make him happy.

"Not here," he said, extricating his head from her hands. "Your body might be here but your soul is elsewhere."

Her mouth was dry, yet full of saliva. "Where is it?"

"In Baron's Court."

She knew then that he would come back with her.

On the night before they were due to fly to London, he took her to his office in the financial heart of the city. The building was anonymous and empty, except for two burly security guards in the foyer who saluted them when they arrived, their other hands resting on the holsters at their sides. The bottom floors of the building were flooded with light. The rest were in darkness. They took his private elevator to the penthouse.

She stepped out on to soft carpet into a high glass chamber lit by the myriad lights of the city below. His figure was shrouded in grey, outlined by light, as he strode ahead of her and keyed in a code on the panel opposite. He stood aside, holding the door open, and she passed through into complete blackness.

Then, light rising like the first rays of the sun, she found herself in a windowless room hung with treasures. She could be in the Tate, but a Tate more seductive, more secret, bathed in a glow of pearl and rose so tangible she seemed to be moving through scented satin. Each painting had its own illumination, the spaces between them shadowed, so that it seemed she only existed, with the painting, in that place and time. Each one was exquisite, and each better than the last. He, or his agents, had scoured the world for its treasures before they knew they were treasures, and here they were, preserved for eternity against corruption and greed and the predations of advertising. Here they existed as art, to make the spirit sing.

And not just paintings either, but sculptures picked out by spotlights, their lines defined against blackness. As she progressed, more rooms bloomed into light. The next was full of conceptual art. And the next of portraits. And yes, there the two Bellings, side by side, their colours and lines even more delineated, the girl's face etched forever in its sadness, the pig in its inquisitiveness, both in their obstinacy... She noticed these were hung on an otherwise blank wall, as if awaiting companions.

She moved onwards as he had in Gali-Leo's, giving every picture the same detailed scrutiny. But this collection surpassed any gallery she had ever been in. His taste was exactly the same as hers. There was nothing here she wouldn't have itched to possess herself.

The final room. She hesitated, steeling herself, aware that he was at her back. The Murchison room. Again, it was in darkness until she crossed the threshold, and then the pearly light dawned. There, facing her, was what Laurence had called Wheels Two, the painting Dominic had acquired from Freddy, just as breathtaking as she had expected. A huge canvas but hung to one side of the wall, awaiting another to be hung alongside it. She stood in front of it for a long time, unable to pass on, just as

Laurence had described himself doing all those years ago in Whitechapel. But eventually she did. Passed on to the seaside pictures, Maudie's river scene, all the others she had crated up and shipped off over the years. Yet here they looked different, more alive, more vibrant, than she remembered. It was almost as if Will had painted them yesterday; he was in the room, he was lifting his eager face under its mop of light curls, ready to welcome her home...

His strong arm was around her, keeping her steady. She was gulping air, trying to breathe. She lost the battle. She buried her head in his chest and wept.

She wept until she was dry of tears. He held one arm round her waist, the other was at the back of her head, holding her against him. When, eventually, she lifted her face, she was surprised to find her contacts still in place.

"I loved him," she said. "He was like a son to me."

"This is his shrine."

"Yes. Thank you."

"I have one more room to show you." He took her hand and led her through an archway into a small side room still in darkness. Again, the light rose as soon as she entered. On the left hand wall were the two pictures in tones of grey that she vaguely remembered but had had to leave Rosemary in charge of; on the opposite wall were the five Studies in Blue and Green, hung side by side and close together.

"This is what I call the Juvenile Room," Dominic said.

"Not the grey studies, surely." She moved closer; these were so unlike Will's usual output that she felt quite composed now. Although, looking at them, a lump came into her throat; these must have been painted when he had been in a period of depression, perhaps when he first arrived in Wapping. Those toppling cranes, that empty water; that would have been his mood before the manic energy took over. But something of the energy was still there in one picture; it was entirely missing from the other.

At first glance this should have more power; it at least had boats, albeit at anchor, and birds, although not in flight. But it lacked that vital spark somehow. She looked at the bottom right hand corner. Yes, there was Will's signature in a rather shaky hand, and the date. March 75.

"That's strange," she said.

"I thought so too. Two works of the same subject, painted so far apart. But the difference is obvious."

"Yes." She looked from one to the other. In one, she saw Will; in the other, nothing.

"It's obviously a juvenile work, though. Compare it to the others." He indicated the row of Blue and Green paintings opposite. "These are strikingly similar in technique, but they're unsigned. Why would he sign one piece, and not the others?"

She was unwilling to look at them yet. "Those were painted a year or so before this one. Perhaps Will only started signing them later on."

"But in my humble opinion, the Blue and Greens are the more accomplished pictures. Look at them carefully, Deborah. What do you see?"

She couldn't put it off any longer. She couldn't let him see her discomfort; he could distinguish between grief and guilt. Oh, why had she allowed Laurence to give her one of the sequence of early works, when she knew they had all been sold to Denver? Because she wanted something of Will, even if only an unsigned early painting. But it obviously belonged here, with the others. And the other two, the one Laurence had sold to Cyril and the one he gave to Dermot, also belonged here.

"They're a sequence," she said. "They do work separately, but together – there's a natural progression, almost like a landscape…"

"Very like a landscape. But unfinished."

Yes, she saw it. The first three pictures belonged at the beginning of the sequence; without them, it was unbalanced.

"You agree, Deborah?"

"Yes."

"There's at least one missing; probably two. Possibly, I think, three."

"They could have been mislaid," she said, "or his mother kept them, or – they were given away…"

"Oh, any number of reasons. But it's a great pity. Even though they're not in the first rank of Murchisons, they make a very interesting group." He was looking at her, his eyebrows raised. She had a feeling she had disappointed him in some way.

But he didn't pursue the matter. They retraced their steps through the rooms, the lights dimming behind them. When she reached the door there was total blackness at her back.

10. November 1986

In the event, he didn't fly back with her. He had a call to attend a conference in Geneva and of course he had to go. Deborah flew back alone.

At first she was rather relieved. She needed a breathing space to get her thoughts in order. She wasn't a silly sixteen-year-old; she was a woman of fifty-two who had been independent all her life. These last weeks had been an idyll, a little bubble of existence set aside from the real world; it was better to keep it like that, behind the glass walls of memory, to be let out and revisited whenever she wanted. Thank goodness she had not been carried away! – because, if she never heard from him again, at least she could say it hadn't been because of her failings between the sheets.

Gali-Leo's had been looked after by a very capable girl. Her salary had been taken care of and would be, if Deborah would like to keep her on. She – Jacqui - would be perfectly prepared to look after the showroom downstairs, while Deborah ran the business from Laurence's office. It was an arrangement she couldn't refuse. If Dominic called again, as he'd intimated, to invite her to visit his favourite bolt holes around the world…

Would he call again? Or had it been enough for him, those two weeks of tentative kissing? But he was used to call girls, high class hookers. What was kissing compared to the things he did with them?

She had been like a Fifties schoolgirl, she thought, allowing him to go so far and no further. He must have been laughing at her. Bored, certainly. How could a man like Dominic King be kept at arms' length by a prudish old maid?

But, when she ran through those weeks in her mind, she couldn't think of an instance where he had acted as if he were bored. If he had been, surely he would have made work an excuse? He needn't have taken her on those trips, or walked through the park, or showed her his collection of art. He wouldn't have bared his soul.

As the days passed with no call from him, she began to despair.

******

"I'm having a bit of bother," Hilary said. "He's certainly a mystery man."

"But wasn't he in the music business before he went to California? Surely there's something to be found there."

"Nothing with an address on it."

"Well, keep looking, Hilary."

"There is another angle I can try. The brother. Dominic."

"Ah…"

"It might be easier to trace what *he* was doing in the mid-Sixties."

"Well, I'm not sure…"

"Could be your only hope, Laurence."

Laurence felt a little uneasy as he put down the phone. If Dominic King knew he was meddling in his business… but how would he find out? Not through Deborah, surely. Although the thought of what had gone on between them in Denver, in the two weeks she was absent, was troubling. Had she told him about the three unsigned Murchisons? But why would she? She wouldn't want to give up the one she possessed. It was all she had left to remind her of Will. Although of course it wasn't Will. Had she realised it was a fake – had she seen Dermot's so-called signature? She was more astute than an A-level student. And if she had seen through it, how would she feel about him, Laurence, having pulled the wool over her eyes? Would she tell Dominic King about Wheels One, to get her revenge?

No. No, no. Deborah would never do that. The old Deborah would never have done that. This new Deborah, though…

…oh God, what had gone on in Denver?

He'd heard nothing more about Dermot's book.

******

Fri 7 Nov 7.28pm

So here I am, in my room, on a Friday nite. Thank goodness I have you, deer Diary. No one else seems to want me. Huwie has been taken over by Podge and Tony has taken Gemma off to the pub before she flies off to Bratislava or somewhere and he's off to Devon. They asked me to go with them but I said I had plans of my own.

I wish I'd never told her to go out with him. Altho she says he's not interested in her in that way, how does she know? He could be saying that just so she keeps seeing him. He's such a pussycat he'd do anything... O, I must stop imagining things, wot they're doing, wot they're getting up to. At this rate I'll be as gloomy as Daddy.

He's not getting on with his book. I went in there last nite and he was reeding a medical encyclopeedia. He's worried about his arthrytus and says his knees are creeking. I called him a silly old hypocondriak.

******

The private phone rang. She let it ring half a dozen times before she picked it up. She waited.

"Deborah?"

The breath expelled from her throat. "Hello, Laurence."

"Are you all right? You sound a bit breathless."

"No, I – I've just come up the stairs."

"We're both getting old. The quack says I should get my knees sorted out soon. Keep putting it off." When she kept silent, he said, "So how are you?"

"Fine."

"How was New York?"

"Wonderful. The opening went very well. I think the exchange of views and products will benefit both..."

"And how was Denver?"

She had to pass her tongue round her lips to moisten them. "Fine."

"You were there for a long time."

"Yes. There were things..."

"Business? Or just sightseeing?"

"Oh, a bit of both."

"Where did you stay? In a hotel?"

"Something like that... Laurence, I'm sorry, but the other phone's ringing. I'll have to go. Pop in sometime." She replaced the receiver and took a few long, deep breaths.

******

"Had more success with Dominic. The first records are an address in Kilburn, then he disappears for a time. Then he pops up in Chiswick. Buys a property there, stays five years or so. Then he must make a bundle, because he moves to Holland Park."

"When is this, Hilary?"

"Sixty-two. Buys one of the big Georgian pads along Holland Park Avenue. But he's not there most of the time. He lets rooms out. That tells me he has an agent, or someone he trusts, on the premises."

"Patrick, you think."

"Could be. That's as much as I can tell you, I'm afraid."

"Thanks, Hilary. You've been a big help."

Was he any further forward? Perhaps. Perhaps not. It was all supposition, anyway. But what if Deirdre had rented one of these rooms in the Holland Park house? And Patrick King was living there? It could be feasible. He felt in his bones he was right. This Patrick King, he was sure, was the kind of man she would have fallen for, although so much older. (As he himself had been.) Or had King taken advantage of her? (As he himself had done.) Whatever had happened, Gemma had been the result.

What should he do now? Ask Deirdre? Tell Gemma? Or keep quiet? After all, this was just supposition. And look what had happened the last time he'd failed to verify the facts.

He would keep quiet, of course. As always.

He spent long sessions studying *Blue & Green #2*. There was certainly something mesmerising about it; if Dermot had painted it under his own name, it would have sold for a good sum (not as much as he'd made from the five fakes sold to Denver, however). All three of them – all eight – would have boosted Dermot's flagging reputation. Had this knowledge, that the best paintings he had ever produced were forever to be attributed to the wrong artist and hidden from public gaze, precipitated his love affair with the bottle? That it hadn't been his, Laurence's, fault at all?

Those green and blue swirls, broken by the yellow and brown dots, induced something like hypnosis. If he stared long enough, they ceased to be swirls and dots. They became… but he didn't know what they'd become, only that he needed the bigger picture, the other two, the final five, to complete it. Oh God, why hadn't he shipped them all off to Denver? What gremlin, what devil, had made him keep three back? Greed? The need to keep some shred of self-esteem, by cheating Dominic King? He didn't know. He couldn't put himself back six years, to the aftermath of Will's death. His only excuse now was that he must have been slightly mad.

It was after one of these long sessions of gazing at the picture that he had the feeling he was being watched. And not only by the horned man, safely locked in the cabinet. No, this was a prickling at the back of his neck, that sixth sense you get when you know someone has crept up behind you, however silent their approach. He was careful not to look round. He bent down and slid the painting under the desk. Then straightened, took two or three deep breaths, and turned to the window.

No one was there.

Although – after a minute or two, Mr Wainwright walked across the lawn from the patio, wheeling a wheelbarrow and whistling one of his tuneless ditties between his teeth.

******

He didn't telephone.

So she would be doomed to spend the rest of her life wondering what might have been. If only she'd been more – what? She couldn't be what she was not. And hadn't it been him

338

who'd decided to take things no further? He said her soul was in Baron's Court. But she felt, although her body was now here, her soul was in Denver.

She went out most lunchtimes leaving Jacqui in charge, as she'd taken to doing more often. She walked round the shops, already gearing themselves up for Christmas, then went back to her desk. If this was to be the pattern of her life for the next few years until she retired – and what then? - she didn't know how she would bear it.

"He's upstairs," Jacqui said, when she arrived back from her lunch break.

She didn't ask who. It would be Laurence, of course.

So she didn't hurry. She went to the ladies' toilet and brushed her hair, redid her make-up. Stared at her face in the mirror. It looked older, sadder, but more interesting, somehow. She was a woman who had been loved. She had a past. No one would know, of course. No one would care.

It was a good five minutes before she mounted the stairs and opened the door to the office. He was sitting in his high leather chair facing the window. It was *his* chair, of course, *his* office – but for an instant pure hatred coursed through her. If he thought he could just walk back in and take over, after all these months…!

The chair swung round. Dominic said, "Hello, Deborah."

She was weightless all over again; made of air, of glass. He caught her before she fell. Their mouths joined like two homing pigeons. She sucked him in like a drowning person sucks in air. Her hands held his head; tracing his chiselled, bullet-like skull under her fingers.

"I'm sorry," he said, at last. "I'm so sorry. My darling."

"You've been cruel."

"I'm a cruel man. I enjoy cruelty. I was cruel to myself, too."

"Why?"

He held her between his strong hands, one at each shoulder. "I wanted you to suffer like I suffered. I didn't want to feel like this. I fought against it. But in the end, you won."

"Shall we go to Baron's Court?"

"I think so. Don't you?"

She said, "I think it's time."

He was as nervous as she was, then. That was why he had kept her waiting.

"I've only ever had sex," he told her. "I've never made love."

"Neither have I."

"Never, Deborah?"

"I'm still a virgin, Dominic."

"I find that hard to believe."

"But I've made a man happy. I believe I've done that. I can make you happy."

"I hope," he said, taking her hand, "I can make *you* happy."

They were in the kitchen at Hurlingham Mansions, sitting at the table drinking coffee. A surreal setting, she felt, for such an intimate discussion.

She smiled. "Have you ever initiated a fifty-two-year-old virgin into the joys of sex before?"

"No. But I think I once taught a very young girl those joys. She wasn't quite a virgin, though." He still sat clutching his coffee mug. There was something more on his mind. "Deborah," he said, "I have another confession. Oh, don't look so appalled. It's a small thing compared to – the other."

"Then let's get it out of the way."

"I've never…" he hesitated, then said, "…fully undressed in front of a woman." He lifted his eyes and must have seen her expression, because he laughed – a very rare sound, a kind of gurgling in his throat. "No, that's not the small thing I meant. I believe I'm as well endowed as the next man – possibly better than some."

"As I said," she murmured, "I've only seen one to compare it with."

His smile was that of a reticent schoolboy. "I'm a very vain man. I've always been proud of my strength, my – virility. I used to go to the gym, I swam, I played squash. Kept myself in good trim. Obviously as you get older… I'm probably not as vain as I was. I probably don't have as much to be vain about."

"You're still a fine figure of a man, Dominic."

"But that made it all the more – galling – to be less than perfect. I know it's ridiculous, to be ashamed of something one can't help, but there it is. You'll be the first woman to have seen my shame. Because I want you to have all of me, Deborah, as I want to have all of you."

Their mugs were empty. They still sat clutching them. She waited for him to make the first move. Where to? Not to her bedroom, with the crisp white sheets on the bed. With *Study in Blue & Green #1* back on the wall. Not to mother's room – Will's room – with its memories and musty old furniture. There was only one other room left.

******

Thurs 27 Nov 3.49pm

Spooky Mrs Wainrite has been snooping around in Daddy's library. She didn't know I hadn't gone out today, I'd stayed up in my room, so she thort she had the house to herself. Daddy always keeps the library locked so I don't know how she got the key. I know he's told her not to go in there, he doesn't even like me going in there, he's got very sneeky and short tempered lately. Anyway I woke up with a headache and throat like sandpaper so I spent most of the morning in bed and I'd only just got up and put my dressing gown on to go and get a drink and was coming down the stairs when I saw her backing out of the library. When she saw me she got all flustered and said, your father wanted me to dust, altho if she had permission why did she feel obliged to say anything?- and I know he didn't want her to dust, he calls the library his sanktum and he wouldn't want that old bat to go in anyway.

Daddy's gone to see a frend today. Shall I tell him when he comes in? It mite give him an excuse to get rid of the pair of them. I'll see wot sort of mood he's in when he gets back.

10.26pm *He didn't tell me where he was going but this frend has cheered him up. He came in quite chirpy. When Daddy's in a good mood he's the best fun in the world and I love him so much it hurts. We sat over dinner for* *hours, him telling me all the old stories of his telly quiz days. We just sat and larfed. Just him and me, like the old days. He didn't even go into the library. So I didn't tell him.*

******

"So you've worked it out." Dermot laughed and swung the empty whisky bottle by its neck. "Easier, of course, when they're all together. Whoever bought them – and I don't want to know, Larry, keep me out of it – must be a bit of a klutz not to have fallen in. Art expert, is he?"

"American."

"I never made it big over there, did I? Never made it that big over here. That explains it then. Damn good pictures, though. Best I ever did."

"I thought you'd given up the drink."

"It never gives *you* up, dear boy. That's the bugger."

Laurence stared at his own half-finished glass, then downed it in one gulp. "Well, I must be off. I'm sorry to see you like this, Dermot. How's – how's the book going?"

Dermot, lying along a threadbare old sofa surrounded by empty bottles and cigarette packets, wagged a finger at him. "Ah, so that's it. Haven't come to see me at all, eh? Just come to find out about the," he gave a hiccup, "b-book. It's going well, old love. Very well. Nearly f-fin-finished…"

Laurence heaved himself, with difficulty, out of the equally threadbare old armchair and walked on stiff legs to the front door. Pain shot through his right knee. He groaned and bent down to rub it, putting out a hand to the wall to steady himself. He thought he'd grabbed a walking stick, but it turned out to be a baseball bat, leaning against the doorframe.

"My protection." Dermot, having also managed to stand upright, stood swaying behind him, the bottle still clasped in his hand. "Can't be too careful. Country's not as safe as it was, yobs everywhere. People hang-hanging around… peep-peeping toms…"

The poor old sod was getting paranoid, Laurence thought, opening the door. Dermot hung over his shoulder, sweeping his eyes up and down the lane.

"Don't let anyone in," he slurred, "except my good friends. Like you, old chap. They get in, though. They've been in." He clapped Laurence on the shoulder. Pain, like a red-hot poker, shot through his left knee. "Spot of advice, old love. Trust no one. Get yourself some prot-protection. Shady characters around. Want to get at the book, you see. Don't want me to fin-finish the book…"

Which was probably, in all likelihood, just a figment of Dermot's imagination, Laurence thought, driving away from the bungalow (the thought crossing his mind that he might be well over the limit himself). He felt happier. If Dermot was back on the booze, the book (if there was one) would never be finished. Dominic King had obviously not seen through the Studies in Blue and Green, which he, Laurence, had only just worked out. He was worrying unnecessarily. His reputation was safe.

******

It was up to her to make the first move. Dominic sat there as if paralysed.

She took the key from the drawer and went along the hall to the third bedroom. She only entered the room once a month now to dust, and she didn't light the lamps. Without the red glow the room looked seedily ordinary – like a brothel would look in daylight, she thought. But now she turned on the lamps, and drew the curtains across the windows, and plumped up the cushions. If he was going to show her all of himself, it was only fair he should see all of her.

She opened the wardrobe and wondered what uniform he would prefer.

"Miss Routledge." He stared at her from the kitchen table. She revealed herself in the doorway as she had never revealed herself to Laurence. When she'd worn the satin basque and fishnet

343

stockings he'd always been safely strapped face down and she was in darkness. She wore the mask anyway. It was her disguise, her protection.

He got to his feet, rather unsteadily. She came forward and took his hand, led him up the corridor to the third bedroom. He was as nervous as a schoolboy on his first initiation. She shut the door behind them and watched him as he turned his head to take in the crimson bed, then the metal table. "Be gentle with me," he murmured.

And she was. She undressed him slowly, with plenty of kisses. Behind the black mask she was someone else, Miss Routledge, not Deborah. But Deborah was there, too. Deborah was there in the kisses and the gentle divesting of garments – his jacket, his shirt, his trousers. She hung them tidily on hangers, knowing he would do this instinctively. His barrel-like chest was as she had imagined it, muscled, smooth and hairless, and she kissed that too, right down to the navel. But Miss Routledge had to take over when she came to his boxer shorts. Not striped like Laurence's, but a plain navy-blue. Miss Routledge noticed the bulge at his groin, and slipped her fingers through the opening. He was right. It wasn't a small one. And she kissed that too.

It was Deborah, though, who slid the shorts down to his ankles, and knelt in front of him as he stepped out of them, and stayed kneeling while she kissed his thighs and knees and shins and feet. Then came back to his groin and, gripping his buttocks, took him into her mouth.

He came almost at once, in great shuddering heaves. And she swallowed it as she had never swallowed Laurence's. He gripped her shoulders as if he was drowning, and she rose and led him over to the crimson bed. She lay him face down, and he sobbed into the pillows.

She knelt beside him and ran her fingers over the length of his body. Those square shoulders, chiselled shoulder blades, the ridge of the spine leading down to the tapering hips, the gentle swell of his buttocks… she kissed each milestone of the journey, each vertebra, the flat area above where the cleft began, then pressed her lips to the virgin surface of his right buttock, furthest

344

from her. And then, when she had kissed every centimetre of that one, she took off her mask and did the same to the other. The one with the mark.

"It's beautiful," she said. It was, too. It was like the map of Africa, a portwine stain, a congenital naevus, covering almost the whole of his left buttock. It matched the crimson duvet.

Here, though, on the virginal white sheets of her own bed, the stain was that of her blood.

He had lifted her up and carried her back to this room, and she couldn't do anything to stop him. Miss Routledge had been in control in the Red Room, but here he had taken over. He had undressed her gently, with kisses on her throat and shoulders and then, when he'd expertly unhooked the red satin basque, her breasts. He left the G-string and stockings in place until she was lying on the bed and he lay beside her, rolling her left nipple between thumb and forefinger.

"You remind me," he said, "of one of my favourite hookers. She always kept her knickers on too. Gusset-less ones, fortunately."

"You're still keeping me waiting, Dominic."

"Ah. I want to keep you waiting as long as possible. That's the only control I have over you."

"And this is the control I have over you." She touched his penis. Although he'd come twice, in her mouth and then, when she'd sat astride him on the crimson bed, between her fingers, it obediently began to stiffen. He groaned.

What happened after that became, in her memory, just a string of sensations. It wasn't what she had expected. She had read that a first deflowering always hurt and was a bit of a disappointment. She had steeled herself for that. And of course she wasn't young; she must have toughened over the years. But although he was obviously ready, he didn't penetrate her at once. He used his hands, his fingers and, while his mouth occupying hers, he brought her to an orgasm that made her shout out loud while he held her head fast to his chest; and then, while she still lay gasping, he entered her as easily as if they had done it a thousand times. And, just as easily, she rode the waves of sensation for the second time, each one taking her higher and higher, until, trapped into a thunderous fizzing climax, she cried out in triumph, her legs wrapped round his waist, her feet clenching his buttocks.

Far, far from disappointment - it had been the most wonderful experience in the world. And yes; oh yes, yes, yes. It had been well worth waiting for.

He didn't mention the painting until they were back in the kitchen. She had cooked an omelette and uncorked a bottle of red wine. They had eaten at opposite ends of the table, their eyes fixed on each other, their mouths fixed, it seemed, in permanent smiles.

"Number One," he said quietly, laying down his fork, wiping his mouth on a napkin. "Is on your wall."

"Yes."

"Why, Deborah?"

"It's the only thing I have left of Will." She was glad to see he was still smiling. "I was going to tell you about it. I was going to give it to you."

"No, I don't want it. It's enough for me to know where it is." He took a sip of his wine. "And the others, Deborah – Numbers Two and Three?"

"I – I don't…"

He remained smiling. "I admire your loyalty, Miss Routledge. You don't need to tell me. I know exactly where they are."

It was as much as she could do to keep her glass steady. Power *was* an aphrodisiac. She was ready to start all over again.

11. January 1987

Wed 7 Jan 5.47pm

Happy New Year! A bit late but I haven't been in the mood to rite anything over Xmas and NY. It's been the most miserablest Xmas ever and as for NY Eve – well, I could have gone partying with G&T but that would have been groosome. So I stayed here.

At leest the Wainrites took the time off. Huwie had Xmas dinner at Podge's and Gemma went down to Sussex. She said we'd been invited too but Daddy said he wouldn't be good company so it was just us left here and he was like Ebeneezer Scrooge before he turned jolly. At leest I tried. I cooked the horrible turkey which was tuff like old boots and the sprowts were boiled to buggery. Daddy ate it all up and said it was delishus but it was horrible.

O well. Let's see wot 1987 has in store.

Titian had gone the way of Leonardo.

He would try Caravaggio. At least he died young.

And he had some sympathy for the poor bugger. Pursued by devils, self-exiled, stalked by retribution, he'd painted most of his best pictures in a state of torment. Perhaps he could find some inspiration there.

Or perhaps it was too near the knuckle.

He hadn't gone to Gali-Leo's since Deborah had come back from Denver. She hadn't got in touch with him either; he'd had to make the first overture. She had joined the enemy camp, obviously. She'd become embroiled in vipers.

But she wouldn't have told King about Wheels One. Or the three Blue and Greens. He could be quite certain about that.

He could cut his losses quite easily. Sever all ties with the gallery. He could sell it – give it – to Deborah and retire from the fray. Let her carry it on, shoulder the whole bloody mess. If she had thrown her lot in with Dominic King she was safe; her ignorance would be her shield. She *was* ignorant about the fakes, of that he was sure. Even Deborah, with all her expertise and qualifications, hadn't seen through them.

He, Laurence Bassett, at least had the satisfaction of having pulled the wool over the eyes of the so-called experts in the art world. Perhaps he, like Dermot, would think of writing a book exposing the whole sordid business for what it was. Art should be enjoyed for its own sake, not bought and sold like tins of beans. A great picture should be enjoyed by the masses, should belong to the nation. Yes, so he had Wheels One in his library, but rather than sell it for megabucks – and King would pay megabucks, he was sure – he would bequeath it to the Tate.

Bequeath? That was a strange word to think of.

But death had been on his mind a lot lately. He knew why. The quack had persuaded him to have a bilateral knee replacement and had put his name down on the waiting list. Of course he wouldn't have to wait long, being in the private health sector.

"You're too young to go hobbling around like an eighty-year-old," he'd been told. "After the operation you should be jumping around like a spring lamb. But try to lose at least a couple of stone first. And of course lay off the booze."

He hadn't been near a hospital in years, not since he'd had his tonsils out as a lad. He didn't relish the thought of being wheeled into that torture-chamber of steel and chrome and hideous instruments. Oh, he was a coward, he'd always known that.

But at least it had galvanised him to change his Will. He'd called on old Cardew of Trafford, Cardew & Wilson, and drawn up an appropriate document. It had been easier than he'd thought.

He didn't have many liquid assets; all his wealth was bound up in the gallery, the house and his car. He'd signed the Barbican flat over to Huw and gifted the Wetherbys a sizeable sum for their property, much against Cardew's advice. He'd handed most of Will's estate back to his mother and put the proceeds of Deirdre's paintings into a trust fund for her. He was, Cardew dryly observed, a bit of a plonker, finance-wise.

He would leave Leo the lion's share of the Hampstead house and its contents, and divide Huw's with Gemma. Huw had the Barbican flat and Gemma – well, she deserved something. She was, he now knew, the daughter of Patrick King who'd died penniless. Her mother, if she took up painting again (and surely she would, when Nick was released), would be able to sell her work for megabucks. To Dominic King? Well, he was Gemma's uncle.

But she would never know that. Deirdre had wanted to keep it secret, and for obvious reasons. Gemma's father had died of a heroin overdose and had been dragged from the Thames like a pauper. Not something you would want your daughter to know about.

The fate of Wheels One he decided to defer for a while. At the moment it was all his; he wanted to keep it that way. To mention it in a Will, in cold legal terms, would somehow take it away from him. Would make it a product, a tin of beans. Wheels One, and the two Blue and Greens, and the heads, and the only other Belling portrait now in existence, would remain locked in his library, unknown to the world, until he decided what could be done about them.

Sat 10 Jan 3.29pm
I can't beleeve it. He's only known her 3½ months.
Huwie's got himself engaged.
Podge – Pudge – has really got her claws into him.
So wot else can happen? I daren't think. Good job Gemma's going off again soon. If THEY don't get engaged before she goes, I mite stand a chance.
The Man will be releesed fairly soon. Then she won't want Tony any more and I'll be on hand to jolly him up when she dumps him. I'm good at that.

"Have you thought this through?" Laurence asked his son. "You're only twenty-three. She's a nice girl but – marriage? And you haven't known each other that long…"

"Oh, we're not getting married for a long while."

"Then why get engaged?"

Huw shrugged. "It's what she wants."

He wanted to ask, do you love her, but somehow he couldn't get the words out. He'd have no trouble asking this of Leo, but he felt awkward asking it of Huw. And he knew the answer to that. Huw didn't love Pudge; he loved Gemma.

He was only getting engaged because he couldn't have Gemma.

But did Gemma love Huw? Oh, did it matter? He couldn't see his son getting married to a woman he didn't love, simply because he was in love with his half-sister. Who wasn't.

He would tell her the truth when she got back from wherever she was off to this time. Poland? Bulgaria? It would be better if he sought Deirdre's advice before doing so, although that might be awkward if she asked, as she would, why it had taken so long for him to realise he wasn't Gemma's father. And if Gemma asked, as she would, if he knew who her real father was, what could he say?

He was prevaricating as usual.

He realised he was hanging fire, waiting for news of Nick's release.

Fri 16 Jan 7.15pm

Wotching the news tonite when Dermot Timberlake came on. Not him but his photo, taken in his younger days when he was, as they say, at the hite of his fame. The newsreeder was speeking in those sepulkral tones they use when someone has died.

And he had.

I said, Daddy, come here, becoz he was in the kitchen making tee.

Dermot Timberlake has snuffed it, I said when he came in. Becoz by the time he came in, the newsreeder was talking cheerily about some forun disaster.

Christ, said Daddy, are you sure.

Yes, I said.

How did he die? asked Daddy.

Of drink, I said. They found him in his house surrounded by empty bottles. He'd been dead a couple of days they think.

O thank God, said Daddy. Then he said, I ment thank God it wasn't berglers or something.

O, I said, they said it looked like the place had been broken into.

O, said Daddy. Yobs, I suppose.

They didn't say, I said. Just that the place was ransacked and he was lying on the sofa with his eyes and mouth open and reeking of wisky.

Christ, said Daddy.

So I don't suppose he finished his book, I said.

Thank Christ, said Daddy.

He rang Hilary the next day. Yes, she said, Dermot Timberlake died of acute alcohol poisoning. The autopsy report hadn't been issued yet but judging by the stench, he'd drunk enough to sink a ship.

"I heard the place was ransacked," Laurence said. "Was anything taken?"

"Not as far as I know. Don't think there was much of value, judging by the state of the place."

Except the book, thought Laurence. If it existed. Who, besides himself, would not want Dermot's autobiography to see the light of day? Only one other, as far as he knew. Dominic King.

If Dermot had confessed in the book to having painted the second grey study and the eight unsigned Murchison juvenilia, King's collection would halve in value immediately. And King himself would be held to ridicule. And yet – Laurence had always suspected Dominic King knew they were fakes all along. Possibly he had only just worked out who had painted them.

So perhaps it wasn't the book they were after.

"Cyril," he said into the phone, "daft question, but have you had any enquiries about your Murchison?"

"Enquiries?"

"Anyone been trying to buy it off you?"

"No. Why do you ask?"

"Oh, just a feeling I've got that someone's after it. Let me know, will you, if you get approached? And just for the sake of interest, would you be willing to sell?"

"The price would have to be right, Larry. No, I don't think so. I've got very fond of the thing. Drives you mad looking at it, but it's got something."

"Right. Thanks. Love to Cynthia."

"Haven't seen you for a while. You hiding, or something? Come round when you have a minute, Cyn would love to see you."

"Thanks, Cyril. I will. Just got a lot on at the moment."

Laurence put the phone down. A large stone seemed to have lodged in his gut. His hand went automatically to the drawer where he kept a bottle but, remembering Dermot, he withdrew it.

It couldn't be Deborah. If Deborah had told Dominic King where to find the three Murchisons, Cyril would have been approached, he was certain. But if King knew only that she had one of them, he would in all likelihood have assumed Laurence had another, and Timberlake the third… but this was all wild supposition. He was getting as paranoid as Dermot. There was no earthly reason for Deborah to have told Dominic King she possessed one of the Blue and Greens. Unless…

Unless she was in love with the fellow. Unless he had seen it, in Baron's Court.

"I don't want you to give the business to me. If you're really serious, I'll buy you out."

"Can you afford it, Deborah?"

Her violet eyes gazed steadily at him. "Oh yes." Laurence couldn't read what was going on in her mind; she kept her face expressionless. They hadn't spoken of Dermot's death or his memoirs, although she must have heard about it. Rumours were still circulating but the more time passed, the more he hoped the thing would blow over.

He shifted his buttocks on the green velvet seat of the ladderback chair. "I'm drawing up my Will. I want to make sure everyone gets what they deserve."

He was glad to see her eyes widen in horror. "Is there something you're not telling me, Laurence?"

"No, no. I'm going under the knife soon, that's all. The old knees."

Her face softened. Well, it softened more than it was soft already. There was something about her – some aura of something – sexiness? – that rendered her almost beautiful. Very beautiful. She had never looked like that for him. "Don't worry. That operation's like having your tonsils out these days."

"Ah. I had trouble having my tonsils out. Something to do with the anaesthetic."

"It's different now. Medicine's moved on."

"Yes, so they tell me."

She suddenly rose from behind the desk, came round to his side, bent down and kissed him. On the lips. Just a quick, fleeting kiss, but it made his heart skip a beat. "Dear Laurence." She patted his knees, very gently. "You're such a baby."

And then she poured him a scotch. He sat there, hands on his knees, tears pricking his eyes, feeling as if he had lost something irrevocably precious.

Fri 23 Jan 4.17pm

Another shock. Got home early today and there was this big black car in the drive. A Daimler, with windows you can't see throo. It gave me a turn coz I knew I'd seen it before. There was no one in it.

I knew Daddy was out, he'd got an appointment at the hospital.

No one was in the sitting room but Mrs Wainrite was in the kitchen. I said, wot's that car doing outside?

O, she said, someone's come to see your father.

He's not here, I said.

I know, she said. I told him to wait in the library.

The library, I said.

Yes, she said.

The library's always locked, I said.

I have a key, she said. I have keys to all the rooms in this house. And she looked at me in such a funny way I just floo out of the kitchen and went down the hall to the library.

It was the man in the sunglasses who'd been looking thru the window when I'd been hoovering. (See Diary 1986 Vol 3.) He was sitting in Daddy's chair behind Daddy's computer.

Wot are you doing in here, I said, it's private, go away. He just flipped his sunglasses up and smiled and said Hallo again, nice to see you.

It's not nice to see you, I said, go away.

And then I herd Daddy's footsteps in the hall and I floo out to him and said don't go in the library, just tell him to go, O pleese Daddy don't go in.

He looked pale and shaken but he pushed me away and said it's alrite Leo, don't worry it's alrite, but I know it's not.

They're still down there. Daddy's still in the library with that man and I'm shaking all over, I don't know why.

At least David Symons had the grace to get up out of his chair when he walked in. Laurence seated himself in it, hoping to gain the advantage, but instead of taking the hard chair in the corner Symons perched himself on a corner of the desk. He was wearing a dark charcoal suit with white shirt and virulent red tie. The tie matched his socks, Laurence noticed, as he crossed one leg over the other, hugging the ankle.

"Nice to see you again, Larry."

"I wish I could say the same."

"Mind if I smoke?" He lit up a cigarette before Laurence could answer. "I hear you've retired from business, right?"

"Not quite."

"But a good idea. You got a nice house here, why not spend time in it? Don't look as if money's the problem." He indicated the wall with a sweep of his arm. "Good collateral, know what I mean?"

"Not really."

Dave grinned. "I like you, Larry. I like your daughter. She's got spirit, I like that."

"Keep my daughter out of this." He kept his voice steady, but his heart was racing. "How did you get in here?"

Dave shrugged. "Knocked at the door and was let in. Ain't that how most people get into places?" He drew a long drag of his cigarette and sent smoke spiralling slowly towards Wheels

One. "Just thought I'd call in for a chat. See if our investments are being took care of."

Laurence was silent.

"Way things are going, insurance-wise, you can't be too careful. Lot of thieves about, know what I mean?"

A fist of anger was punching up from his stomach. Before he could think better of it, Laurence asked, "Did you have anything to do with Dermot Timberlake's death?"

"Who?" Dave shrugged again. "Never heard of him. Why should I have?"

"Not you personally. Your thugs."

"Thugs?" Dave's grin stretched from ear to ear. "Oh dear, Larry, been watching too many gangster movies, huh? Thugs, eh. And what were these thugs supposed to have done?"

Laurence felt suddenly weary. He sagged back in his chair, aware of pain shooting into his pelvic region.

Dave was looking at him in amusement. "Let me tell you a story," he said at last, rubbing his chin. "Hypothetical story. Concerns someone who tried to pull the wool over someone's eyes. Not a nice thing to do, when we're all supposed to be friends. All pulling in the same direction, so to speak. But this guy thought he could be smart, see. Saw an opportunity to make a bit of money – a lot of money – and not tell anyone. Kinda unfriendly, I think you'd agree." He finished his cigarette, got down from the desk and sauntered over to the window, opening the catch and flicking the butt out on the flowerbed. He shut the window and turned to face Laurence. "Maybe that's what this Timberlake guy had done to his friends, huh?"

"He didn't deserve to die for it."

"But maybe he had a death wish, anyway. Might not have took much to finish him off." Dave shrugged. "As I said, hypothetical. Let's talk about the real world here, shall we?"

"By all means. What do you want from me?"

"Just your co-operation, Larry. As I said, we got to protect our investments."

"Investments?"

"Don't piss me about. You know what I mean." He strolled over to the wall and stood under the painting. His head touched the bottom of the frame. "My client is a little upset with you, Larry. He's given you plenty of time to consider. But he's getting a little – twitchy. He thinks you're not looking after them as well as you should."

"Meaning?"

"Anyone can just stroll in here, can't they? I done it, no trouble."

"This room is kept locked. No one should have let you in."

"Ah, but they did. And I could have cleared this place out and been on my way before you knew it."

Laurence said carefully, "But nobody knows what's in here. I don't let anyone come in. It's perfectly safe."

"You got good insurance?"

"The contents are well insured, yes."

"Every picture separate and described?"

"Not all." Oh God, he was no good at this. His brain had seized up. He'd never been any good at thinking on his feet; he'd got away with it in the past, but not now.

"That's right, Larry. Not all. This one, for instance," jerking a thumb above his head, "and others that rightly belong to my client. Now if they were to go missing…"

"I get your point." He sighed. "All right, I admit it. I've kept a couple back that I should have told him about. But the one on the wall was a gift. It's mine. Will painted it for me."

Dave nodded. "Okay, okay. Listen, my client's a reasonable man. He'll offer big bucks for it, but if you don't want to sell – well, no one can make you. The other ones, though…"

"I've only got one other one."

"My client thinks there are two missing. He's located the third."

Laurence took the key from the top drawer and unlocked the bottom drawer of his desk. He drew out Blue & Green No 2. Thank God he had kept it separate from the Belling portrait, locked in the cabinet. "I think this is what you're after. Timberlake gave it to me. He didn't have it."

"So," said Dave, his eyes following the painting as Laurence laid it on the desk, "we're still missing one."

"Yes."

"But I bet you know where it is."

"I can locate it, yes."

"Then you better had, Larry."

"I don't think the owner wants to sell."

"The *owner* is my client. He paid for all the Murchison juvenilia. You cheated him, Larry." Dave came forward and stood in front of the desk. He was quite a few inches shorter than Laurence. He had a pronounced stoop to his right shoulder – some form of kyphoscoliosis, possibly (Laurence had become quite an expert on osteopathy) – but his thin, bony figure exuded menace. "He's willing to overlook it this time, but he wants all three. Next time I'm in the area, I'll call in for it."

"Why," said Laurence, wearily, "is he so keen to get them all? He must know…"

"Know what?" Dave was grinning again.

"That they're not – worth what he paid for them."

"You'll have to ask him that, Larry. Search me. They look shit to me, you know? All that green and blue. But he sees something in them, I guess."

"All right then. Take it. I'll try and get the other one."

"Try's not a word my client understands." Dave hefted the painting under his arm. "I'll be in touch in a month. Should give you enough time." He walked to the door, paused, then turned. "Oh, one more thing. That painting on the wall – apparently that's worth more than all these put together. That's what my client's twitchy about. He wouldn't like to see it get stolen, even though it's not his. He told me to give you this." He put his hand in his pocket and drew out a small squat object, threw it on the desk. "Next time someone comes in uninvited, you got something to protect it with."

Laurence didn't see him go out. The library door opened and shut and a few seconds later the front door slammed. He didn't lift his eyes from the desk.

4.36pm *The front door's just closed. He's gone. I'm going down and see wot's happened.*

4.47pm *I don't know how I can rite this. My hand's shaking.*

Daddy was standing by his desk looking at something. That horrible old head, I thort, but it wasn't. I must have startled him coz he went to cover it up with his hand but nocked it on to the floor.

So I dashed over and picked it up becoz of his nees.

It was a GUN.

Quite a small one, quite pretty really, but a GUN.

I stared at it and then at him and he said I got it becoz of berglers.

Berglers, I said.

You can't be too careful, he said. Yobs. Peeping toms.

It's a gun, I said.

Yes, he said. Then he gave a kind of smile and said don't worry Leo, I don't know how to use the thing anyway.

It was a funny feeling, holding it. It was heavy and snug, it fitted my hand as if it belonged. I can see why some people get hooked on them.

But Daddy hates guns.

He had opened the top draw of his desk so I went over and put the gun in it and he locked it away.

Don't tell anyone, Leo, he said. I don't have a lisense.

But I can't not tell anyone. I'll have to tell Huwie. It's too much to ask of me, not to tell Huwie.

12. February 1987

He should ring Cyril and offer him megabucks. But he didn't have megabucks. He could sell the Jag. He could raid Deirdre's trust fund. He could take out a mortgage on the Hampstead house. There were a thousand things he could do. He didn't want to do any of them.

All he did was to write a letter and give it to old Cardew. On the envelope he wrote: *To my dear daughter Gemma, to be opened after my death.*

If he survived this blasted operation, he would tell her face to face.

The gun he never allowed himself to consciously think about. It lay in the top drawer of the desk as the portrait of the horned man lay under the partition in the bottom of the cabinet, a permanent unacknowledged presence. He didn't even allow himself to wonder why Dominic King would want him to have it. He had compartmentalised that part of his brain as he'd compartmentalised other things – Will and the fakes. Deirdre. Dermot. Gemma and Huw. Deborah and Dominic. It was the only way he knew how to get through life.

He was aware now of a nagging restlessness that overrode everything else. He kept the calendar in front of him and crossed off the days. He wondered whether to telephone Nick's solicitor but decided against it. Nick would get in touch with Gemma, of course, on his release; but would it be this month, or next? Or would he have to wait longer?

******

"Deborah."

The sound of his voice always sent shocks, like little electric currents, through her. "Hello, Dominic."

"How are you?"

"Missing you."

"I'm missing you. Come over to Denver."

"When?"

"Soon. I have something to show you."

There was telepathy between them. "You've got the other Blue and Greens." She had given him hers; he hadn't wanted it, he said, but she had couriered it over when she'd flown out at Christmas, wrapped as a gift. A tangible piece of her heart was now in his possession. And the painting belonged with the others, in the Juvenile Room with the rest of Will, although she hadn't seen it hung there yet.

"Yes. Almost. Still awaiting delivery of one." There was a note in his voice that set a tiny doubt tingling in her brain. A questioning, testing note.

She hesitated for a fraction of a heartbeat, then said, "So Cyril Lyttleton was willing to sell?"

There was a longer pause at the other end of the line while the cogs turned. Then, "Oh yes. He was persuaded. Eventually."

******

"Like you said, Larry. Megabucks."

"Who got in touch with you, Cyril?"

"Some agency on behalf of a client. Well, I just couldn't refuse. I'll miss it, but Christ – couldn't turn down what they offered. It's only canvas and paint, after all."

Canvas and paint. If he took a cloth saturated in cleaning fluid and scrubbed at Wheels One, it would eventually become merely a blurred canvas. Cyril was right. The world had gone mad.

******

He didn't send the Learjet. She caught a British Airways flight from Heathrow to Denver, first class. At Christmas he had sent a car, but this time he was waiting beside the Daimler.

The sight of him sent tremors through her whole body. Did he feel the same, seeing her? He didn't come forward to meet her. He waited, standing by the car, until she came up to him. They stood two feet apart.

"My darling." And then he had clasped her to him, and their mouths met like two starving oysters.

"You enjoy keeping me waiting."

"Oh yes. It keeps both of us on our toes."

All the way to the house they held hands, exchanged kisses, remarked on the changing scenery. In some indefinable way she felt she had come home. London was strange to her now. Here, among the mountains, the wide open spaces, she felt cleansed.

As she entered the huge portico she knew she was back where she belonged. His staff treated her with respect; the butler obsequient, the little maid awed. There was the housekeeper and the cook, who wished her goodday and bobbed their heads. They all scurried away as Dominic entered, and the chauffeur brought in her luggage.

They spent the whole afternoon and the following nights in the huge circular bed in his suite. Oh yes, she'd come home.

******

Sat 7 Feb 9.47pm *There's someone lerking at the end of the drive, under the lite. I'm sure it's Him, tho I can't see properly becoz of the hedge. If he hasn't gone in 10 mins I'll call the police.*
Mon 9 Feb 9.22pm *He's back. I'll wotch to see wot he does.* **9.24pm** *He's still there.* **9.28pm** *Still there.* **9.31pm** *Ditto.* **9.34pm** *Ditto* **9.37pm** *He's gone. He's hoping to see Gemma of corse, but she won't be back for another 12 days.*
Tues 10-Fri 13 *Ditto*
Sat 14 Feb *Went to party. Didn't enjoy. Kept thinking of the Man. Bet he was there.*
Mon 16 Feb 9.27pm *Gemma's come back early. She told us she was staying on for another week but she arrived back this a.m. Perhaps she knows he's been let out. Shall I tell her he comes here about this time every nite? No, I'll wait to see wot happens.*
9.31pm *There he is. He's looking up at Gemma's window but she's not looking out or else her curtains are drawn. But he's seen the lite on. Now*

he's walking up the drive – no, he's turned back. Why doesn't he just come up and ring the bell like a normal person? I wish I knew what she thinks of him now. Her feelings mite have changed. Perhaps he's afraid of that too...

Her door has opened. She's running along the landing. She must have seen him.

I'm looking out the window, I've kept the lite off so they can't see me.

She's running up to him, throwing her arms round his neck. Now they're walking off like a couple of lovebirds.

Wot about wot he's done? Wot about the aborshun? I don't understand wot she sees in him.

And she's off to Russia again in a few days.

So the Coast is Cleer. Operation Hooking Masterson will swing into acshun.

******

So Gemma had arrived back early. She'd planned to stay on at least a week after her assignment came to an end; she needed a holiday, she said. But she'd arrived home this morning, looking tired and wan but somehow strung up. Had she heard anything about Nick's release? She had left Laurence the number of her hotel in Warsaw in case Nick rang while she was away. But no phonecall had come. He didn't really expect it.

Laurence had wondered if he should ring Deirdre, but decided against. Barbara? – she might have heard something. But best not to stir things up. He was as certain as he could be that Nick would first come to see Gemma; he would think he owed her that much.

So here he was in the sitting room at the front of the house, its big bow-fronted windows giving a good view of the drive but not the end of it, not the street light. He was pretending to read but not seeing a word. Thank goodness Leo was up in her room, as usual; she would wonder what on earth he was doing here, skulking by the window watching every shadow that passed.

He was there, skulking, when footsteps clattered down the stairs. He had time only to throw himself into the armchair and pick up his book, red-hot pokers shooting through his joints, before Gemma raced through the hall, out the door, down the drive. Ignoring the searing pain in his knees, he heaved himself up with the aid of the stick he'd been using more and more lately and hobbled to the front door. The street light cast a glow across one end of the drive, and in it he saw two shadows entwined. They stayed that way for a long time. Then they separated and, still joined, walked out of the light.

He waited until he heard the sound of a key in the front door, at half past midnight. She was alone but her face was radiant.

"He's out?"

"Yes. He was released a week ago. Oh Laurence, if only I'd known!"

"Why didn't he ring you?"

"Oh, you know what he's like. He has to do things his way. And guess what! He's got a job in London, he'll be around for a few months. I wish I wasn't going away, but he'll still be here when I get back. Oh Laurence! I'm so happy!"

He was pleased for her, of course. But there was no doubt she was in love with him. So what about Huw? What about Deirdre?

"Where is he working?"

"He wouldn't tell me. Well, I asked but he didn't answer."

"So when," Laurence chose his words carefully, "are you meeting him again?"

"Every day until I go to Moscow. We'll meet lunch time in the café on Euston station, he says it's about the same distance for both of us."

He left it a couple of days, but on the Wednesday at midday he drove the Jag to Euston and parked in the exorbitant car park, and walked on to the concourse. He took up a position where he could see the entrance to the café, and stood with a newspaper covering his face. After half an hour the pain in his knees was excruciating but he didn't dare to move; and then, just as he was about to give up, Gemma came out, alone. She walked quickly towards the tube and disappeared down the steps. Laurence folded his paper, tucked it under his arm, grasped his stick and made his painful way into the café.

Nick was scraping back his chair at a table over by the far wall, about to leave. Laurence hobbled up to him.

"Ah," said Nick, sitting down again.

"Gemma didn't tell me," he said, lowering himself heavily into the seat opposite. "I followed her."

"Want a coffee?"

"No thanks. Well – yes, actually."

"I could do with another." Nick rose and joined the small queue at the counter. Laurence gazed down at the tabletop. He felt old, and suddenly drained. He didn't know what he was doing here. He couldn't change anything. He couldn't help Nick or Deirdre or Gemma or Leo. He had become a useless old man before his time in a world that had left him behind, floundering to keep up. He had become part of the flotsam on the revolving wheel that would either be doomed to ride the same circle or dropped off and left behind, crushed and withered. He passed a hand over his eyes, pulled at his nose. A mug slid into his field of vision. Nick said, "So what do you want?"

For a moment Laurence couldn't speak. He cupped his hands round the mug, unable to raise his eyes to those deep brown ones fixed on him with that steady, considering gaze. When he did, he got a shock. Nick looked older, more – worn. There were streaks of grey in that unruly brown hair. His usual healthy tan had faded. He looked tired and pale, and somehow diminished.

"I just need to tell you two things. My son's in love with Gemma."

"Is he."

"He, of course, thinks he's her half-brother."

Nick lifted his mug. "But he's not." He drank, looking at Laurence over the rim.

"No."

"And you're not going to say anything."

"I can't say anything, Nick. You see – I know who her real father was."

Nick frowned. "That's more than I do."

364

"I've worked it out. I think I'm right. It was that hippie fellow, Patrick King."

Nick put down his mug, tapped a fingernail against it. "So?" He didn't sound surprised.

Laurence sighed. "I know it doesn't mean anything to you, but it means a lot to Gemma. Knowing where she comes from. Not just that, but – *who* she comes from, if you see what I mean. She was happy to think it was me. I can give her what she needs – security, stability – and yes, a certain amount of social standing. You might not think much of me, but I've done my best for her. Even after I realised she wasn't mine."

"And what was the other thing?"

"It's about Deirdre. She misses you, Nick. If you stay in London she's not going to get better. She's not going to paint again."

That quick smile, the smile that softened his features and made him seem like a boy again. "Ah. So that's it."

"I'm not being selfish. All right, I admit that if she starts painting I can sell whatever she produces, for a lot of money. There's a buyer who'll pay…" He stopped, took a long mouthful of the hot, bitter liquid. "Well, let that be. I'm just concerned about her. About her welfare."

Nick sat back. He stirred his coffee in long, slow circles. Then he threw down the spoon. "I've got a job," he said. "Jobs won't be easy to come by. I'm an ex-con, and people remember. So I'll have to stay here until it comes to an end. It shouldn't be long, a few months. Then I'll go to her." He smiled again. "That is, if she'll have me."

Laurence took a deep breath. "Do you love her? Gemma, I mean?" He didn't expect Nick to answer; he rarely answered personal questions.

"Yes." There was no hesitation.

"And Deirdre?"

"Yes, but in a different way." He took his gaze from Laurence and stared down at the table. "Don't worry. Gem and I – we've talked it over. She knows it's not possible. I'll always be here for her, she knows that, but - that's all. So you can tell your son there's hope for him."

"But only if I tell her I'm not her father."

Nick shrugged. "That's up to you." He finished the rest of his coffee, then stood. "I've got to go. Some of us have work to do." He pushed his chair in, deftly skirted the next table and walked quickly out of the café.

Laurence sat staring at his mug of cooling coffee, remembering another time, another place he had done likewise. At Caernarvon, in 1971. With Francine Everett, who lived in Gloucestershire.

******

They rode the elevator to the top floor. Dominic pressed the buttons on the panel by the door and held it open for her to enter. She stood on the threshold, staring into blackness.

He placed a hand under her elbow and guided her forward. The rooms bloomed into light, one after another, as they progressed. She found herself breathing deeply as the last room appeared, Wheels Two blazing into gigantic life. But she couldn't stop, even if she'd wanted to. He was guiding her inexorably towards the Juvenile Room.

The eight Blue and Greens were lined along the wall, complete. Hers started the sequence. How would Will have painted them? Altogether, she was sure. She could see a younger Will tentatively loading his brush and starting at one corner of the first canvas, the others lined up blank and virginal, until he'd worked out what he would do. And then – he would paint in a frenzy, filling them all. But he would have started with hers. She had given birth to them.

The effect was overwhelming. Great sweeps and swirls of green, mirrored in the blue beneath – but blue also at the top, little touches of it peeping through like sky through branches, and those random brown and yellow dots, joining up now to form a continuous chain, threading along – yes the whole picture

366

made sense now, it was coalescing into a whole in front of her eyes.

"It *is* a landscape," she said. "Trees and water." But even as she said this, Will disappeared. It had not been painted in a frenzy. It had been painted slowly and deliberately. It could not have been a young Will who'd done it; this was a painting of maturity, of someone at the height of their powers.

She swayed. His arm was round her waist, holding her up.

"I'm sorry, my darling. But you had to see it."

"You knew."

"I suspected. I had to be sure."

All these years. All these years she had been trying to find Will in a painting that wasn't his.

"Did Laurence know?"

"He attributed them all as unsigned Murchison juvenilia."

He couldn't have known. But how would Dermot Timberlake have been able to pass them off as Murchisons, without his knowledge? She thought Laurence couldn't be hoodwinked; but he had been, with that Study in Grey on the other wall, which she knew now was Dermot's. But surely he wouldn't have been tricked by eight canvases, each carefully scrutinised and authenticated by a Gali-Leo's sticker and his signature. Even if he had never seen them together in sequence, so that the trees and water were unmistakeable – timber/lake – he would have known they weren't Will's.

The money had not gone through the books. He'd told her that he'd sent it, less his commission, to Will's mother. Why should the Inland Revenue, he'd said, get a share in paintings that nobody would know existed?

She was aware that something was curdling and hardening inside her. Not withering; affection, love, whatever it had been, what she had felt for Laurence, that couldn't wither. Something else was happening. It was said that love was very near hatred. What she felt for Laurence at this precise moment was something very near hatred.

"Timberlake died," Dominic said, "of cirrhosis of the liver brought on by an excess of ethanol."

"I heard his house had been broken into."

"The police think that someone took advantage of his demise. Found him dead, decided to see if there was anything worth taking."

"Would there have been?"

"Possibly." He looked steadily at her. "A few canvases, perhaps. And a manuscript."

They were sitting drinking cocktails in the Garden of the Gods, looking out over the majestic Pikes Peak. Another surreal setting, this time to discuss a death.

"And did they find anything?" She kept her voice steady, its tone merely interested.

"No."

"Not even a manuscript?"

"Ah," Dominic smiled. "He'd already finished that."

"You have it?" She tried to conceal her surprise. He was always surprising her, but she should know better; he seemed to know everything. He hadn't known the whereabouts of the third Blue and Green, however; he had misled her about that.

"A copy is in my possession." He sounded neither smug nor triumphant, just matter-of-fact.

"Will you have it destroyed?" Of course he would. Dominic King couldn't afford to allow the whole art world to realise he'd been hoodwinked; that he'd bought a whole series of Timberlakes thinking they were Murchisons.

"Oh no." Those steel grey eyes were fastened on her face, assessing her reaction. "It will be published fairly soon to great public and media interest."

And now she couldn't conceal her surprise. "But everyone will know of the fraud. Laurence's reputation will be in pieces." Did she care about that? Why had she said that? The drink must be more potent than it looked. She went on hastily, "Your collection…"

"Will go up in value." He smiled thinly. "The world has gone mad, Deborah. Notoriety is prized above talent. Your poor Will would never have survived if he'd lived. Dermot Timberlake will live on, overshadowing him, merely by pulling off a scam. People will flock to see the Blue and Greens and forget about Closed Circuits and Stoned Seas."

"So you'll put them on show." Voice neutral, face blank.

"I think so. But," he smiled, "only if you agree."

She sipped her cocktail slowly. She would never let him exhibit the fakes, he must realise that. And not because of Laurence (or not entirely), but because of Will. She couldn't allow Dominic to betray Will just for the sake of his art collection. No, she would prevent him publishing the manuscript and exhibiting the Timberlakes. She had the power. Dominic King might be able to hold the world to ransom, but she, Deborah Routledge, controlled Dominic King.

******

Mon 23 Feb 6.03pm *Operation Hooking Masterson offishully opened. Gemma floo off at the weekend so the Coast is well and trooly Cleer.*
Tony was at the shoot today. He saw me and waved. I waved back. But I left it till lunch time to approach.
Hallo, I said.
Hallo, he said.
Gemma's got there all rite, I said.
Good, he said.
Then we just smiled at each other until he was called away. I couldn't think of a thing to say and nyther could he. It's not offen I'm lost for words.
Still, early days yet. I'll work on it.

Tues 24 Feb 8.17pm *Am worried about Daddy. He spends all day in the library and I can't get in. He told me at brekfast that he's signed the gallery over to Deborah Routledge.*
So it won't be Gali-Leo's any longer, I said.
O it will for a wile, he said.
I think that's wot the bloke came about the other nite. But I don't think that's wot Daddy's so sad about. I think he's sad about the Man not having foned or nocked at the door, but skulked about outside. And now Gemma's

gone the Man won't come any more until she gets back, but he still won't come to see Daddy. They've cut Daddy out of their lives and that's wot he's sad about.

I hate the Man and the Mad Mother and Gemma, too, becoz it's all her folt.

But I hate the Man most of all becoz he hates Daddy.

******

The appointment letter was lying on the hall table. He would be admitted to hospital on Monday, 2nd March, the operation to take place the following day. To see it written in black and white gave him a shock. He'd given up the whisky since Dermot's death; hadn't touched a drop, apart from the one Deborah had poured him. He hadn't lost weight, but he hadn't put any on. But surely the quacks knew their job; they wouldn't operate on an unfit man. And if he didn't have the operation, he'd been told he'd soon be in a wheelchair.

Deborah had flown off to Denver. Jacqui, from VP Associates, was in charge of Gali-Leo's which soon wouldn't be.

Dominic King now owned all the Murchison juvenilia. Which wasn't. Which he knew wasn't. And soon Deborah would realise it wasn't.

He didn't care about his reputation. But he did care what Deborah thought of him.

Huwie was engaged to a woman he didn't love.

Leo was missing out on life because she was worried about him. She rarely left the house now, or only for work.

Gemma had flown off to Moscow. She had her own life; at least he had given her that.

Nick wouldn't come again. He would never again set foot in this house. When his job came to an end he would go back to Deirdre, who would soon be well enough to leave Sussex and return to Suffolk. Or would he go back to Francine Everett, in Gloucestershire? In either case, he had lost him.

And he was being watched. Mrs Wainwright watched him from the house, Mr Wainwright from the garden. They had seen

Wheels One and Dermot's picture. The only thing they hadn't seen was the portrait of the horned man, the only other Belling painting now in existence.

Dermot Timberlake, he was convinced, had been killed. Someone had held him down and poured whisky down his throat, all for a painting and a manuscript. But the case had been closed. There had been no suspicious circumstances, as far as the police were concerned.

He had taken to opening the drawer and staring at the gun. It exerted a weird fascination. One day he would get up the courage to pick it up. One day. Perhaps.

13.   Sunday 1st March 1987

"I'm a little bit scared, Deborah."

"Oh, Laurence. It's nothing. It'll be plain sailing."

"I need someone to hold my hand. I can't worry Leo."

"We've only just arrived back."

We? "Oh. Sorry. I just rang on the off chance…"

A pause. Then, "I'll come over if I can. It might be quite late."

"No, no. Don't worry."

"Don't *you* worry. It's really nothing to be worried about."

"Yes, I know. I'm just a big fat coward, as Leo would say. Listen, forget it, Deborah. Did you have a good time?"

"Wonderful."

"You sound happy."

"I am."

"Good. Have a happy life, Deborah. You deserve it." He dropped the receiver and held his head in his hands.

She replaced the receiver, stood looking at it for a second or two before going back into the kitchen. She'd left Dominic to open the wine.

He was looking in the drawer where she kept the keys. He said, "I couldn't find the corkscrew."

"You've got it in your hand."

"Ah yes." He shut the drawer and, smiling at her, pulled the cork.

"I'll have to go out for a while."

"Oh?" He paused in the act of filling her glass.

"It's Laurence. He's got himself in a bit of a twist about this operation."

He said quietly, "I thought you were over him, Deborah."

"I hated him in Denver. It's different here." She felt tears pricking her eyes. The thought of Laurence in his library, all alone, worrying…

"I don't like rivals." He said this smiling.

She went to him, kissed him. "It was a long time ago. You mustn't be jealous."

"Oh but I am. I'm a jealous, cruel man."

"And I love you for it."

"Forget the wine. Let's go to bed. You must be tired."

Never too tired to hold him, caress him. He was as precious to her as breathing. But she was tired. She fell asleep, her arm over his chest. When she awoke, in the early hours, her arm was flung over the pillow, and he had gone.

******

He didn't hear the front door open.

The first time he knew there was someone in the house was when the library door was unlocked. From the outside.

"Good God." He was looking into the pale grey eyes of Dominic King.

"Hello, Larry."

"How the hell did you get in?"

"With a key. I have keys to all the rooms in this house." He came in, closed the door behind him. He turned his head to the left, lifted his chin in profile to study Wheels One, hung high on the wall. That smooth forehead, straight nose, well-shaped eyebrows…

Laurence felt as if he had turned to stone.

Dominic stood unmoving for a long moment, then moved closer to the painting. His eyes hadn't blinked. Laurence had that profile offered to him for maybe a whole minute. Then he said, "No wonder you kept this under wraps. I can't blame you. But I think you know where it belongs."

"It belongs here." These words seemed to come from somewhere outside himself, outside the block of stone he'd become.

Dominic turned back to him, that small smile on his mouth but not in his eyes. "It belongs with Closed Circuits Two. But let it be. I can wait."

"I'll never sell it."

"I'll never buy it." He turned from the painting and walked up to the desk, stood looking down at him, fists resting on its surface. "I like you, Larry. I wish I didn't, but I do. I can quite see why Deborah can't let you go, even after I'd shown her the Timberlakes. I thought she would cut you out of her life like rotten flesh, as I would have done. But she's worried about you. And your knees."

Laurence said nothing.

"It's always the thought of something, not the thing itself, that one dreads, don't you find?"

Laurence said nothing. His brain was racing, however. Dominic King had also lived at the Holland Park house. Two brothers, Dominic and Patrick. But surely it would have been Patrick that Deirdre would have been attracted to, not Dominic the much older, richer, colder brother…

But Deborah had seen something in him. Deborah obviously loved him.

"Do you love her?" he said suddenly. "Deborah?"

"She's as necessary to me as oxygen."

"You won't hurt her?"

"I would cut off my right arm before I hurt her. And that's not easy for me to admit, Larry. I never thought I would, or could, admit it."

"But I have, haven't I. I've hurt her."

"Yes. Deeply. She wept."

"Ah God." Laurence leaned forward and held his head in his hands, ran his fingers through his hair. "Tell her I didn't mean it. The whole thing – snowballed. I only wanted…"

"What?"

"I don't know. To be cleverer than you, I suppose. To feel more alive, after Will died. Possibly to help Dermot. I don't know."

"Greed, Larry. It gets us all in the end." He paused, then said, "I have the manuscript, by the way. I believe it'll enhance my reputation – Timberlake mentions in the last chapter that I'd seen through the fraud years ago – but it'll ruin yours. You don't come out of it at all well, I'm afraid. He accuses you of making him paint the pictures under duress. You might even be looking at a prison sentence, if I decide to press charges."

Laurence was silent.

Dominic went on, "I'm thinking of publishing it soon. Although I could be persuaded not to publish at all."

Laurence licked his lips. His mouth had gone dry. "What would persuade you?"

"Ah. That rather depends on you, Larry."

"How?"

"Oh, come now. I thought you were an intelligent man."

"Sometimes I think," Laurence said slowly, "it would be best if I didn't survive this damn operation. I'm no good to anyone now. If it wasn't for Leo…"

"Your daughter? From what I've heard, she'd get over it. A little fighter, apparently."

Laurence smiled. "Yes." Then, after a deep breath, "Is that why you gave me the gun?"

"I didn't. But Dave thought it might come in useful."

"I've sat looking at it. The thought has crossed my mind… but I'm sorry, I can't do it."

"Not even to protect your reputation?"

"I'm not worried about that." But he was, of course. He was a vain, selfish man. But he was also a big fat coward. "I wouldn't know how to use it, anyway."

"Then I'll have it back."

Laurence opened the drawer, took out the gun and laid it on the desk. Dominic stretched out a hand and picked it up. It was then Laurence saw he was wearing gloves.

The barrel was pointing at his forehead. Dominic's thumb was pulling back the safety catch. His finger was squeezing the trigger…

"Bang," he said. The chamber clicked, whirled round. He smiled. "It wasn't loaded."

"Jesus." Laurence slumped forward, clutching his head.

"I didn't really want you dead, Larry. Not then. I just wanted to put the idea in your mind. To get you used to it."

And the idea that was now in his mind was that he could have been dead; he should have been dead. It would have been all over. All the whole bloody mess…

He lifted his eyes to see Dominic loading bullets into the chamber. He placed the gun on the desk. "Now it is loaded. And it's easy to use. Just point and pull. Even an idiot can do it." He moved to the door. "I'll leave you alone to think about it. I can't have rivals, Larry. Especially ones I like."

He sat and thought about it for hours. Or what seemed like hours. Probably only minutes. Him and the gun, locked in mutual contemplation.

He couldn't do it, of course. Anywhere else, but not here. There was only him and Leo in the house. He couldn't do it to Leo. Not to his Leonora, his one and only precious princess.

When the door opened he didn't lift his eyes from the gun. He said, "I'm sorry, Dominic. I can't do it."

But it wasn't Dominic King who stood there. It was someone else.

14. June 1987

Leo gets up early the next day, steeling herself for the task ahead. She had rung the gallery yesterday, expecting Deborah Routledge to answer the phone. But an American voice said, "Good morning, you're through to VP Galleries London and New York, how can I help you?"

Miss Routledge wasn't there, she'd been informed, but would be in first thing the next morning. Mr Bassett's daughter? Oh, of course she'll be pleased to see you, I'll pencil you in for ten-thirty, that will be no problem, have a nice day.

She had left the painting on the desk, face down. She would have to pick it up and wrap it and tie string around it to make carrying easier. But she couldn't live in the house now while that thing was in Daddy's cabinet. The heads she will have to think about. She will discuss them with Tony, who'll be back, thank goodness, tomorrow. Tony will know what to do.

Leo knows nothing much about art, but she knows the portrait is a Belling, painted by Gemma's mother. So it could be worth a lot of money. But who would want such a thing? It's horrible. It gives her the shivers.

As does Miss Rottweiler. Leo has never taken to her, doesn't know what Daddy saw in her. She's always thought of her as a dried-up old prune who Daddy had felt sorry for, keeping her on all those years. And now she has Gali-Leo's and turned it into something else. She had taken advantage of Daddy's generosity, his good nature, his failure to see bad in anybody. Why do those sort of people get away with it, when people like Daddy…

Anyway. She has got a swathe of bubblewrap, and a large piece of brown paper, and brown tape, and string, and a pair of scissors. So here goes.

******

"Leonora Bassett?"

"I thought you'd want to see her. I've made it ten-thirty."

"Oh. Well…"

"Was that wrong?" Jacqui looks mortified.

"No. No, of course not. Send her up when she arrives."

Deborah mounts the stairs to the office. This will probably be the last time for a few months – possibly years – that she will do this. Although nominally in charge of the two VP Galleries, London and New York, with more openings planned in Toronto and Sydney and Barcelona, she knows that Dominic won't want her spending too much time out of his sight. She is flying out to Denver tomorrow for good. Their waiting game is over.

Seating herself in the high leather chair, Deborah spreads her hands on the desk top. The diamond on the third finger of the left, the twin of his, sparkles. He had proposed, with all the panoply of tradition (he'd knelt at her feet, kissed her hand, offered her a perfect red rose) and, of course, she had accepted.

She has become like Laurence, she thinks. Compartmentalising her life. She has moved on. She doesn't want to see Leonora, to be reminded of that old existence she has thankfully left behind. The Baron's Court flat had been put on the market and is now under contract; until her marriage, she has rented a small mews in Chelsea.

Until her marriage. She smiles.

She is still smiling when Leonora Bassett enters the office. She hasn't seen her since the funeral, and is surprised at the change in her. For the better. In fact they both stare at each other in mutual surprise.

"Leonora." Deborah feels emboldened to get up, approach the girl and embrace her. The girl responds as well as she's able with a large flat parcel under one arm. "I'm sorry I haven't called on you. I haven't felt the time was right, somehow. How are you?"

"I'm fine. Really. The first couple of months were awful…"

"I know."

"But it's all right now. I'll survive."

"Good. We'll never forget him, but time does heal."

"The next thing's the inquest."

"Yes." Deborah hesitates; the subject is a thorny one. "I won't be able to attend, I'm afraid." She sits down and the girl takes the ladderback chair opposite. For a moment Laurence is there, hands on his knees, looking rueful. Deborah sighs. She won't be sorry to leave this place.

"You don't have to, do you? You've already done your bit." This is a trace of the old Leonora, Laurence's brat of a daughter.

Deborah says carefully, "Do you still believe...?"

Leonora shakes her head vigorously. Deborah takes that to mean she doesn't still think her father was murdered, but it could merely mean she doesn't want to talk about it. Either way, the subject can be left there, unexplored.

"I'm glad you've come. This is my last day here, Jacqui's taking over as from tomorrow."

"Oh."

"I shall be based in the States."

"Oh."

"So it's nice that we've met again just in time, isn't it?"

"Yes." There is something on the girl's mind, obviously. Deborah waits. Leonora hesitates, then says, "I wanted to ask you something. I don't know if you can help, but – I think some of Daddy's paintings and things have been stolen."

"What makes you think that?"

"They've disappeared. The painting on the library wall – the Murchison – and some others, we think."

"Think? Don't you know?"

"No." The girl looks discomfited. "Well, after Daddy... I didn't want to go in... and then things were so awful... It wasn't until yesterday we realised they'd gone missing."

Deborah smiles. "They haven't gone missing, Leonora. Your father arranged for them to be sold before he died. He was obviously settling his affairs..." She pauses, then says gently, "I don't know if you realise, but he had debts. The sale of his collection paid them off so you wouldn't have to worry."

"Daddy had debts?" The girl swallows. "He never told me..."

"Well he wouldn't, would he? Your father loved you very much, he didn't want you to know."

Tears fill Leonora's eyes and plop down her face. She fists them away with a fierce little-girl gesture. Deborah's heart leaps out to her. In fact Leonora seems much younger now with her hair soft and frizzy and her face unmade-up. She can see Laurence in that face, beyond those dark flashing eyes and the pursed-up lips holding back sobs. Her own eyes fill in sympathy.

She hasn't cried since the night it happened. Dominic had allowed her those tears, but no more. He knows how she felt about Laurence (but what did she feel?), but he doesn't want to be reminded of it. Whatever she felt for Laurence is in the past; her future is with him, all her feelings must now be for him. And they are. Except…

She will allow a few more tears, to keep the girl company. They sit facing each other, trying to smile, getting their emotions under control.

"I'm sorry," Leonora says eventually. "I don't mean crying, or even upsetting you. I mean I'm sorry I doubted you. You loved him too, didn't you."

"Yes. Very much."

"And he knew it."

"Yes. He did."

"Good." She takes a deep breath. "I was always a bit jealous, I suppose. That you spent so much time with him. But I'm not any more. I'm glad he had someone else who loved him when he wasn't with me." She bends down and places the flat package on the desk. "I found this in his library. In a drawer. I think it might be valuable."

Deborah hesitates. Dominic had told her everything of value had been cleared. Dominic isn't usually wrong.

She is aware of the girl's eyes on her as she cuts the string and parts the brown paper, slides off the bubblewrap. The canvas is upside down. She sees the girl flinch as she turns it over, and understands why.

"It's horrible, isn't it."

Yes, it is horrible. But also magnificent.

"It's a Belling." She touches it with her fingers, feeling a slight moist stickiness. "Where has it been? It's not been very well looked after..."

"I don't know. I know nothing about it."

The face is compelling. Smiling yet sneering. Beneficent yet evil. And the horns... You don't notice them at first, but when you do – it all fits. And it's a face that seems familiar, although it's no one she knows.

"What do you want to do with it?"

Leonora shrugs. "I don't want it. I thought you might be able to do something with it."

"I know someone who'll pay a lot of money for it." She takes her eyes off the portrait, with difficulty, to look across at the girl. "Do you know Drusilla Belling? Do you know where she lives?"

"Oh yes."

"But she's not painting at the moment."

"No. She's not been well. But I think she might take it up again fairly soon."

"When she does, will you let me know?"

"All right."

"And the daughter, Gemma – does she know about this?"

"No, I don't think so."

"Shall we keep it secret? For the moment? Just until I get some idea how valuable it is."

Leonora nods. She gets up. Her face is streaky from the tears, but she is composed, a little combative. "Well, I'll go then. Thanks. I feel much better now." She walks to the door, then turns. "Oh, I hope you get on well in America. Good luck." And she disappears.

Deborah is left with the portrait of the horned man leering up at her as he had presumably leered up at Laurence. Who is he? Did Laurence know him? And will Dominic want such a portrait, even if it is a Belling? She knows the answer to that one even as she poses it. He wants to possess them all, every last one. He's a possessive, jealous man.

She sees the diamond glitter on her finger and, for a moment, a shiver runs down her spine.

******

She had awoken in the early hours of the morning. He wasn't by her side. The flat was empty of his presence. They hadn't made love, but he'd kissed her goodnight with his usual tenderness. She hadn't been disloyal. He hadn't wanted her to go to Laurence, so she hadn't.

But he had been looking in the drawer...

It was strange how, in the short time she'd known him, she had become so attuned to his needs and his thoughts. He was a twin of herself. She knew exactly how his mind worked.

She dressed, grabbed her keys, caught the lift down to the car park in the basement. She drove through the silent London streets, passing taxis and the odd night bus. How would he have got there? – he had dismissed his driver. But of course he could just click his fingers and things would fall into place. He would have lifted the phone and ordered a car...

The street was in darkness. Laurence's house was in darkness. There was no car in the drive. She cruised past, looking for the Daimler. But it wouldn't be the Daimler, the Daimler would be too distinctive. She parked round a corner, leapt from the car without locking it. Hurried up the street, turned into the drive. And bumped into someone who stepped out of the hedge.

A hand was across her mouth. She was held in a grip of iron.

She was held in a grip of iron against his chest; his mouth, not his hand, now pressed to hers. His hands were blocking her ears. But she heard it, even as his tongue was gagging her mouth. A sharp, single note, muffled, gone almost as soon as it reached her ears. A sob was wrenched from her body but he stifled it, holding her against him, forcing all his iron will into her.

Then he let her go and she sagged into the hedge, held on to the trunk of a tree for support. On the periphery of her vision a figure slipped through the front door which closed silently behind it. She had the impression that it had a large head that seemed too big for its body.

But it might have been her imagination, because when she looked again it seemed to have melted into the shadows and the drive was empty. She was being led away, taken through the gateway and back to her car.

"I'll drive," Dominic said.

They didn't speak all the way back. They didn't speak until they were in the flat at Hurlingham Mansions, and he was putting the kettle on for coffee.

"Never do that again," he said. "Never check up on me, Deborah."

She said nothing. She felt dead inside.

"He was an unhappy man. You couldn't have done anything for him."

"I think I could…"

"No, Deborah. He'd gone beyond help. Even yours."

He allowed her to cry. She wept for five minutes, while he made the coffee. He gave her a handkerchief. Then, looking at his watch, he said, "I never want to hear his name on your lips again. It's time to move on."

He allowed her to attend the funeral. It would have looked strange if she hadn't. A month later he sent for her from Barbados, where, after she'd promised to prove her love was for him alone, he proposed.

And she, of course, accepted.

15. July 1987

They are all together again in their best suits and frocks, just like at Daddy's funeral, except not so many. Hilary Frost, the Lyttletons, Ralph Weinstock, Gemma, Huwie (Pudge, fortunately, couldn't come, apparently Lord Havergo couldn't spare her), and her and Tony. As they congregate in the lobby of the Coroner's Court, Leo catches sight of another figure on the periphery, someone vaguely familiar. She is about to let go of Tony's arm to get a better look when Gemma suddenly breaks away from Huwie and runs up to him. She takes his hands in hers and kisses him on both cheeks. Huwie scowls.

It is Julian Montfort, Sebastian's elder brother.

Leo squeezes Tony's elbow. "Just a moment," she says. "There's someone I must speak to." She goes over to them and offers her hand, which Julian touches briefly. "Hello again."

Physically Julian takes after his father, a fairly short, thickset fellow. But Sir Denis, she remembers, was a bluff, no-nonsense type of person who brooked no argument. Julian is much more reserved, like his mother. He has a grave and courteous manner and gives a formal bow from the waist. "It's the least I could do. I wanted to offer my condolences. Obviously I know exactly how you feel. My father also wanted to come but mother's health prevents him."

Gemma asks, "Are they still in Switzerland?"

"Yes. The air seems to suit her there." He hesitates, then says, "I'm hope they reach a verdict. It's better for all concerned. Mother hasn't been allowed to grieve properly. I'm sure that's part of her problem."

"Does your father still think it wasn't an accident?" Gemma's tone is calm, but Leo hears the faint tremble behind the words.

"I don't know. He's very stubborn. I shall try to talk him round when he comes back – when *they* come back." Julian's voice is similarly measured and Leo, on impulse, flings her arms round him and kisses his cheek.

"Thanks so much for coming. Daddy would have appreciated it."

She is grateful for Tony's reassuring presence at her side as they file into the court. He holds her firmly round the waist but she feels strong and in control. The proceedings are short and to the point, not like Sebastian's. Daddy had been in good health, apart from his arthritis; a little overweight, but all organs were in working order. So there was nothing physical that might explain his depression. He may have had financial problems. His business had been sold and there were rumours that his professional judgement could be called into question. He had recently changed his Will. He had access to a gun.

And of course there is the note, which Huwie had told her about only a few days ago when he couldn't put it off any longer. It had been sent to him two months ago by Deborah Routledge, who had originally received it through the post the day after Daddy's death. She had told Huwie she had hesitated to send it to him; she had even been going to destroy it, but had realised it was valuable evidence. Huwie, of course, had told the authorities immediately. He hadn't offered to show it to her and Leo hadn't asked to see it.

The verdict is suicide while the balance of mind was disturbed.

She is aware that people are looking surreptitiously at her, watching for her reaction. But she won't question the verdict. She must have been mistaken about the noises she'd heard. She must have been dreaming. She will leave Daddy to rest in peace and get on with the rest of her life.

Back out in the corridor she breaks away from Tony and goes up to Huwie. He is comforting Gemma, who has broken down in tears. Julian Montfort is nowhere to be seen.

"Daddy's note," she says. "Have you still got it?"

He nods. "It's in my wallet."

"Can I see it?"

He hesitates. "I don't think you ought to, Leo. It'll upset you."

"Please." She feels strong enough now to look at it. It's the last thing she must do so she can wrap the whole thing up and file it away.

Still with one arm around Gemma, he puts his hand into his inside jacket pocket and brings out his wallet, flips it open and holds it out to her. "It's in the first compartment. Are you sure about this, sis?"

She delves into the wallet and brings out a small piece of paper. It's only a scrap, cut off top and bottom, but she recognises Daddy's loopy handwriting, although the words are neater, less ostentatious than usual. He obviously didn't write it while his balance of mind was disturbed. She has the feeling it has been written over and over again until he was satisfied.

She reads: *I haven't been a good man. It's not enough for intentions to be good, I know that now. I've thought through my entire life and it doesn't add up to much. All I want to say is that I'm so very very sorry. I know that nothing I can do or say will change anything. If I could make amends I would, but there's nothing anyone can do now. I'm in despair.*

She folds it up and tucks it back into Huwie's wallet. Something about the note strikes her as anomalous, but she doesn't know why. She won't even try to analyse it. There was obviously a side to Daddy she didn't know existed, but it doesn't matter. Her feelings for him will never change. He was, and always will be, her beloved father and she will always and forever be his one and only precious princess.

"Okay, Leo?" Tony is beside her, lovely Tony who will help her get over her loss, just as Huwie will help Gemma. Poor Gemma, who has had her own losses to contend with. They must all help each other now. And Nick is with Dee in Sussex with the dear Ws. Somehow it has all turned out well; Daddy has put everything right.

"Oh yes," she says. "I'm fine." And threads her arm through his, ready to face the little band of media hyenas who have gathered outside the court.

The third part of *Closed Circuits, Cluttered Minds,* will be published shortly by PETAN PUBLISHING.

The TRILOGY
CLOSED CIRCUITS, CUTTERED MINDS

Riding the Wheel

1st in trilogy *Closed Circuits, Cluttered Minds*

Gemma Belling is bringing her boyfriend Sebastian home to
meet mother. But Drusilla is no ordinary mother, and her
Suffolk cottage no ordinary home. And as Sebastian is soon to
find out, meddling in things that don't concern him can lead to
revelations that might be better left undiscovered.

Why doesn't Drusilla, a talented painter, want to be famous?
What is the nature of the relationship between her and Nick?
Who is Gemma's real father? And why does Laurence Bassett, a
London art dealer, think there are dark secrets hidden in the
past?

From Drusilla's isolated cottage the web of tangled relationships
and motives reaches out from Suffolk to London and Wales,
from the mid-eighties back to the mid-sixties, when society's
rules were being overthrown and times were certainly a-changin'.
But, as this novel reveals, the past still has power to affect the
future, if nothing has been
resolved.

Wheels and Circles

2nd in trilogy *Closed Circuits, Cluttered Minds*

Laurence Bassett, West End art gallery owner and TV quiz show
host, is found one morning in March 1987 shot dead in his
library. Did he commit suicide? Or, as his daughter Leonora is
convinced, was he murdered?

As Leo tries to hunt down his killer, secrets are unearthed from
the past. Is Laurence's long-lost daughter Gemma really his?
Why does he keep valuable art locked in his library? Who is
buying up the paintings of a talented artist, Will Murchison? And

how much does his assistant, Deborah Routledge, know of his secret life?

In this second part of the trilogy *Closed Circuits, Cluttered Minds,* past and present shadow each other as the wheels and circles of fate bring in their revenges.

Full Circle
3rd in trilogy *Closed Circuits, Cluttered Minds*

The identification of a dismembered body on a Welsh farm is the start of a domino effect that will leave nobody unscathed. As skeletons fall out of cupboards, lives are irrevocably changed. And Dominic King, confidant of governments and a broker between nations, finds that he is just as vulnerable to the curses of love and jealousy as anyone else. As he pursues the object of his affliction, he begins to find out exactly what love is…

In the last part of the trilogy *Closed Circuits, Cluttered Minds,* the story is brought full circle as retribution stalks the footsteps of the guilty.

Now read the first part of the first chapter of *Full Circle*:

Full Circle

Part One – Sex and Death

1.   November 1985 - Gloucestershire

There is someone lying beside him.

Although of course it might still be the dream. He's again been staring into dark depths of black water terrified of what is underneath and has woken up with the usual jolt, heart pounding, mouth dry. But no, he's not hallucinating. There is someone beside him.

Okay. Count to ten. Think of possibilities.

Cassie? Vague recollection of her whispering something at some point in the evening. But their affair had wound up – or down – over three years ago. She is newly married, for God's sake. He can't have taken up with her again – can he?

Gina. Remembers seeing her on the edge of his vision as he greeted Beverley, the hostess. Kept out of her way after that. Fairly plastered when he arrived and must have downed a good few bevvies after... *Bev?* – ah God, surely not. No, no, she is ancient, at least sixty-five, and he is surely in his own bed. The broken spring is pressing against his third rib. Whoever it is is on the side he usually sleeps, so at least he's been considerate in that respect.

Last thing he remembers? Greeting Bev; shaking hands with Stu, her toy boy husband; spotting Gina and lurching in the opposite direction; fetching up against – who? Who? Cassie? Okay, Cassie, who had whispered – what? – and yes, sinking into one of Bev's squashy sofas beside... Nigella? Antonia? Harriet? *Alex?*

Oh no. No, no, not Alex. After all the trouble – and money – it has taken to offload her, he can't have allowed... no, she won't have allowed... he can't remember seeing her and anyway surely

389

Bev wouldn't have invited her knowing he would be there unless out of spite (has he fallen out of favour with Bev recently?) – but if Alex had been there, and if she'd been as hammered as him, as totally wiped out, wasted, paralytic, leg-tremblingly brain-numbingly gut-wrenchingly bladdered, anything might be possible...

Turn head. Open eyes. Okay, just open eyes for the moment. Yes, it's his ceiling, that damp patch he must do something about is directly above his head although it must be coming from the flat upstairs and surely that's their problem, not his, because he's not here most of the time...

Right. Process of elimination. Definitely not Nigella or Bev. Probably not Antonia or Harriet. Possibly not Gina or Cassie. Hideously possible, Alex.

The someone is turning towards him; breath fans his face. He can't pretend to be asleep. A voice murmurs, "Peter...?", fingertips are being lightly trailed across his chest.

American? His name sounds as if it's in italics, with a *d* instead of a *t,* a rolled *r* on a rising inflection. Does he know any American women?

"Um," he says, stalling for time.

"Do you feel up to it now?"

"Ummm," – ending on a downward note.

"Alex did warn me," she says, "so I'm not disappointed." Definitely American. East coast, not west. "And it's not surprising given the amount of alcohol you poured down your neck last night."

Christ. Brain beginning to work. Memory coming back. "Um?"

His head lowering as the pillow sinks. Her head rising, propped up on one elbow. Blonde. Long obviously peroxided white-blonde hair tickling the side of his face. Wide almond-shaped blue-green eyes framed by long brown lashes. Now he remembers. Not last night, no, that is still a blank, but maybe six months ago...

"So I figure you may need some assistance." The hair and eyes disappear. The bed grows choppy her side.

He lies still, merely raising his hands and plaiting his fingers behind his head. She is burrowing like a mole, making her way down the underside of the duvet. He draws in a breath as her mouth finds his groin. Busy mouth, busy fingers – these American chicks certainly know the business. He should relax, enjoy it. But somehow...

"Hey, loosen up." The duvet rises as her head lifts like Aphrodite from the waves. "You're too tense, bud."

He grins. The irony strikes him as funny now, but later... oh hell. He pushes the duvet sideways, looks fondly down at his limp John Doe nestling like a hopeful orphan between her thumb and index finger. "Sorry, sugar," he says. "I need a pee."

"Alex's shrink," he says later, in the kitchen, while she fixes coffee and something called French toast. "Is that ethical?"

"Alex's *former* psychotherapist and life counsellor."

"Ah."

"She told me all about you, obviously. And I figured maybe you were more in need of therapy than her."

"Is that what you call it?"

"That," she says, efficiently dipping slices of bread into a gloopy mixture of milk and beaten egg, "was sex. The therapy comes after." She throws the slices into the frying pan where a knob of butter has melted. They sizzle and smoke.

"Do you offer all your clients the same deal?"

She smiles. She is attractive, yes – well, beautiful – but he's never fallen for perfectly-groomed women. His first two wives had endearing flaws – Mel's crooked teeth, Isobel's lumpy thighs. Alex – well, Alex is physically near-perfect but inside a bundle of neuroses. The only woman who is both beautiful and uncomplicated he has let slip through his fingers.

"Ditch that thought, buster," she says. "My clients are always female. Until now."

"So you're willing to take me on?"

"If you're willing to pay."

"How much do you charge?"

She flips the slices over in the pan as expertly as she can with a bent fork. ("You have no spatula?" she had marvelled, surveying his meagre selection of utensils with disbelief.) Which she now prods at the flies of his jeans. "Give me sex like that before every session," she says, "and you have yourself a deal."

Yes. To lie back and let someone guide him through the wreckage of his life, a non-judgmental confessor for the psyche if not for the spirit – he can see now why Alex had been so enthusiastic a convert. And if they can get through the basics before the wonderful sex becomes stale and commonplace – before he starts drifting off in the middle of it...

"You're on," he says, stuffing himself with the beautifully crisp golden toast she's holding out, tasting the delicate flavours that melt in his mouth as he reaches the crust and then questing on, licking her fingers, each perfectly manicured glossy-tipped greasy finger dripping with warm butter and runny cheese until her mouth has replaced the fingers and oh God it starts all over again...

"Wrap it up nice and safe," she says like a good Girl Guide, whisking another condom out of her purse.

392